The Autopsy of planet Earth

A SCI-FI NOVEL

R.J. EASTWOOD

"I am more convinced than ever that we are not alone."

-Steven Hawking-

Theoretical Physicist

This book was published in paperback and e-book formats.

The Autopsy of Planet Earth is a work of fiction. Names, characters, Places, and incidents are the products of the author's imagination or are used fictitiously. Any resemblance to actual events, locales, or persons, living or dead, is entirely coincidental.

Join us online: **http://TheAutopsyofPlanetEarth.com**
Email: rjeastwood@theautopsyofplanetearth.com

For my wife Susanne, Dick Jacobs, and JoAnn Lilla who read early drafts and provided invaluable feedback.

Thank you.

On April 12, 1961, the Soviet Union launched Cosmonaut Yuri Gagarin into space. The flight lasted a single orbit. Gagarin's courageous exploits set in motion a full-throttled space race between the Soviet Union and the United States. It culminated in triumph for America when on July 20, 1969, astronauts Neil Armstrong and Buzz Aldrin successfully landed on the Moon. Bolstered by this monumental human achievement, the search for intelligent life beyond Earth went into overdrive. In the years that followed, probe after probe scanned the heavens. Although Earth-like planets were found in the "Goldilocks" zone—where the temperature is just right to support life as we know it—alien life was never discovered.

As the quest to locate extraterrestrials accelerated at warp speed, life on planet Earth was fast deteriorating. The world's population continued its unchecked, explosive growth, placing an enormous and dangerous strain on natural resources. Changing weather patterns led to devastating droughts in major food growing regions. Mass migrations began as more and more of the destitute fled areas plagued by famine, lack of fresh water, and nature's fury.

As far back as 1987, then President Ronald Reagan shrewdly recognized the human race was traveling a perilous and destructive path. During a speech before the United Nations, he spoke longingly of the unity that would surely come about if the world were to face a common enemy.

"Perhaps we need some outside universal threat to make us recognize this common bond. I occasionally think how quickly our differences worldwide would vanish if we were facing an alien threat from outside this world."

-Ronald Reagan- 40ᵗʰ President of the United States

He now realized where the beam was coming from; the sun was reflecting off whatever was out there.

Curiosity got the best of him.

He stepped down into the drainage ditch, then up to the barbed wire fence, slipped between the two strands, and began trekking across the fallow field. Curious, 100 feet or so of hard, winter ground leading to the object had been chewed up. Before he could get close enough to determine what lay ahead on the ridge, his right foot sunk into a gopher hole and his ankle twisted hard to the right. He cried out in pain and fell flat on his face. "Jesus H. Christ!"

His glasses had flown off into the brown, withered grass. He pulled his foot out of the hole—his ankle hurt, but nothing felt broken. Rising slowly and brushing himself off, he went looking for his glasses. On his second step, he heard a sickening crunch and snap. "Son of a bitch!"

He scooped up the spectacles from beneath his left foot—the right lens was shattered and the metal frame twisted.

"Wonderful, just goddamned wonderful!"

Straightening the damaged frame as best he could, he slipped them on. With only one good lens—his right eye was out of focus—he forged ahead. Nearing the spot where the meadow sloped downward gave him his first good look at what lay there. His eyes bloomed and his mouth opened wide like he was going to scream—instead, it came out as a hard whisper, "*holy shit!*"

Back-peddling, he stumbled and landed flat on his back. Frantically shoving his shaking right hand into his jacket pocket, he pulled out his cell phone, and with a quivering finger tapped in 911.

3

Thursday, February 23rd, Georgetown, Washington, D.C.
Twenty days after the Michigan jogger's discovery,

It was 5:30 AM. Thirty-eight-year-old Gabriel Javier Ferro, the lone offspring of Cuban immigrants Isabella and Javier Ferro, stepped out of the shower. His piercing brown eyes and thick, brown hair topped a physically fit six-foot-one frame. Since he was divorced, he was viewed as one of Washington's most eligible bachelors, a title he neither dwelled on nor took advantage of.

On this cold February morning, fate would intervene in Gabriel's life in ways he would soon wish it had not. Before the day was out, he would become an involuntary accomplice in an attempt to alter the human race from one stage of being to the next.

Standing naked in the well-appointed kitchen of his fourth-floor Georgetown condominium, he sipped a cup of black coffee and nibbled a cream cheese smeared poppy seed bagel—his morning ritual. A casual observer would take note of the spotless, orderly kitchen and correctly deduce that no serious culinary creations took place there.

Coffee and bagel in hand, he entered his cream-colored living room with its shiny, dark Brazilian hardwood floors, brown leather sofa, matching chair and glass-topped coffee and end tables. A painting of an ancient, three-mast sailing vessel navigating rough seas hung over the sofa, and a 52-inch, flat-screen TV was mounted on the wall to the left of the glass patio doors. That was it. The room looked like a carefully decorated builder's model than a bachelor pad.

Seemingly oblivious to his nakedness, he paused by the patio doors. A light snow yawed lazily to the already white-packed Wisconsin Avenue seven floors below.

At the far end of the living room, he passed through French doors to a small windowless study. This room looked totally lived in. The left wall was covered with photos of him posing with political bigwigs, famous entertainers and athletes. A photo of his parents hung over the desk next to an autographed photo of United States President William Jordan Conrad. The inscription read, *To my trusted third hand … your loyal friend, William.*

Flush against the right wall, magazines and books filled a four-shelf book-case. Many were the scribblings of the famous and infamous that permeated the Washington political scene, past and present. On the floor was a regulation bas-ketball, a pair of well-worn sneakers, a crumpled dark blue T-shirt, and a baseball cap. The latter sported the Washington Nationals logo.

Setting the bagel and coffee down, he eased into the black leather chair and winced. An old college basketball injury—a posterolateral disc bulge in combina-tion with facet arthropathy at L2-3 of his spine—continued to dog him.

Leaning back and folding his arms across his chest, he allowed his thoughts to wander back to the final days of the presidential election. Despite his age, early polls predicted seventy-three-year-old two-term Senator William Conrad was the odds-on-favorite to win. And win, he did with 302 electoral votes. His first act was to appoint Gabriel his Chief of Staff, one of the youngest to ever serve in that key position.

From the beginning of the presidential campaign, Gabriel had kept a journal in a brown, pocket-size notebook. It was to be a cache of his private thoughts and observations, which he hoped to turn into a book one day. On election eve, while still in their suite at the Chase Park Plaza Hotel in St. Louis, Missouri, President-Elect Conrad took Gabriel aside, and they spoke privately. When Conrad left to deliver his victory speech in the ballroom, Gabriel wrote in his journal what Conrad had told him.

> *Gabriel, I see it as my duty to cut open and laid bare a flawed and dreadfully dysfunctional government; not only the visible one, but those anonymous, greedy, scoundrels that influence government policies with the*

complicity of corrupt politicians. President James Madison said it best: "The truth is that all men having power ought to be mistrusted." I'm just the son-of-a-bitch to tackle the problem. I have nothing to lose, I have zero political ambitions beyond the next four years. So, put your hard hat on son, it's going to be one hell of a bumpy ride.

Twenty-seven long months of rough sailing through mine-laden political waters had elapsed since President Conrad had made those remarks.

With his journal entry still fresh in his mind, Gabriel placed his fingers on the keyboard and began documenting his latest musings.

Working with the White House and working in the White House is akin to being shipped off to a foreign planet. We suddenly found ourselves making decisions that would affect an entire nation, not to mention the rest of the world. When we took over, the political atmosphere inside the Beltway was dark and mean-spirited to the point of cruelty. Unfortunately, not much has changed; it's worse than it looks and worse than it was. Congress keeps stonewalling President Conrad at every turn. There is a total disregard for the welfare of citizens beyond what is required to secure votes, while the masses continue to cling to dreams no longer within their reach.

As for me, I'm at the peak of my game standing toe-to-toe with the man in charge. So, what's with these thoughts of doom and gloom that shadow me? Have I allowed myself to be hypnotized by political possibilities, but blind to political truth? Sometimes, when I'm alone, I flush all the political garbage from my brain. I find those fleeting moments liberating almost to the point of euphoria. But it is a dangerous mindset I embrace, for it could cause me to reject the convoluted rules of politics and fail the task at hand; to stay in the game and fight on at the President's side.

He stopped typing, cupped his hands behind his head, and pondered what he had written. "Nice going Ferro, negative introspection never got the job done."

He thought for a moment of a quote that would best describe what he was feeling. It was a habit he had picked up from President Conrad, who often used quotes to make a point.

"Ah, got it." Positioning his fingers over the keyboard, he wrote:

Russian novelist Fyodor Dostoevsky said it best: "Neither man or nation can survive without a sublime idea."

Well, Fyodor, I fear humanity has no new ideas; I pray President Conrad does. But daily I question whether I am the best person for the job.

Silently, he reread what he had written before adding:

What are we if not...

Deleting the line, he replaced it with:

Where is humanity going? When will we know we have arrived? The journey has been long and arduous. When will it end?

Grim-faced, he hit the "save" key and closed the laptop.

Gabriel had attended the University of Missouri Law School on a partial aca-demic scholarship. There he received a combined law degree and a master's in political science. In his final year, he was awarded an internship in the office of Missouri Governor, William Conrad. The Governor was known for his rough-and-tumble, straightforward, speak-your-mind persona, as well as his legendary skill in twisting political arms without deflating overblown egos. His shock of mostly unkempt, snow white hair reminded Gabriel of an old mangy lion.

Fueled by the demands, the drama, and perils of politics, Gabriel excelled. His offbeat and sometimes brash sense of humor appealed to Governor Conrad, and the two men quickly bonded.

"You have a questionable future as a bad comedian, kid," the governor once told Gabriel, "but a promising one in politics, so allow me to pass on this single piece of advice. Someone once said governing requires one to arrive ready to get their hands dirty, not bring dirty hands to the job. Remember that and you just may survive this cockfight called politics."

Upon graduation, Gabriel was offered the position of junior legal aid to Governor Conrad. He readily accepted. When Conrad ran for the U.S. Senate and won, he appointed Gabriel his chief of staff. Together, Conrad told him, they would go to Washington to fight in the biggest cockfight arena of them all.

Conrad had requested Gabriel join him in the Oval Office at 6:00 AM the morning following his inauguration. He arrived five minutes early, knocked, but there was no response. Entering quietly, he found the President peering out over the snow-covered Rose Garden. The new day's sun, rising in a clear azure sky, illuminated the treetops, casting long shadows to the west and dappling the iconic room with splashes of deeply saturated colors.

Gabriel greeted the President with, "Good morning, Governor, good morning senator... good morning *Mr. President.*"

Conrad smiled broadly. "God, can you believe this: you, the son of Cuban immigrants, and me, the son of a dirt-poor Missouri farmer, standing here like we own the bloody damn place? Hell, let's make lots of important decisions before someone makes us out to be frauds."

"Mr. President, I want to begin this journey by thanking you for the confidence you've shown in me."

"You earned it, Gabriel, you earned it."

"Thank you, sir."

Conrad strolled to the highly polished presidential desk and ran the tips of his fingers lightly over its surface as if somehow that would link him to its storied history. Lowering himself to his chair, he washed a hand over his face and sat quietly for a long moment.

Finally, as if speaking only to himself, he said, "We are mere mortals, flawed in so many ways, and yet somehow the human spirit drives us on." He raked his fingers through his white hair. "Damn, I wish I could remember who said that gem." And then he went silent as if far too many priorities were flooding his brain all at once.

Gabriel waited, but Conrad's mind had wandered.

"Mr. President?"

"Humanity is in serious trouble," Conrad finally said. "We ignore what is best for people and the planet in favor of corporate profits, GDP growth, and political power." And then, out of the blue, like a long-lost memory found, he said quietly, "In 1841, a fourteen-year-old girl by the name of Atiya was hijacked from her small village in East Africa and sold to white slavers. This innocent young lady ended up on a Virginia plantation where for some damn reason they changed her name to Emma." He shook his head and repeated, "Emma. Back then it was the practice of plantation owners to personally impregnate their slaves; some to work the plantation, others to be sold to shore up the bottom line. Can you imagine anything more barbaric?"

Having no idea why Conrad related this tale, Gabriel said, "Yes, I'm aware, sir. The offspring they sired were treated like any other personal asset."

"Barbaric! Anyway, when Emma turned 16, she gave birth to a son sired by her owner. She was simply bred like other farm animals. It was customary the offspring be given the last name of the plantation owner, so Emma named the boy George... George Conrad."

Gabriel was surprised by the last name but made no comment.

"Emma was unusually light-skinned for a Negro. Her coupling with a white man produced a child that could have damn well passed for white. When George was 14, just a couple of months shy of Lincoln's Emancipation Proclamation, he ran off and eluded all attempts to capture him. That's all documented in the plantation's records. In his flight to freedom, George came upon a young, childless, immigrant German woman named Helena Heinz. Just 23 years old, Helena was living on an isolated patch of scrubland in Hillsville, Virginia, near the North Carolina border. Sadly, her husband had died, leaving the widow Heinz to work the land alone. George, who looked older than his 14 years, told her he was a runaway Union soldier. Desperate for help, she offered him meals and a place to sleep in a small shed in exchange for his labor. George worked that land night and day like it was his own. Over time he and Helena grew close, nature took its course, and Helena gave birth first to a boy and then a girl. By then, the Thirteenth Amendment had been ratified, and slavery was no more. Whatever you're thinking son, you're correct."

"You are—"

"A direct descendant of Atiya." Conrad opened the lower right drawer of his desk and withdrew a small, weather-beaten cloth-bound book. "Helena Heinz kept a diary, God bless her. It's all documented in here. Anyway, things got really bad one year in Hillsville because of a severe drought—no water, no crops. Desperate, Helena and George upped and moved to Missouri and started all over again... and here I am."

"That's an amazing story, sir."

Conrad set a flat hand on Helena's diary. "If only Emma—*Atiya*—had known that one day one of her descendants would become the President of these United States." Conrad brushed a finger over the back of his left hand. "The simple fact is, under this thin, protective veneer, we all emerge from the same soup." He chuckled softly. "Now, why in the living hell did I bring this up?"

"Obviously, Mr. President, you are proud of your heritage."

Conrad rose and sauntered slowly toward Gabriel, his shoulders bent, his steps measured. "You can see as well as I where things are heading; there's a political crisis on the horizon that could very well lead to a breakdown of constitutional government and our democratic structure. So, it falls to us now to reverse the zigzag course mankind is traveling and restore human equality, dignity, and freedom—and it has to start right here in the USA. I'm going to take a good run at doing just that. Remember, a goal without a plan is just a wish, and I have a plan. Okay, enough of my pontificating. Give me another 10 minutes alone before the cockfight begins."

"Yes, Mr. President... and welcome to the White House, sir."

Conrad smiled. "Let's hope it's still standing when we leave."

I can trust with what is the most terrifying threat I have ever encountered. You're booked in the morning at 8 AM on AA flight 2286 out of Dulles to Flagstaff. Pick up pre-paid ticket at the AA counter using enclosed ID. Someone will meet you at ground transportation in Flagstaff.

The last line was underlined.

Imperative you tell no one of your destination, not even the President. Please, Gabriel, if you trust me, now is the time to prove it.

Mystified, Gabriel read the note again, searching for any clue he may have overlooked. He could find none.

Damn it, Owen, what am I supposed to make of this? What could be so threatening, so secret, for me to lie to the president and sneak off like a thief in the night?

For a few brief seconds, Gabriel's thoughts flashed back to college and how quickly he and Jennings had bonded like inseparable twins. Post-graduation, Gabriel stayed with politics, while Jennings pursued a career as a psychologist until the CIA claimed him as one of their own. It was Jennings, the perennial bachelor, who stood as Gabriel's best man at his wedding. He was also Gabriel's rock during his painful divorce.

Reaching for a slip of paper, he jotted down the name *Owen Jennings*. "Betty," he called over the intercom.

Betty stuck her head in the doorway. "You bellowed?"

"Call David Flagler at CIA, I need to know where this agent is. If I call, he'll make a big deal out of it."

"So, you want me to call?"

"Right."

"And tell him what?"

"Well, tell him… wait, I need to think this through."

"Give it to me, I'll figure something out. I'm if nothing else, I'm discreet."

Gabriel handed her the slip of paper. Glancing at the name, Betty's face lit up with recognition. "It's your friend, Owen Jennings?"

"Yes, yes, it's Owen."

"When's the last time you saw him?"

Gabriel shot her a keen look. "I need the info while I'm still young."

"Okay, okay, I'm on it."

"And be discreet."

Leaning back, he read Jennings's note twice more, but the abbreviated message was simply too vague to glean any more than what had been written. "Damn you, Owen, damn you," he murmured.

He waited seven long minutes before hollering, "Betty! Get through to Flagler yet?"

Betty appeared at the door. "Hold your horses, Sparky. Mr. Flagler said the agent in question was—"

"The agent in question?"

"He never referred to Mr. Jennings by name. He simply said the agent in question was on a classified assignment."

"Where?"

"The agent's file is sealed for reasons of national security—he doesn't have access."

Gabriel's forehead furrowed. "And the White House doesn't have sufficient clearance? Goddamnit!"

Betty shook her head disapprovingly, "Don't cuss."

"Why not?"

"You sound juvenile."

"They're just *words*, Betty. Why would *words* upset you?"

"They are crude and uncalled for," she scolded.

"That's because you were raised Catholic."

"And if I were Protestant?"

"You might find the words *less* crude."

Betty's left eyebrow went up. "You're incorrigible!"

"I hear that all the time—mostly from you."

The good-natured raillery between them was a daily routine, a game they played to see who could best the other.

16

"Please clear my schedule for the day."

"You have a full schedule."

"Other than immediate staff, no visitors, no calls. When's the president due back from that Congressional lunch?"

"You know when—2:30 PM."

Gabriel glanced at his watch; it was 11:32. "I'm going out to lunch."

Gabriel's decision to venture out raised a red flag with Betty. He was far too disciplined when it came to his daily routine to be acting impulsively.

"You always eat with staff in the White House mess."

"Want to send a service dog with me to be sure I return?"

"Not funny, dear boy. Has this got anything to do with Mr. Jennings?"

"You're helicoptering again, Betty."

"I'm what?"

"Hovering."

"And if I don't, who will?"

"Do you trust me?"

"Most of the time—not always."

Gabriel took a deep breath and for one brief moment considered showing Betty Jennings's cryptic note.

"Well?" Betty asked.

"Nothing." Gabriel stood, reached for his overcoat, and breezed past her.

"Where are you going?"

"I told you—out to lunch."

"Bring me back a cappuccino," she teased. "And there's no such word as *helicoptering.*"

Jennings's ambiguous note had left Gabriel's stomach in proverbial knots—the last thing on his mind was lunch. He simply needed to escape the never-ending din of the West Wing and breathe fresh, cold air to snap his brain clear. He had to decide what to do about the enigmatic plea from his most-trusted friend.

Slipping out of the seventeenth street NW gate, he walked south to Constitution Avenue, crossed over to the National Mall, past Constitution Gardens to the reflection pool of the World War II memorial. The massive structure honored the 16 million men and women who served in the war, the only twentieth-century event to be commemorated on the National Mall's central axis. He stood pensively against the cold wind, scanning the impressive structure until a passing congressional staffer recognized him.

"Hello, Mr. Ferro."

A young, petite, brown-haired woman was approaching. "Hi, ah—"

"Shirley Graham. We met at a House meeting a couple of months back. I work for Congressman Halley."

Gabriel had no memory of her. "Yes, of course, Shirley. How are you?"

"Fine, thank you. Aren't you cold standing here?"

Gabriel tapped at his temple. "Clears the cobwebs."

Shirley eyed the memorial with visible admiration. "Pretty impressive, isn't it?"

Gabriel nodded in agreement.

Shirley's gaze settled on the Freedom Wall of gold stars that commemorated the more than 400,000 who perished in the war. "So many lives lost."

"Too many... for all the wrong reasons."

She shot Gabriel a questioning look before turning back to the monument. "My great, great grandfather's name is on that wall."

Gabriel had not anticipated that and regretted having referred to the lost lives the way he had. "You, ah, you must be proud of him."

"I would have liked to have met him. What did you mean when you said they died for all the wrong reasons?"

"A bad choice of words, I'm sorry."

"I don't mean to put you on the spot, but what did you mean?"

"I misspoke."

"But did you mean what you said?"

He drew in a long, slow breath and exhaled a stream of vapor. "I have never understood the basic concept of war. Two opposing factions slaughter one another until one force is depleted or surrenders. How does that advance society? It's barbaric—like what took place in the Roman Coliseum was barbaric. What's worse, we learn nothing from the savagery of war. If we did, we wouldn't fight new ones now, would we?"

Shirley shook her head in agreement. "Can't argue with that."

"But it doesn't in any way diminish the courage and sacrifices made by these brave men and women."

"No, it doesn't."

"It's always been this way; one war ends, eventually another begins, and the vicious cycle just keeps on cycling. We ought to start a crusade to ban war."

Shirley nodded in agreement. "Sounds like a winning idea. Well, I better be going. Nice talking with you, Mr. Ferro. Have a great day and my regards to President Conrad."

"Take care Shirley, my best to the Congressman."

The young woman tossed a friendly wave over her shoulder, then stopped and turned back. "Say, if you decide to pursue that anti-war movement idea, count me in."

Gabriel smiled, waved, and watched her disappear around the far side of the monument. He stood against the cold wind, his eyes scanning the magnificent structure, knowing full well that some future generation would raise yet another memorial to yet another bygone battle.

The ambiguity of Owen Jennings's note weighed more heavily on him now. What was he to do— what was the right thing to do? His loyalty to President Conrad was absolute, but so was his loyalty to Owen Jennings, his oldest and most trusted friend. Jennings, he knew, would have never sent such a dire message unless it was a matter of life or death.

Charcoal clouds were rolling in from the west. A storm was coming. With one last lingering glance at the war memorial, he pulled his coat collar high before heading back to the White House with a brisk, determined stride, confident now of which course of action he was compelled to take.

At 2:45 PM—against everything he held sacred—Gabriel lied, first to Betty, and then to the President. He had received a call from his mother on his personal cell phone, he explained. She was experiencing severe stomach pains and her doctor ordered an overnight hospital stay while they ran tests. Since his father had died three years earlier, he thought it best to be at his mother's side. He would fly to Miami in the morning and return Sunday night.

"Would it damage your ego to know we can run things without you for a few days?" The President said. "Go, be a good son, be with your mother."

"Tomorrow is Friday. You have the Wall Street speech."

"I can handle those bloodsuckers just fine."

The dreaded conversation had taken less than five minutes. Gabriel prayed he had not committed the biggest blunder of his young life.

Late that night, Gabriel lay in bed in a mental fog. REM sleep refused to kick in. He would doze off and then awaken with a start. The process kept repeating until finally, totally frustrated, he rolled over onto his back and cursed, "Damn you, Owen Jennings!"

Sleep finally came just before 3:30 AM, and he immediately began dreaming. His eyelids fluttered rapidly, his lips pinched together like he was in pain. Whatever the dream, it was disturbing enough to wake him yet again. He shot to a sitting position, sweating and gulping breaths. It felt as if only minutes had passed, but in fact, it was now 4:25 AM. Thoroughly pissed, he rolled out of bed, put on his slippers and robe, and made his way to the kitchen.

At 4:37 AM with a cup of coffee in hand, he entered his study, opened his journal file, and stared at the computer screen unsure of what he wanted to say. Finally, arranging his fingers on the keyboard, he began typing.

> *There are times when you get a sick feeling deep in your gut—that unexplainable warning, there's trouble on the horizon with no clue as to what it might be. Thanks to Owen Jennings, this is one of those times. He's the coolest, calmest human I know and not prone to irrational behavior. I just pray whatever is going on justified my having lied to the president.*
>
> *Can anything ever justify that?*

He pondered what he had written, hit the save key, and turned off the computer.

5

Friday, February 24th. Gabriel's flight left Dulles International Airport, arriving in Flagstaff, Arizona a few minutes past noon. He proceeded directly to the outside transportation area, set his overnight bag down, and retrieved his journal from the inside breast pocket of his blazer. He was about to make a notation when a voice called out.

"Dr. Constanza?"

The bogus name took a moment to register. "What?" He turned to find a tall African American man standing a few feet away.

The guy looked to be in his mid-forties, with close-cropped dark brown hair that topped a six-foot-three frame worthy of an intimidating NFL linebacker. In his right hand, held close to his beltline as if trying to conceal it, he flashed his credentials. "I'm Agent Rod Sanford. Did anyone recognize you?"

"I don't think so."

"You're on TV a lot with the President."

"No one paid me any attention."

"Good."

"Your credentials, Agent Sandford?"

"Yes."

"You're with the NSA?"

Sandford confirmed with a nod.

"Owen Jennings is with the CIA."

"I'm quite aware of that."

Confused as to why an NSA agent had met him, Gabriel hesitated.

"Is something wrong, Mr. Ferro?"

"Ur, no, I guess not if you were sent by Jennings."

"I assure you, sir, I was."

"Where are we going?"

"About a half hour from here—Mr. Jennings will meet us there."

"Where's *there*?"

Stoned-face, Sandford said, "About a half-hour from *here*."

As they traveled down the highway, very little passed between them in the way of conversation. Gabriel fired off several questions, but Sandford simply nodded or offered one or two-word replies.

"You don't talk much, Agent Sandford?"

Sandford shot Gabriel a sideways glance.

"At least tell me where we're going."

"We're almost there, sir."

"Is this some sort of a joint operation between the CIA and NSA?"

"We're almost there, Mr. Ferro."

And that is where any attempt at reasonable conversation ended.

They traveled south for about 30 minutes before turning into the million plus acres of the Coconino National Forest, a place Gabriel had never visited. The diverse terrain was alive with rich colors of red rocks, sandstone buttes, crimson cliffs, stone spires, and river-sliced gorges.

As they entered a heavily forested area, Sandford's eyes darted to the rearview mirror. Confident they were not being followed, he made a sharp right turn onto a narrow, pothole-riddled, dirt road, so narrow overgrown weeds and low-hanging tree branches brushed against the vehicle. Tall pine trees formed a dense overhead canopy causing the sun to punch in and out like a strobe light. A hundred yards in, they came to an area wide enough for an average-sized vehicle to turn around. A warning sign read: *No Outlet. U.S. Government Facility. Turn Around Now. Violators will be met with force.*

"Well, that's pretty straightforward," Gabriel mused.

From his inside suit jacket pocket, Sandford retrieved two white badges attached to long, blue ribbons. Other than a black barcode running along the bottom edge, the badges were blank. Sandford slipped one around his neck and handed the other to Gabriel. "Put this on."

They traveled a couple of hundred yards down when suddenly the undercarriage of their vehicle was bombarded by what sounded like small firecrackers.

Gabriel stiffened. "What in the hell is that?"

"A section of the road is covered with pebbles. It lets them know someone is coming—low tech but effective."

A high, chain-link fence came into view. It fanned left and right into the surrounding woodlands for as far as Gabriel could see. Just behind the gate was a small guard shack. On the corner of its roof, a conspicuous video camera spied down on them. Two men in unmarked, black, military-style uniforms, accompanied by a German Shepherd on a leash, swung the gate open and approached.

"Mr. Sandford," A guard said politely.

Sandford nodded.

"May I see your badges, gentleman?"

The guard swiped both badges through a small electronic hand device. Once verified, he handed them back. "Thank you, gentleman, have a good day."

Sanford proceeded up the dirt road until they came to an undistinguished one-story, windowless, gray cement block building that could have easily been mistaken for a forestry office. A chain-link fence, topped with multiple strands of razor-wire, encircled the small structure. The only visible entrance to the building was a steel, gray door. The roof was slightly pitched to a center peak except for a ten by ten-foot-high extension on the far-right side. Video cameras were mounted on both corners of the roof and above the door. Two ground-mounted satellite dishes sat to the left of the building next to a dark blue Chevrolet Express van with heavily tinted windows, and a black Chevrolet Impala identical to the one Sandford was driving.

In the center of the chain-link gate, yellow lights pulsed on either side of a sign that warned: CAUTION: ELECTRIFIED FENCE. Below the sign was a small metal box with a golf ball size red pulsing light. Sandford punched four numbers followed by the pound sign into his cell phone. The red light turned green, and the gate opened.

"Ah yes, another Smartphone app."

Sandford ignored Gabriel's wisecrack. "Inside, they'll verify your identity again and issue a clip-on badge in place of that one. Just answer any questions—don't elaborate."

"I have no idea where we are or why I'm here, so there's little chance of me volunteering anything."

"Good," Sandford muttered as if patting a dog for good behavior.

At the entrance, Sandford placed his right thumb flat on an opaque glass scanner. A couple of seconds later the metal door swung inward.

"After you, sir."

Gabriel crossed the threshold into a room that appeared to take up the entire footprint of the small building except for an elevator door on the right wall, which explained the elevated roof. A large half-circle console was positioned dead center of the space and held a bank of video monitors. Two armed guards dressed in unmarked, black military uniforms stood by it.

"Mr. Sandford," one of the guards said.

Although the guards' uniforms displayed no identification or rank, Sandford replied, "Sergeant."

Motioning to a hand scanner, the sergeant addressed Gabriel, "Sir, please place your right hand flat."

Gabriel flashed a wary look to Sandford who nodded his approval. Dutifully, Gabriel placed his hand on the scanner. Seconds later his official government photo appeared on the computer's monitor. Personal statistics identified him as Dr. Andrew Constanza, Director of Biological Control at the Centers for Disease Control and Prevention. His home address was confirmed as the 7502 Pines Drive, Atlanta, Georgia, along with home, work and cell phone numbers. His security clearance was listed as 1.1.1-Top Secret (TS).

The guard took their badges and handed them new clip-ons. "Please wear these at all times while in the facility." He tapped three computer keys and the elevator doors quietly opened.

"Thank you, Sergeant. This way Dr. Constanza," Sandford instructed.

As they reached the elevator, an addled Gabriel whispered, "Where are we going?"

"Four stories down."

In the elevator, Sandford entered a five-digit code into a wall-mounted key-pad. The doors closed and the lift quietly descended.

"At least tell me what you people do here."

"The government's dirty work." A stone-faced Sandford answered.

Gabriel wanted to press Sandford for more, but before he could, the elevator came to a stop. Sandford entered another five-digit code and the doors opened to a long, dimly lit passageway.

Sandford stepped out first. Gabriel hesitated.

"Something wrong, sir?"

"Uh, no." Gabriel stepped onto the gray cement floor of the narrow, cloister-like passageway. It was humid, and a damp odor permeated the air. Whitewashed walls raised high to an arched ceiling. Bare bulbs encased in metal mesh ran down the center of the ceiling to the far end, which was a good fifty to sixty feet away.

A bit bewildered, Gabriel said, "This place is a hell-of-a-lot bigger than the ground level structure suggests."

Either Sandford did not hear, or he chose to ignore Gabriel and walked off. When they reached double steel doors at the far end, Sandford lifted the cover of a wall-mounted metal box and entered a series of five numbers.

"How do you remember all these codes?"

Sandford swung open the right door to an ominous-looking dark hole.

"Please, sir, step in."

"There's no light."

"There will be."

Gabriel stepped into the dark space, and Sandford pulled the door shut.

"I can't see," Gabriel bemoaned.

"Wait here, please."

Sandford disappeared into the dark passageway, his footsteps echoing for about eighteen steps before stopping.

"Agent Sandford?"

No answer.

The sharp crack of a lock snapping open startled Gabriel. A door swung open and blinding light flooded the hallway, followed by a blast of frigid air.

"Okay, sir, come ahead."

The abrupt change from total darkness to bright light had momentarily blinded Gabriel. He blinked several times before he made out Sandford's silhouette at the far end.

"The cold air is escaping, sir."

"Hold your horses."

Sandford allowed Gabriel to enter the new space first. The first thing that caught his eye was a large array of rack-mounted computer servers that lined the right wall. They were covered top-to-bottom in semi-transparent plastic, suggesting whatever the equipment's purpose, none was in current use. A massive, shiny steel vault door—the old type once used in banks—dominated much of the far back wall. To his left, dead center of the room, a half-circle console housed the only working equipment: eight video monitors, a computer, a telephone, and a flex-stem mounted microphone. Four monitors displayed visuals of the building's exterior, another of the outer guard station and the ground floor guard station above. The image on the last monitor, identified simply as "vault," was too dark to make out any details. A mule deer came into view on monitor four and briefly nibbled on something semi-green, then scampered off into the pine woods.

But what caught Gabriel's attention was a three-foot by six-foot glass window on the left wall. Moving to it, he peered in. In the center was a standard size surgical operating table covered with clean, crisp white sheets. A surgical light hovered three feet above. Mounted on two separate rolling pedestals were medical monitoring devices. Running the length of the back wall, a stainless-steel table held a tray of shiny surgical instruments, two microscopes, a box of surgical gloves, and a piece of equipment about the size of a large breadbox labeled *RapidHIT 200 DNA Identification System*. Two oxygen tank cylinders rested on the floor, and white lab coats hung on wall hooks.

"Sir?"

Gabriel turned to find Sandford inches from his face.

"We need to move on, sir."

"All this medical equipment, what's it for?"

"The facility is a deactivated biological testing facility."

"Why would they leave a fully equipped operating room—what did they use it for?"

Sandford eyebrows rose. "I don't know, maybe for testing animals?"

"Must have been some big animals."

"We really do need to move on, sir."

"How big did you say this facility was?"

Sandford shrugged. "I didn't. Mr. Jennings is waiting."

They moved along a dimly lit hallway. There was three offices on either side equipped with desks, chairs, computers, phones, and file cabinets, but absent any human presence.

"Where is everybody?"

Sandford ignored the question and kept moving until they reached a door at the end of the hall. A small sign read *Conference Room*.

6

The conference room was small and undistinguished. A large map of the United States filled the upper half of the off-white wall to the left of the entry. On it, a conspicuous red stick pin marked a spot in the southwest corner of Michigan. A black Formica-topped table ran down the center of the room along with six, black, leather-covered captain's chairs. On the table was a laptop computer displaying the CIA logo and a manila file folder. A 32-inch, flat-screen TV rested atop a two-shelf cabinet. On the lower shelf was a video disc recorder/player.

CIA Interrogator Owen Jennings, clutching a cup of coffee, stood pole straight on five feet ten inch frame of not more than 185 pounds. He was dressed casually in gray slacks and a long-sleeved, vertical striped blue and white shirt. Bronze-rimmed glasses framed his thin face and piercing blue eyes. Only four months older than Gabriel, Jennings's thinning brown hair displayed strands of white at his temples.

With a quick unsmiling glance at Gabriel then to Sandford, Jennings said, "Get lost?"

For the first time since Gabriel had encountered Sandford, the man actually smiled. "The gentleman found the facility arresting." Sanford's smile faded. "Yell if you need anything,"

Jennings nodded. "Thanks, Rod."

Gabriel waited until Sandford was out of earshot. "Agent Sandford needs to get a life; at the very least a personality transplant."

Jennings grinned. "Yeah, he's buttoned-up most of the time."

"You mean borderline rude like maybe he's got an ingrown hair up his ass that requires surgical removal."

"But in a dark alley on a cold night, he's the guy you want at your back."

"Nice trick with my credentials. I always wanted to work for the CDC."

"Happy to oblige." Jennings set his coffee on the table and encircled Gabriel in a bear hug. "Damn good to see you, Cuban boy." He planted a playful kiss on Gabriel's forehead. "Nine months ago, in D.C. I recall we got wasted."

"You left me with a nasty hangover."

"Duty called."

"Where have you been?"

"Getting dirty in the dry, dusty Middle East. How are you surviving the Washington piranha?"

"Like a dime-sized cold sore."

Jennings tossed his head back and laughed. "And you expected better?"

"Would civility and common decency be too much to hope for?"

"How anyone keeps their integrity intact in that cesspool is a mystery to me. I warned you back in college to stay clear of politics, but *nooo*, you didn't listen. Still smoke?"

"Thought you quit?"

"I did." Jennings made a *'give me'* motion with his fingers. Gabriel tossed him a pack of Marlboros and a lighter. Jennings lit one, sucked in a long drag, closed his eyes, and held in the smoke as if the poisonous carcinogens were a rare aphrodisiac.

"Why are you cohabitating with the NSA? Where the hell are we? And why am I here?"

"As always, you're full of questions. First, this place. It was originally built for biological warfare testing. Since we're not supposed to do that anymore, the guards think they're protecting a legit government viral research center."

"And they're not?"

"Now, it's a go-to destination when—how I shall put this—when a bit of privacy is required to converse with a person of interest."

"Jesus, Owen, a *Black Site* on American soil?"

"More precisely, it's called a Communications Management Unit—CMU for short." Jennings grinned and doused the cigarette in his coffee cup. "It gets the job done."

"More importantly, I lied to President Conrad because your note said, and I quote: '*I have come face-to-face with the future—it is terrifying beyond words, beyond all human apprehension.*' Pretty frightening choice of words."

Stuffing his hands in his pockets, Jennings walked the length of the conference table and stood for a long moment.

"Still with me?"

Jennings did a slow turn—his expression had turned grim. "We're in the middle of a global civil war, one far uglier and darker than the average chump realizes. You know as well as me the nut-jobs, living on the fringe in their perverted reality, stand ready to off the rest of us at their first opportunity."

"We deal with it on a daily basis," Gabriel said, "but you make it sound more dystopian than we do."

"You wouldn't say that if you'd been crawling around in the sewer of humanity like I have..." Jennings's eyes went to the floor, "... been asked to do the things I've done. There isn't one whit of difference between any of us, yet because of where we were born and raised, our customs and traditions, we believe our tribe is better than the other guys, and the only way to prove it is to kill one another." Jennings' hand went to the back of his neck, his fingers rhythmically tightening and loosening around the muscles there. "We're just a piss-ant of a planet in a big universe, and billions ignorantly believe we're at its center. How oversimplified and narcissistic is that?"

"Where's this going?"

"How about the collapse of civilization as we know it?"

"Owen, friend, I have no idea what you're talking about."

Jennings turned to the wall map. Dragging in a long, deep breath, it seeped slowly from his lungs as a long sigh. "What if the world as we know it was to end?"

"End how?"

"I don't mean we all die, but what if everything we hold to be sacred and true turned out to be one big lie?"

"I'm not sure we hold anything to be sacred and true anymore, and you're still not making sense."

"Yeah, I know, I'm rambling." His eyes went to the map briefly before turning back to Gabriel. "What I'm about to lay on you is either a new beginning or the beginning of the end. At the very least it will transform humanity's destiny forever."

Jennings moved back to the map. Gabriel waited, but Jennings stood quietly staring at the red pin. His right arm rose slowly like it was heavy. Extending his index finger, he set it firmly on the head of the red pin. "This is Three Oaks in Berrien Country in Michigan's lower west peninsula, population 1,822. An event occurred there that defies human definition." He lowered his arm to his side. "Right there… in a remote meadow…" His eyes shifted from the map to Gabriel, "… contact was made."

"Contact with what?"

"A single entity not of this world."

Neurons in Gabriel's brain raced to connect Jennings's bone chilling words. With a hesitant grin, he said derisively, "Right, little green men?"

"*Gray*, Gabriel, not green."

Gabriel's grin faded. "Gray—that *is* what you said—no joke?"

"No joke—*gray*—and it's alive."

The words ricocheted in Gabriel's skull like an errant bullet. He wanted his friend to begin again, only this time there would be no reference to a gray foreign entity.

"Are you processing this?"

"I'm trying. When did this happen?"

"Just over three weeks ago."

"Jesus, Owen! President Conrad has no knowledge of this!"

"Are you so sure of that, Gabe?"

Jennings was the only one who would dare call Gabriel, *Gabe*. It was a thing with Gabriel, like James objecting to being called Jimmy, or Robert, Bobby.

"I'm positive!" Gabriel answered forcefully.

"Well, don't be."

"What the hell does that mean? I'm telling you the president has no knowledge of the existence of an alien."

"As far as *you* know."

"For Christ's sake Owen, you're interrogating me!"

Jennings took several quick steps closer to Gabriel. "If I've made a bad call, if anyone even knew you were here—" He left it hanging, scooped up the pack of cigarettes and lit another one. "It has two legs, two arms, and two eyes. He walks, he talks, he's light years ahead in the intelligence department, and no he's not an ugly ogre. He looks like—"

"My God! Where is this thing?"

"Back there in the vault."

"Jesus!"

Of all the threats facing humankind, the idea that a captured extraterrestrial was now at the top of the crisis list was beyond imagination. Gabriel blew out a breath, loosened his tie, and freed the top button of his shirt. "Give me the details."

Jennings dropped his half-smoked cigarette in the coffee cup. "I was in Damascus when Director Downing himself called. He wouldn't tell me why or where I was going, just that a CIA jet was waiting for me at Damascus International. When the Director of the CIA calls, you do as he asks. The following day I arrived here and was greeted by two young CIA agents, Zack Young and Kenneth Mitchell."

"Did you know these guys?"

"Never met either one. Agent Young put me on a secure line with Director Downing, who informed me I was to be lead interrogator on an ultra-secret CIA-NSA joint operation. Then he tells me what's in the vault. *Holy shit* was my reaction. How the hell do you interrogate an alien? I'm good, but not that good. About an hour later the rest of the team shows up. Rod Sandford was first. He's one of NSA's top field agents and computer code writers and communications wizard. Then there's Ethan Daniels, an NCIS/DNA forensic specialist, and Dr. Catherine Blake, a scientific, medical professional; she works for the Navy in San Diego. There's six security guards who bunk on level two and have no access to this level. They're clueless to what's we have down here in that vault. Once our team had arrived and were fully briefed, poof, Young and Mitchell left."

"That's it? They left four of you in charge of a captured alien?"

"You got it," Jennings replied. "This place should be crawling with experts looking to play with a live alien. So, I get Director Downing back on the line and I expressed my concern. He seemed pissed that I even asked—says the President ordered the operation be below the radar going in to avoid leaks that would panic the public. We were to get the ball rolling before the operation was expanded; a week, two at the most, Downing says. Okay, I understand the need for secrecy, especially something this colossal. Like a good soldier, I saluted and followed orders."

"The guards—who are they? There's no identification on their uniforms."

"I have no idea—contractors I suspect—I was instructed not to ask. Rod Sandford and I were to conduct videotaped interrogations, Dr. Blake and Ethan Daniels DNA testing and physical examinations. A CIA jet flies in and picks up our reports and tapes for analysis back at Langley. That's how I contacted you; we gave the pilot a second package to be delivered via the CIA Mailroom directly to you. If you hadn't shown up today, I'd know the jig was up, and I was going to Leavenworth.

"And you trusted the pilot?"

"They're bus drivers, Gabriel, they shuttle stuff around and don't ask questions. So, now we're expecting that within a week or two a team of NASA scientists, medical experts, intelligence personnel, and psychologists would swoop in and take charge." Jennings pursed his lips and made a smacking sound. "Today marks day 27 and counting."

"Maybe Langley needs more information before—"

Jennings waved him off. "That's bullshit. From the first day, our distinguished guest made it clear he would only reveal the reason for his being here to the US President. He said so in our first taped interview, so Downing knew that from the get-go. Knowing full well the President of the United States wasn't going to meet face-to-face with an alien, I suggested they connect via teleconference, thereby not exposing Conrad directly. Without explaining why, Downing nixed the idea." Jennings scooped up Gabriel's cigarettes and lit another one. "He says his name is *Legna* and claims to be from a planet called *Ecaep*."

"Legna?" Gabriel voice spiked up, "*E* what?"

"E-C-A-E-P... Ecaep."

"Where the hell is Ecaep?"

"I have no idea."

"This is coming way too fast, back up."

"To where?"

"The beginning—how did they find the alien in the first place?"

Jennings pointed to the red stick pin. "A lone jogger spotted something odd in that remote Michigan meadow late one afternoon and decided to investigate. When he realized it was a UFO, he called the Berrien County sheriff who showed up with a deputy. Seeing that it was an honest-to-god UFO, the Sheriff called NASIC."

"The National Air and Space Intelligence Center."

"Yeah, at Wright-Patterson Air Force Base outside of Dayton. The Sheriff connected with a Lt. Colonel Gil Robinson, the ranking night duty officer. Robinson requested a photo to confirm it wasn't a prank. The sheriff sent one on his cell phone, but the sun was already over the horizon, and the image was pretty dark—it could have been anything. But since the site was only a little over an hour and a half away by helicopter, Robinson sent an investigative team of three headed by Captain Andrew Lewis."

"Only three people to investigate a possible downed UFO?"

"Because the alleged site was so remote and only the Sheriff, his deputy, and the jogger were witnesses, Colonel Robinson made the decision to keep a low profile until they had hard evidence."

"Unbelievable!"

"When Lewis and his guys arrived, they put on Biohazard suits and approached the craft—that's when an opening appeared."

"And opening?"

"Lewis described it as a dime-sized, white light that splayed into a doorway and ramp. His words, not mine. The alien appeared and in precise English told them there was nothing to fear."

"In English?"

"Once they confirmed the alien was alone, Lewis and his guys secured the creature and—"

"How'd they do that?"

"I have no idea, Gabe. Maybe they wrestled him to the ground, zapped him with a Taser, handcuffed him, and read him his rights."

"Stop already, will ya."

"Now here's where the story takes a left turn when it should have taken a right. At 9:02 PM Captain Lewis fired off his first communiqué to Colonel Robinson confirming they had secured a UFO and a live ET. Here's where the left turn comes in: I don't believe Colonel Robinson ever received Captain Lewis' transmission."

"Why not?"

"As soon as Robinson received Lewis' confirmation, procedure dictated he alert others at NASIC, which would have kicked in top-secret protocols. A half-hour later Lewis receives a reply from Robinson; they didn't want the alien transferred back in the helicopter. Lewis was directed to take him to South Bend Regional Airport in Indiana, 25 miles from Three Oaks, where an aircraft would be waiting. When Lewis' helicopter arrived at the Airport, it was directed to an unmarked jet on the far side of the airfield. It turned out to be a CIA aircraft. Lewis and his team were greeted by agents Young and Mitchell, who presented written authorization stating the CIA and NSA were to take immediate control of the alien. Captain Lewis was told his assignment ended there—he and his team were to return to Wright-Patterson and never speak of what they had seen. The CIA then flew the alien to this facility."

"Wait, now I'm confused. You said you don't believe Colonel Robinson received Captain Lewis's confirmation communique. So, who sent it?"

"Try a wolf disguised in sheep's clothing."

Gabriel scratched the back of his head. "You lost me."

Jennings picked up the manila folder, withdrew a sheet of paper, and handed it to Gabriel. "Maybe this will turn on a few lights."

It was a copy of a memo on White House stationary addressed to William Downing, Director, CIA, and Jonathan Benthurst, Director NSA. The one-line of text authorized the immediate transfer of the alien from Air Force Intelligence to the custody of the CIA and NSA.

With quiet acquiescence, Gabriel said, "That's President Conrad's signature."

Jennings took the memo and slipped it back into the file folder.

"Owen, I never saw that memo."

"Why would you?"

"Conrad would have taken me into his confidence."

"You're sure about that?'

"Positive."

"I'm not saying Conrad did or didn't sign that."

"Then what are you saying?"

"Let's remove the President from the equation for the moment and attack it from another angle. Inter-agency spying happens with all too regular frequency. For the sake of argument, assume the NSA intercepted the sheriff's initial contact with Colonel Robinson and shared it with Downing. From there, it's not much of a stretch to connect the dots: the CIA, in cahoots with the NSA, decided this discovery had to be under *their* control. If I'm right, Captain Lewis's instructions were coming from two spy agencies and not NASIC."

"Jesus, Owen, that's a bit of a stretch. You're charging your own agency with—"

"I know exactly who I'm charging and what with."

"How did you come to be in possession of that White House authorization?"

"Agents Young and Mitchell showed it to Rod and me. We had no reason to doubt it. When Young and Mitchell hit the men's room together, Sandford, who trusts no one, lifted the memo from Young's briefcase, made a copy, and put the original back. If there's a smoking gun, I've got a copy of it."

"But if this operation is not on the up and up, why in the hell trust you guys, why didn't Downing and Benthurst put their own people in here?"

"Sandford, Dr. Blake, Daniels, and me, we're the best at what we do."

"That's too simple."

"Okay, try this, we are the *very* best at what we do. But maybe we were never meant to leave here alive once our work was completed."

That grim thought brought a brief silence.

"You're asking me to believe the directors of the CIA and NSA are plotting against their own government. I need a solid motive, Owen, or none of this makes it to a court of law."

"Process this hairy thought; the alien made it clear to us he's here to assist what he referred to as a failing society. Now consider there are those who prefer the ET's mind their own damn business."

"But why?"

"Commerce, Gabe, commerce—economics 101, follow the money. You know better than I, special interests, mega corporations, wealthy individuals, and political policymakers are all one in the same."

"I know all too well."

"Now assume they would prefer no one, let alone an ET, upset the proverbial apple cart. What if the alien was to show us a new and improved energy source? What happens to the existing energy companies and their profits? How about medical advances that lead to cures? What becomes of pharmaceutical company profits? Those are just the tip of the iceberg. It's an easy jump to connect Directors Downing and Benthurst, two of the most powerful men in government, as protectors of the power brokers who manipulate the system for personal, corporate, and political gain."

"That's absurd. We're talking about the most life-changing event in the history of mankind. The very thought these men would be involved in such a conspiracy is unimaginable."

"Is it, Gabe? Wealth and power are potent aphrodisiacs."

"We could put this to bed one way or the other with a call to Conrad."

"And what if he's a member of the hunting party?"

"He's not." Gabriel scooped up the pack of cigarettes and lit one. "Give me something besides a theory."

7

"You want hard evidence, here it is," Jennings said. "Encrypted communications between the CIA, NSA and us are channeled through SIGNET, NSA's
code-breaking unit. We begin each communication by typing OTEN."

"OTEN?"

"O-T-E-N. Think of it as a slot machine. Each time they or us send a message,
we begin with OTEN, which sets off a random numerical code authorizing us to
send, and from that point on it's encrypted. Once it's read, the receiving end types
in OTEN again and poof, the communication is gone forever."

"Does OTEN stand for something?"

"It does." Jennings lit another cigarette. The air in the small room was beginning to reek of stale smoke. "By the end of week two, we're getting nowhere with
our alien friend, and I'm losing patience with Langley. I'm thinking, what in the
hell is going on? Why isn't the brain trust here already? A little sleuthing was
in order. Rod has full security access to NSA's databases. I asked him to search
SIGNET using the four letters we had—OTEN. Exactly 35 minutes and nine seconds later, four letters were placed in front of OTEN—V-E-R-B."

Gabriel's eyes widened with discovery. "Jesus, *verboten,* German for forbid-
den! That's almost too simple."

"In the spy game, simple throws the bad guys off every damn time. *Verboten*
took us to an NSA file titled *Verboten: Magna Security/Executive Signals Intercept.*
Low and behold, it contained the actual communiqués between Lewis and
Robinson, or more accurately, between Lewis and the NSA. Everything was documented—that's how I know what I know. Would it surprise you to learn that first

report from Captain Lewis to Colonel Robinson stated that no UFO was found? Who wrote that?"

"At this point, nothing would surprise me."

"Based on Lewis' account of no UFO, Robinson assumed Lewis' team would return to base, so he goes about his business."

"Didn't he get suspicious when they didn't show up?"

"Patience, Gabriel, patience. The next page in the file contained the names of all those who came into contact with the alien. Rod ran a search on each of them and…" Jennings hesitated. "… they're all deceased."

Gabriel's head snapped up and back. "What?"

"Colonel Robison's shift ended before Lewis would have returned. At home, he fell down a flight of stairs and split his head open like a ripe watermelon. An accident? Who knows? But that ended any possibility he and Lewis would come face-to-face and compare stories. And remember, Lewis and his crew were sworn to secrecy, so they wouldn't have told anyone anything back at NASIC. Smell a rat yet?"

"My God!"

"It gets worse. A massive heart attack took Captain Lewis' life, one of his team died of a cerebral hemorrhage, the other choked on a sandwich and suffocated, one of the helicopter pilots in a hunting accident, the other ran off the road into a telephone pole. The sheriff and his deputy were gunned down in a robbery attempt. The jogger supposedly died of natural causes; all within two weeks from coming into contact with the alien. Mere coincidence?"

"And the two CIA agents?"

"Never saw them again."

"Unbelievable! If your assumptions are right, something has to be done."

"And there's the rub. The rogues will claim they captured an alien suspected of being an advance scout in advance of a full-scale invasion. The gullible public would hail Director's Downing and Benthurst as heroes who protected the world from aliens."

"This is simply too bizarre."

"We're talking aliens here, Gabe, nothing's too bizarre. I thought I had come face-to-face with just about everything this world had to offer, but when I stepped into that vault for the first time..." His eyes flashed with renewed excitement. "... To actually stand in the presence of, and communicate with, a super-intelligent alien being, well..." He shuffled close to Gabriel and spoke in a hushed tone, "I have never once felt threatened in his presence. There is a gentle, calming aura about him. When I'm with him, I experience a serenity like never before. Rod, Dr. Blake, and Daniels feel the same. I know this sounds crazy, but his demeanor toward us is almost paternal, as if in some strange way he feels responsible for us."

"Clearly, you're captivated by this creature."

"He has my undivided attention, yeah."

Gabriel pulled a chair back from the table and sat. Jennings took a seat next to him.

"This much I do know," Jennings said, "... an aura of mysticism surrounds him. I don't mean in a religious or spiritual way—damn, I can't explain it."

"Are you sure you're not confusing spirituality with sorcery?"

"You'll change your mind when you meet him."

Gabriel pushed back from the table. "Whoa, back up! Show me a picture, one of your videos, but I'm not prepared to step into that vault."

"But because of your position, your relationship with the President, maybe this creature will reveal to you what he has denied us. Hell, negotiate with him if need be."

"I have no authority to negotiate on behalf of the U.S. government, let alone an alien."

Jennings leaped to his feet. "Stop thinking like a damn lawyer!"

"I *am* a damn lawyer!"

"Then stop thinking like one. There's no laws governing this, no second half to this game. Down the hall from here, behind a steel door, is a life-changing event waiting to happen. If President Conrad is out of the loop, we need to act. And if he's involved, we need to know that too. Either way, the clock is running down fast. So, get off your Cuban ass and do this."

"Listen to us, will ya'! We're yelling at one another."

Jennings' head bobbed back, and he laughed. "It isn't the first time—it won't be the last."

There was no denying that Jennings had presented a feasible scenario, one that Gabriel knew he was compelled to consider. The counter argument—which he rejected—was that President Conrad was aware of the alien's presence and, for reasons yet to be revealed, had chosen to keep Gabriel out of the loop. If so, it would be the first time; they were just that close personally and professionally.

Because of his unquestioning trust in Jennings, Gabriel relented and agreed to meet with the alien. But first, he wanted assurances that Sandford, Dr. Blake, and Ethan Daniels would support whatever actions he and Jennings might take.

"Does this Dr. Blake and the NCIS guy know I'm here?"

"I briefed Dr. Blake late last night. She's with us on this. I haven't told Daniels yet, and neither of them knows what we found in that Verboten file."

The door swung open and in walked Dr. Catherine Blake. "Owen, Rod said you wanted to see me." She spied Gabriel. "Sorry, didn't mean to barge in."

"Catherine, come in."

Dr. Catherine Blake stood around five-foot-four on a trim and fit figure. She was dressed in black slacks and a light gray blouse under an unbuttoned, knee-length, white medical coat. Her medium-brown hair was pulled back in a ponytail, which made her look younger than her thirty-five years. Rimless glasses framed her hazel eyes, and minimal makeup enhanced her fresh 'girl next door' look that encouraged men to steal a second glance.

"Dr. Catherine Blake, this is Gabriel Ferro."

Gabriel smiled politely like everyone does when introduced to someone for the first time. "A pleasure, Dr. Blake."

Her response was cool and straight forward. "Thank you for coming."

Gabriel offered his hand in greeting, but Catherine turned to Jennings.

"I pray we're not making a monumental mistake, Owen," she said. "God forbid we've misread this."

"I don't think we have," Jennings answered.

She turned to Gabriel. "Owen tells me you were college roommates, Mr. Ferro?"

"We were."

"Best friends ever since?" Jennings said.

Gabriel smiled. "Yes."

Catherine pivoted to the wall map and the red stick pin. "Isn't it interesting how much we humans think we know, yet it keeps changing until we realize what we thought we knew is outstripped by what we *don't* know. In the grand scheme of things, we are nothing more than unlearned children in a vast universe of unknowns."

It sounded like something a politician might spit out at a news conference to confuse reporters.

Gabriel shot Jennings a *what the hell is she talking about* look.

"I'm trained to examine the unknowns from strictly a scientific approach," She continued. "In this case, the absolute living proof is sitting in that vault. The transition will be—"

"Transition?"

"Eventually, Mr. Ferro, the truth will surface, and life as we know it will end. Hence, a transition like no other mankind has experienced."

Blake was in lecture mode, and Jennings wanted her back on track. "Catherine, bring Gabriel up to speed on what we've learned from Legna's DNA."

The very thought that the alien volunteered a DNA sample surprised Gabriel. "He gave you a sample?"

Before Catherine could answer, Rod Sandford entered with Ethan Daniels in tow. Daniels looked 40-ish, slight of build, fair complexion, with closely cropped blondish hair. Black rimmed glasses sat slightly low on the bridge of his nose.

Gabriel's presence surprised him. "Hey, what's going on?" He glanced at Gabriel's security badge. "New member of the team? We sure as hell can use the help." He scrutinized Gabriel's face. "You look familiar, have we met?"

"This is Gabriel Ferro," Jennings said. "A close friend and President Conrad's chief of staff."

"Yeah, yeah, now I know, I've seen you on TV. So, what gives?"

"No one authorized his visit and no one outside of this room knows he's here." Jennings said

"Really? Why?"

"Ethan, it's been three weeks. We were told it would be one or two; that raises lots of red flags. And it may be that President Conrad has no knowledge of what's going on here."

"Jeez!" Daniels bleated. "Mr. Ferro, want to weigh in here before we all get our asses in slings we can't get out of?"

"I'm afraid I only know what Owen has told me so far."

"He's agreed to meet with Legna," Jennings said.

"And do what?" Daniels asked.

"Once Legna learns he's President Conrad's right-hand man, maybe he'll be more forthcoming."

"And how will I know he's truthful? I can't just take an alien's word at face value now, can I?" Gabriel grinned. "God, I can't believe I just said that."

"Let's take one step at a time," Jennings cautioned. "Ethan, Catherine was about to explain Legna's DNA. Why don't you pick it up?"

Daniels smiled. "Ah, the DNA question. Our DNA is identified by four letters... *G, C, A* and *T*. Information is stored as a code made up of four chemical bases—guanine, cytosine, adenine, and thymine. More than 99 percent of those bases are the same in all humans."

"I'm aware of what DNA is, Mr. Daniels."

"Yes, right, well, the little bugger refused to give us a sample. Hell, he wouldn't even allow Catherine to conduct a basic physical exam, let alone a mouth swab. So, we went high-tech. I held his arm down long enough for Catherine to get a fingernail clipping."

"A fingernail?"

"Yeah. Boy did that piss him off; he didn't speak to us for the rest of that day. Anyway, we ran the sample through the Rapid HIT™ DNA Identification System."

Anxious to know what they might have found, Gabriel asked, "Does he have DNA as we know it?"

Without missing a beat, Daniels said, deadpan, "He doesn't have any DNA."

Gabriel looked befuddled. "What? How can that be?"

Catherine picked it up. "As crazy as this may sound, his body shows nothing that would indicate its flesh and blood as we know it."

"You mean like a robot?"

"Not exactly. His body does function exactly like ours, but he doesn't contain the same genetic material as us. His chemistry, his entire makeup, is unrecognizable." Catherine tapped at her temple. "It's possible his brain is encased in a physical structure we don't understand. Unless we run more tests, we're stumped."

"I won't allow forcing the issue" Jennings said. "We can't take the risk that he'd fight us and in the process, we'd hurt him."

"What about food? Does he eat?"

"Well, now, that's a strange one," Daniels said. "He's never requested food, although we've offered to get him whatever he wants. We have a camera in there and one of us is always monitoring him. We've never caught him sleeping—never."

"I wish we could provide you more, Mr. Ferro," Catherine added, "but without more tests, we've hit the proverbial brick wall. In case you haven't noticed, we're shorthanded. The four of us are essentially playing babysitter to the most extraordinary discovery in history."

"So, Ethan," Jennings said. "I need to know where you stand?"

Daniels hesitated, glanced at Catherine, then to Sandford, and finally back to Jennings. "I trust you're basing any action we might take on more than just your intuition."

"Rod found incriminating data in an NSA computer file that backs us up."

"Like what?"

"Like a conspiracy to keep this from the rest of the world. Rod will brief you. You'll find it convincing enough."

"Look, gentleman," Catherine said impatiently, "I don't know left from right when it comes to politics, spies, secret files or conspiracies. All I care about is Legna's well-being. That's my job—that's our job." She moved close to Gabriel, close enough for him to detect a pleasing scent. Perhaps it was nothing more than fragrant soap, but for an instant, it distracted him. "You should meet with him, Mr. Ferro, if for no other reason but to draw your own conclusions. Hopefully, he'll share with you what he hasn't with us."

"Okay," Daniels said, "it appears we have a consensus, albeit one that could lead to a shitload of trouble for all of us. In for a penny, in for a pound, as the saying goes. If you're going in there—"

Gabriel stepped back. "Hold on! I cannot present myself as an official representative authorized to speak on behalf of the U.S. government."

Jennings touched Gabriel's arm. "At the moment, you're the next best thing."

Everyone's eyes went to Gabriel. He hesitated, took in a quick breath, and released it just as quickly. "Okay, okay, I'll do it."

"Houston, we have a decision," Daniels said with a chuckle. "We shouldn't just spring Mr. Ferro on His Highness. Let me go in first and prepare him for a visitor."

"Just pretend you're meeting with another member of Congress, and you'll be right at home." It was Jennings's attempt at a bit of humor.

Gabriel frowned.

8

Gabriel stared into the men's room mirror examining his reflection and won-
dering if the alien would take note of his flaws: the small birth mole on the ridge
of his right jaw, or the half-inch scar just over his left eye, a lingering gift from a
neighborhood bully back in Little Havana. "That," he said aloud, "has got to be the
most juvenile thought you've ever had. We're talking about an alien here. God only
knows what *it* looks like."

He adjusted the hot and cold-water taps until the water was warm to the touch
and washed and rinsed his hands. Turning the hot tap off, he splashed cold water
on his face three times. Water dripped to his tie, leaving a two-inch mark across
the middle of the silk fabric. "Nice going."

He dried his face and hands with paper towels and blotted the water-stain.
"Listen to me carefully, big boy. This is nothing more than a fallacious dream, so
wake up!"

"Trust me, this is anything but a dream."

Spinning around, he found Jennings leaning against the door frame. "How
long have you been standing there?"

"Long enough to remind me of how you talked in your sleep back in college;
it drove me nuts."

"Huh, I could give you a laundry list of your bad habits." Gabriel dabbed at the
wet necktie with a paper towel. "I dripped water on my tie."

"As attractive as that tie is, it's the least of our problems."

"You're quick with the witticisms."

"Just about now, you're wishing we were back in that college dorm."

47

"If we could turn back the clock, so help me I would. Washington is a shit-hole. I wonder sometimes if Conrad made the right decision in giving me the job. Each day is like walking a tightrope ten-stories up without a net. One slip and—"

"You paid your dues. You're the best man for the job, so stop obsessing."

"If not for the President, I wouldn't be where I am. It was Conrad who—"

"Yeah, yeah, but if you had never met William Conrad, you would have risen to the top in other ways. Right now, I need you to focus on this because it's *the* big one, *the* game-changer. I'm convinced there is deception at work, and we have to stop it. So, is it game on or what?"

Gabriel ran his hand through his thick, brown hair. "Tell me what this creature looks like."

"It's best you meet him like we did without preconceived notions."

"What's that mean?"

"You'll see."

Gabriel frowned. "Great. In that case, let's get this dirty deed over with so you'll leave me the hell alone."

Jennings grinned. "Not much chance of that, Cuban boy."

A soft laugh before Gabriel said, "Chuck you, Farley."

In the 27 days that Legna had been their "guest", Catherine was, for whatever reason, the one he was most comfortable with. For this reason, Jennings chose her to introduce Gabriel. She led Gabriel through the dimly lit maze of passageways to the electronics-laden control room. The ominous vault door loomed large on the back wall.

Ethan Daniels was seated at the monitoring console. "I told him he was about to get a visitor. Ready to go?"

Gabriel eyed the steel door warily. "They kept deadly viruses in there at one time?"

"Yeah, back when they were figuring out how to effectively kill the enemy in easy, quick steps with chemicals," Daniels said, deadpan.

"And it *is* safe?"

Catherine shot him a cold look. "Would we be going in there if it weren't?"

"I suppose not."

"I understand your hesitancy Mr. Ferro, it's only normal."

"Nothing about this is normal, doctor."

"Mr. Jennings believes you can succeed where we have failed."

"Why do I get the feeling you don't share his confidence?"

"I'm a medical scientist working to find cures to save lives. Like you, I'm out of my element here. But here I am, and here I will stay to ensure that no harm comes to him. Now, we really need to go in."

"I assume we won't contaminate him, nor he us?"

Catherine shot him a stern look.

"I'll take that as a yes." Gabriel eyed the steel door with apprehension. "What do I need to know?"

"Just be yourself," Daniels called out.

Daniels had tossed that line off all too casually, and it unnerved Gabriel. He sucked in an uneasy breath and muttered, "I haven't a clue as to what I'm supposed to do in there."

"Listen and learn," Catherine said. "There is an enigmatic, almost holy, aura about him. To be in his presence is to experience wisdom and knowledge far beyond our own. On the other hand, he can be too cute for his own good—like dealing with a spoiled, cantankerous two-year-old at times."

"We are talking about an alien, right?"

"Just keep your wits about you. Don't let the force of his personality overwhelm you. Talk to him as you would anyone else."

"Easy enough—got it," Gabriel murmured.

Stark images of silver screen aliens portrayed as grotesque monsters out to destroy everything in sight raced through Gabriel's mind. *You're being silly,* he told himself. *Surely what's behind that steel door isn't a monster, or they wouldn't allow me in there. But how do you greet an alien? Welcome to our planet, sir, how about a pizza and a movie?*

Daniels' voice broke the silence like cracking ice. "Say when, Catherine."

That only served to amplify Gabriel's misgivings. "What's that mean?"

"The door's locking mechanism is controlled by the computer. Okay, Ethan."

Daniels tapped several computer keys. A sharp crack sounded as the door's locking mechanism was set free. Slowly and silently, the one-foot thick steel door began to glide open. A hot, prickly flush coursed from Gabriel's head to his toes. His legs felt weak like maybe his muscles would give out and he'd slump to the floor in a sweaty heap.

The vault door was now fully extended, revealing a dark cavern ahead. Catherine stepped into the void. As she did, an overhead, amber-colored light automatically came on. About eight feet in front of her, there was another steel barrier, this one the size of a standard interior door.

"Step in, Mr. Ferro."

Gabriel placed one foot in front of the other; his legs felt heavy like weights were strapped to his ankles. The outer vault door closed with a deep, disturbing metallic clang. Suddenly, Gabriel felt small and insignificant.

He was startled yet again when the tumblers on the second door were released. Despite the sweat beads that had gathered on his brow, he felt cold. Running a finger along the inside of his shirt collar, he felt dampness. *I'm intelligent enough to accept that if intelligent life exists on Earth, it's only reasonable it exists elsewhere, so get your act together.* "Get a grip, Sparky," he whispered.

"Did you say something, Mr. Ferro?"

Gabriel coughed. "Clearing my throat."

As they stepped clear of the second door, it closed behind them, and the sound of the tumblers locking kicked in. The sudden realization they were sealed away from the outside world scraped at Gabriel's already frayed nerves. He checked the Windsor knot of his tie and tugged at the hem of his navy blazer.

The vault was dark; the only illumination came from a gooseneck floor lamp by the left wall. He felt a cool breeze, looked up, and saw a ceiling vent overhead and another 10 feet further down. He scanned the area looking for anything that might be lurking there. In the low light, he was barely able to make out a three-foot high wooden table near the lamp. Perched on it was a large flat-screen monitor, a DVD player, an assortment of DVDs, and a stack of books and magazines. To his right was a brown leather sofa and a matching chair faced it. He couldn't be sure, but what looked like a child's bed and a small table was pushed up against the far back wall some twenty-feet from where he and Catherine stood.

There was no sign of an extraterrestrial, which only served to heighten his anxiety.

Several agonizing seconds of eerie, dead silence passed—enough for his imagination to run wild. Like conjured up visions in an all too realistic dream, more grotesque images raced through his mind's eye.

Catherine's voice jolted him back into his reality. "You have a visitor."

There was no response—that rattled Gabriel even more.

"This is Gabriel Ferro, Chief of Staff to the President of the United States."

It was a straightforward introduction; no fluff, no formality, just, *here he is*. They waited—silence—seconds suddenly felt like minutes. Then something was moving in the shadows back in the far-right corner near the table and bed. Gabriel sucked in a quick breath, blinked several times, and squinted. To his horror, whatever it was slowly lumbered toward them.

His skin felt ice cold—his heart kicked hard at his chest.

Ever so slowly, the very future of the human race inched toward them. At that moment, he wanted to backtrack, to leave this cold, dark chamber of horror as fast as his feet would carry him. He felt a deep fear, the kind that sticks to the back of one's throat, bubbling up like hot lava as a primal scream or a choking gasp. *Come on,* he heard his inner voice screaming, *one more step! Move into the bloody light. Get this nightmare over with!*

The alien stopped just short of the light. Gabriel strained to make out facial features, but he could not. He waited—seconds passed—more cold sweat formed on his brow.

Finally, the alien took two steps forward into what little light there was. Every imagined image that had raced through Gabriel's consciousness turned out to be a miscalculation. Like a shot of adrenaline pumped straight into his veins, his whole being snapped alive. His mouth gaped, his spine went pole straight, and he took one brisk, involuntary step back.

The creature standing before him topped out at no more than four feet. Surprisingly, its facial features were remarkably humanoid, smooth, and cherubic, like that of a fresh-faced twelve or thirteen-year-old boy—except its skin was pale gray. Its hairless head was just a bit large for its bantam body. The slightly almond-shaped eyes were light gray against the white sclera. There were no eyebrows or eyelashes. The nickel-sized holes on either side of the head lacked any outer structure like human ears. Gabriel assumed they functioned as audio receivers. A one-piece jumpsuit of shiny, silvery material reminiscent of sharkskin covered the creature's lean body.

Even when the alien finally smiled at him, it was nothing more than a slight stretch of the muscles on either side of his thin lips. It would happen a number of times before he realized it was, in fact, a smile and not a smirk. Despite the fact that he was standing in front of an alien, he couldn't get past the idea that it looked like a young teenage boy.

"Mr. Ferro, may I present Legna, an emissary from the planet Ecaep." Catherine announced it with a flair, as one might when introducing nobility.

Gabriel stood stiff and speechless. The alien locked eyes with his, its stare intense and penetrating. Its right hand began to rise. Gabriel's eyes shot to it, his brain spinning now like a free-running flywheel. He recoiled. *Jesus! Is this thing going to shake my hand? Is that what it's doing?*

What he was staring looked like a hand, but the fingers were long and bony—far longer than those of a human. A one-inch flap of skin protruded between the index finger and thumb. The flesh—if in fact, that's what it was—was gray and smooth. Perhaps it was nothing more than an involuntary reflex, but Gabriel's clammy and trembling right hand reached out to meet the alien's. Ever so gently, the creature's long digits enveloped Gabriel's, causing his entire muscular system to become as rigid as steel.

The alien withdrew his hand, but his eyes remained locked on Gabriel's. "He... is... frightened... of... me... Catherine."

The voice was a couple of octaves higher than normal, the words delivered slow and deliberate. It wasn't so much a halting pattern as it was a precise rhythm that commanded complete attention. Each word was released with clear pronunci-ation in a voice that was gentle and soothing and, oddly, had a slight feminine tone to it, like that of author Truman Capote. Strange, Gabriel thought, that he would think of that now, considering Capote died back in 1984, 10 years before Gabriel was born.

"Mr. Ferro is a high-ranking member of President Conrad's staff and—"

The alien's thin lips curled ever so slightly. "How nice for Mr. Ferro."

"Mr. Jennings thinks it is best if you and Mr. Ferro meet alone to—"

"Wait a minute!" Gabriel shot Catherine a wild-eyed look.

"Yes, by all means, Catherine, *wait a minute*," Legna mocked, dropping his voice an octave.

Catherine touched Gabriel's arm reassuringly. "You'll be fine. He doesn't bite, and he's not contagious." She gave Legna a stern look. "But he does think he's amusing."

Legna laughed a low, guttural laugh. "There, you see, Mr. Ferro, I do not bite, you need not fear for your safety. Catherine, assure the gentleman I am a kind and gentle soul."

"Sometimes yes, sometimes no." She flashed a modest smile that suggested she did indeed enjoy an easy relationship with this creature. "I'll stay until Mr. Ferro is comfortable."

"I would prefer to converse with this emissary alone."

"It would be best if I remained for a few minutes more."

"Dear Catherine, please leave us," Legna said with finality.

"Are we in a foul mood today?"

"Perhaps."

Catherine feigned a sigh. "All right, if that is what you wish."

"That is what I wish."

But it wasn't Gabriel's wish. "I… I think it would be better if you stayed."

"There's a buzzer to the right of the door." Catherine pointed. "Press it when you want to leave."

"But I… I really prefer you stay." Gabriel stuttered.

Catherine stepped close to him, so close he caught a whiff of her fresh scent again. "There's no cause for alarm," she whispered. "We'll be watching and listening." To Legna she playfully scolded, "Behave."

Another throaty laugh. "I always do, Catherine."

"Says you."

Gabriel's mind raced. *What the hell is happening here? They talk to each other like kids on a playground. No, she can't leave me alone with this... whatever it is.*

Before Gabriel could plead his case, Catherine was pressing the buzzer that would signal Daniels to open the doors. The sharp crack of the locks reverberated and he flinched. Catherine slipped out and the door closed and locked. Seconds later he heard the disquieting clunk of the outer vault door securely locking.

He was alone with the alien now, and it left him with a feeling of dread. *What is the protocol here, and who goes first? If it's me, what am I supposed to say?* His thought process disintegrated into complete disarray.

The alien's hand rose again, only this time it did not stop until it reached Gabriel's face, causing Gabriel to sway back on his heels ever so slightly. He swallowed hard as a single long, bony finger traced along his cheek, down along the ridge of his jaw, and under his chin.

Sensing Gabriel's increasing uneasiness, Legna withdrew his probing finger. "You proffered a mistruth to your president."

Gabriel's eyelids narrowed. "I beg your pardon?"

"Did you not tell your president your birth mother was ill?"

"How would you... how could you know that?"

In that instant, Gabriel realized what had occurred; *this creature is able to invade my thoughts.* He quickly diverted his eyes to the floor. Several seconds ticked away before he gathered enough courage to meet Legna's stare again. As he did, the muscles on either side of the alien's tiny mouth twisted into a smile. Clearly, the alien was playing him. He would have to be on point if he was going to survive the encounter.

For a few moments, neither spoke. Legna looked away with disinterest.

Is he waiting for me to say something? The best Gabriel could come up with was, "You articulate our language very well."

"I articulate in all languages," Legna said matter-of-factly. "For example, Bahasa, the official language of all of Indonesia. It is a standardized register of Malay used as a lingua Franca in the multilingual Indonesian archipelago for many of your millenniums. Are you familiar with it?"

"Actually, no."

"I thought not. Your world's highest level of linguistic diversity is in the area known as Papua, New Guinea."

Gabriel replied sheepishly, "I did not know that either."

Legna brushed it off with a wave of his hand. "No matter." He ambled in the direction of the steel door, his movements fluid and smooth.

"You once visited the land known as Italy and wished to learn its language, did you not?"

Legna had reached into Gabriel's subconscious again.

"Yes, I ah… please don't do that."

"Forgive me, I have little control over such innate abilities. *Se lo si desidera, posso trasmettere la lingua italiana alla corteccia cerebrale. Sarete abile in tutti i dialetti regionali.* I offered to convey the Italian language to your cerebral cortex. You would then be proficient in all regional dialects."

No way am I going to let him mess with my brain, "Thank you, but no."

"As you wish." Raising his arms high, palms open, fingers outstretched, the alien said, "I have been incarcerated within these walls for over three of your weeks. How long must I endure such effrontery in these less than desirable accommodations?"

Lost for an answer, Gabriel simply shook his head.

"Cat got your tongue, Mr. Ferro?" The alien's lips curled into that crooked grin again. Then, just as quickly, his face went slack. "Are they planning to end my life force?"

"Why do you assume that?"

"Because I withhold the knowledge."

"The knowledge?"

"Those who imprison me are not prepared to receive the knowledge, not now, perhaps never." He glanced at the small video camera mounted above the door. "They are watching and listening. They wish to prick me with their needles and probe my anatomy with their primitive instruments." He snapped his fingers and playfully waved at the camera. "Check, check, testing, one, two, one, two." A low guttural laugh escaped his throat. "What is your mission, Mr. Ferro?"

"My mission?"

"It is a simple question, is it not? Why are you here?"

Gabriel shifted his weight uneasily. "To be honest with you, I—"

"Honesty begets truth. Truth represents the supreme reality, the ultimate meaning of value and existence. Let us recline and converse like reasonably intelligent citizens and seek truth."

The alien ambled to the sofa, crawled up, and sat. Because of his short stature, his feet dangled several inches above the dark-gray cement floor.

Gabriel hesitated. His back ached from his old injury. To sit would bring welcome relief. Accepting Legna's offer, he lowered himself to the chair facing the alien. Legna glanced at him briefly, then looked away. Gabriel seized the opportunity to swipe at the sweat on his brow, hoping the creature had not noticed.

Is he waiting for me to begin, or do I wait for him? Gabriel waited for what felt like a lifetime, but the alien continued to gaze blankly across the room, his right index finger slowly tracing along the smooth gray skin of his right temple

"You are an important person within your government?" Legna finally asked.

Gabriel shifted uneasily and rubbed his hands together. "I am the president's Chief of Staff, an administrative, organizational, and advisory position."

"Then you are a person of great influence."

Gabriel shifted his weight again. "I have daily contact with the president if that is what you mean."

"Your president has yet to summon me. Why might that be, Mr. Ferro? Am I not entitled to a reverential reception?"

Gabriel cleared his throat. "Please forgive me. But I, uh… what I mean is, we have spent a lifetime searching. There have been many credible reports, and yet…"

"Know that all life is bound together through cause and effect, traceable to the beginning of all that exists or ever will." Legna's right hand swept through the air. "Life seeks to be everywhere in number and variety, and then, in complexity. For humans to assume they were the sole inhabitants of an endless universe, I would say to them, as there are five sextillion atoms in a drop of water, so are there worlds encompassing unimaginable wonders, civilizations that savor what humans have yet to assimilate; the joy of peace, harmony, and balance."

Gabriel swallowed hard, angry with himself for not asking more probing questions. *Damn it, is this the best you can do? Try again with something sounding halfway intelligent.*

"You appear distressed, Mr. Ferro. No need, we are simply sharing a quiet conversation."

"Forgive me, I—"

"Forgive you for what?"

"You are ... I mean, I am—"

"Overwhelmed to be in my presence?"

"To be perfectly honest, yes."

"You have nothing to fear, Mr. Ferro, for I am of the same origins as you."

"I find that difficult to believe... I mean, understand."

"Why might that be, Mr. Ferro? The building blocks of life are assertive on all levels. There exist no defined boundaries. For you to assume that life beyond your planet is disparate from yours would be a misconception."

Gabriel waited for an expanded explanation, but none came. A single drop of sweat rolled down his brow, past his left eye, and along his nose to his upper lip. Instinctively, he wiped it away. *Say something at least semi-intelligent. Convince him you are not a complete imbecile.* "May I ask a question?"

"Certainly, Mr. Ferro"

"When Mr. Jennings inquired as to where you were from, you offered no explanation other than the name of your planet."

"Your question, Mr. Ferro, should be... in which universe might I reside. There are many."

"Yes, well, perhaps you could enlighten me."

Legna's eyelids closed. "Because the distant light of wisdom has yet to reveal itself to your species," slowly his eyelids reopened, "a chapter and verse summary is beyond your present sphere of knowledge."

In a sudden burst of confidence, Gabriel shot back, "Perhaps not."

The alien's brow arched. "Tell me again, what was your question?"

"You're mocking me."

"You do not find me amusing?"

"Not when it's at my expense. Dr. Blake warned me about your—"

"Did she now?"

"To your point, the theory of multiple universes is known to us."

"It is hardly a theory, Mr. Ferro."

"Might some of these universes support life similar to ours?"

Legna laughed a guttural laugh that sounded more cryptic than joyful. "Oh, Mr. Ferro, I find it daunting that life beyond your planet would mirror a troubled humankind."

"You're mocking me again."

"Perish the thought. Now then, like those who imprison me, you wish to be enlightened to life's deepest mysteries, do you not? That is not possible until mankind has achieved a higher level of understanding. I suspect that will take many moments."

"Is that your way of labeling us primitives?"

"Does not a child crawl before it walks?"

Gabriel half-smiled at the analogy and nodded.

"There, you have your answer."

"Can you at least tell me why you are here?"

"Such definitions are reserved for your president," Legna answered smugly. "I have expressed a desire to meet with him, yet he has not summoned me. Instead, I am in the custody of Mr. Jennings, waiting, waiting, for what, I am unsure."

"Mr. Jennings suspects that certain people may be acting independently of our government and that in truth, our leaders, specifically President Conrad, know nothing of your existence." He flicked his tongue over his dry lips and swallowed. "Some people—very powerful people—mistrust what they are unable to control. There are those who would fear you, fear that you would diminish their authority."

"They are of little significance."

"Oh, but they wield much influence and dominance over others."

"That is because humans acquiesce to the most emphatic, most ego-driven of their species."

"It's not that simple. Those who wield power beget more power, and it becomes difficult, often impossible to—"

"Success derived from privilege, wealth, and influence hardly defines a life, Mr. Ferro. One must be judged by one's actions. If such actions prove injurious to others, you are obligated to terminate the offender." The alien raised his right hand to his temple, slowly running the tips of his fingers along the smooth gray skin there. "Rapacious desire for riches, possessions, and power sets human against human, reinforcing the same cycle of greed, indifference, and ignorance."

Gabriel was ready to argue, to present a defense on behalf of his fellow man, yet he knew all too well the alien had spoken words of truth, however painful to acknowledge. *On the other hand,* he thought, *who is this arrogant pint-sized alien to act as judge and jury?*

Before he could present a rebuttal, Legna continued his censure.

"Earth's ability to support its citizens is rapidly diminishing; once plentiful resources are dangerously deficient. The planet's climate is rapidly changing, and not for the better. A logical query would be; Why have humans allowed the planet to be systematically destroyed by those who would prosper without regard for the well-being of either? Piece by piece, mankind's fragile assets have been strewn about like discarded scraps." He washed a hand slowly over his face. "I find it untenable that you fret over weapons of mass destruction while turning a blind eye to your deadliest weapons: poverty, racism, prejudice, and fear—all weapons of self-destruction. Yet, it is within your realm to end wars, hunger, poverty and the exploitation and destruction of your environment, but you fail to do so."

"We are painfully aware of our shortcomings, but—"

"Reserve your rhetoric, Mr. Ferro, for whatever defense you wish to present will surely diminish you. Learn from your failures, otherwise you are destined to repeat them, in which case you have no future." Legna placed his right hand flat atop his head. "Your most valuable yet untapped resource resides here." He placed a finger to his right eye. "Your eyes fail to see." The finger slipped to his ear canal. "Your hearing instruments fail to listen." He tapped lightly at his temple. "Because you have yet to fully engage this treasure."

However accurate Legna's assessment, the alien's continued demonization inflamed Gabriel. *Just who the hell is this creature to judge? What does he know about the struggle of life on this planet, the fragility of our minds and souls? And yet, to argue the point is to dismiss the red flag warning me to slow down, to handle him with diplomacy, or he'll verbally eat me alive.*

"One of the few humans of consequence," Legna plowed on, "with the melodious name of Mahatma Gandhi, quite rightfully said, 'Earth can provide enough to satisfy everyone's needs, but not everyone's greed.'"

"Great Soul."

"What is, Mr. Ferro?"

"The word 'Mahatma' translates to 'Great Soul.'"

"Are the eloquent words spoken by the 'Great Soul' so difficult a concept to grasp?"

The discomfort in Gabriel's lower back had increased. Shifting his weight, he crossed and uncrossed his legs and absent-mindedly swiped at the perspiration on his forehead—a move he instantly regretted. "There is an element of truth in what you say."

"Just an element, Mr. Ferro?"

"Before any society can achieve its full potential, it has to forge a lasting peace among its tribes—we are still working at that."

"That objective remains unattainable as long as humans insist on clinging to their archaic traditions and, as you point out, their insidious tribal mentality. Such practices spew ugliness, destruction, and death, often in the name of doctrine based on ambiguous fables. I find it quite amusing, for example, that you each pray to your imagined creator to champion your efforts over those of your perceived enemies. How presumptuous is that?"

Defiantly, Gabriel set his jaw and straightened his aching spine. "There are evil forces at work in the name of theology that wantonly kills innocent men, women, and children."

"Please, Mr. Ferro, your self-righteous indignation is but a shallow attempt to justify those you annihilate."

"Look, you're twisting my words. We retaliate only against those who would destroy us."

"Ah yes, an eye for an eye; a particularly distasteful human condition that all but guarantees an endless cycle of revenge and bloodshed."

"Can you stop with the platitudes long enough to tell me what it is you want from us!" It was the wrong thing to say at the wrong moment. At the very least, Gabriel wished he had tempered his tone.

If Legna had taken Gabriel's belligerency as an affront, he failed to show it. Instead, the alien settled against the sofa back. "I am not what you envisioned. I apologize if I have failed to meet your expectations." His eyes crinkled and his lips curled in amusement. "But alas, like you, I am but a humble creature of the universes."

Despite Legna's demoralizing tongue-lashing, Gabriel was in awe of Legna's undeniable insight and historical knowledge of human society. He decided a better strategy would be to pursue the alien with respectful curiosity. "With all due respect, your very existence will have an enormous impact on our society."

"I am no more or less than you. Only the eons of our being separate us."

"You make it sound simple."

"Oh, but it is, Mr. Ferro. Life is to be celebrated and revered in its basic simplicity wherever it flourishes; peace, harmony, and balance are the very definitions of simplicity." He slid from the sofa and ambled toward the steel door, leaving Gabriel fearing the meeting had ended. Without turning back, Legna said, "Mr. Ferro, would you please stand?"

Gabriel twisted in his chair, "What?"

Legna thrust his hands up. "Stand up."

Placing the palms of his hands firmly on the chair's side arms, Gabriel attempted to stand but was unable. He struggled, pushing forcefully but to no avail. "What the—?"

Legna's thin lips curled into a smug grin. "Please forgive the theatrics I have employed to make this simple point; all that divides us is the enlightenment attained over millions of eons of evolution. It is no more or less complicated than that. You may stand now."

Gabriel pushed at the chair again and was able to stand without difficulty. Taking several threatening steps toward Legna, he blurted, "Damn it, who are you?"

"Best to listen, Mr. Ferro, for I fear you have nothing of consequence to offer." Legna's hand reached for the wall buzzer that would signal Daniels to release the locking mechanisms. But the alien hesitated. "Know that all beings emanate from the same provenance, a source of continuous creation on all levels; you stand before me as proof of that. Those who ascend to peace, harmony, and balance bask in the light of life; I stand before you as proof of that." His voice dropped an octave. "Am I moving too quickly, Mr. Ferro? Have I left anything out?"

"You're patronizing me again."

The alien's lips twisted into a grin and his eyes crinkled. "I would not think of it."

"You condemn our race when in truth not all of humanity is at fault. There are millions upon millions of honest, decent people who are powerless in the face of adversity heaped on them by others."

The alien shook his head from side to side. "Come, come, Mr. Ferro, each of your subsequent generations turn a blind eye to the lessons of antiquity, do they not? I would think mankind would find that burdensome."

Gabriel had no snappy reply, but he plowed on anyway. "Because you speak of our society with deep knowledge, you must know we are a race of many diverse cultures, beliefs, and philosophies; some will accept you, but many will fear and reject you."

"Ah, yes, the fear factor; is my presence a divine light at the end of the tunnel, or a speeding train bringing death and destruction?" He smiled. "Praise the human who first spoke those insightful words."

Gabriel glowered, but held his tongue.

"To those who would reject my hand, I say to them, shun the charlatans who have promulgated falsehoods. To those who would accept my hand, they shall be bathed in peace, harmony, and balance." For a moment, Legna's eyes strayed as if once again he had retreated into a hidden place deep within himself. "It is not lost, Mr. Ferro."

"What?"

"The years of your youth."

"My what?"

"Phantom images remain as enduring portraits, whether real or imagined."

"I have no idea what you are referring to."

"Do you recall your dream during your last sleep period?"

"No! What is your point?"

"It is possible to relive your dreams… if you know how."

"Why would I want to?"

"Dreams can be quite revealing."

Suddenly, an image of himself as a ten-year-old in a schoolyard flashed in Gabriel's mind's eye. "Whoa! What's happening?"

"Your most recent dream, Mr. Ferro."

Gabriel's hands went flat to his temples. "Make it stop!"

But the dream continued. Four boys were taunting him. One took a swing at his head and missed. He backed away, but another pulled Gabriel's arms behind him and held him tight. The others pushed and grabbed at him until he fell to the ground. Like a pack of jackals in a feeding frenzy, they descended on him, biting and chewing his face until it was a bloody mass of torn flesh.

"Stop it!" Gabriel closed his eyes. "Stop it!"

"As you wish, Mr. Ferro, I meant no malice."

A quickly as it had begun, the conjured-up dream stopped. It had never actually happened; it was simply a bad dream.

Gabriel's voice jumped up. "If I'm to trust you've come in peace to help us, then you are obligated to provide something of substance I can present to President Conrad."

"Clarity is reserved for your President only." Legna's hand extended to the wall buzzer. "I welcome your return if you resolve to safely deliver me."

With an extended bony finger, Legna pressed the buzzer, and the unlocking sequence began. Without making further eye contact with Gabriel, the alien ambled to the side table and tapped the CD player *ON* button. Instantly, the symphonic sounds of *Beethoven's Seventh* engulfed the room.

The meeting had come to an unceremonious end.

9

It felt like the most bizarre day of his life, and it had only just begun. Removing his jacket and tie, he dropped them haphazardly on a chair and paced up one side of the conference table and down the other. "This is absolutely nuts! We're supposed to engage ugly, fire-breathing, mechanical-driven aliens, not cuddly, doe-eyed creatures that looks like a ninth grader who talks funny."

Jennings smiled. "You've been watching too many movies."

"And he listens to Beethoven, for heavens sake."

"He likes it, plays it over and over again."

"Damn it, Owen, he dismissed me like a discarded hooker!"

"In the end, like us, he didn't trust you."

Gabriel tossed his hands up. "It was like having a conversation with Truman Capote."

"The dead author?"

"Oh, that effeminately high-pitched voice and agonizingly slow delivery, all calculated to make me look like an asshole. Truth is, the little son-of-a-bitch was conceited, contemptuous, and displayed insufferable moral superiority."

"He treated us the same way at first."

Gabriel clenched a fist. "I wanted to punch his twisted little mouth for some of the things he said." He sucked in a quick, quivering breath. "And me? I was tongue-tied and clumsy at a time when I should have been at my diplomatic best."

"Like us, you were intimidated."

"Look!" Gabriel held out his hands. They were oscillating like an electric toothbrush. "I handled it badly, and it was my job *not* to handle it badly. Damn it, you can't lie to him! He reads minds, for Christ's sake!"

Jennings exhaled. "We know."

"What? And you sent me in there without a warning?"

"I didn't want your defenses up, or you would have never grasped the full gravity of the situation."

"Gee, thanks, friend." Gabriel paced again. "Why would he be so antagonistic toward me when I'm in a position to help?"

"Don't beat yourself up, we'll try again later, sit down."

Gabriel sat across from Jennings and ran his hands over his face and up through his hair. "To add insult to injury, your Dr. Blake didn't make things easier. She's abrupt and condescending. The good doctor needs an injection of bedside manners."

"There you go again, making flash judgments."

"What the hell is that supposed to mean?"

"You're quick to judge people."

"It's a prerequisite if you hope to function in Washington."

"Somalia, three years back."

"What about it?"

Jennings folded his hands and set them on the table. "Four American businessmen were held for ransom."

"Yeah, by Al-Shabaab, what's your point?"

"A Navy Seal team was sent to extract them. Everyone made it out... everyone except the team's leader. Captain Andrew T. Blake came home in a body bag."

"Don't tell me he was—"

"Catherine's husband of four years. I'm not making excuses for her, but she still carries the pain as if it happened yesterday. She doesn't mean it, but she has this icy exterior that turns people off."

"I had no idea."

"She gets under my skin too, but consider what I just told you and cut her some slack."

Rod Sandford stormed in; his sullen expression spelled trouble. "Better check your email."

Jennings head snapped up, "What?"

"A message from Long Reach."

"Who's Long Reach?" Gabriel asked.

"Director Downing." Jennings reached for the laptop and opened his email. His face registered shock. "Holy mother of god!"

"What is it?"

Jennings spun the laptop toward Gabriel. "See for yourself."

Gabriel leaned in and read the brief message. It was from CIA Director Downing to NSA Director Benthurst: *COS GF at Arizona Site: Offensive Action Initiated.*

"COS GF," Sandford said grim-faced, "Chief of Staff, Gabriel Ferro."

Gabriel's face went pale, and he sucked in a quick breath. "How could they possibly know I'm here?"

Jennings shot him a hard look. "Your secretary's call to CIA for starters."

"Oh, shit!" Gabriel muttered.

"We weren't meant to receive this," Sandford said. "The CC has to be a screw-up."

Jennings pulled the computer back and read the message again. "Pray Downing doesn't discover his screw-up."

"He will," Sandford said low.

"How long do we have?"

"Expect company sooner than later."

"Company?" Gabriel asked

Sandford said low, "A cleaning crew."

"A cleanup crew?" Gabriel repeated.

Jennings grimaced, "Yeah, and it's exactly what you're thinking."

The frightening thought they might have to fight their way out swirled through Gabriel's mind like a fire racing through dry brush. "The guards—they'll defend us?"

"They're clueless contractors," Jennings droned. "Whoever comes will be under orders not to leave witnesses." He sprang to his feet. "Rod, find Catherine and Ethan and meet us in the control room. Gabriel, I need you to focus."

"On what?"

"You'll take Legna and Dr. Blake and hightail it out of here."

"Me? Go where? I can't—"

"Yes, you can." Jennings gripped Gabriel's shoulders firmly. "You'll take the van and follow the dirt road out back. There's an electronically controlled gate in the chain-link fence; we can open it from here. A couple of miles out you'll come to a paved road that'll take you out of the Coconino."

"And go where?"

"The hell away from here—stay off highways, stick to back roads."

"Why can't we go together?"

"There are files and videotapes we need as evidence. Don't worry, we'll meet up."

"Owen, I don't know if I can do this."

"There isn't time not to know!"

Jennings and Gabriel swept into the control room.

"Catherine, did Rod fill you in?" Jennings barked.

Catherine, her expression betraying her fear, simply nodded.

"Rod, where's Daniels?"

"In with Legna. I'm getting him out now." Sandford tapped several computer keys, and the vault door swung open.

Jennings moved to the console, followed by Gabriel and Catherine. Jennings' eyes went from one monitor to the next in quick succession. He blew a quick sigh of relief. "Nothing yet."

"Ethan's out," Sandford said.

"Ethan, escort Legna out here."

There was no response from Daniels.

"Ethan, did you hear what I said?"

"Loud and clear, Owen."

It was Daniels' tone and controlled response that sounded a warning bell. Turning to Daniels, Jennings came face-to-face with a 45-mm pistol pointed at him. "Ethan?" He took a step toward Daniels.

"Far enough, Owen."

"What in hell are you doing!?"

The urgency in Jennings' voice caught everyone's attention.

Catherine swung toward Daniels. "Ethan—what?" She looked to Jennings. "What's he talking about?"

To Daniels, Jennings said, "You want to enlighten her, Ethan, or should I?"

"I think you've got it figured, go for it."

Wide-eyed, Gabriel said, "Will one of you explain what's going on?"

"It would appear Mr. Daniels is their mole."

"Mole?" Gabriel almost swallowed the word.

Jennings sighed and shook his head. "How sloppy of me not to realize they'd have someone watching us."

Daniels tossed his head back and sneered. "Everyone is watched by some- one, it's the new world order you helped create, Owen. You just couldn't leave well enough alone, could you? You had to play super-spy and stick your nose where it didn't belong."

"That's what they pay me for."

"As long as you did what you were sent to do, everything was copasetic." Daniels waved the handgun at Gabriel. "But you had to bring Mr. Chief of Staff here—that sealed your fate."

"You're not a DNA expert?"

"Oh yes, Mr. Ferro, that part's true—one of the best NCIS has. I'm also a patriot sworn to protect this country against all enemies."

"Your definition of patriot doesn't square with mine," Gabriel hissed.

"Because you're an idealist, a dreamer, Mr. Ferro. That makes you, not me, dangerous."

"We were never meant to leave here alive, were we?"

"Now, now, Owen, what do you think?"

"Directors Downing, Benthurst, and whoever else is involved, are committing treason."

"I doubt they would agree with you. The allure of our guest is not to be denied, I'll give you that. But he and his kind threaten the very structure of human society." Daniels' waved his gun at the surgical room window. "Enough chit-chat, line up there. We'll have company soon."

Legna's head appeared at the edge of the open vault door. With a clear line of sight past Daniels, Gabriel was the first to spot him. His heart skipped a beat as Legna began to slowly move toward Daniels.

Daniels said, "Like an invasive parasite, this threat has to be eliminated before the infection kills the host."

Legna crept closer to Daniels. Now he was in Catherine, Jennings and Sandford's line of sight.

"You're committing a grievous crime against all humanity by keeping this from the world."

"Brave words, Mr. Ferro, but humanity commits enough crimes against itself without any assistance from us, so spare me your acrimonious denunciations. Your self-righteous pursuit of high and noble principles has blinded you to the reality of risk and peril. Even if their intentions were benevolent, they can't be presented to the unwashed masses—the ignorant bastards would worship them as gods."

Legna was within a foot of Daniels' left leg. He reached for it just as Daniels took a step forward.

Daniels chortled. "The world will thank us for preserving life as we know it."

"You mean *your* way of life."

"Yes, *our* way of life, Mr. Ferro."

With the speed of a striking cobra, Legna's left hand snapped around the muscled flesh of Daniels' left calf. Daniels mouth flapped open and his head jerked back hard. His body vibrated as if high-voltage was coursing through him frying muscles, bones, tendons, and nerves. A blood-curdling scream escaped his throat, and his gun hand shot up over his head. An involuntary jerk of the trigger finger sent an errant shell exploding into the ceiling. His arm slumped downward, his finger jerked a second time discharging another round. It missed Catherine's head by an inch and shattered the glass window behind them.

"My God, my God!" Catherine shrieked.

Daniels slumped to the floor with a loud moan and a thud, his body shuddering violently before becoming still.

Rushing to Daniels' body, Jennings pried the pistol from Daniels' hand and tossed it to Sandford. He held a finger to Daniels' neck. "No pulse."

With dispassion, Legna said, "A permanent disruption to his nervous system. He is of no further threat."

"We don't have a second to waste." Jennings barked to the others, then to Legna, "There are men coming to do us harm. Our only choice is to leave."

The alien hesitated, his eyes flitting first to Catherine and Gabriel and back to Jennings. "Will you spirit me to your president?"

"If what you've told us is the truth then—"

"I have been truthful."

"Then yes, we'll try."

"Logic demands we depart this uninviting structure."

Sandford checked the monitors again. "Still clear."

"Okay, set the alarm—tell them we have a breach."

"I'm on it." Sandford's fingers raced across the computer keyboard and the room plunged into darkness. Two seconds later, emergency lights flooded the space with an eerie amber glow, and an ear-splitting alarm sounded, signaling the guards above a lab breach had occurred.

"Sergeant," Sandford barked over the intercom.

"Sir, what's going on down there?"

"We were working with a contagious virus and the container seal was breached."

"Is there contamination?"

"We can't be certain; we're taking no chances—start the shutdown."

"Once shutdown begins on level four it happens whether you're out of there or not."

"I know how it works, sergeant."

"How about levels two and three?"

"Hold off, we have to retrieve critical records on three."

10

They shoehorned Legna into a large aluminum virus storage container, slapped a hazardous material label on its top and sides and padlocked it.

At ground level, all six security guards were waiting.

"Sergeant!" Jennings instructed. "Place this container in the van, and be careful with it.

"Sir, level four is sealed. Where's Mr. Daniels?"

Jennings looked to Sandford. "Did you see Daniels?"

"I thought he was right behind us."

"If he's still on level four, sir, he's sealed in."

Sandford feigned concern. "Jesus! I'll try contacting him from your station."

While Sandford dashed back into the building, Jennings motioned to Catherine and Gabriel to follow him out of range of the guards. He handed Catherine the container key. "Get him out of there as quickly as you can. Gabriel, give me your phone."

Gabriel retrieved his cell phone from his pants pocket.

"They'll be scanning yours for sure." Jennings handed Gabriel a new phone. "Take this one. My number is programmed in, but do *not* call unless it's your only option."

"This is insane! I'll call the White House and end this here and now."

"The hell you will!" Jennings snapped. "If the CIA and NSA are acting on Conrad's orders, your call will seal our fate."

"Conrad would never do anything to—"

"Damn it, Gabriel, right now we come down on the side of caution, not who we think we can trust. What's in that container is *the* game changer. Trust no one."

"You'll join us?"

"I'll call. You'll tell me where you are without telling me where you are."

"How do I do that?"

"You'll figure it out. Now put some miles between you and this shit-hole."

"Owen," Catherine pleaded, "the security guys."

"I'll order them out with us. Go now!"

As Jennings promised, the electronically-controlled gate behind the building swung open as they approached. Gabriel sped the government van onto the narrow dirt road and into the deep woods. A half-mile out they stopped and freed Legna from the metal container and tossed it behind nearby bushes.

Legna showed no emotion or fear, seemingly undaunted by the urgency of their plight.

For the next several minutes, they sped down the dirt road. Small arteries branched to the left and right and Gabriel had inadvertently taken one. He failed to realize his mistake until the trail became too narrow to navigate. Slapping the steering wheel hard with both hands, he cursed, "Goddamnit, I think we're on an ATV trail."

Catherine's voice quivered. "We have to go back."

Gabriel blew a hard breath and shifted into reverse, but before he could move there came the unmistakable *whap, whap, whap* of a helicopter. It sounded alarmingly close like it was skimming the treetops nearby.

Catherine's spine went straight. "Is that—"

"*Shh!*" Gabriel turned off the engine. "Hopefully, these high spruce trees will provide cover." His eyes shot to the rearview mirror. Legna met his gaze, but appeared untroubled by their predicament.

Catherine peered out the window up through the trees. "Can they spot us electronically?"

"I don't know, I'm not sure… yeah, maybe," Gabriel whispered.

The *whap, whap* of rotor blades sounded like the helicopter was directly overhead.

An anxious minute ticked away before the sound began to dissipate. It was another nerve-wracking three minutes before it faded entirely.

Legna appeared unruffled. "They have departed. We may leave now."

"The lab," Gabriel whispered.

"Owen, Rod and…" Catherine stopped mid-sentence.

"We need to go."

Gabriel backed the van along the narrow path until he came to an area wide enough to turn around. They followed the road they had originally been traveling another two and a half miles before they reached an exit that freed them of the vast Coconino National Forest. Turning right, they rode in edgy silence for fifteen minutes before Gabriel pulled over to the side of the road.

In a brusque tone, Catherine asked, "Why are we stopping?"

"To breathe, to think." Gabriel sucked in a long, slow breath. "We'll drive East until I think it's safe to stop and wait for Jennings' call."

"And what if that call never comes?"

Gabriel frowned and shot Catherine a sideways glance.

She shot him a look back, folded her arms tight across her chest, and stared out the window.

Avoiding major highways, Gabriel drove east on back country roads. Not a word passed between them until Catherine began haranguing him again.

"There must be one person in this big world you trust. For God's sake, call someone, anyone."

Gabriel hit the brakes and veered hard right onto a tractor path leading into a fallow corn field, stopping abruptly under a cluster of tall pine trees on the edge of the field.

Catherine tossed her hand up. "What was that all about?"

Despite his safety belt, the hard turn had pushed Legna far to his left. Straightening himself, he waved. "I'm fine."

"Damn it!" Gabriel cursed and ran his hands over his face and through his hair. "I need to think!"

"Do not to raise your voice to me, Mr. Ferro!"

"Play nice, boys and girls," Legna chimed in.

Unbuckling her seatbelt, Catherine twisted and glared at Legna. "Unless you have something to contribute, be quiet."

And that is exactly what they did for several long, anxious-filled minutes.

Unbuckling his seatbelt, Legna scooted his bantam body forward. "Our circumstances have extracted an emotional toll on you, Catherine."

"You are the indisputable master of the obvious."

The alien placed a gentle hand on her shoulder, but she brushed it away.

"What is of the utmost urgency is to ensure my safe delivery to your president."

"I'm open to any suggestions that won't get us killed," Gabriel grumbled.

"I assure you, Mr. Ferro, I am in no position to provide solutions. I remain at your mercy."

Legna grappled with the seatbelt latch. For all his wisdom, he seemed confused by the two metal parts.

"The male part—it's in your right hand. Slip it into the female receptacle," Catherine instructed.

"Yes, yes, of course." After several failed attempts, Legna succeeded and seemed quite pleased with having done so.

Gabriel drummed his finger nervously on the steering wheel. His usually reliable thought process was now as clouded as a pool of stagnant water. He had no idea what their next move should be. He glanced at his watch. "We'll give Owen another ten minutes. If he doesn't call, we'll keep going East."

"And from there?"

"Dr. Blake, please, sit quietly and let me think."

"Do it quickly before we're all be dead."

"Listen lady, if you have any bright ideas, now's the time to share. Otherwise, like you I'm out of my safe zone here, so cut me some slack."

Catherine's eyes narrowed and her lips pinched. If looks could kill, hers would.

Gabriel tried to concentrate, but his brain kept spinning the same question over and over; what might have taken place back at the lab site? *Stop and focus,* he told himself, but it was useless. He couldn't get Jennings, Sandford, and the guards out of his head.

Pushing back against his seat, his thoughts drifted back to his roots, back to Miami's Little Havana where he grew up. It was called Little Havana, but in reality, the area was a composite of refugees from the Caribbean and Central American countries. Most spoke little English and lived in sequestered ethnic groups that dared not venture far from the relative safety of their own streets. As a short and skinny kid, he was often the target of local bullies. He once confided in his father in the hope that Javier would lodge a complaint with some of the parents. Instead, Javier, with affirmation and encouragement, offered wisdom only a father could pass on to a beloved son.

"This life is not for the faint of heart, my son. Do not expect others to fight your battles."

It was hardly the solution Gabriel was seeking. "I don't want to fight anyone, Papa."

"Then learn to use your wits, show them you are not afraid and stand firm. Bullies fear those who stand up to them."

Here in this cold, dormant winter field, with danger a heart-beat away, his late father's simple words of wisdom echoed with renewed clarity. He made the decision to act, to use stealth over speed.

"They'll be expecting us to go east."

"What?" Catherine asked.

"Why didn't I think of this? They'll be expecting us to go east. Let's take the first road north and pray that throws them off."

They traveled in silence through sparsely populated areas until they reached the small town of Winslow, Arizona. There Gabriel swung north on State Road 87, which would take them northwest to where Colorado, New Mexico, and Utah merged.

11

The White House—the same day

Despite the near freezing temperature, the afternoon sun cast a warmish glow over the Oval Office. Looking tired, President Conrad sat at his desk studying a report from the Intergovernmental Panel on Climate Change.

There was a faint knock at the door.

"Come."

His secretary Helen entered. "I checked on Mr. Ferro's mother as you asked, sir."

Without looking up, Conrad responded, "Great, how is she is doing?"

"I called Miami's Mercy Hospital where Gabriel said her tests were being conducted. They had no record of Mrs. Ferro being admitted. I called her home and lo and behold, she answered. She had no earthly idea why I was calling and hasn't spoken to her son in over a week."

Conrad's head popped up. "What?"

"Mrs. Ferro had no clue what I was talking about."

"Good God." Conrad stood and strode to the window.

"Mr. President?" Helen said softly.

"Something's wrong." He swung his hands behind his back. "What the hell is going on?"

"Shall I call her back, sir?"

"Call her back and tell her that you misunderstood, that it was another West Wing staffer not Gabriel."

"Yes, sir."

"Tell her Gabriel is fine and out of town on an assignment."

"Yes, sir, I've got it."

"Tell her he's in California or someplace out west."

"Really, sir, I'll take care of it."

"And Helen—"

"Yes?"

Conrad stuffed his hands into his pockets and stared blankly out the window.

"Mr. President?"

"Yes, right, uh, get FBI Director Hendrickson on the phone."

"Right away, is there anything else I can do for you, Mr. President?"

"What?

"Is there anything else?"

"Oh, no thank you, Helen. Uh, keep this between us."

"Thank you, Mr. President. I'll get the FBI Director on the line."

In the snow-covered Rose Garden, a news crew from one of the cable news channels was preparing to tape a segment. Spotting the president standing at the window, they trained their camera in his direction for an unexpected photo opportunity. Conrad smiled and waved—a sound technician waved back. The President's smile faded, his thoughts switching to back Gabriel. *What could have been so immediate, so secret, to compel Gabriel to mislead me about his mother's medical condition? What?*

12

Gabriel drove some 470 miles through sparsely populated areas of northeast-
ern Arizona making only two quick stops: a two-pump, ramshackle gas station to get gas, drinks, and snacks, and a roadside rest area with nothing more
than questionable toilets and rusting vending machines. Back on the road, dark
clouds smeared the sky, and they soon found themselves enveloped in a violent
thunderstorm.

"Sooner than later we have to reach out to someone."

"I've told you ten times now, Catherine, I have no idea who we dare trust."

"Then I suppose we'll just continue to ride the back roads of America in this
storm until we run out of gas and money."

"Listen, lady, zip your lip!"

Catherine's whipped her head around. "Temper your tone, Mr. Ferro."

"Look, I'm sorry, I'm tired, you're tired, and—"

"At the risk of sounding redundant, call the president, your *trusted* friend."

"Need I remind you that what's sitting in the backseat cuts through all friend-
ships, *Ms. Blake*?"

Legna feigned a loud sigh. "Once again, you speak of me as if I were not
visible."

Catherine twisted in her seat and stared icily at Legna. "Just about now, I wish
you were."

"Dear Catherine, if only I could make your wish my command."

"There's nothing humorous about this," Catherine squawked. "Nothing at all."

At ten past midnight, with the storm still raging, they rolled into the sleepy town of Vernal, Utah, population 13,800. Gabriel brought the van to a stop directly across from a used car lot.

"They'll be searching for this van for sure."

Crossing the rain-soaked pavement onto the car lot, he stopped in front of the small, pale-green, white-trimmed sales office. There were two rows of used vehicles. Gabriel spotted a black GMC SUV parked at the far end of the first row.

"That one, the green SUV. I don't suppose either of you knows how to hot-wire an engine?"

"Surely, Mr. Ferro, you jest," Legna muttered from the rear.

"I know how," Catherine volunteered, "assuming we *have* to do this."

"You can?"

"I have a number of attributes you know nothing about, Mr. Ferro," she said smugly.

As luck would have it, the door to the SUV was unlocked. In short order, Catherine had the vehicle running. Gabriel switched the government license plates from the van to the SUV.

"We passed a closed supermarket a few blocks back," Gabriel said to Catherine. "Drive the van there and park it behind the building."

They continued on in the stolen SUV, uncertain of where they were heading. They were exhausted and hungry, and to make matters worse, the storm had intensified. Strong, sideways-driven rain stung their vehicle like shotgun pellets, and gusts of wind buffeted them violently, forcing Gabriel to slow to a crawl on the dark, two-lane road.

Seven miles east of Vernal, Gabriel spied a one-story motel bearing the incongruous name of *Rainbow Inn* nestled under a canopy of tall quaking aspen trees. The motel's vacancy sign blinked erratically like something out of a low-budget horror movie. He brought the SUV to a stop just short of the motel's driveway.

"We're lost?" Catherine asked.

"It's impossible to keep driving in this storm—we need food and rest." Gabriel bobbed his head toward Legna. "And I'm determined to see no harm comes to *that.*"

Catherine fumed. "Are you suggesting I'm not?"

"Your concern for my well-being is most reassuring," Legna chided. "However, I would encourage more thought for our well-being and less antagonism between you."

"Let' do this." Gabriel pulled into the motel's driveway and stopped by the office. "I'll book a couple of rooms."

The small, cramped motel office smelled of burnt coffee. Gabriel spied a coffee pot on a side table to the right of the door, its red *on* button glowing, its glass container a quarter full of the black brew. An older, portly man, wearing a sweatshirt that read, "Grandpa Rocks," sat with his feet propped up on a footstool. The sound of deep, throaty snores confirmed the man was fast asleep.

Gabriel roused the old guy and booked two rooms. He inquired where he might find food and clothing at that hour of the night.

The manager rubbed the sleep from his eyes and pointed to the window. "There's a 24-hour Wal-Mart on the outskirts of Vernal. Go back toward town about four miles, it'll be on your right. Big sign, you can't miss it. Be careful in this storm."

Gabriel and Legna's room could only be described as early Goodwill. The musty smell of all things old permeated the unsightly, depressing space. Its dark maroon walls looked as if they had been painted with a mixture of whatever combination of colors had been laying around. The soft, lumpy twin beds were impregnated with the off-putting odor of human bodies that had previously rested there. One nightstand, a two-drawer blond dresser, a chair, and a desk—with any number of previous occupants' initials scratched into its surface—made up the balance of the sparsely furnished room. A single framed picture, hanging slightly askew between the beds, depicted an attacking tiger painted on black velvet. A 24-inch, flat screen television and a fading cardboard sign touting free HBO sat atop the dresser, as did a show card offering pay-per-view, feature-length, X-rated movies for $10.95 each or $19.95 for twenty-four hours.

Legna sat alone on one of the beds watching football highlights on ESPN. As the referee made the "time-out" sign, Legna brought his hands together and mimicked it and emitted a low, guttural laugh. But an off-putting sound coming from the adjoining room distracted him.

Through the slightly open connecting door, he heard Catherine gagging, coughing, clearing her throat, and blowing her nose. The toilet flushed, and water ran in the sink. A few moments later, Catherine appeared, her eyes red and watery, her complexion pale. She was holding a damp hand towel to the right side of her face. Her hair, in need of combing, hung loosely around her shoulders.

"Are you well?"

Catherine shot Legna a caustic look and said in a raspy voice, "As well as one can be while running for one's life."

"Human sarcasm."

"That would be correct." She planted herself on the opposite bed and cupped her head in her hands. "I have a throbbing headache."

"You must rest."

She shrugged. "I'll be fine."

Legna mimicked her shrug and turned his attention to the television just as two linemen sacked the quarterback. He winced. "The challenge appears to be the amount of physical violence one human can inflict on another human."

"That's why they call it a contact sport. Do you really need to watch that?"

"Does it distress you?"

"It does." Scooping up the remote, she clicked off the television and began massaging her temples with her fingertips.

Legna scrutinized her for a long moment as if he was seeing her delicately sculptured features for the first time: high cheekbones, round, wide eyes, full lips, and nearly perfect nose and chin. Despite her pleasing features—at least for a human—she looked raw, exposed, and frightened.

"Shall we talk, Catherine?"

She rested her hands in her lap. "Sure."

"We have become intimate, have we not?"

"Intimate? I suppose so—kind of."

"Then we may speak without reservation?"

"Depends."

"On what, Catherine?"

"Intimates share each other's thoughts, feelings, and knowledge. You have chosen to share none with me. Not only that, you seem okay with us risking our lives trying to save yours."

Legna lowered his eyes.

"Right, have it your way. Let's talk about something that's stuck in my craw."

"I am not familiar with this term?"

"A point I wish to clarify."

"Yes, what might that be?"

"Let's discuss emotions. You know what emotions are?"

The alien thought for a moment. "Emotions are an affective state of consciousness in which humans experience feelings of joy, sorrow, reverence, hate, and love. These responses represent nothing more than a state of mental agitation, often brought on by physiological changes in one's existence."

"Thank you for that textbook dissertation. Now, these physiological changes, do they not exist where you come from?"

Legna looked away.

"There, you see, you evaded my question. In the short time we've been together, you have demonstrated a deep, almost affectionate understanding of who we are, but you also hold us in contempt for who *you* think we should be. It is not that straightforward here. There are variables associated with being human that I think you fail to grasp."

"That is a rationalization."

"No, it's just how it is. Our lives are integrated, complicated, and unknowable; sometimes we are good, sometimes not so good. And although we are burdened with our share of troublemakers, there is a core decency, and we demonstrate love for others. Love is the glue that makes us whole and empathetic. It's what separates us from the insects and beasts."

"Emotional attachment is not an acceptable concept; peace, harmony, and balance are."

Catherine closed her eyes and swayed her head. "If you have never known love, I feel sorrow for you."

"You also hate... I feel saddened for you."

Catherine swallowed and looked away.

"Do not be disheartened, Catherine, for I am no more or less than you."

Her eyes came back to him. "Right, next you'll tell me about all the things we have in common."

"You wish our present predicament to end." It was a statement, not a question.

Catherine made a slight smacking sound with her lips. "Good guess."

"I assure you again, I do not command such ability. I remain in your charge."

"Do I really look stupid to you—do I?" Catherine scooped up the damp towel, ran it across her face, and tossed it back to the bed. "Where are your buddies? Hell, even we despicable humans would send a rescue team to save one of our own."

If Legna understood the question, he avoided answering it. He took her hand in his and gently squeezed. "Much remains beyond your understanding."

Catherine jerked her hand away. "Then feel free to explain what it is that I don't understand."

Legna reached for her hand again and held it tight. "Be trustful, for I have come as a messenger of peace and goodwill."

There was an urgent pounding at the door. Instinctively, Catherine stiffened.

Legna released her hand. "It is only Gabriel."

The pounding sounded again, this time more urgently. Moving quickly to the door, Catherine peered through the peephole. Gabriel stood in the rain dripping wet and shivering. His arms were wrapped around two Wal-Mart shopping bags. Swinging the door open, Catherine was assaulted by a gust of wind and a spray of rain, and she stepped back.

Gabriel dashed into the room. "Who the hell builds a motel without an over-hang outside the rooms? It's not fit for man, beast, or aliens out there."

"Humor—I approve." Legna mused.

Gabriel was wearing a new, blue windbreaker, but the rain had soaked completely through to his shirt.

Catherine took the shopping bags and set them on the desk. "Get out of those wet clothes."

Spying the towel on the bed, Gabriel scooped it up and rubbed it vigorously through his wet hair. "There are sandwiches and fresh clothes for both of us and a jacket for you—it's a kid's size."

Legna feigned indifference. "My protoplasm self-regulates in changing environments. I do not require additional garments."

Gabriel feigned a smile. "How convenient."

He had bought a dark brown, long-sleeved shirt for himself, a high-neck, gray wool sweater for Catherine, and jeans and blue windbreakers for them both. Reaching into one of the bags, he pulled out two wrapped sandwiches, a large bag of potato chips, two cans of soda, two toothbrushes, and a small tube of toothpaste. "They tell me you don't consume our food, so I didn't get you anything."

"I do not require human sustenance." Legna said.

"Gabriel," Catherine instructed, "hang that jacket in the bathroom to dry."

Gabriel playfully saluted, scooped up the new jeans, and went off to the bathroom to change.

Catherine sat on the bed and unwrapped what turned out to be a ham and cheese sandwich on rye with mustard. She eyed it dubiously. "Gabriel, how old is this sandwich?"

"Beats me," he called from the bathroom.

Afraid of another unwanted circling of the commode, Catherine nibbled on the edge of the sandwich until she felt Legna staring. "It's not polite to stare."

"I was contemplating the human thought process."

"Reach any conclusions?"

"Several."

"Go for it."

"Humans squander precious moments justifying their flawed history in an attempt to infuse meaning into their lives."

"Whoa, where did that obnoxious statement come from?" Gabriel snickered as he exited the bathroom. "Is there a point?"

"He's very short on specifics," Catherine said waggishly.

"You wish me to provide clarity?"

"Yes, considering just mere minutes ago, you sidestepped my questions."

"What questions? Can I get in on this?"

"Catherine is seeking clarity."

"This may surprise you," Gabriel chimed in, "but we humans *do* seek clarity no matter how painful it might prove to be."

Legna's brow stretched upward. "More precisely, humans practice duplicity, choosing between right and wrong, truth and lies when it favors their position while dismissing others whose appearance, lifestyle, and beliefs do not reflect their own."

"There you go again, wrapping all mankind into your perception of what our moral, psychological, and aesthetic qualities ought to be."

Like a giddy child, Legna clapped his hands. "Bravo, Gabriel, well said on behalf of a declining society."

The alien's hurtful remark proved one too many for Gabriel, and he blurted, "Go straight to hell!"

In that split second, with those four hurtful words, Gabriel had expressed his growing acrimony with the alien's continued condemnation of the human race. He waited for Legna to retaliate, but the alien simply looked away.

"Cat got your tongue, Citizen Legna?" For the first time since they had met, Gabriel had addressed Legna by name.

"Stop it, both of you!" Catherine scolded.

"Don't yell at me, he started it."

"Gabriel, stop!"

"Let us heed Catherine's advice and be finished with this unproductive discourse." Legna strolled across the small space and stopped mid-room. "To be the master of one's fate, one must embrace the free will that has been bestowed upon them."

"Free will does not always dictate how humans make decisions."

"Come, come, Gabriel, do not sugarcoat it, as you say. At the moment of decision, one must realize they command the free will to have done otherwise."

"That makes a great sound bite, but there are forces that often negate free will."

"Only if one allows one's self to yield to such odious forces. Your life is purposeful, but only if you accept responsibility for it."

Catherine saw an opening, and she seized it. "If what you say is true—that our lives are purposeful—then something or someone had to create that contrivance. I have faith there is a dynamism behind all there is or will be. Even though your very existence places many of our fundamental beliefs in question, I still trust there is *something* rather than *nothing* guiding our existence."

"Then you are conflicted, Catherine. You profess faith in a divinity you cannot see, hear or touch. I find that curious from one trained to seek authentication as the basis of knowledge."

And then Legna fell silent, his gaze wandering aimlessly as it often did.

"Well, that's it? I wouldn't dare stop you now!"

"Catherine, let him explain." Gabriel scolded.

"Hopefully, in my lifetime."

Legna's gaze came back to Catherine. "Faith in a divine creator is a human concept, a hypothesis that demands that one expresses his or her fidelity beyond their range of knowledge or understanding. It is that very mystery that drives you. If it were not so, humans would not engage in so many diverse doctrines."

"Now that you pose the question," Gabriel said, "I have an opinion on the subject."

"I'm sure you do," Catherine seethed.

"Hear me out. Most of us follow a particular doctrine by default, one taught to us as children, mostly based on dogma promulgated by ancients."

Catherine sighed. "Where are you going with this?"

"Just this; consider that to most, death is a terrifying final act. Can we agree on that?

Catherine conceded with a nod.

"So, to counter that final, fatal act, we created a safety net."

Catherine feigned a sigh. "What are you talking about?"

"I think we can agree we humans lack a built-in stop mechanism that warns us not to give in to anger, pettiness, ego, and greed. So, to counter those weaknesses, we created a path to redemption, a fairy-tale ending called heaven. But what if we all followed a strict code of ethics, morality, and conscience to begin with? The redemption and reward we seek would be here on Earth, and not in some enchanted hereafter."

Catherine countered. "If our existence is to be validated, there has to be a grander scheme."

"As one who seeks authenticity," Legna offered, "your conjecture on the subject is bewildering."

"Don't assume that I automatically negate what I cannot authenticate. Your very existence makes my point."

"I assure you, dear Catherine, you will find no solace in the mysteries you seek to define."

"You say that with surety as if you know something we don't. Okay, prove me wrong."

Legna brow edged up, "My counsel is reserved for your president."

"Well, now," Gabriel intoned, "considering our present outlook is precarious at best, it's in your best interest to enlighten us first."

A burst of lightning illuminated the room, followed by a loud crash of thunder. Then all went eerily quiet except for the rhythmic *tap, tap, tap* of the rain against the window. Finally, Legna spoke just above a whisper. "Perhaps the parallels that bind all living creatures to their source will provide enlightenment."

"Considering that no one in his or her right mind would waltz you into the office of the President of the United States without first knowing why," Gabriel challenged, "enlightenment is strongly encouraged."

13

With his shoulders slumped and his eyes to the floor, Legna strolled to the window. As if ordained, a lightning strike exploded with such force, it encircled the alien with an ethereal glow. He placed the fingertips of both hands firmly against the condensation that had gathered on the cool window glass.

And then he did something quite odd.

Bringing his right hand to his face, he sniffed his fingers as if the dew held some abstract meaning known only to him. "Your world is quite captivating after a renewing rain." He inhaled long and slow as if the musty scent stimulated his alien senses. "The air is sweet and fragrant, the land more sharply defined." After a long pause, he said just above a whisper, "What I reveal now, I do now I do with reservation, for it is enlightenment no other humans possess."

"If you want our help," Gabriel said, "best you come clean, as us humans say."

Gabriel and Catherine waited breathlessly. But, Legna's gaze went to the floor. He became silent as if he had slipped into a state of being available only to him, swaying ever so slightly from side to side for several agonizing moments before turning and staring fixedly at them. Yet, he said nothing—not a word, not a syllable.

They waited.

Seconds ticked away.

Finally, Legna spoke, delivering each word in a precise, monotone, clinical rhythm. "Your planet—your very being—is but a blink of an eye in the vastness of existence."

"Our planet is 4.5 billion years old, hardly a blink of an eye."

"And you know this how, Catherine?"

"Scientific methods—primitive to yours, I'm sure—measures time passed quite reliably."

"You are misguided, Catherine."

"Am I now? Damn that unreliable science."

"Your present perception of time and time past is but an illusion, a temporary linear mechanism in a non-linear environment. It allows you to arrange sequential relations that one event has to another. Advanced civilizations function within an all-encompassing dimension in which all activity moves in but one direction—forward—moment by moment, perpetually renewed and transitory. It cannot be captured or retained."

"The human mind reacts to example," Catherine said. "Without a memory of past events, we would have never advanced beyond our primitive ways."

"And yet, Catherine, humans have repeated the same missteps from generation to generation—so much for making decisions by example. However, there is good news; as your civilization advances to a higher state of consciousness, the perception of time and time past will cease to exist. Until then, time and memories are nothing more than a temporary paradox."

"*If* what you say is true," Catherine challenged, "then I go back to my earlier point; something or someone had to create the devices that you suggest govern our existence."

Legna stood silent and still.

"Rearrange my last statement as a question."

The wind and rain continued to lash against the window with increasing force. Turning back to the window, Legna pressed his palms flat against the glass. He stood pole-straight, his head arched back slightly, his eyes closed.

"Have we lost you yet again?" Catherine hissed.

The alien's head bent forward. "You wish me to reveal what I wish not to reveal."

"If you expect our continued support, best you take us into your confidence here and now," Gabriel said.

"You must not speak of what I reveal this day," the bantam creature cautioned, "for mankind is unprepared to accept such truth." His hands slid slowly down the glass to his sides. "As it is and always has been… we were merely repeating an unwavering cycle in the cosmos." His head arched up sharply, his eyes opened wide. "The created shall one day become…" He paused, drew in a slow breath, and held it briefly before ending with, "the creators."

The significance of Legna's last two words descended upon Gabriel and Catherine like a frightful epiphany. Speaking with calm and candor, the alien proceeded to unravel the most astounding parable either of them could have imagined. It was the inconceivable final piece of the human puzzle.

Or was it a clever artifice to secure their support to expedite a more sinister agenda?

Saturday morning, February 25th

Catherine and Gabriel were nowhere to be found. Except for the dim light spill-ing from the small desk lamp, the room was eerily dark. A young girl wrapped in a brown winter coat sat on the edge of one of the beds. She was pretty and fair-skinned with shoulder-length, silky, blond hair that ended just above her shoulders in small curls. Her eyes were as blue as a cloudless sky. But there was a disturbing two-inch wide swath of red and purple scar tissue running from her right temple, down over her cheekbone, her jaw, and her neck.

Legna was seated on the edge of the bed opposite her. "What is your name?"

The girl smiled. "Kristen."

"That is a pretty name."

"What's your name?"

"Legna."

"*Leg-na*? That's a funny name."

"Yes, it is. What is your age, Kristen?"

She held up her right hand and wiggled her fingers. "Five."

"That is a nice age. Where are your mommy and daddy?"

Kristen twirled the end of one of her blond curls. "Mommy cleans the rooms here—her name is Flora. Daddy's working—his name is Frank." She held her hands up and apart. "He drives a *big* truck, and when he's not working, he parks it in our yard."

"Ah yes, I see," Legna hesitated. "Are you frightened of me, Kristen?"

Kristen giggled. "You're a little funny looking."

"Yes, I am."

She tossed her head back and laughed. "Like Kermit."

"And who is Kermit?"

"He's a frog, silly, everybody knows that. But you're not the same color."

"What color is Kermit?"

"Green!" Her eyes crinkled. "I was just foolin', you don't look like Kermit." She giggled. "You look like my brother Evan. He's twelve."

Legna pointed a long finger to the child's facial disfigurement. "Did someone hurt you?"

Kristen ran the tips of her fingers along the scar. "I was in a *veery* bad fire when I was *veery* little. Mommy told me."

"I understand."

Legna slipped to the floor and climbed up beside Kristen. She studied the alien's face with a child's curiosity. Extending her right hand, she gently touched Legna's left temple, slowly tracing downward, over and under his thin lips. That seemed to delight her, and she giggled.

Legna wrapped a finger around one of Kristen's golden curls. "You are a very pretty little girl with very pretty hair."

"Mommy says I'm a special angel. Do you know what an angel is?"

"Yes, Kristen, I do."

"Have you seen one?"

"Yes, I have."

Kristen face lit up with excitement. "Do they really have wings?"

"The good ones do."

"Wow!" Kristen exclaimed clasping her hands together.

"May I touch your face?"

"Sure."

Legna slowly raised his hand to Kristin's face. With the tip of his index finger, he gently traced along the scar with his fingertips. She did not seem to mind and sat very still. He opened his hand and placed his flat palm over the scar, closed his eyes and kept them closed for several seconds before his eyelids rolled back. What had been gray pupils against white were now solid pools of black. He pressed his hand firmly against Kristin's scar. Her head jerked slightly left, and she gasped. Her eyelids stretched wide, and her eyeballs rolled up and back until only white was exposed. Then her head lurched sharply back, and she let out a low, throaty moan.

There was a knock at the door.

Legna's head whipped in the direction of the sound. He blinked, and his eyes instantly returned to gray and white.

"Good morning. Housekeeping," a woman's muffled voice called out.

Then came the unmistakable sound of a key in the lock followed by the door swinging open. Bright morning sunlight spilled in like warm, melted butter. A young woman in her late twenties stood there carrying a box of cleaning supplies. A vacuum cleaner sat on the cement sidewalk by her side.

Spying Kristen on the bed, the woman said, "Honey, how did you get in here?"

Kristen sat wide-eyed and still, as if in a trance.

"Kristen, honey," the woman scolded, "answer me when I talk to you."

Kristen did not respond.

"So, young lady, you think this is funny?" The woman set her cleaning supplies down and stepped into the room. "I don't have time for this nonsense, I have work to do."

Legna was crouched in the corner just beyond the desk with his arms wrapped around his knees and pulled tight against his chest. "Good morning," he called out cheerfully. "Would you be Kristen's mother?"

There was a moment of confused hesitation as the woman tried to determine just what was smiling at her from that dark corner. Then it registered that whatever it was, didn't belong there. She gasped and let loose with a bloodcurdling scream.

"Please, do not fear me, madam!"

At the sound of the creature's voice, she screamed again and her motherly instincts kicked in. She propelled herself to the bed, scooped Kristen into her arms, and ran out the door nearly tripping over the cleaning supplies.

No sooner had the woman cleared the doorway, Gabriel and Catherine appeared. "What in the hell?" Gabriel exclaimed.

Off in the distance, they heard Kristen's mother's urgent call for help.

Lunging into the room, Gabriel grabbed Legna's hand. "Come on," he ordered. "Move, in the car, now! Leave everything—let's go!"

They escaped from the motel before anyone could respond to Kristen's mother's calls for help.

"What were you thinking?" Catherine barked at Legna. "We stepped out for a simple cup of coffee."

Like a child scorned, Legna hung his head down. "I saw the female child outside the room and I—"

"You invited her in?"

"I did so."

"Are you trying to get us killed? Did that ever occur to you?"

"Her young girl's name was Kristen. She said she was playing Hop Scotch. What is Hop Scotch?"

"Oh, for God's sake, this is nuts!"

"Catherine," Gabriel said, "what's done is done. I didn't list the vehicle's license plate number on the registration. The manager won't be able to provide any details."

"That solves everything, doesn't it?" Catherine groaned.

14

In an open field bordering the rear of the Rainbow Inn, a Black Hawk and an Apache helicopter sat with their rotor blades whirring. The NSA had intercepted a call to the Uintah Country Sheriff's Department describing how an unidentified creature had been found in one of the Rainbow Inn's rooms.

There was frantic activity as the paramilitaries swarmed the place. Having been instructed to stay out of the way because this was—for reasons unexplained—a federal matter, the local sheriff and two of his deputies stood by their vehicle looking rather sullen.

Several men were sweeping the rooms where Gabriel, Catherine, and Legna had spent the night. They found nothing more than the remnants of what had been left behind.

Kristen's mother Flora, visibly shaken, held Kristen tightly to her side while speaking animatedly with one of the men. "It was short and kind of human looking! Like a young boy, but bald with no ears and gray skin."

"Did it make any sound, ma'am?"

"Yeah, yeah, it said good morning!"

"Good morning—anything else?"

"I didn't hang around long enough to have an intimate conversation. I grabbed my child and hauled my butt out of there. Have you seen my daughter's face?"

Confused, the man glanced at Kristen. "What about it?"

Flora turned Kristen's head toward the man so that the right side of her face was clearly visible. "There! Explain that, if you can!"

Having no idea what the woman was talking about, the guy examined Kristen's face, but saw nothing out of the ordinary "What is it I'm supposed to see?"

Flora pointed to Kristen's face. "There!"

Kristen's burn scar was completely gone.

A second uniformed man approached. "Sir, the Sheriff said an auto dealer in Vernal is reporting a stolen vehicle—a late-model green GMC SUV. The motel manager saw one parked in front of these rooms last night."

"Did he get a plate number?"

"No, sir, but a blue government van minus its license plates was found in a grocery store parking lot in Vernal. It's registered to the government."

The man blew a breath. "Okay, what's the major route going east from here?"

"Route 40."

"Load up, let's go."

Gabriel followed backcountry roads until he came to the town of Loveland, Colorado. There he ran into Route 40, which ran East and West through the center of town.

"We'll try going East again."

He turned right on Main street until he spotted a two-pump gas station and convenience store on the right and pulled in.

"We better gas up and get something to eat. You need to use the facilities?"

Catherine sulked. "No."

Gabriel twisted in his seat and pointed to the only item they had taken from the hotel—an old, brown blanket. "*You!*" he said sternly to Legna. "Cover up and stay out of sight. Catherine, lock the doors and keep them locked until I return and gas up."

Gabriel slipped out and closed the door, making a downward motion with his index finger until he was sure Catherine had engaged the lock.

Twisting in her seat, she opened her mouth to say something to Legna but hesitated.

The alien lay across the back seat with the brown blanket pulled up to his neck. "You wish to question me, Catherine?"

"I've given serious consideration to what you told us last night—I cannot accept it."

"Why might that be, Catherine? I did not mislead."

"I refuse to allow the essence of our existence to be defined by you. You are not God!"

"Are you so certain?"

It was not the answer she expected.

"I have bestowed upon you what no other human knows."

"You are *not* God!"

Pushing the blanket aside, Legna sat up. "Hear me well, Catherine. We are all manifestations of a single, all-powerful force—the omniscient *Originator*—the Imperator of all universes and galaxies, a force that always was and always will be. Embrace this truth and be free of the parables that constrain you."

In defiance, Catherine shot back, "I refuse to blindly accept—"

She was interrupted by Gabriel's urgent tapping on the window.

"This conversation has only just begun," Catherine said through clenched teeth as she unlocked the door.

Gabriel handed her a plastic store bag. "There's bottled water and snacks—not much to choose from in there. Be right back."

"Where are you going?"

"Be right back."

Gabriel strode off across the parking lot toward an elderly white-haired man smoking a cigarette by an aging Ford Taurus.

The commander of the Apache helicopter had committed to following Route 40 East. It was a calculated risk, and he knew it. If he were wrong, they would lose precious time. They had not been flying long when they spied what appeared to the stolen green SUV ahead.

"Goddamn, that looks like it!" The Commander yelped. "Drop this thing down in front of them. Cut them off!"

The Apache overflew the van and set down on the highway just ahead of it, causing the van to screech to a stop some fifty feet short of the Apache. The Black

Hawk landed directly behind, cutting off any chance of escape. With traffic stacking up quickly, three armed men jumped from the Black Hawk with their weapons trained on the SUV.

"Take out a tire," the Commander ordered.

The first shot exploded the SUV's left rear tire.

With a bullhorn in hand, the Commander called out, "The next shot will be through a window. Get out of the van with your hands high where I can see them."

A few anxious seconds passed before the driver's door partially opened, and a hand flew high in the air.

"Get out now!" the Commander yelled into the bullhorn.

The driver's door swung wider, and the old, white-haired man Gabriel had approached back at the Loveland gas station, slipped out. His feet hit the ground, and his hands shot up as high as his arms would allow.

"What in the hell?" the Commander wailed.

Two of the armed men rushed the van, forced the old man to the ground, and handcuffed him. Weapons at the ready, they swung the van's doors open. It was empty.

The Commander crossed the road and got in the old man's face. "Where did you get this van?"

"I didn't steal it, honest to god. I traded it for my old Ford."

"What?"

"Back in Loveland at the gas station, the guy traded this here van for my Ford Taurus and gave me a seventy-dollars to boot." The old man was on the verge of tears. "That's the god's honest truth. Listen, mister, if you want the van, take it, just give me my Ford back."

"Was anyone with the guy?"

"A woman—he said it was his wife."

"Anybody else?"

"I didn't see nobody else."

The Commander stuck a photo of Gabriel in the man's face. "Is this the man?"

"Yeah, yeah, that's him. Listen, I don't know why the crazy damn fool wanted my old Ford. All I know is this one here is better, and I can sure as hell use the seventy-dollars."

The Commander threw up his hand and stormed back across the highway to the Apache. "Goddamnit!" he cursed and flung the bullhorn across the highway.

15

They drove in silence. There was little to be said and much to contemplate con-
sidering the fantastical tale the alien had related the night before.

They were nearing Evans, Colorado. Gabriel knew he had better come up with
a plan to end this misadventure, and the sooner, the better. Even if they were able
to avoid capture, they would never make it to D.C. in the ramshackle Ford. The
dark blue paint had long lost its luster, and visible rust had invaded the lower
frame beneath the doors on both sides. Abruptly, he steered the Ford to the side of
the road within a few feet of a roadside billboard.

"What's wrong?" Catherine asked.

"We can't keep running. The odds are one-hundred percent against us."

Catherine scoffed. "I couldn't agree more. What do we do?"

Gabriel thrust a hand into his windbreaker and retrieved the phone Owen
Jennings had given him.

"What are you doing?"

"My neighbor Zack Worley, he works for the State Department. I've known
him since Conrad was in the Senate." Gabriel stared at the phone like it was an
enemy to be avoided at all costs. "Understand that if I do this, it could come back
to bite us."

"We're out of options. Do it."

He powered the phone up. A few seconds later he had a dial tone. "Bingo!" He
punched in Zack's number.

In a barely audible voice from the back seat, Legna cautioned, "An unwise
decision, Gabriel."

Gabriel hit *send* and waited. Five rings later Zack's answering machine clicked on:

"Hi, this is Zack and Jennifer. We cannot take your call right now, but if you leave a phone number and a message, we will get back to you as quickly as we can. Thanks, and have a great day."

"Zack, this is Gabriel. It's urgent I speak with you. I'll try your office, but if we don't connect, call me ASAP at…" He turned to Catherine with a bewildered look. "I don't know the number."

"Didn't Jennings tell you?"

"I have no idea what the number of this phone is!"

"Then call Jennings!"

"Bad idea, he would have called us by now if…" He left it hanging.

Twenty-seven seconds had expired since Gabriel first placed the call. Legna unbuckled his seat belt, lurched forward, snatched the phone from Gabriel's hand, and broke the connection.

"Why the hell did you do that?" Gabriel barked.

Legna tossed the phone in Gabriel's lap. "You have foolishly defied Mr. Jennings words of caution."

"But I—"

"But nothing, Gabriel," Legna scolded. "You held in your hand a locator device."

Deep within the bowels of NSA headquarters, in the Signal Intelligence Section, rows of men and women sitting in small cubicles hunched over expansive arrays of computers and video monitors. One young technician's eye was glued to his audio waveform monitor; something had caught his attention. The words "Audio Match" popped up in bold, red letters.

"Gotcha!"

The young man's fingers flew over his computer keyboard with urgency. Seconds later, Gabriel's photo and stats popped up. A second monitor displayed a satellite feed of the western United States. The image zoomed in on Colorado showing a fifty-mile radius surrounding the towns of Evans and Greely: Greely to the north of State Route 40, Evans to the south.

"Hello, Colorado, how's the weather?" the operator whispered with a satisfied grin.

A passing supervisor spotted Gabriel's photo. "That's the president's Chief of Staff."

The technician flinched. "Jeez. I didn't see you there."

"Isn't that Gabriel Ferro?"

"Yes, sir."

"Why are we tracking him?"

The operator held up a yellow Post-it with Gabriel's name written on it.

The supervisor examined it. "Who authorized this?"

The technician's shoulders raised and contracted. "Director Benthurst handed it to me with instructions to contact him immediately if—"

"I haven't seen the Director down here today."

"I was called to his office just before my shift began."

"And you didn't think that odd?"

The technician shrugged.

"What's going on here, tracking requests come through me?"

"The director instructed that I report directly to him on this one."

"Did he now?" The man thought for a moment. "So, what have you found?"

The technician pointed to the monitor. "He's somewhere in that area of Colorado."

"Colorado?"

"Yes, sir."

"And the Director ordered this personally?"

"Yes, sir, he did."

The supervisor thought for another moment. "Okay then, do as you were instructed."

Two miles from where they had stopped by the billboard, Gabriel pulled over to the side of the road.

"What's wrong now?" Catherine asked.

He pointed to a sign that read *Skip's place* with a large black arrow pointing down a dirt road to their right.

"What about it?"

"There was an arrow on that billboard back there pointing in this direction."

Catherine looked at the sign. "What's Skip's Place?"

Without responding, Gabriel swung down the dirt road until they came to a gabled-roofed barn that looked like it might have sheltered farm animals in a past life. The structure's brown, faded façade was in dire need of a fresh coat of paint, as was the sign that read *Skip's Crop Dusting*. A new black 4X4 Dodge pickup was parked next to a vintage Huey UH-1H military helicopter, its olive-drab paint discolored and dust covered. The name *Irene* was splashed across its nose in bright red letters.

Catherine eyed the helicopter with a look of dread. "You can't be serious!"

"Apparently, he is," came Legna's disinterested voice from the rear.

"Apparently, I am. Cover up," he called to Legna.

"Wait a minute!" Catherine protested. "You're going to trust a total stranger? Are you mad?"

Gabriel slipped out of the Ford.

"Gabriel!"

Ignoring Catherine's plea, he entered the barn through the large, open sliding doors. The air inside was thick with the pungent smell of oil, grease, and aircraft fuel. Several fifty-five-gallon drums of insecticide lined the left wall.

"Hello," Gabriel called out, "Anybody here?"

The distinct sound of a toilet flushing and clothes rustling echoed throughout the cavernous space. From a semi-dark corner in the rear, the door of a small cubicle swung open.

"What can I do for you?" a deep, gravelly voice called out.

"Are you Skip Galinski?"

The man strode slowly out of the shadows into the daylight that streamed through the open doors. He looked to be in his late sixties, six feet tall, broad-shouldered with a full head of unkempt, white hair, and a several-day-old white stubble of a beard. Yellowing teeth tightly gripped the stub of a thick, half-smoked cigar. His slightly paunchy waistline pushed at a light green-gray, military-style Eisenhower jacket. A patch on the right shoulder identified the 129th Helicopter Assault Company.

"Who wants to know?" Galinski called out

"I saw a billboard on the road advertising your services."

"And you followed the arrows."

"I did."

Galinski strolled slowly across the cement floor, eyeing Gabriel suspiciously with every step. "Kind of early in the year for spraying crops."

"I don't need crops sprayed."

"What then?"

Gabriel shifted his weight from one foot to the other. "I, uh, I would like to pay you to transport a few people."

"Does this look like a Delta Airlines terminal? I spray crops, son."

"But you can transport people."

"You don't hear so good do you, fella'? I spray crops. But just for the sake of politeness, where do you need to go?"

"Washington, D.C."

Galinski removed the cigar and spit on the floor. His lips curled into a grin. "Not hardly, son."

"Why not?"

"Well, even if I did agree, Irene can't make D.C. on a tank of gas. Now, if you're serious about getting to Washington, here's what you do. Get back in your car, and go east on Tenth Street in Greely—that's US-34. Take a slight left onto US-85 and continue to County Highway 37; that becomes US-85 south. Take the ramp toward tollway E-470, then merge onto Nome Street toward Aurora, and finally, take the Pena Boulevard West exit—number 28— toward Denver International

Airport where they'll put you on a real airplane with wings that'll take you to Washington, D.C."

"I can't do that, sir."

Galinski returned the cigar to his mouth. "Well, if ya' can't remember them directions, I'll gladly write 'em down for ya.'"

Galinski dropped the ending syllables of just about every other word that spilled from his mouth. The cigar made it even more difficult to follow his clipped Western cadence.

"Just a minute, sir." Gabriel slipped his hand into his back pants pocket.

Galinski took a step back. "Whoa, what are you doin' there?"

From his wallet, Gabriel whipped out his White House ID card and handed it to Galinski.

Galinski retrieved a pair of reading glasses from his shirt pocket and scanned the card. He shot Gabriel wary glance. "The White House?" Slipping his glasses back into his pocket, he said with a straight face, "I've always been of the opinion that Washington—especially those pre-teens in Congress—could benefit from a few well-placed heart attacks. Some intellectual type once said that—he was right."

"I don't work for Congress; I work for President Conrad. I'm his chief of staff."

"Well, goody for you, young man. I work for Skip Galinski, and I'm *his* Chief of Staff." He walked past Gabriel, removed the cigar from his mouth, and spit on the floor again. "You seem a bit nervous, son. What's eating at ya'?"

"You were in the military, sir?"

"Why would you want to know that?"

"You wouldn't be wearing that patch unless you had been in that specific outfit."

"So what?"

"I'd like to show you something outside."

Galinski laughed. "Now here's a young fella' who comes waltzing into my business establishment and says he works for what's his name."

"President Conrad."

"Yeah, him—goddamn liberal. Now then, let's see if I have this right: You, who I never met before a few minutes ago, wants to show me something outside, but you haven't told me what it is. Have I got this badass story straight so far?"

"Yes, sir."

"All right then, here's what I'll do. If you promise to stop calling me, sir, I'll take a peek outside to see what the hell's so important to ya."

"Thank you, Mr. Galinski."

"Skip." Galinski waved a hand impatiently. "Go on, I'll follow you."

As they exited the barn, Galinski reached into a wall-mounted cabinet by the door, retrieved a 9-mm pistol, and slipped it in his belt at the base of his spine.

Outside, Galinski spied Catherine sitting in the passenger seat of the Ford. "That your wife?"

"No." Gabriel proceeded to the rear door of the Ford and wrapped a hand tightly around the handle. "Can you come a bit closer, Mr. Galinski?"

Gilinsky's right hand slowly snaked back toward the pistol. "I thought government folks drove fancy new cars?"

"Come closer," Gabriel encouraged.

"What are you doing, Gabriel?" Catherine fussed.

That spooked Galinski even more. He shot a quick glance at Catherine then back to Gabriel. "This is as far as I'm goin', son."

"Okay, okay, that's good." Gabriel's grip tightened on the door handle, and he swung it open.

Legna was lying flat on the seat covered up to his neck with the brown motel blanket. Whipping it off, he sat up and smiled.

It took Galinski a second or two to conclude that what he was looking at, and what was looking back at him, was not quite human. His eyes bulged, and his jaw dropped. The cigar slipped from his lips and spiraled to the ground. "Holy mother of god, what in the living hell is that? The damn thing's gray!" He gasped and groped for the pistol. With his hand firmly wrapped around the gun's grip, he swung his arm out and around and took aim at Legna.

When Gabriel saw the pistol, his eyes bloomed, and he thrust his hands high in the air. "God, wait! Don't shoot!" He positioned himself in front of the open door. "Wait!"

Catherine spotted the gun and her head bobbed forward toward the dashboard.

Legna slid across the seat and peeked around Gabriel. "Good morning, sir."

"Jesus, God Almighty, it talks!" Galinski propelled himself backward, stumbling over his feet and losing his balance. As he toppled backwards, his finger jerked on the gun's trigger. There was an ear-piercing blast and a puff of white smoke. The errant bullet missed Gabriel by an inch shattering the window of the open car door and sending shards of glass flying. Gabriel dove for the ground, Catherine screamed, and Legna fell back and yanked the blanket over his head.

"Sweet Jesus! Who the hell are you people?" Galinski wailed in a shrill voice.

16

FBI Director Stanley Hendrickson sat solemn-faced next to the presidential desk. President Conrad, standing by a window, balled his right hand and punched hard into his left palm. "Damn it, people don't just disappear off the face of the bloody damn Earth for no good reason."

"They do, sir," Hendrickson responded quietly.

Conrad's head snapped in Hendrickson's direction. "What?"

"People disappear almost every day for any number of unexplained reasons."

"Not Gabriel!"

A moment of awkward silence.

Finally, Hendrickson said, "We mustn't discount the fact that Gabriel is a valuable asset to this administration."

"What's that mean in English?" Conrad strode quickly to his desk and sat.

"Well, sir, Mr. Ferro could have been abducted by foreign terrorists or a domestic militant group looking to get to you."

Conrad placed his hands flat on the desk and pushed himself to his feet. "Wait just a bloody damn minute, Stanley. Someone told Gabriel to waltz in here and tell me his mother was ill?"

"Crazy as it sounds, if her life was threatened, he might have turned himself over willingly to protect her. It demands serious consideration until we know otherwise.

"That's the craziest damn notion!" Conrad slumped to his chair. "All right, all right, use all of your resources. Just find him. And until you do, keep this between us until I say otherwise."

"I don't know how long we can—"

"If the bloodhound press sniffs this out before we know something, it'll turn into a media circus and could jeopardize Gabriel's life."

"Yes, sir, but at some point, we're going to have to consider—"

Conrad's right index finger pointed down. "For now, this remains in *this* office."

"Yes, sir. There's another matter. Sorry to burden you with it now."

"What is it?"

"Day before yesterday there was an explosion at a facility in a remote area of the Coconino National Forest. It appears to be government property. The structure was totally destroyed."

"I haven't heard about this. What agency, what was it used for?"

"Well, sir, that's just it, we don't know. It may have been a classified location."

"Arizona is still a state, isn't it? How in the hell can we not know which government agency has an operation in the middle of a National Forest?"

"As you are aware, sir, there are agencies that maintain off-the-book sites for reasons of national security. We think this might have been one."

"You think, Stanley!"

"Sorry sir, but no agency has yet claimed ownership."

"Were there fatalities?"

"Only one male was found. He's badly burned and in a coma."

"Was he identified?"

"He wasn't carrying an ID. He's in Bethesda's burn unit as of this morning. As soon as he's awake, we'll question him."

"Good God!"

"Sir, until we know who was running the place and for what reason, we should say nothing publicly."

Conrad shook his head. "Wonderful, just wonderful! Apparently, it's our day not to know anything about anything. All right, keep me informed. Now, for the love of God, go find Gabriel."

17

Skip Galinski wanted nothing to do with the oddball trio and threatened to call the authorities.

However, Gabriel, ever the politician, prevailed. He recounted their plight step-by-step except for the unprecedented tale Legna had shared with them in the Utah motel room.

"Jesus, that's the wildest damn story I ever heard!" Galinski wailed, "A real live alien!"

"If we don't get him to Washington..." Gabriel's voice trailed off.

The old soldier slipped into military mode. "Maybe I got an idea."

"No disrespect, Mr. Galinski, but we don't know you and—"

"Let's hear him out, Catherine!" Gabriel said.

"No, what we need to do is end this nightmare by contacting someone who can pull us out of this ditch."

"And who might that be?" Gabriel countered.

"For crying out loud, Gabriel!" Catherine bellowed. "There's no conspiracy if everyone is in on it. There has to be someone you trust. If not, I will call someone *I* trust."

"Damn you, Catherine, you're in denial."

"No, *you're* the one who's in denial, *Mr. Ferro!*"

Galinski growled. "You two sound like kids in a sandbox fighting over a pail. It's counterproductive to military tactics. Now, if someone is chasing you as you say—"

"They are," Gabriel piped up.

"That's an assumption. We have no proof," Catherine argued.

"Catherine, I understand and share your fear. If I could wish our situation away, I would, but I can't. So, until there is a clear sign that we're out of harm's way, we should hear Mr. Galinski out."

"This is madness—I want no part of it!" She huffed and stalked off toward the open doors.

"Not that I necessarily agree with the lady," Galinski said, "but it does seem kind of strange that this creature from somewhere other than this troubled planet needs us to protect him. Who the hell travels through space all alone anyway?" Galinski scratched the back of his head. "And how?"

"I trust the man who got me involved in this mess. If he says there's a conspiracy, there's a conspiracy."

Galinski sucked in a long drag on his cigar. "Okay, let's proceed like you're right."

First, to shield the Ford from prying eyes, Galinski had Gabriel move the Taurus into the hangar. Legna remained quietly in the back seat, which struck Galinski as odd, considering all the drama swirling around them was about him. But Legna remained unfazed.

Distancing herself from what she labeled insane, Catherine paced in silent protest just outside the open barn doors.

Galinski spread a map of the United States across the Ford's hood and eyed Legna warily. "He doesn't say much, does he?"

"No."

Galinski took in a long drag on his cigar and blew perfect smoke circles in Legna's direction.

Legna smiled.

"Since we don't get to make a non-stop trip to D.C. in the Huey…" He drew circles on the map around Oberlin, Kansas; Seymour, Indiana; Winchester, Virginia; and Washington, D.C., then drew a straight line between each location, "… we'll stop at each of these oil-stained spots run by fellows from my old squadron—people I know and trust. If we can, we'll change aircraft at each place to keep our trail cold as iced beer." He nodded in Legna's direction. "My boys will be will go ape when they see ET there, but it'll shake out okay."

"I really don't care if your *boys* are astronauts," Catherine growled from the open barn doors. With her feet spaced apart and her hands firmly on her hips, she looked like she was itching for a fight. "Have we lost all common sense? We can't do this and expect to keep breathing air."

Galinski removed the cigar from between his yellowing teeth. "Sure, we can."

She charged across the cement floor, her heels echoing throughout the barn like blasts from a pistol. "You *do not* get a vote, Mr. Galinski. This is *not* a war zone," she snapped.

"Sure it is, you just ain't accepted it yet. Now then Mr. Ferro, have you used a phone since you hit the road?"

Catherine fumed. "You are not addressing my concerns, Mr. Galinski."

"I made one call to a trusted friend in Washington. I got his answering machine."

Galinski plowed on, "Where did you call from?"

"Out on the road by your billboard. Why?"

Galinski sucked air through clenched teeth. "*Ooh,* that was bad. If the spooks nailed your signal, they know you're somewhere in the area."

"You see?" Catherine snapped. "This sinkhole gets deeper, darker, and uglier."

"If they did fix your location, they'll be combing every inch of this little patch of heaven. Give me that phone."

Gabriel dug into his pocket and handed the phone to Galinski who dropped it to the floor and stomped on it with the heel of his boot.

Gabriel was horrified. "Why the hell did you do that?"

"To keep you, Dr. Blake, and that there creature alive, Mr. Ferro. Now then, we should stop the jibber-jabber and skedaddle to Oberlin before whoever's chasing you shows up here."

Catherine softened her tone. "Look, Mr. Galinski, with all due respect, I appreciate what you're trying to do, but—"

"Missy, with all due respect, we can stand around shooting the bull, or we can get our collective asses movin'." He stuffed the cigar between his lips, smiled and added, "Or you can resort to plan *B*."

Gabriel said, "We don't have a plan *B*."

"Precisely my point, son," Galinski dropped his spent cigar to the floor and pointed to Legna sitting quietly in the Ford. "I don't know what in the livin' hell you got there, but it's obvious to anyone with eyes that it's unique to this here planet of ours. So, either you trust that you're doin' the right thing, or you don't. It's that simple." He scooped up the map and began folding it. "While you two squabble over whether the moon is made of Swiss or Provolone, I'm gonna call Jimmy Gillford in Oberlin on a landline. Once in the air, we keep radio silence." Still uncomfortable with a live alien occupying his hanger, he smiled and gave the Ford a wide berth and said, "Howdy."

Legna smiled back as Galinski shuffled off to his office.

Catherine fumed. "You don't get to make this decision alone."

"Catherine, for god's sake, what the hell do you want from me?"

"Pardon me." Legna was standing by the Ford. "Since this conversation embodies my well-being, might I inject a thought?"

Catherine wagged a finger at Gabriel. "Only if you can talk sense into General Ferro here."

Legna made the football sign for time out—if the situation had not been dire, it would have been funny. "Need I remind you of the urgency of my mission? If it requires we take evasive action, then it shall be."

Catherine wagged her finger at Legna. "Why aren't *you* doing something?"

Legna stepped closer to her. "Catherine, dear Catherine, you are experiencing fear, a distressing emotion aroused by impending danger, whether real or imagined. It promotes a destructive state of consciousness, impairing your ability to prevail against a perceived adversary. But know that your fear *is* conquerable." He tapped lightly at his temple. "You are in command." He gently touched her arm. "We shall not permit fear to triumph. We shall prevail."

The sun was high in the western sky. The aging Huey lifted noisily into the air, kicking up a mini dust storm from the downdraft of the rotor blades. Gabriel sat in the co-pilot's seat, stiff-backed with his legs pulled tight against the seat. With safety straps in place, Catherine and Legna were in the rear seat. To facilitate communications over the noise, Galinski had provided each of them with headphones.

As they climbed to altitude, Galinski lit a fresh cigar.

"Aren't you afraid you'll blow us all to hell." Catherine yelled.

"She wouldn't dare." Galinski tapped at his headset. "No need to shout, Missy, I can hear you just fine. If you're wonderin, this old bird's official name is the Bell UH-1 Iroquois, nicknamed *Huey*. A lot of brave souls made it home from wars thanks to this workhorse. In case you were wonderin', the name on her nose is that of my late wife, Irene."

He took a long drag on his cigar and blew perfect smoke circles.

18

By the time the Huey's skids kissed the ground at Jimmy Gillford's airfield, the rim of the far western horizon sky was smeared an orange, green, and blue patina. Gillford's place of business eight miles west of Oberlin, Kansas and was home to seven private single-engine aircraft, two owner-built experimental planes, and a single-engine Beech CT-134 Musketeer Canadian Air Force trainer, which Gillford had purchased at auction to train local wannabe pilots.

"Let me talk with Jimmy alone before exposing you all," Galinski said in his best-sounding military voice.

"You trust this guy?"

Galinski shot Catherine a strained look. "With my life, Missy." He slipped out and slammed the door hard.

Jimmy Gillford and Galinski had served side-by-side in the 129th Helicopter Assault Company until both had retired. Gillford was three years younger and three inches shorter than Galinski. A few hairs shy of being bald, he sported an ample waistline that pushed at his belt.

He greeted Galinski with a smile and a wave. "Hey major, it's been a while."

Galinski chortled. "How the hell do you make a living in this mouse-infested hole?"

"I overcharge like hell."

The two old friends wrapped their arms around one another.

"What's so important that you couldn't tell me over the phone?" Gillford said.

"Come, let me introduce you to my passengers first, Jimmy."

"When did you start carrying live bodies?"

"Now, just stay calm and don't go into a tailspin."

"What's that supposed to mean?"

When they reached the Huey, Galinski swung open the pilot's door. "This here's Gabriel Ferro, and back there is Dr. Catherine Blake."

Gabriel smiled, and Catherine half-heartedly waved.

Galinski set a firm hand on Gillford's shoulder. "Jim, there's one more."

Legna popped up from the floor and pressed his smiling juvenile face against the window.

Gillford's immediate reaction was no reaction, staring blankly at whatever it was smiling at him before his brain caught up with his eyes. His mouth flapped open, he took a step back, and he squeaked in a high-pitched voice, "What the *hell* is that?"

"Damned if I know partner. What say we all gather in your office so Mr. Ferro here can relate the damnedest story you're ever goin' to choke on."

Gillford's office was just short of a pigsty: a few pieces of oiled-stained furniture, a paper-cluttered desk, aircraft parts, a CB radio, and a small TV covered in a layer of dust. Up against one wall was a well-used, cast iron, wood-burning stove.

"Cleaning lady holding out for more money, Jimmy?" Galinski wisecracked.

As soon as they had settled—Legna made himself at home in an over-stuff, faded, aqua blue Lazy Boy rocker. Gabriel laid out his story for a dazed and confused Gillford how they had come to be traveling in the company of an honest-to-goodness extraterrestrial.

"It looks like a bloody damn kid!" Gillford stammered.

"Given that I am actually in the room Mr. Gillford, you may address me directly."

"I was right all along," Gillford said smugly. "I believed those things existed, but everyone labeled me a nut-job."

"I assure you, sir; I am not a *thing*. And Mr. Gillford, may I caution you from doing that."

"Doing what?"

"You wish to share this with your female mate and friends to confirm that you are not a nut-job. Doing so would place us in peril."

Gillford looked to Galinski. "How'd he know what I was thinking?"

"Jimmy, buddy," Galinski interrupted, "don't waste time tryin' to figure out what you're never goin' to understand. Just *don't* blab about what you've seen and heard this fine day."

"And you're taking *that* to the White House?" You're all crazy as loons. The Secret Service will shoot him on sight."

No one commented on Gillford's prediction.

"Now then …" Galinski said, "if they trace these good folks to my place and find the old Ford, they'll be searchin' for the Huey, so I need to borrow the Beech."

"Will I get it back?"

"What kind of a question is that?"

"One my insurance company would ask, Skip."

"You can pick it up all in one piece at Harry's. Call him, but don't use my name. Just tell him the major's comin' his way and needs a bit of assistance. Now, let's roll Irene into your hangar, lest the prying sky-eyes spot her. And you need to take a photo of the three of us with that cuddly little creature. If we were to vanish from this good earth, give it to the press and tell them what Mr. Ferro told ya' and what you've seen with your own eyes."

While they waited for Gillford to return with drinks and sandwiches for the flight to Harry Wilson's in Seymour, Indiana, Catherine made the mistake of pushing Galinski's button.

"Can we assume this Harry Wilson is yet another one of your war buddies?"

Galinski's neck muscles thickened, his voice jacked up. "Little lady, you're in bad need of an attitude adjustment."

"Do not raise your voice to me, Mr. Galinski!"

"Wait!" Gabriel jumped in. "This will get us nowhere."

"Right!" Galinski snapped. "So, decide what the hell you wanna' do, cause it ain't my job to talk you into nothin'. Make up your collective minds before we find guns stickin' up our asses."

Turning on his heels, Galinski stomped to the door, yanked it open, and slammed it hard behind him.

"Nice going, Doctor." Gabriel chided.

Gabriel stormed to the door and slammed it behind him.

An angry Galinski was marching toward the airstrip.

"Skip, wait up," Gabriel called to him.

Galinski spun around so fast that Gabriel recoiled.

Galinski thrust a stiff finger in his face. "I put my sorry ass on the line for you people, and I don't appreciate havin' it handed back to me. You understand what I'm sayin', boy?"

"Yes, yes! I'm sorry."

"This ain't no friggin' softball game, this is hardball. What's sittin' in that office is goin' to flip this wacky screwed-up world on its ass *forever!*"

"You think I don't understand that?"

"No tellin' what you and that dizzy dame understand. Now, these people you suspect are chasing you, you're sure their motives are less than honorable?"

"Yes!"

Galinski moved within inches of Gabriel's face. His breath smelled of stale cigar. "So, make a damn decision one way or the other—go or no go."

Gabriel took a step back. "We're going—we're going to do this."

"Maybe you should check with *Miss Prissy Tight Ass,* first."

"She's scared as hell, Skip, that's all."

"Sounds like you're makin' excuses for her like a teenager who's thinkin' with his crotch. Maybe you got the hots for her—you're not thinking clearly."

"Skip, stop it!"

Galinski took a step closer to Gabriel. "Any further bullshit from either of you and I cut you loose."

Gabriel shook his head vigorously. "I understand."

Galinski lit a cigar, took a long drag and blew smoke in Gabriel's face. "Now then, go tell the Dragon Lady that if she mouths off during the flight, she better sprout wings, 'cause I'll shove her tight ass out." He thrust his right index and little finger at Gabriel's eyes. "Focus, boy, focus. This mission is all about protecting that little creature!"

Gabriel nodded.

"Okay then, let's get this goddamn freak show in the air."

19

Harry Wilson was the same age as Galinski, trim and fit with bushy white hair and a full beard to match. He was a skilled pilot who had flown missions alongside Galinski. During one offensive in Yemen's Abyan Province, he had rescued Galinski, his co-pilot, and four Marines when Galinski's Huey was downed in a U.S. led attack on terrorists.

At sight of the alien along an explanation from Gabriel, Wilson's reaction was even more extreme than Jimmy Gillford's. "And just where in the hell are you taking that, that thing?"

"The White House."

Wilson shot Galinski an incredulous look. "Right, the Marine band will be playing, and the President and First Lady will greet you with milk and cookies."

Galinski laughed. "Wouldn't surprise me if they did."

"Jesus, you're dense, why in the hell are *you* putting *your* life on the line?"

"Because Mr. Ferro and Dr. Blake have placed themselves in the line of fire to save that creature. Or maybe it's because I'm just plain stupid. Now, give Frenchie a holler and tell him the major is comin' his way, but *do not* tell him why. Jimmy will be comin' to reclaim the Beech."

"How are you getting to his place?"

"That scrap heap you call a helicopter will do nicely."

Wilson owned an original 1980 Polish-built Swidnik Sokol helicopter purchased from an air museum in Omaha, Nebraska. It had taken a year to find original replacement parts and another year to restore the aircraft to its former glory.

Like Galinski's Huey, the Swidnik was rigged for crop spraying to ensure the old bird earned its keep.

"Are you serious?" Wilson said. "You're going to Winchester, Virginia in a helicopter I don't dare take more than thirty-five to forty miles from here?"

"Yeah, even though that sorry excuse for a helicopter belongs on display alongside the Spirit of St. Louis."

"You my point. You still want it, or you don't?"

Galinski stuck his cigar between his teeth. "Gas her up."

"You're incorrigible." Wilson smiled and wrapped his arms around his old war buddy. "Godspeed, Skip."

Wilson took a photo of the four of them with instructions to take it to the press if they turned up missing.

Sunday Morning, February 26, Winchester, Virginia

Galinski powered back and began his descent to French Stewart's small air-field, located eighty-one miles southwest of Washington, D.C. Fifty-feet from touchdown the engine sputtered, skipped a beat, followed by a loud pop that sounded like a shotgun blast.

Catherine looked to the window. "What was that?"

Gabriel squirmed in the seat. "Somebody shooting at us?"

Legna sat beside Catherine, unfazed by whatever it was that had caused the noise.

"That would be the carburetor," Galinski said. He cut engine-power and dis-engaged from the rotors which continued to spin in autorotation from the upward flow of air. With only a few feet to go, the old veteran guided the Swidnik down to a hard landing. "Everybody okay?"

Catherine, sitting stiff-backed with her hands tightly wrapped around her knees, was first to respond "I'm okay… I think."

Gabriel was white as a sheet. "Me, too."

"Doing just fine, Skip," Legna called out as if nothing of consequence had occurred.

French "Frenchie" Stewart came running across the airfield to see what all the noise was about. He was tall and thin with a ruddy complexion and thinning salt-and-pepper hair. He suffered from a mild form of obsessive-compulsive disorder, causing him to repeat words.

No sooner had Galinski introduced him to Legna, followed by yet another explanation from Gabriel, Stewart sputtered, "Good God in purgatory, in purgatory."

"Relax, Frenchie, the little creature is as friendly as a puppy."

With eyes locked on Legna, Stewart mumbled, "Yeah, like a wolf hybrid, hybrid!"

By the time the sun had set, the temperature had dropped to a chilly forty-five degrees. Ground fog hugged the airfield like a wet, gray blanket. Catherine and Gabriel camped out in Carter's small, cluttered office, which was at least warm and with a working toilet. Legna, on the other hand, chose to sit alone in the rear of the Swidnik while Frenchie worked on the Swidnik's engine with Galinski looking over his shoulder.

"I checked the serial number on the Internet; this one was built in 1972, for Christ's sake. Harry should retire this antique before it kills him.

"Got something else that will get us to D.C.?"

Frenchie pointed to several single-engine aircraft barely visible through the fog. "Nothing out there belongs to me, so that settles that. D.C. is only eighty or so miles. You could drive there— It would be safer."

"I wanna' land this thing on the White House lawn and shake 'em all up."

"Are you nuts? They'll shoot you out of the sky, the sky before you get there."

"The hell they will," Galinski grumbled.

Except for the refrigerator compressor that whirred like an idling motor scooter each time it kicked in, it was quiet in Frenchie's office. Catherine was slouched on the sofa with her eyes closed.

"Coffee?"

Her eyes opened. "What?"

Gabriel stood over her holding two cups of steaming coffee. "Sorry, I didn't mean to wake you."

"Just resting my eyes."

"Coffee?"

She took one of the cups. "Thanks."

Gabriel pulled a rusting metal folding chair over and sat opposite her. "How are you holding up?"

She forced a smile and shrugged.

"I'm sorry if I yelled at you, it's just—"

"No, no, it's me that should apologize. I know you're doing what you think is right."

"Owen would have known how to handle this."

"We can only wonder what might have happened back at the lab." Catherine's gaze went to her lap.

They were quiet for several moments.

"So, tell me, what makes Dr. Catherine Blake tick?"

"Hmm… my life consists of only a few short chapters—nothing much to tell, really."

"Fill in the blanks."

"Well, … I was born an only child in Denison, Iowa."

"I'm an only child, too."

"That makes us spoiled brats. Mom and dad were high school teachers— mom, English and dad, history." She became pensive—her eyes drifted across the room. "They died in a horrible auto accident when an 18-wheeler slammed into their car at 65 miles an hour. I was eighteen."

"I'm sorry."

"It was the worst time of my life, an emotional roller coaster I thought I would never get off. My dad's brother and his wife—Steve and Margorie—they had no children of their own and they took me in. It was their nurturing, their love, that helped me return to a somewhat normal life… one day at a time. My dream since I was 13 was to become a doctor. I worked my way through medical school with

Steve and Margorie's help and a few grants, went on to get my master's in scientific medicine, and landed a job with a major pharmaceutical company in the R&D department right out of school." She turned wistful. "A year after I graduated, Steve and Margorie died within six months of each other from cancer. Five years later the Navy came knocking with an offer I couldn't refuse."

"Jennings says you're one of their best and brightest."

She appeared embarrassed by the compliment and looked away. They were silent until she sensed Gabriel staring. "Is there something on my nose? You're staring."

"I was just thinking that—"

"Oh no, not another idea?"

Gabriel grinned. "No… what I was hoping was… well…"

"What? Just say it."

"Can we call a truce to our bickering; I'm really not the bad guy here."

"I never said you were." Catherine blew gently on the steaming coffee.

"So far the decisions I've made have kept us alive." Gabriel cocked his head to one side. "Do I get points for that?"

Catherine raised a hand and wiggled two fingers.

"Out of?"

She wiggled five fingers.

They laughed.

"There, you see," Gabriel said, "you can laugh. I like it when you do."

Catherine smiled and looked away, her thoughts drifting to happier times. A few moments passed before her eyes met his again. "I'm scared, Gabriel, really scared."

Considering how antagonistic they had been toward one another; her vulnerability was surfacing in a way Gabriel had not anticipated. Now she appeared exposed and fragile. His first impulse was to wrap his arms around her, to reassure her all would be okay. He reached out and touched her hand gently with the tips of his fingers, "I'm scared too," he said. Immediately, his inner voice screamed—*You're scared too? That's the best you can do to comfort this woman? If you had any chance in hell to make peace with her, you just blew it. She must think you're an idiot.*

Another awkward silence followed. It was Catherine who picked up the conversation. "Jennings told me your parents came here from Cuba."

"In a 25-foot boat with 12 adults and 4 children. Can you believe that? They left everything behind. My dad owned a small restaurant in Cuba. It broke his heart to leave, but once they arrived in America they never looked back. I still have relatives in Cuba that I've never met."

"To become chief of staff to the President of the United States, well now, that's pretty heady stuff."

"Huh! Sometimes, not always. It can be intense, rewarding, and all too often deceptive. You learn quickly that political arguments are hardly ever about the issues being argued, but subterfuge for what is going on behind closed doors. Washington reeks of third-rate people who should never be in positions of power. And yet they're the first to abuse that power on behalf of themselves and their benefactors. It's a game of hypocrisy practiced openly without guilt." And then he blurted, "Jennings told me of the loss of your husband. I'm very sorry."

Catherine recoiled, "I wish he hadn't done that. It's not something I talk about."

Gabriel had touched a raw nerve. "Sorry, I shouldn't have brought it up." *Damn it, I said the wrong thing again. Diffuse this before you put your other foot in your mouth.* "There, you see! That's what you get for accepting a cup of coffee from a socially insensitive Neanderthal."

"No, no, I'm the one who should apologize. Sometimes my mouth engages before my brain kicks in and I come off sounding like the proverbial shrew."

"Apology offered, apology accepted." He extended his right hand. "Let's be friends, let's shake on it, what do you say?"

Catherine's smiled warmly and took Gabriel's hand. For the first time, he was seeing her in a new light, someone other than the women he had initially come to dislike. In that moment of ambiguity, she revealed an inner softness and vulnerability he had not previously witnessed.

"His name was Jeffrey." she whispered.

"Don't relive it."

"I relive it every day at 3:07 in the afternoon, the exact moment a colonel and a chaplain arrived to break the news. First, I lost my parents, then my aunt and uncle… and then my husband." Her eyes began to mist and she looked away. "I was convinced I was jinxed, so I turned inward. If anyone dared get too close, I pushed them away for fear I would lose them too. Emotionally bankrupt, I disappeared deep into my work where I felt safe. Even now, I find it difficult reining in the anger, the bitterness, the mistrust—it's always there just below the surface. I'm making progress—baby steps actually. I'm not all that good in social situations yet, so forgive me if I scratch and bite."

Gabriel smiled and nodded.

"I feel so small right now, like whatever problems I have, they're petty compared to what is happening. The human race is facing the most challenging chapter in its history; for all we know, maybe the final chapter. What must Legna think of us?"

"I fear he sees who we are: a morally corrupt, warring species whose greatest legacy thus far has been body counts; a race that has yet to use its hardwired intellect to right all that is wrong. Perhaps he will take pity on us and lead us out of the darkness that is our existence. So here we are—you, me, Captain Midnight, and an extraterrestrial that looks like a teenager—running for our lives in a broken helicopter."

Catherine set her coffee aside and reached for Gabriel's right hand and encircled it in hers. "So, while we're waiting for the third act, let's you and I be friends."

She began to withdraw her hand, but Gabriel held it firm. He was not sure why, but he wasn't ready to let go.

Catherine cocked her head and smiled. "Can I have my hand back now?"

The soft, inviting timbre of her voice contrasted from the tough-talking lady Gabriel had come to know. At that moment, he no longer saw her as a thorn in his side. Now she was open, warm and accessible, and he responded in a way he could not explain. Finally, reluctantly, never taking his eyes from hers, he withdrew his hand, his fingertips gliding softly over her palm. "We're going to make it."

The clock ticked past midnight—it was Monday, February 27th. The temperature had dropped another couple of degrees and fog continued to cover the airfield. French Stewart went off to his small hangar to find a part—a spring clip, he said.

"A damn spring clip?" Galinski grumbled. "Get some chewing gum and double-sided tape while you're there, why don't ya'?"

Puffing on what was left of his cigar, Galinski zipped his jacket to his neck to stave off the chill. Like a feral cat on the prowl for its next meal, he paced the length of the Swidnik in measured, purposeful steps. On his third pass, he stopped by the sliding door and peered through the window. Frenchie had set up a work light, and except for a narrow shaft that snaked across the alien's face, the aircraft's interior was opaque. He dropped his cigar and snubbed it out beneath his heel. Wrapping a calloused hand around the cold door handle, he slid it open until it locked with a loud clang.

The noise startled Legna, and he flinched.

"Didn't mean to frighten you, partner." He planted his backside on the chopper's floor, keeping his feet firmly on the ground. "It's pretty chilly out here. Wouldn't you be more comfortable inside?"

Legna sat still and silent.

Determined to drive a conversation, Galinski sniffed the air, "I smell hay— must be a farm nearby." He sniffed the air again before lighting a fresh cigar.

Legna studied Skip's unshaven, emaciated face with its craggy creases and extra folds beneath his eyes, which all came together in a loose configuration of skin and bones that suggested a life thoroughly lived.

"You were a hero in your war?"

Surprised by the question, Galinski cocked his head back. "Now why would you want to know that?"

"I am curious."

"Was I a hero? No, just damn scared like every other able body." He took a long drag on the cigar. "They have wars where you come from?"

"Only peace, harmony, and balance."

"Ah, Nirvana!"

"Did you kill humans in your war?"

"I intensely dislike the word *kill*. Makes it sound like we were murderers, which we weren't. We took the lives of those who were trying' to take ours, that's all... although at times we acted with less than compassionate. That's what wars do to people, ya' know; strips 'em down raw and leaves 'em naked and dead inside."

"And yet you were of the same species."

Galinski flicked ash from his cigar. "Yeah, well, that's what we humans do to each other. My theory is that wars are conspiracies created to distract people from whatever the real truth is. Too many are caused by religious differences. Dictators who have little respect for human life start them. Politicians start wars, often for all the wrong reasons. Now don't get me wrong, there are times when you have to stand up against evil forces—God knows there's plenty around. But in the end, wars are stupid human blunders that disrespect life."

"Why do humans not learn from their missteps?"

"The $64,000 question." Galinski scratched at his chin. "One school of thought is that we never solve problems intellectually, but instead let our primitive emotions take center stage every damn time. That's just a fact with us, I'll be damned if I know why."

"You have yet to question me," Legna finally said.

Galinski blew perfect smoke circles. "Well, it's not that I don't have any, but folks a lot smarter than me will be askin' you a bunch before this three-ring circus folds its tent. There's just this one itty-bitty itch that I keep tryin' to scratch—one detail that continues to nag me." He tapped at his left temple. "I keep playin' it over and over in my mind."

"Yes, I know, Skip," Legna said in a whisper.

"Right, Gabriel warned me you read people's thoughts. Well, here's that itch anyway; if you traveled through space and time, how come you, ah—"

"Does the thought challenge you?"

"Well now, here I sit with whatever or whoever the hell you are, and you're lookin' to me, Gabriel, and Miss Catherine to get you somewhere safe." He smacked his lips and shook his head. "Strikes me as being a little *Star Trekish*, if you know what I mean."

"What is Star Trekish?"

"Science fiction stuff."

Legna's small mouth twisted into a full grin. "Yes, I see—*Star Trekish*—like your films."

"Gabriel told me how wretched you think we humans are. Yeah, there's plenty of bad, I'll concede that. But there's a lot more good, ya' know, 'cause no matter what obstacles are tossed our way, the human spirit always wins out over evil on this planet—*always*. It would be a major miscalculation for anyone to underestimate our resolve."

"I would never do that, Skip."

Galinski ran a weathered hand through his tousled white hair and brushed cigar ash from his lap. "They have flowers where you come from?"

"We do."

Galinski laughed and slapped his knee. "Well then, there you go partner, we have somethin' in common. There's nothin' more beautiful than flowers in full bloom, all sizes and colors, so intricate you can't imagine how they came to be. And animals, hell, there's over 62,000 vertebrates and over a million invertebrates roaming around this planet. Amazing! Absolutely, amazing! Now, how do you think all that came about?"

"How do you believe it did. Skip?"

"I was hoping you might tell me."

Legna emitted a throaty laugh. "You are a clever, educated man who delights in causing others to believe otherwise."

Galinski's smile faded. "You know, Mr. Legna, you told Gabriel and Catherine you came to our cozy little corner of the universe to help us. Well, maybe you did, maybe you didn't. It's not for me to decide, but for me to wonder." And then, as if to confirm he was in fact an educated man, he said, "Let me not be *ambiguous* about this. Like any good neighbor, consider staying out of our business. Feel free to go back to your planet and allow us to navigate this world of ours for ourselves." He stood, drew on the cigar, and blew a series of smoke circles. "Just a thought, you understand."

Galinski closed the door, only this time he did so quietly.

Frenchie pronounced the carburetor whole again at 4:40 AM.

"Glad you got it done while I'm still breathing," Galinski cracked.

129

"Major, you always were one big pain in the ass."

"Yeah, but I'm *your* pain in the ass."

Frenchie slapped the engine cover. "Let's hope the hell I got this right."

Since Washington was only eighty miles away, Galinski decided to wait for first light before waking Gabriel and Catherine who were sleeping in Frenchie's office.

At 6:30 AM the new day's sun made its morning debut with a splash of warm gold smudged across a vivid blue sky. Gabriel, unshaven and disheveled, could have passed for a vagrant. Catherine had removed her makeup, and her uncombed hair fell loosely to her shoulders.

Galinski greeted them with a fresh pot of coffee. "We need to get going as soon as your hearts are pumping."

"Skip, is flying in the smartest move?" Gabriel said.

"The worst that can happen is they make us land outside the restricted zone. Down that coffee and let's skedaddle."

Galinski had Frenchie snap a group photo with the same instructions; present it to the press if any harm came to them. Then he bid Frenchie goodbye and glanced at Legna standing by the Swidnik like a kid anxious to hit the road. "Some badasses want to control that little fella'. We're going' to do our damnedest to see that doesn't happen."

"Batman, Bat Girl, and Superman are ya'?"

Galinski laughed. "I wish that were true." Galinski encircled Frenchie in a bear hug. "Take care of your old self, partner."

"Godspeed, Skip, Godspeed."

"Godspeed, Frenchie."

The area around French Stewart's airfield was open farmland. For a while they could fly low to avoid radar detection before all hell loose when they neared the 13-15 nautical mile restricted area around Washington.

As soon as they were in the air, Galinski called to Gabriel. "Okay, son, do like we talked about before somebody shoots us down for violating their precious air space."

Gabriel withdrew a cell phone from his jacket.

"Where did that come from?" Catherine asked.

"It's Skip's."

"Who are you calling?"

"The President."

Catherine's face lit up like a flood light. "Finally!"

Gabriel punched in the private number that would connect him to the Oval Office. After what felt like an agonizingly long wait, the president's secretary answered. "Helen, this is Gabriel."

"Gabriel!" she cried! It sounded like a cheer. *"Good god, is that really you?"*

"Get him on the phone."

"Oh my, the president's in a meeting in the Roosevelt Room."

"Helen, get him on the damn phone."

"Yes, yes! Someone get the president back here! It's urgent! Gabriel, Are you there?"

"Yes."

"What's all that noise?"

"A helicopter."

"A what?"

"Helen, what's the emergency?" President Conrad could be heard booming in the background.

"It's Mr. Ferro!"

"Gabriel? Good God!!"

"I'll transfer him to your desk, sir."

With as much speed as his old legs could muster, Conrad dashed across the ornate Oval Office rug and scooped up the phone. "Gabriel? Gabriel? Are you okay, my boy?"

"Mr. President, listen carefully."

"I can hardly hear you! What's that noise?"

"I'm in a helicopter, and—"

"In a what?"

"*A helicopter!*" Gabriel shouted. "*Sixty-five miles or so southwest of Washington in line with Winchester, Virginia. We could use a military escort.*"

"A military escort? Damn it, Gabriel, what's happening? Where have you been?"

"*Mr. President, we need to land on the White House lawn!*"

"Where?"

"*The White House lawn!*"

"What? For god's sake son, make sense. Helen, find Agent Wilkinson, quick! And get the FBI director on the line."

"*Sir, we just left Winchester, Virginia in a helicopter heading straight to Washington. We need an escort. On-board this aircraft is an ali—*"

There was a loud, sharp *ping*, scratchy crackling, then nothing.

Looking bewildered, President Conrad dropped into his chair. "Hello! Hello? Damn it, damn it! I've lost him!"

His secretary rushed in. "FBI Director Hendrickson is on line 2."

Conrad switched to line 2. "Stanley, Gabriel just called. He's in a helicopter southwest of here and wants to land on my lawn."

"*Sir,*" The FBI Director said, "*the survivor of that Coconino Forest explosion is conscious and talking. He's a CIA Agent by the name of Owen Jennings and—*"

"Jennings? That's Gabriel's friend."

"*He knows what happened to Gabriel. Before he could explain, he slipped back into a coma.*"

"Damn it, the call dropped!" Gabriel's hand was shaking badly now. "This phone is dead!"

"Dead?" Skip yelped.

"When did you last charge it?"

"Don't remember."

"Well, it's dead!"

Just then, Galinski's attention was drawn to the left outside mirror that allowed the pilot to monitor the release of insecticide.

"Skip, did you hear me?"

"Hold on!" Galinski's eyes remained locked on the side mirror for several seconds.

"What is it?"

"Thought I saw something."

"What?"

"Uh, was nothing." Then, as he was about to look away, he saw a dark object slip into his view. Whatever it was, it was pretty far back. His first thought was a flock of birds flying in formation. But the wavering, shimmering shape was gaining on the Swidnik way too fast to be a flock of birds. "Holy crap There's a helicopter on our tail!"

"Where?" Gabriel pressed his face flat to the window.

A second image, taking up a position alongside the first, appeared in the mirror.

"Damn, there's another one."

Gabriel strained to see. "I don't see anything."

"Tighten your seat belts," Galinski commanded. His eyes stayed glued to the mirror until the two objects were close enough for him to identify. "Maybe the president's not your best friend after all. Looks like an Apache gunship and a UH-60 Black Hawk!"

Hearing those words, a shutter went through Catherine. Legna showed concern at all.

Gabriel said, "Maybe it's the escort I asked for."

"We'll find out soon enough—hang on!"

Galinski pushed the control yoke forward, forcing the aircraft into a stomach-churning plunge toward the ground. Down and down they went until he pulled back hard, leveling off one-hundred feet above a wide-open field. With little effort, the fast-approaching Apache and Black Hawk easily matched the Swidnik's maneuver. Now they were a mere 200 or so yards behind the Swidnik. To Galinski's horror, the Apache let loose a burst from its nose mounted M230 chain gun. The 30-mm rounds undershot the Swidnik by inches.

Galinski bit down hard on his cigar. "That answers that."

Jesus!" Gabriel shouted. "Are they shooting at us?"

"Oh, my God!" Catherine screamed.

Legna continued to sit quietly.

With the cocksure confidence of a seasoned military pilot, Galinski pushed the Swidnik into a series of moves that would have caused the most pilots to lose their lunch. First to the right, then a bone-jarring turn to the left, then straight upwards until the Swidnik almost climbed horizontally, then rolling forward and down into another nose dive before leveling off twenty feet above the ground. But the aging Swidnik proved to be no match for the Apache, which repeated with precision each of Galinski's stomach-churning moves.

"We're sure as hell not going to outrun them," Galinski hollered.

The Apache sped wide left then hard right then forward, a move that placed it parallel and slightly ahead of the slower moving Swidnik with only a 1000-feet now separating the two aircraft. The Black Hawk maneuvered directly behind the Swidnik.

Galinski looked to Gabriel. "They're going to box us in—one in front, one in back."

But that is not what happened.

The Apache rolled hard right, which put it on a straight path toward the Swidnik. In that split second, Galinski realized what the Apache pilot was up to and his eyes grew big. But it was too late to react. The Apache's chain gun spewed 30-mm rounds that tore into the Swidnik's outer skin aft of the cockpit. Catherine screamed and tried to crouch forward, but the safety strap across her chest held her fast. Gabriel covered his head with his hands and pushed forward, but his safety strap held him in place also.

Catherine flung her arms around Legna in an attempt to shield him. Her right hand was flat against his chest, and it felt wet. Pulling her hand back, she found it covered in sticky crimson-colored goo. A single round had ripped into the alien's chest just below his left shoulder. He moaned, and his hand went to the wound.

"Gabriel! Skip! Legna's been hit!" Catherine cried out.

Legna's chest heaved as he sucked in quick, shallow breaths.

"Hang on!" Galinski dropped the Swidnik to just above the ground. The fast-approaching Apache over-flew the Swidnik, forcing it to circle around before it could reposition itself in front of the Black Hawk.

Catherine's hand pressed hard against Legna's torn flesh. "Look at me! Look at me!" she shouted.

Gabriel tore off his headphones and snapped open his seatbelt and struggled to make his way to the rear just as Galinski started another series of death-defying moves. The increasing g-forces caused him to lose his balance and he tumbled to the rear floor, landing hard at Catherine's feet.

In an attempt to out-maneuver the Apache, Galinski banked to the right, then upward, then down, then leveled off, but the Apache pilot followed each of Galinski's moves with ease and fired an AGM Hellfire missile from its M261 rocket launcher. Galinski pulled back hard. The missile, fired from a too close range to correct for Galinski's sudden upward swing, zoomed under the Swidnik exploding in a frightening ball of orange and red flames when it hit the ground.

Gabriel removed Legna's headset and placed them on himself. "Jesus, was that a missile?"

"As God is my witness!" Galinski barked. "And it's royally pissed me off. I'm gonna' let the sons of bitches have it with both barrels."

"You have weapons on this thing?"

"Not exactly, son."

Galinski drove the aircraft downward, leveling off and skimming daringly close to the surface. His eyes shot to the side mirror just as the Apache fired a second missile. He yanked the yoke back hard and climbed to the open sky like a cannon shot. As was the fate of the first, the second missile hit the ground and exploded, causing the Swidnik to rock wildly in the resulting turbulence.

Galinski dove again to 20-feet above the surface and leveled off. The Apache, easily matching the Swidnik's moves, lined up directly behind. "Come on, sweetheart, just a little closer. Come to daddy."

As Apache closed the distance between them, Galinski pulled the Swidnik's throttle back cutting its speed in half. Before the Apache pilot could react, he was within 30-feet of the Swidnik's tail.

To Galinski's left, protruding from the dashboard, a raised metal plate held a single toggle switch on the left, and a small, T-shaped handle mounted to the right. He flipped the toggle switch up. From either side of the Swidnik's undercarriage, eight-foot aluminum tubes, each with eight protruding nozzles, sprang out and locked into position like mini-wings. He yanked the T-handle out. Instantly, thick, gooey, yellow insecticide flowed from the nozzles, streaming through the air toward the Apache like a swarm of angry African killer bees and splattering yellow-like vomit over the Apache's windshield.

His view obstructed, the stunned Apache pilot swerved left and throttled back hard, placing his aircraft directly into the path of the Black Hawk. Unable to stop its forward momentum, the Black Hawk ripped into the Apache's rear vertical rotor blades shedding them like papier-Mache. Flying debris filled the air as both helicopters spun out of control, plunging the short distance to the ground and cart wheeling end over end in a blistering inferno of orange, red, and blue flames.

Galinski raised a clenched fist. "There's to ya', fly-boys!"

Gabriel was still on the aircraft's floor. "What happened?"

Galinski whooped. "I sprayed 'em with bug juice. If those tanks had been empty, we'd be up shit creek without a you-know-what."

"How did you know the tanks were full?"

Galinski chuckled. "I didn't, son, I didn't."

With tears streaming down her face, Catherine cradled Legna in her arms and rocked him as a mother would a sick child. "Too late," she said under her breath. "Too late."

Neither Gabriel or Galinski had heard her.

"Hang on, we're gonna' make it." Galinski gained a couple of hundred feet and put the Swidnik through several minor maneuvers to ensure the controls still functioned normally. Despite the stress he had placed on the aging aircraft, the controls were in working order. He planted a kiss on the side window. "I take back all the bad stuff I said about ya', you sexy bitch, you." In the distant, Galinski could see the outline of the iconic Washington Monument came into view. "Damn, that's one hell of a beautiful sight. How's our passenger doin'?"

"We've lost him!" Catherine wailed.

20

Galinski yelled out, "Holy crap!"

Gabriel, still on the floor at Catherine's feet, twisted toward the cockpit just in time to see two F-35 Lightning III fighters screaming toward them. With a loud whoosh, they passed alarmingly close, one peeling left and the other right. Their powerful wake tossed the Swidnik about like a rag doll, causing Gabriel to lose his balance again. His full weight slammed against the right door.

"Goddamn it!" Galinski cursed. "You okay, Gabriel?"

Gabriel's right shoulder had taken the brunt of the impact, and he rubbed it. "It hurts like hell, but nothing feels broken!"

Galinski's eyes widened in disbelief. "What now!"

Gabriel struggled back to the co-pilot's seat and strapped himself in just as two Marine Apache attack helicopters approached.

"We're in a goddamn war zone!" Galinski hooted.

One Apache passed left and the other right. In short order, they made sharp U-turns and within seconds had taken up positions on either side of the Swidnik, but neither displayed aggression.

"What the hell are they doing?" Galinski grumbled.

"I could be wrong, but I think they're escorts!" Gabriel howled.

The F-35 fighters roared overhead again and within seconds were dots on the far horizon beyond the Washington Monument.

The Apache pilot on Skip's left rocked his aircraft and, mimicking a microphone, raised a cupped hand to his mouth.

"This one wants to have a conversation," Galinski spoke into his headset microphone. "Hey, this is Skip Galinski. I have passengers on board, Gabriel Ferro from the White House and—"

The Apache pilot shook his head and tapped at his helmet.

"Shit!" Galinski cursed. Changing radio frequencies, he tapped at his headset. "How's that, partner?"

The Apache pilot shook his head again.

"One of those 30-mm rounds must have knocked out the antenna." Galinski shrugged at the Apache pilot.

The pilot acknowledged with a nod, made a fist, circled it above his head, and pointed forward and down.

Galinski gave the pilot a thumbs-up. He banked left and began a slow descent toward the Washington Monument. The landing spot on the White House lawn was now in sight.

Catherine was crying as she cradled Legna's limp body in her arms.

"Gabriel," Galinski barked, "try that phone again."

"The battery's dead!"

"Pop it out and reset it."

With shaking hands, Gabriel removed the battery, rubbed it on his pant leg, and reset it. This time it worked. "Got it!" A couple of anxious seconds later the call was going through. "It's ringing!"

In the Oval Office, President Conrad paced and four Secret Service agents paced along with him: one front and back, one on each side.

The president's secretary entered in a flurry of excitement. "Sir, sir! It's Mr. Ferro again!"

"Oh, thank God!" Pushing past the agents, Conrad scooped up the phone. "Gabriel, Gabriel, the military reports they found you."

"Yes, they have. Sir, listen carefully. Are you aware that the Directors of the CIA and NSA have had an extraterrestrial in their possession and—"

"A what? You're not making sense."

"An alien—an extraterrestrial. You're going to want to clear all media from the property. You don't want them seeing this just yet."

"See what, Gabriel?"

And then the line went dead.

"Gabriel? Gabriel? Damn it, I've lost him again!" Conrad turned to Agent Denver Wilkinson. "Clear that aircraft to land on the lawn."

"But, sir—"

"Do it! Helen, get the FBI Director here now. And get the press secretary in here." Then, with a befuddled look, he said under his breath, "He said something about…" He swallowed. "… an *alien*."

In the excitement of the moment, no one heard him.

A loud pop that sounded like a firecracker echoed throughout the Swidnik's cabin.

Gabriel pressed his face to the window. "What was that?"

"Carburetor!" Galinski yelled. "We either set this old rig down, or she's gonna' go down on her own."

There was a second pop followed by rapid sputtering, and then the engine ran smoothly again. That lasted for a few seconds before the engine sputtered again.

The Apache pilot on Galinski's left rocked his aircraft.

Galinski waved a hand. "Yeah, yeah, I know, something's wrong!"

The on-again, off-again fuel-starved carburetor continued to work sporadically for another fifteen seconds before the engine simply stopped altogether. It was eerily silent except for the ominous *whap, whap, whap* of the free-whirling rotor blades turning in autorotation. Galinski tried controlling his descent by increasing the drag on the blades, but no matter how honed his skill, the Swidnik was going down fast.

"Brace yourselves!" Galinski yelled. "Brace yourselves!"

Gabriel stiffened and checked his seatbelt. He looked back at Catherine: her arms tightly wrapped around Legna.

Working to avert a full-pitch nosedive, Galinski tapped into every trick he had ever learned. There was only 1000 feet or so between them and the ground, leaving zero room for error. But despite his valiant efforts, the Swidnik was slowly nosing over into an unstoppable dive.

And then suddenly, the Swidnik gently nosed up and leveled before stopping midair as if it had landed on solid ground.

"What in the Hell?" Gabriel gasped.

Galinski's head swung first to the left window, then to the right and finally through the windshield. "Am I imagining this?"

In their excitement, no one noticed that Legna's eyes had opened. In a barely audible voice, he whispered, "Man the controls, Skip."

Despite his bewilderment at hanging dead-still midair without power, Galinski heard those words as clearly as if the alien had whispered in his ear. "What are you talkin' about? We have no power!"

"Skip, guide us down," Legna whispered again.

Through her tears, Catherine realized it was Legna who was speaking. "He's alive!"

Gabriel twisted in his seat. "What did you say?"

"He's alive!"

"Skip!" Gabriel said excitedly. "Legna's alive!"

Galinski wrapped both hands tightly around the yoke and attempted to coax the aircraft forward. To his utter astonishment, the Swidnik was responding as if it still had engine power. He whistled long and slow. "Well, I'll be damned."

With Apache gunships on either side, Galinski guided the Swidnik left past the Washington Monument, over Constitution Avenue, past the Ellipse and set the Swidnik down ever so gently on the snow-covered White House lawn.

Uniformed and plain-clothed Secret Service agents surrounded them.

Wiping a hand across his sweating brow, Galinski dug into his shirt pocket and whipped out a fresh cigar and lit it.

With their attention now on the Secret Service who had their weapons pointed at them, they failed to notice what Legna was doing. He pressed the palm of his right hand just below his left collarbone where the bullet had ripped into his gray flesh. His eyelids closed. When they rolled back, the sockets were solid black. He pressed his hand hard against the entry wound and held it there for a several seconds before removing it. In his palm was a spent 30-mm bullet. It had all happened in less than 30 seconds.

Catherine's attention turned back to Legna just as he blinked and his eyes returned to gray. He held his hand open for Catherine to see. It took a second before she realized the spent bullet was in his hand.

"Oh, my god!" She probed the area where the lethal projectile had entered Legna's shoulder. There was no sign of an entry wound, just smooth, unbroken gray skin. And then before her very eyes, the crimson goo stains and the rip in Legna's clothes disappeared. She checked her hand and her clothing and the stains were gone there too.

21

White House staffers jammed hallways and windows trying to get a glimpse of the odd contraption that had landed on historic ground.

"Sir," Agent Wilkinson said, "I'm ordering the White House into lockdown. You and the vice president will be moved down to the Doomsday Bunker."

"I'm not going anywhere," Conrad scowled.

"Mr. President, we have no idea who's on that aircraft."

"For heaven's sake, it's Gabriel."

Vice President Cross burst in with his Secret Service detail. "What's going on?" he bleated. "What's that contraption doing on the lawn? Who's on it?"

Calmly, Conrad said, "Stick around, Alan. We'll find out together."

Agent Wilkinson was listening intently to his earpiece receiver. An odd look came over his face as if he had not fully understood. "Say again?" His eyes grew large.

"What's wrong?" Conrad asked.

"Gabriel is on the aircraft with a woman and the pilot. He says everything's under control."

"Gabriel!" Vice President Cross bellowed. "What the hell is he doing on that helicopter?"

Wilkinson's brow furrowed. "There's something else, sir,"

"What?" Conrad asked impatiently.

"Not sure I understood correctly, sir."

"Damn it, what didn't you understand?"

Wilkinson seemed hesitant to repeat what he thought he had heard. "Uh…" he stammered. "There's a fourth person on the aircraft, sir."

"Well, damn it, have them brought in here now."

"Sir, I cannot allow you and the vice president to be exposed to—"

"Damn it all to hell, Denver, get them in here!"

"You're overruling me, sir?"

"Yes, I am, do it now."

Reluctantly, Wilkinson whispered into his communication device. "Okay, bring them in."

After what seemed an eternity, the portico door swung open and a contingent of grim-looking Secret Service agents filed in. They had formed a tight circle around Gabriel, Catherine, and Galinski.

Legna was nowhere to be seen.

At the sight of Gabriel, Conrad's face broke into a relieved smile. "Gabriel, thank God you're safe!"

Rumpled and unshaven, Gabriel simply said easily, "I'm fine, sir."

Conrad's eyes probed Gabriel from head to toe. "What happened to you? You look like hell. Where have you been?"

"Mr. President, Mr. Vice President," Gabriel began, "this is Dr. Catherine Blake and our pilot, Skip Galinski. If I may sir, there's someone else." Gabriel nodded to the Secret Service agents. "Gentlemen, please."

The agents moved aside, and there stood Legna—all four feet of him.

At first, neither the President nor anyone else reacted. Then it registered that what stood before him possessed some very non-human features, not the least of which was that its skin was gray.

Conrad gasped and took a quick step back. "Good lord!"

"What the—!" Alan Cross breathed.

"Sir, this is Legna from the planet Ecaep. He had come to see you, Mr. President."

"Me?" Conrad stammered. "Where did you find it? Does it… does it speak?"

Legna's lips scalloped into a broad smile, "C'est un honneur de faire votre connaissance, Monsieur le President."

Conrad's eyes bloomed and his brow rose up. "Good Lord!"

"Did *it* just speak French?" Cross sputtered.

Legna repeated the greeting in Spanish, "Es un honor conocerle, Senor Presidente." Then in Italian, "E un onore per conoscerla, Signor Presidente," as well as in German, "Es ist eine Ehre, zum du, Herr President zu Kennen," and then in Indonesian Bahasa, "Kesenangan menemi kamu, sir." Finally, he finished with, "It is an honor to meet you, Mr. President."

Flummoxed to the point of being unable to assemble words into a coherent sentence, Conrad faltered. "I, uh, you, uh…"

Legna bowed his head slightly. "Mr. President, it is you I seek."

His eyes shifted quickly to Gabriel. "Are there others?"

"I have traveled alone, Mr. President."

"How is that possible?"

The alien's right hand began to rise and it appeared as if he was going to touch the president. Instinctively, an agent stepped between them.

"Hold on," Gabriel said to the agent. "Mr. President, he wants to shake your hand."

The room went dead silent except for the *tick, tock, tick, tock* of the grandfather clock. Conrad's face went pale. He shot a nervous glance to Gabriel.

"It's okay, sir."

Agent Wilkinson quickly stepped between them. "Nor, sir, you shouldn't do that."

Conrad looked to Gabriel—Gabriel nodded.

"Objections duly noted, Denver. Please step aside."

With a defiant stare, Wilkinson took a step back. Ever so slowly, the right hand of the President of the United States and the hand of the extraterrestrial, Legna, intertwined.

With his eyes squarely fixed on the creature standing before him, Conrad said simply, "Welcome."

"I have come as an ambassador to aid the citizens of Earth in achieving peace, harmony, and balance."

Wide-eyed, Conrad repeated, "Peace, harmony, and—"

"Balance," Legna said.

It was all too surreal to be believed.

There are seminal events in time that have sharply defined mankind's history, but the magnitude of this event would prove to be the most defining of all.

President Conrad, grasping the gravity of the situation, took control. "It is necessary, sir, for me to act quickly to protect the world from false rumors."

"I comprehend, Mr. President."

Turning to Catherine and Galinski, Conrad said, "I assume along with Gabriel you each played a role in whatever's behind this?"

Catherine nodded. "Yes, Mr. President."

"Then before I go to the media, I need you to fill me in. Leave nothing out."

Except for Allan Cross, Denver Wilkinson, Catherine, Gabriel and Ship and another agent, the room was cleared. Gabriel took the lead, explaining the alien had been held captive by the directors of the CIA and NSA, how the three of them had escaped from the Arizona site, and finally, their subsequent dash across the country courtesy of Skip Galinski.

Without reservation or hesitation, Conrad took a bold step, decreeing Legna be treated with the same obeisance afforded all foreign dignitaries. He instructed his staff to make arrangement for Legna to be sheltered at Blair House under the tightest security.

"I express my gratitude for your generosity and your kind welcome, Mr. President. I look forward to our deliberations with great anticipation. Before I leave, may I have a moment with those who rescued me?"

"By all means, sir. Do I call you, sir?"

"Please call me Legna."

"Fine, Legna."

Legna took Catherine's hands and pulled her to him. "You are blessed, Catherine. I will miss our enlightening conversations."

"Perhaps we will meet again one day soon."

"I would cherish that." Legna turned to Galinski. "Skip, you are an original."

Galinski chuckled. "Look who's talking."

Finally, Legna said to Gabriel, "Gabriel, if not for your determination and courage, I would have failed my mission."

"Let's just say I was drafted involuntarily."

And that is how the encounter ended. Under tight security, Legna was spirited off to Blair House. Catherine and Galinski were whisked away to FBI headquarters for debriefing after which they were to be sequestered at Washington's Hay-Adams Hotel under guard to keep the media at bay.

As fir CIA Director William Downing and NSA Director Jonathan Benthurst, Conrad directed they be taken into custody.

When everyone had cleared the Oval Office, Conrad, VP Cross, Gabriel, FBI Director Stanley Hendrickson, and National Security Advisor, Charles Bregg, met privately to discuss how best to prepare the world at large for the arrival of an extraterrestrial. As Gabriel expected, it was Alan Cross who would prove to be the chink in the armor. He was the kind of politician people liked to vote for: well groomed, ruggedly handsome, and always nattily dressed. His well-deserved reputation was that of a brash, unyielding but expert negotiator whose language was more often than not peppered with profanity. Despite Cross' over-the-top persona, Conrad was confident that if called upon Cross, a career diplomat and a former secretary of state, could step in and successfully lead the country.

Gabriel and Cross had only met on two social occasions prior to his selection as Conrad's running mate. Early on in the campaign, Gabriel became aware that Cross found his close relationship with Conrad troubling. Conrad often sought Gabriel's counsel before consulting with either his advisers or Cross. It came to a head during a campaign stop in Bangor, Maine. Cross verbalized his resentment to Gabriel in a profane tongue-lashing. Incensed by Cross' audacity, Gabriel refused to speak directly to him until Conrad finally stepped in and ordered a ceasefire between them. From then on, Cross and Gabriel maintained a professional, if distant, relationship.

"When I requested a briefing on the subject of aliens and UFOs, the damn fools at the Department of Defense brushed me off like I was a crackpot," The president grumbled. "Now who's laughing?"

"The DOD has never trusted presidents fearing one might spill the beans," National Security Advisor Bregg said.

"That's a bunch of hooey!" Conrad spit out. "How the hell am I supposed to do my job if you guys keep secrets from me?"

No one answered.

"Blair House—in the middle of Washington?" Cross blurted. "We've welcomed an alien into our midst like royalty, one who we know nothing about."

"Alan, Alan," Conrad said. "We are witnesses—now participants—to the most prodigious event in the history of all mankind. This is not a time to react out of fear."

"But we have absolutely no proof he's telling the truth, or whether this is a clever guise masking something more sinister. To be sure, you'll get no support from Congress on this."

"Congress?" Conrad shook his head. "Nothing that bunch of thieving bloodsuckers might do matters much now."

Cross' neck muscles thickened and his face reddened. "Damn it, you're shooting from the hip, placing the entire world in danger. You're just one man, William, you cannot be allowed to make a decision of this magnitude alone."

"Choose your words carefully, Alan."

"Look, all I'm saying is, we literally know nothing other than what Gabriel and this creature has told us, which at this point amounts to nothing. There could be thousands of them waiting on the horizon to do us harm. Surely, they'd have stealth capabilities—we wouldn't even know they're there."

"I spent three days with him, and I saw no threat." Gabriel said. "We should treat this emissary respectfully until—"

"Emissary? Is that what the hell you're calling this, this creature from God knows where?" Cross turned to Conrad. "William, listen to reason, you're getting dangerously bad advice here. You simply don't have the authority to make this decision alone."

"Actually," Gabriel interjected, "as commander in chief, he does."

Cross' face flushed with anger and his enmity was swift, shoving a hand against Gabriel's shoulder just hard enough to force Gabriel back a full step. "I'm done listening to you."

Conrad was horrified. "Alan, how dare you! Do that again, and I will personally kick your ass."

Realizing his blunder, Cross took several steps back. "I'm sorry, I didn't mean to—it's just that…"

Conrad cut him short. "I don't care what the hell you meant, you stepped over the line. I intend to meet with this alien as he requested while DOD briefs you on whatever the hell it is that will make you feel secure."

"I'm on record here and now; I vehemently disagree with your handling of this."

"Objection duly noted," Conrad snapped. "Now then, was there something else you wished to add?"

Cross, looking mortally wounded, backed his way to the door, swung around, and left.

To FBI Director Hendrickson, Conrad said, "I need an immediate investigation into the CIA and NSA Director's involvement."

"Yes, sir."

"Gentleman, unless there is something you wish to add, I'd like to speak to Gabriel alone."

"Thank you, Mr. President," Bregg and Hendrickson left.

Conrad, looking tired, strolled slowly to his desk and sat. "Sometimes Vice-President Cross doesn't know when to get the hell out of his own way. But I cannot—I will not— allow us to react out of fear. Not this time… not this time."

"My oldest friend, Owen Jennings, he was the CIA agent in charge and—"

"He's at Bethesda."

"What? He's alive!"

"Badly burned, in critical conditions and in a coma, I'm afraid."

Gabriel breathed a sigh of relief. "Thank goodness. Any word on the others, sir?"

"Agent Jennings was the only one found. The FBI will want to know who else was there."

"Yes, of course."

22

The White House press office released a statement confirming a single extraterrestrial being had arrived on the planet and was the guest of the American government. No mention was made of the alien having been held captive in Arizona or that Gabriel had been involved. The public was simply told that Legna, as he was called, was an emissary from the planet Ecaep, whose location had yet to be determined. It was a quick, brief statement to calm the press and the populace in an effort to deflect false rumors.

And so, it came to be that the alien known as Legna from the planet Ecaep was the sole guest at 1653 Pennsylvania Avenue. Area traffic was rerouted for five blocks in all directions, adding to Washington's already out-of-control gridlock. DC police, Secret Service, the FBI, and a Marine unit was assigned to guard Blair House 24/7.

The area around Blair House resembled a war zone.

To quell the expected hysteria, it was paramount that President Conrad addressed the world without delay. Initially, a news conference was called for at 10:00 PM that same night. However, Conrad squashed that idea in favor of an address from the Oval Office early the following morning at 11:00AM.

Despite the makeup lady's valiant efforts, President Conrad sat behind his Oval Office desk still looking tired from the excitement of the day before. When the camera went live, he began.

"Let me begin by assuring the world that despite the rumors circulating on social media, there has been no alien invasion of our planet and there is no cause for alarm. Our distinguished visitor, whose name is Legna, has traveled to us our on a mission of peace and we have welcomed him as we do all ambassadors of peace. This is an exciting time, for the entire record of past events and times of our civilization are about to begin anew. In the days to follow, I will meet with our distinguished emissary and will share with you all that I learn. Until then, be at peace."

It was short and to the point, perhaps too much to the point, because it left more questions than it answered. That inflamed world leaders as well as the press, who besieged the White House for more details. They were all told to be patient until the President had an opportunity to spend time with the alien.

Conrad had requested Gabriel meet with him privately following his televised address. In the Oval office, Gabriel found the President deep in thought standing by a window.

"Did the FBI put you through the ringer during your debriefing this morning?"

"That they did, sir."

"What are we to make of all this, Gabriel?"

"I'm still trying to figure it out, sir."

"I'm being told by senior advisors, the security spooks, and the military, that I've lost my marbles for receiving him the way we have. So much for not acting out of fear." His shoulders hunched and he shoved his hands into his pockets. "I'll meet with him alone as he requested. If I allow half-witted bureaucrats to participate, it'll become a bloody three-ring circus, and I'll have none of that."

Notwithstanding Legna's admonishment not to betray the revelations he had divulged in the Utah motel room, Gabriel was tempted to do just that. "There are certain elements of this that could sway you."

"Sway me how? Speak freely."

And then Gabriel had second thoughts. *Not yet. It would be better if he heard it from Legna, just as Legna had requested.* He shifted gears. "Legna has certain capabilities that—"

"Like what?"

"Well, for one, he stopped me from getting out of a chair."

"I don't understand." Conrad returned to his desk and sat.

"He was making a point that by simply using his mind he could cause me not to get out of a chair. I was unable to get up, no matter how hard I tried. And then he released me from whatever force was holding me down, and I was able to rise. Clearly, he possesses powers beyond anything we understand. He also has the ability to invade your thoughts."

"Thoughts?"

"He reads minds, sir. That alone could place you at a great disadvantage."

"Jeezzz, how do I avoid it?"

"Try not making direct eye contact any more than necessary. Otherwise, I you should be fine."

"Before they whisked him off to Blair House, he told me privately he could help us end poverty, bring peace to warring nations, and revive our damaged environment."

"Yes, sir, he told me that and much more."

"It is my solemn duty to listen to every last word of wisdom he's willing to share." Conrad rose and moved swiftly back to the window, clasped his hands behind his back, and squeezed his fingers tightly together. Finally, he spoke barely above a whisper. "Someone brighter than me once said, '*We examine our lives in straight lines, and we draw conclusions. But those who believe they have the answers to life's mysteries eventually come to realize they do not.*'"

Gabriel waited, but Conrad just stood quietly, head bent forward, eyes to the floor.

"Mr. President?" Gabriel said softly.

Conrad breathed a sigh. "My god, they've been out there the whole time!"

It was 12:30 by the time Gabriel returned to his office. He agonized over whether he had made the right decision to withhold vital information from the President. Retrieving his journal, he made a quick hand-written entry:

Legna has defined consciousness—our very existence—as moment by moment. Well, right or wrong, this moment in time belongs to President Conrad. The alien's revelation to Catherine and me, as earth-shattering as it may have been, was enlightenment, not a threat. Therefore, I must allow the president to learn this directly from Legna.

Two hours later, Gabriel stood quietly by Owen Jennings's bed in Bethesda Medical Center's ICU burn unit. Jennings, the doctor had told him, had received a single gunshot wound an inch above and to the left of his heart. He suffered third-degree burns over sixty percent of his body and remained in a coma. An endotracheal intubation tube snaked into his windpipe to aid his breathing. Life-sustaining bags of intravenous fluids and antibiotics flowed into his veins. Biosynthetic gel dressings covered his arms, legs, chest, and head. The only parts of his face not covered in bandages were his eyes, nostrils, and lips, and even they were smeared with gel. Except for Jennings's distinctive eyes, the body lying there did not in any way resemble Gabriel's lifelong friend.

Gabriel cupped his head in his hands and wept.

Despite Conrad's admonition that an invasion had not taken place, there was no stopping the high level of hysteria sweeping the planet. As was expected, the fringe element interpreted the alien's arrival as signaling the cataclysmic end of the world as predicted by so many self-proclaimed prophets. Others believed the alien to be God or at the very least a messenger sent by God, in a spacecraft no less. Alien conspiracy advocates, believing they had been vindicated, rejoiced.

Within hours of Conrad's Oval Office address, suicides were being reported from all corners of the globe. The most bizarre, carried out on live television, involved seventeen members of an obscure European cult who, in a display of sheer lunacy, joined hands and leapt from London's fifty-story One Canada Square building. Prior to doing so, their leader, a frail, white-bearded man had stated, *"The Bible is our university, but now the church age has ended and the Great Tribulation, the beginning of the end, has begun."*

Hospital emergency rooms were inundated with reports of exotic illnesses, most dismissed as psychosomatic episodes attributed to stress and anxiety brought on by the revelation that intelligent extraterrestrial life did indeed exist, which millions were unwilling or not prepared to accept.

Using social media to organize, candlelight vigils sprung up around the world. Millions upon millions stood shoulder to shoulder, carrying glowing green candles which had become a symbol, of what, no one was sure. Religious leaders were uncharacteristically silent. Most worrisome, worldwide military forces went into overdrive without the slightest idea of what the actual threat, if any, might be.

The human race responded as expected: When faced with events that by their very nature challenged human survival, react impulsively *before* thinking it through.

23

The meetings between Legna and Conrad were to take place in the Lincoln Room at Blair House. Legna requested no videotape or audio recordings be made stating that his counsel was for Conrad only, and only Conrad would determine what was to be relayed to the public. At the insistence of the Secret Service, who demanded eyes on the President at all times, Legna agreed to a single video camera but there was to be no audio. Against all advice, the President agreed to the alien's terms.

On the morning of Wednesday, March 1, just three hours before his first scheduled meeting with Legna, Federal Marshalls escorted CIA Director Downing and NSA Director Benthurst to the White House Cabinet Room.

William Downing was in his early sixties and came from old-world money; his family owned railroad lines across the northeastern states of Vermont, New Hampshire, and Maine. NSA's Jonathan Benthurst, who had recently turned fifty-two, looked and spoke like he had been raised on the wrong side of the Boston tracks instead of the historic neighborhood of Beacon Hill where his father had been a successful trial attorney.

President Conrad swept into the room. "Good morning, gentlemen," he said brusquely.

Neither man said a word, nor did they stand in respect to the president.

Conrad ignored the slight and strode to the head of the conference table. "I will present to the world what you have endeavored to keep from them."

"And you will be committing a heinous offense against all humanity," Downing said in a rancorous tone.

"So you say, so you say," Conrad shot back. "I only wish we all possessed your infinite wisdom."

In stiff defiance Downing quickly stood. "This is simply another example of your high-minded, ill-conceived concept of governing, that all men are created equal and therefore should be treated as equals. You could not be more misguided."

Conrad shook his head with disgust. "Your opinion of your fellow man is disturbing, to say the least, maybe even psychopathic."

"I'm a realist," Downing snapped back.

"No, you son of a bitch, you are an elitist. Both of you are poster children for what is wrong with society."

Benthurst sprang to his feet and shook a tight fist. "Damn it, you know as well as me there are millions of bottom feeders out there who live off the rest of us and contribute absolutely nothing to society. Despite your misguided progressive convictions, that will never, ever change. Nor will your kissing up to this damned alien change anything other than to upset—"

Conrad waved him off. "There, you see? You prove my point. If you were in charge those *bottom feeders* you refer to would never have the opportunity to rise to your level, but would remain your indentured slaves."

Benthurst's voice spiked up. "What you fail to understand is the danger we now face. You have welcomed an unknown entity into our midst, when in fact you should be distrustful of what is clearly a crisis, one that has yet to fully reveal itself. Why can't you see that?"

Conrad waved him off. "Enough! My ears are burning from your warped oratory! Now then, this planet and its inhabitants are about to take the next step in our evolution, and nothing you or anyone else has to say will change that."

"If you forge ahead with this," Downing warned, "you will have unleashed an evil on society the likes of which has never been witnessed."

"The real truth is you two, and the other vermin in cahoots with you, see this as a threat to *your* way of life. Your actions were ill-conceived and certainly not in the best interest of the people you were sworn to serve and protect. I remind you, it was never your decision to make to begin with."

"And you no doubt will live to regret yours," Downing lashed back.

Conrad shook his head and walked briskly to the door. "I wanted to meet face-to-face one last time to tell you what a vile thing you did. Your selfish interests, your disdain for your fellow man, are contemptible beyond belief." His hand wrapped tightly around the doorknob. "Now then, I am the President of the United States, not judge and jury. Your fate will be determined in a court of law." He swung the door open. "Until then, gentlemen, get your asses the hell out of the people's house."

At 2:00 PM, President Conrad, Vice-President Cross, National Security Advisor Charles Bregg,

And Gabriel, arrived at the heavily fortified Blair House and proceeded directly to the Lincoln Room. President Conrad appeared well rested with his usually tousled white hair neatly combed.

"A monitor has been set up in the Drawing Room. We'll be watching from there," Vice President Cross said. "Good luck, Mr. President."

"Thank you. I'll need all I can get."

Cross stepped close to Conrad and whispered, "I owe you an apology for my inexcusable behavior in the Oval the other night."

"Alan, we've been friends and working colleagues for more years than I care to remember. I know you always have my back. For that I am grateful. Enough said."

Conrad ambled to the Lincoln Room door, but before he could enter, Gabriel sidled up to him and whispered, "Remember what I told you, sir. He sees your thoughts, so be sure to—"

"Yes, yes, Gabriel, I'll be fine."

And with that, the president checked that his tie was tight against his collar, straightened his spine, and strode into the Lincoln Room alone. Two Secret Service agents took up positions at the door.

"What did you say to him, Gabriel?" Cross asked.

"Under no circumstances reveal the nuclear codes."

Cross, Gabriel, Bregg, and Agent Wilkinson gathered around 42-inch TV in the Drawing Room. Cross saw that President Conrad faced the camera while the alien's back was *to* the camera.

"Jesus, who the hell set this up? We can't see the alien's face?"

"Only the president will know what Legna tells him. I thought you knew?"

Cross shot Gabriel an annoyed look. "Damn it, nobody told me."

The meeting ended at precisely 3:00 PM. President Conrad emerged looking physically drained.

His shoulders slumped, and his eyes went to the floor as he moved past Gabriel and Cross without making eye contact or uttering a single word.

"Mr. President," Cross called.

Conrad did not respond. He e Hhuddled briefly with Agent Denver Wilkinson and left.

Wilkinson approached Gabriel, Cross, and Bregg. "Gentlemen, the President requests you return to the White House in a separate vehicle."

"What's going on, Denver?"

"Don't know, Mr. Vice President."

Cross bemoaned, "What do we make of that?"

After hitching a ride with the Secret Service, Gabriel arrived back at his office at 3:25 PM. He had breezed past Betty without saying a word.

Betty followed. "How'd it go?"

"He came out of the meeting and left without a work. The press is screaming for information—we have to tell them something."

"Well, something's up, the President's requested you meet with him at 7:30 in the family quarters."

"Why the family quarters?"

"Don't know, I'm just the messenger."

"And not always the bearer of good news, I might add."

At 7:29 PM, a Secret Service agent ushered Gabriel into the presidential sleep-ing quarters. Conrad was dressed in his blue pajamas and matching blue robe and was sitting quietly reading. He looked tired and older than his years.

"Good evening, Mr. President."

Conrad closed the book and held it up for Gabriel to see. The cover read: *S-P-Q-R, A History of Ancient Rome,* by Mary Beard. "It seems nothing much has changed." Rising slowly, he ambled across the room, and with his back to Gabriel, said, "Do you know what the *Hundredth Monkey Syndrome* is?"

"I beg your pardon, sir?"

He turned back. "The Hundredth Monkey Syndrome simply states that when 100 members of a species accepts an idea, the rest of the pack will accept it is as truth and follow along like lemmings." Conrad shook his head slowly from side to side, sighed and turned away, his eyes going to a photo on the nightstand of him and his wife Victoria. "It goes to the heart of who we are. We make rash decisions based on poor judgment, poor reasoning, carelessness, and insufficient knowledge; the Hundredth Monkey Syndrome at work." He crossed his arms and hugged him. "The eighteenth-century British playwright James F. Barrie said, *'Life is a long lesson in humility.'*" He lowered his arms to his side. "I have been greatly humbled this day by an incredibly intelligent creature that appears to know more about us than we do. He did most of the talking and me the listening. Some of what he told me was so astonishing, if given a choice, I might have preferred not to know." Slowly, deliberately, he turned to Gabriel, his eyes piercing and telling. "You've been like a son to me, Gabriel."

It was the tone in which the president spoke that was so telling. His jaw was set tight, his words delivered in a deep, low timber.

Barely above a whisper, Gabriel said, "He told you, didn't he?"

"The question is, son… why didn't you?"

Gabriel's eyes went to the floor.

"Look at me, Gabriel." It was not said in anger, but a simple request.

Gabriel's eyes fanned up slowly to meet the president's cold stare. "Sir, he insisted he be the one to tell you."

"Well, he did that all right… as well as letting me know that you already knew."

"Please, sir, allow me to explain."

Conrad waved him off. "In any relationship, loyalty and trust are the glue that holds the bond together." Ambling across the room to a side table, he poured himself a glass of water and drank it quickly. "Loyalty—the textbook definition demands one's faithful adherence to a sovereign, a government, a leader, one's family, or a trusted friend. It is an alliance that, if broken, leaves a damaging void. Sometimes, the real or imagined complexities of life become confused, causing us to lose our way. I'm assuming that in the mad rush of all that's swirling around us, you lost yours."

"Please, sir, let me explain."

Conrad waved him. "I'm faced now with a grave decision. I promised the world that I would share all that I learned. I gave my word. But this—how do I begin to explain what I have learned this day?" Conrad's face was vacant now, like a man who had glimpsed the future, but wished he had not.

"Sir, I—"

Conrad waved him off again, the subject was no longer open to discussion. "Legna suggested a way we could best present him to the world, and I've agreed. On Monday, I want the leaders of every country on the face of this planet, their military commanders, their financial and spiritual gurus—every last one of them—gathered in the Great Hall at the United Nations."

"Yes, sir."

"Have the press secretary make a release to that effect. This Dr. Blake, does she know what you and I know?"

"Yes, sir."

"And that pilot, Galinski?"

"No, sir."

"Anyone else?"

"No, sir."

"That's the way it's to remain then."

"I will inform Dr. Blake immediately."

"No, I'll speak with her, you concern yourself with your duties." He turned his back to Gabriel. "That'll be all."

A dispirited Gabriel turned away slowly and walked to the door. He hesitated there before turning back to Conrad. Before he could speak, Conrad raised a hand.

"Say no more, Gabriel."

Gabriel's decision to withhold information from the President, however well-intentioned, had misfired. Conrad viewed it as a major breach of confidence, one that would require time to heal.

Later that evening, Gabriel wrote in his journal.

Note to self: You made a bad call, now leave it alone. You're not the point of focus at the moment, so get over it. This wound can only be healed over time. And do not mention it to Catherine. She'll learn soon enough when Conrad speaks with her.

Galinski and Catherine harbored zero interest in playing the role of hero. But at Conrad's insistence, in an Oval Office ceremony, Galinski was awarded the Congressional Medal of Honor and the Presidential Medal of Freedom. Catherine accepted the Congressional Medal of Honor and the National Science Award. Gabriel accepted honors on behalf of Owen Jennings, but he declined personal recognition. Harry Wilson, Jimmy Gillford, and French Stewart were awarded the Medal of Freedom.

Following the ceremony, Galinski returned to Oberlin, Kansas to retrieve his beloved *Irene*, flew back to Steamboat Springs, Colorado, and immediately went into hiding.

Despite the fear and uncertainty that had gripped the world, Gabriel was anxious to explore his evolving feeling for Catherine. He called her at the Hay Adams Hotel and invited her to remain in Washington as the guest of the government until after the alien's unveiling at the United Nations.

"What brought this on?" Catherine asked.

"Well, considering what we've been through together, I thought we might share some time before you return to San Diego. Besides, you don't want to miss the unveiling, do you?"

"I'm not going to the UN, if that's what you're suggesting."

"Why not?"

"I had enough excitement to last a lifetime. I'm done, kaput, finished with this whole adventure. I leave the next chapter to you."

"You're okay, right, you're not getting depressed on me?"

Catherine laughed. "And if I am, I wouldn't tell you."

Sounding like a young teenager asking for a first date, Gabriel said timidly, "So, what do you say? Spend a few days here, and I'll show you around the big city. I won't take no for an answer."

There was a long pause as he waited patiently for her answer.

"Okay, I can use a few day's rest."

"Fine. Let's begin with dinner tonight."

"Wow, Cowboy, no one will ever accuse you of subtlety."

"The Hay-Adams Lafayette Dining Room at 7:30?"

And so, that evening a boyishly exuberant Gabriel and tough-talking Catherine shared a meal in The Lafayette Room in one of Washington's finest hotels. It would prove to be the beginning of an unlikely romance.

President Conrad continued his daily meetings with Legna without revealing what the alien might be sharing, which left the world wondering what was behind the stall. Under great pressure from allies and foes alike, Conrad relented and made a brief television appearance, first apologizing for not keeping the world informed—for reasons he failed to explain—then vowing that all would become clear during the televised United Nations gathering. World leaders were quick to accuse the United States of duplicity in an attempt to shield America from what many perceived as a deceptive and brazen invasion of the planet. Conrad ignored the rhetoric, preferring instead to remain squirreled away with Legna while the rest of the world held its collective breath.

24

The gold leaf wall behind the podium rose up like a fiery flame. The United Nations emblem—a map of the world as seen from the North Pole flanked by olive wreaths—dominated the center of the wall. Giant video screens hung on either side.

Presidents, kings, queens, chancellors, prime ministers, and dictators represented every country on the planet. Despised dictators sat side-by-side next to spiritual leaders and corporate tycoons in rapt anticipation of the unveiling of the most extraordinary event of their lives. Vice President Cross, the leaders of both US political parties, selected members of Congress, the President's Cabinet, the Joint Chiefs of Staff, Supreme Court Justices, as well as Gabriel, were seated front and center below the podium.

The General Assembly Hall's entry doors were secured on both sides. Only one dozen United Nations security personnel and four members of Conrad's Secret Service detail remained inside the hall. A single, pool camera would serve all broadcast outlets, the Internet, and radio. Translations would be provided in real time in all major languages.

Outside the Hall, it was an entirely different matter altogether. Swarms of Secret Service, FBI, New York City Police, and 200 U.S. Special Ops troops patrolled the area for ten blocks in all directions. Police and military helicopters crisscrossed the sky.

New York resembled a war zone.

Without formal introduction or fanfare, President Conrad strode quickly across the lush green carpet to the podium to polite but subdued applause. Despite rigorous denials by the White House, many in attendance still clung to the belief the United States had forged an unholy alliance with extraterrestrials.

Conrad set his written speech on the podium. He had declined the use of a TelePrompTer, preferring instead to commit his words to memory; the written script would be his fallback if he faltered. He glanced briefly at a privacy screen that had been erected fifteen feet to his right, then turned to the capacity crowd. He was in awe that such an aggregation of allies and foes had gathered under one roof, something never before achieved in modern history.

"As I look out over this historic assemblage," Conrad began in a low, somber voice, "I welcome the political, judicial, military, financial, and spiritual leaders of all nations. Perhaps if we had embraced what unites us earlier in our history instead of what divides us, mankind could have, would have, achieved lasting peace."

He raised a hand to his mouth and cleared his throat.

"A few days ago, someone asked me a simple enough question, one that has dogged us from the beginning of mankind's short journey on Earth: What would be the legacy we hoped to pass on to future generations? I answered this way— equality and opportunity for all. Unfortunately, that goal has continually eluded us."

He took a quick sip from a glass of water and cleared his throat again.

"This past week, I have learned that what we have yet to know about ourselves, our world, and the universe, would fill all of the books ever printed. I have been truly humbled, for in the words of our extraordinary guest, human civilization is but a blink of an eye in a vast, wondrous, ever-expanding universe, and we have yet to establish our rightful place in it. But now we stand at the threshold of a new beginning to transcend our missteps, to rise up to a level of heightened knowledge and understanding beyond our wildest imagination."

He abruptly stopped and seemed disorientated as if he had forgotten the rest of his speech. His eyes shot down to the manuscript. His finger traced along the lines trying to find his place. Then, with a knowing smile, he covered his notes with his hands and looked up. He had made his point and did it well. Nothing further needed to be said.

"Honored guests, it is my distinct honor and privilege to present a valued new ally, one that has traveled through the vast cosmos to aid us in our endless pursuit of peace and prosperity. Ladies and gentlemen, please welcome warmly… Legna from the faraway planet of Ecaep."

The camera operator panned to the privacy screen and re-focused. For several agonizing seconds, nothing happened as the overflowing crowd waited in rapt silence. Finally, Legna stepped clear of the screen, his upper torso bent forward, his eyes to the floor.

The audience sat in frozen anticipation. Not a word was uttered, not a sound made.

The alien walked slowly to within five feet of the podium and stopped. His gaze went first to President Conrad and his face stretching into a wide, welcoming smile. The camera operator pushed in for a close-up. Legna's cherubic face filled the jumbo video screens with such impact that any rational reaction from the crowd was unimaginable. A hush hung in the air for several long seconds. Then whispers and murmurs rippled through the rows of dignitaries until it swelled to a continuous hum of animated voices.

Legna looked to President Conrad, bowed his head slightly, then turned to Gabriel in the front row, and he winked. Gabriel winked back and gave the thumbs-up sign. The alien repeated the simple hand gesture, which brought a spontaneous outburst of applause in a moment of unadulterated, electrified nervous excitement.

Then Legna did the unimaginable. His eyelids slid ever so slowly down over his gray pupils until his eyeballs were completely covered. His lids remained closed for several seconds before the gray skin slowly rolled back.

The eye sockets were now solid black.

What had begun so innocently with much hope, now played like theater of the absurd, a moment of precipitous insanity.

Legna slowly swiveled his head to President Conrad.

For a split second the change in Legna's eyes failed to register. When it finally did, Conrad cried out, "What in the hell!"

Legna's downed craft was poised on an elevated platform in a secret location somewhere in Nevada. A beehive of activity surrounded the sphere as several dozen military and NASA engineers worked painstakingly to unlock its secrets.

Suddenly, as if a light switch had been flipped on, the smooth, geometric, metallic surface began to glow a cloudy white. Stunned workers, sensing a pulsing wave emanating from the craft, quickly drew back. Silently, slowly, the sphere rose up, stopping briefly some twenty-five feet above the hangar floor before exploding through the roof and shooting to an altitude of 20,000 feet. There it stopped and hovered, poised soundlessly against the clear blue sky like a beacon transmitting a deadly signal.

All communications equipment on and above the planet simultaneously malfunctioned.

With his eyes black as night, the alien's childlike innocence had faded—now Legna looked threatening.

In the pandemonium that ensued no one had noticed President Conrad clutching his torso as if a hand grenade had ripped through him. He staggered back and swung to his right, his fingers clawing at the excruciating pain that had invaded his body. His wide-eyed, terrified look met the alien's black-filled eyes. In that final moment of his ebbing life, Conrad realized his worst fear; it had all been an elaborate ruse. His eyes wide with terror, he frantically sought out Gabriel. His mouth gaped as if to call out one final message to his beloved protégé. But no sound came out. Before he could utter a single word—before Gabriel or the Secret Service could reach him—his dead weight simply gave way to gravity. He was dead by the time he hit the floor.

The alien's jet-black eyes penetrated the crowded room as if sending a silent message. With uncanny parity, the entire assemblage fell into a catatonic state unable to move or speak.

Gabriel—spared from whatever debilitating spell that had been cast—reached Conrad and checked his motionless body for a pulse. He could find none. Looking up and locking eyes with Legna, he screamed, "You've killed him!"

Legna blinked, and his eyes instantly returned to gray and white. "I've done nothing of the sort, Gabriel." His tone was devoid of compassion.

Gabriel turned to the packed hall for help, but every last soul lay unconscious. Placing a shaking finger to Conrad's neck, he was unable to detect a pulse. Ripping open the president's shirt, he began to administer CPR.

Legna spoke with disturbing detachment. "His biological energy—his life force—has left him."

"Do something! Help him!"

"His heart has stopped, Gabriel. I am truly saddened."

"You saved yourself, you can save the President!" Gabriel pleaded.

"I cannot."

"Or you won't!" Gabriel spun around to the frozen crowd. "What have you done to them?"

"It is but a temporary paralysis of the central nervous system—they are not harmed." As if his awareness had drifted elsewhere, as if Conrad's death held no significance, Legna's deportment visibly changed. His spine went pole straight as he strode across the rostrum like a victorious gladiator taking his victory lap around the Coliseum. "My transport's unfortunate mechanical malfunction led to my untimely capture. I found it amusing for the time I spent, but as I was about to take my leave, you arrived. But then your discovery by those who imprisoned me required my stratagem be altered."

"Is this all game to you?"

"Not at all, Gabriel, not at all. However, I did find our flight an amusing diversion."

"And amusing diversion? You placed Catherine and me in danger because it was an amusing diversion?"

Legna gazed out over the unconscious gathering. "This was my charge; to gather Earth's leaders here in this emplacement of compromise, concessions, and agreements." His eyes shot up to the high ceiling. "As I speak, our vessels have assumed positions over your planet."

Tears streamed from Gabriel's eyes as he stroked Conrad's lifeless body. In a wavering voice, he barked, "What is the truth? Why are you here?"

"To guide your failing society to a life of peace, harmony, and balance. It is unfortunate that humans are ill-prepared to achieve this worthy aspiration on their own."

Gabriel choked. "I trusted you, damn it. I trusted you!"

"In time, I hope to regain that trust. We shall enlighten humankind to the laws of their universe; not just *how* it works, but *why* it works. Your insidious behavior and reckless conservancy have led to insurmountable social and ecological challenges without attainable solutions. The transformation to a new and pure citizenry will begin with the eradication of archaic traditions and beliefs that have destroyed the very fabric of your society."

Unable to hold back his anger, Gabriel balled his right hand into a tight fist and thrust it above his head. "You are invaders!"

"No, Gabriel… caretakers. Our reformation will bring about cohesion, order will ascend from chaos, and your species shall flourish."

Gabriel's hands trembled, his heart pounded wildly, and fierce defiance rose from deep within him. "This is our planet, not yours. You have no right to—"

"Have you already forgotten about what I revealed in that despicable motel room? We have every right."

"That changes nothing. All of mankind will fight you to the last person standing!"

"However honorable and courageous you believe that to be, you confirm the unbridled, self-destructive human ego. Humans do not get to write the next chapter in their existence, for the day of reckoning is today."

Gabriel wanted to strike out, to physically attack this creature and pummel him until like Conrad, he was laying on the floor dead. But at the moment there were more important consideration. He stepped away from the President's body and cautiously approached Legna. "Listen to me, every living soul on the planet with access to the media will be terrified as to why, in the middle of the most historic announcement ever, all communications abruptly stopped. Have you considered that?"

Legna's head cocked to one side, his small mouth pinched, and his eyelids constricted. "Perhaps a public testimony of our resolve is in order."

The alien turned to the video camera perched on a three-foot platform 25-feet away. Its operator, his eyes open, lay motionless on the floor. Legna aligned himself with the camera, laced his fingers, bowed his head, and closed his eyes. Seconds later the camera's ready light glowed red and his image splashed across the giant monitors above and behind him.

"Citizens of Earth," he began, "we have journeyed from afar, not to ravage your planet but to restore it to its embryonic glory. Conduct your lives without fear, for misfortune will not beset those who comply with the enlightenments that will be promulgated. I offer now testimony if our guidance is not adhered too."

The image on the video screens changed to a massive spacecraft lurking on the edge of the planet's stratosphere. It was configured on three levels—three ovals overlapping one another, so that the top level—the smallest—was slightly forward of the second, and the second slightly forward of the lowest, which was largest. There were no visible markings, windows, or entrances on its dull gray surface.

From the underbelly of the ship, with no visible evidence of a protruding weapon, a single orange beam streaked toward Earth. The image on the overhead TV screens showed the beam striking the uninhabited 450-acre coral island of Howland, located north of the Equator some 1,700 nautical miles southwest of Honolulu. The flat atoll was instantly vaporized without violent fanfare of any kind and was replaced by the surrounding, vast, blue ocean.

The TV screens switched sky-high views of Washington, D.C., London, Moscow, Paris, Beijing, Athens, Canberra, and Madrid as each city was struck by electromagnetic pulses plunging over 100 million people into total darkness. Fifteen seconds after Madrid went dark the blackouts were reversed and full electrical power restored.

The pernicious demonstration served to convey its intended warning; human weapons would prove useless against the Ecaepians.

Legna's face filled the monitors again. "These methods will not be employed as long as peace is maintained and our guidance adhered to. Further transparency shall follow in the days ahead. Until then be at peace, for we have come in peace."

The broadcast abruptly ended without any mention of the sudden death of President Conrad.

"Return now to the city of Washington, Citizen Gabriel. Prepare the presidential ceremonial residence for my arrival."

"The White House!"

"I will conduct my affairs from this structure."

"Never! Americans will see that as an act of war. There will be violent uprisings."

"It would be unwise for the citizens of Earth to reject our will."

Gabriel dropped to his knees and wailed like a wounded animal. "What is happening!?" Placing a gentle hand on Conrad's lifeless body, he lowered his head and openly wept.

With satellites, telescopes, and ground communications all mysteriously disabled, it was impossible to confirm whether more than one alien craft hovered above the planet. Despite the lack of intelligence, within minutes of Legna's broadcast, every nation's military, police, and security forces scrambled to high alert status.

25

With a deceased president on board, returning to America's capital was a top priority. But without functioning satellites and communications, the FAA was shut down, forcing Air Force One to delay its return to Washington.

Vice-president Cross ordered a news release be issued announcing the death of President Conrad. "As soon as communications are restored, release it."

The front cabin section of Air Force One was designed with double doors that would accommodate a coffin for just such a tragedy. Several front row seats were removable as well. With Gabriel at her side, First Lady Victoria Conrad kept silent vigil by her husband's flag-draped casket, while in the aircraft's conference area total bedlam ruled. A fierce debate swirled around the swearing in of Vice President Cross as America's next president.

"We are sworn to ensure the continuity of government," Cross argued aggressively.

"But Alan," Charles Bregg cautioned, "is that wise? He's taking over the White House, for Christ's sake."

Cross' face flushed red with anger. "Americans do not run from potential enemies, whether from our own species or a sawed-off alien."

The debate raged on with Cross arguing for immediate swearing in. Everyone else, fearing reprisals, argued for restraint. In the end, with the alien's superior firepower clearly established, Cross relented, and temporary restraint won out.

For the first time in its history, the United States of America was without a functioning commander in chief.

To demonstrate they had not come as invaders, the aliens restored ground and satellite communications: phones, television, and the internet. Spy satellites, ground telescopes, radar, and all other tracking devices capable of detecting objects in space, remained disabled.

With FAA communications restored, Air Force One departed New York. Fifty minutes later the aircraft set wheels down at Joint Base Andrews in Maryland where a military honor guard, government officials, and the press waited. They were told the president was struck by a massive heart attack—details to follow.

A Marine Helicopter transferred Vice President Cross, Gabriel, and two of Cross' top aides from Andrews to the White House. Cross sat in the presidential seat. Gabriel sat alone in the rear and retrieved his cell phone. He had intentionally turned it off before departing New York to avoid the press. The instant he powered it up, it rang. Caller ID confirmed it was a cable network news reporter. Hitting the *off* button, he tossed the phone into his briefcase and fetched a second one. Only President Conrad, Vice President Cross, his secretary, a few key staffers and his widowed mother Isabella knew its number. He had intended to call her during the flight from New York, but in the chaos and raw emotions of the moment, he had not.

It took three attempts before the connection went through.

"Gabriel, Gabriel, my son, my *hijito, estás bien*?" His mother's voice was quivering.

"I'm okay, *Mama*."

Isabella began to weep. "You were there? You saw it happen?" she said in her thick Cuban accent.

"I was less than thirty feet from the podium."

"Ay, dios mio, *debe de haber sido terrible*."

"*Sí, mama*; it was terrible, it was terrible."

"I am so saddened, Gabriel. He was a wonderful, caring man. I know how close you were."

Gabriel swallowed hard and fell silent at his mother's reference to Conrad.

"Gabriel?" Her crying intensified. "*¿Dios Mio, que será de nosotros?*"

"We'll be fine, *mama*. We'll all be okay, we'll come through this."

"Que Dios nos compadezca y nos mantenga a salvo de esta cosa horrible," she said through tears.

"Yes, it is horrible."

"Come home Gabriel, come to Miami," Isabella pleaded.

Gabriel sighed. "I'm needed here, Mama."

"They are the *Diablo* come to destroy us," she cried. *"Diablo!"*

The White House came into view—the rest of the conversation was a blur.

As soon as they arrived at the White House, Cross called for an emergency meeting in the Situation Room. "Get everybody in before that damnable alien shows up," he told Gabriel.

An hour later, the Situation Room was at capacity. Cross occupied the seat reserved for the president. Gabriel usually sat to the president's right, but this day he chose to sit at the far end facing Cross. The Vice-President began the meeting by announcing he would assume the responsibility and authority of the office of the president.

"You haven't been properly sworn in, Alan," the Speaker of the House, Harry Dorn, voiced.

"Harry, for god's sake, listen to yourself." Cross slammed a hand on the table." We've been invaded, despite this alien's bullshit rhetoric about how they've come to help. What this country needs at this crucial moment is a Commander in Chief, and by law that's me. We'll swear me in, we just won't announce it publicly."

"No, Alan," Dorn said.

"What do you mean, no?"

"You agreed on Air Force One we'd wait."

"You agreed, not me."

"We will wait, Alan," Dorn said with finality.

"Then at least we mobilize worldwide forces for a preemptive strike. I'll be damned if we're going to sit on our asses waiting to find out what they have in mind for us."

"But, Alan, how can we attack what we haven't yet seen?" Charles Bregg asked.

It was the first bit of common sense Gabriel had heard since the hastily called meeting began.

Cross ignored Bregg's caution and nodded to the Secretary of Defense. "Paul?"

"It's reasonable to assume that if all countries act as one, we may have a chance. But make no mistake, it might take every nuclear weapon available, and we just might kill ourselves in the process."

"Whoa!" Gabriel said. "Have we forgotten Howland Island and power outages? Neither incident was a mirage."

Cross folded his hands on the tabletop. "And you would be the one to know."

"You assume I know more than I actually do."

"Well, if not you, then who? You helped him to escape."

"I had no reason to believe his intent was hostile."

"Jesus, Gabriel, our president is dead, they've seized control of the planet, and that damnable creature is moving in here."

"I never felt threatened by him, and neither did Dr. Blake."

"And your point would be?"

"That we act not out of ignorance or fear until we're certain there's something *to* fear."

"Oh, for Christ's sake Gabriel, don't be so goddamn naive!"

"Alan," Charles Bregg cautioned, "there's no need to get personal. Let's stay on message."

"Offense, not defense!" Cross spit out. "If we show weakness, that's the end of us." He turned to the Chairman of the Joint Chiefs. "Mack, in the volumes of military contingency plans, is there one that supports a response to an alien invasion?"

"Well, kind of," the General said meekly.

"What's that mean?"

"Since we've never been invaded, the strategy is based purely on speculation."

"Share it with us."

Before the General could respond, the large wall-mounted video screen behind Gabriel came alive with an image of a massive spacecraft presumably somewhere over the planet.

"Good God!" Charles Bregg shrilled.

It was the same craft they saw just before the destruction of Howland Island.

Cross made a short convulsive noise and jumped to his feet. "I thought our satellites were down?"

"They were!" The Joint Chiefs General gasped.

Cross slumped back to his chair. "Then where in the hell is that feed coming from?"

A second later, the screen went dark. It was clear now they were being listened to.

Bregg waved his arms to get everyone's attention. Reaching for his notepad, he hurriedly scribbled something and held it up for everyone to see. *We are being listened to*, the note read.

Gabriel rose to his feet, rounded the table until he was at Cross' side. Laying a hand on Cross shoulder, he winked and placed a finger to his lips. "Look, we have nothing to lose by taking Legna at his word that they are here to help us."

"Yes, yes, I agree." Bregg tapped his ear and winked. "A military response at this time is unwarranted."

Cross nodded. "Ur, right, that makes sense—we'll wait."

"Look, Since Gabriel has a relationship with this alien," Bregg added. "Let's give him time to explore what they actually have in mind. Gabriel?"

"As I said, I never had reason to doubt Legna's motives."

"Right, I'm in agreement." Cross said.

26

Gabriel and Agent Wilkinson stood shivering in the cold by the West Colonnade entrance. Legna's instructions to Gabriel was to meet him there that at the appointed time. All non-essential White House personnel had been instructed to vacate the complex.

"How'd it go in the Sit-Room?" Wilkinson asked Gabriel.

"I don't know how, but we were being monitored."

"Jeez, this is just short of unbelievable." Wilkinson looked up at the clear night sky. Not a cloud marred his view of the stars. "We're standing here waiting for an alien to make his grand entrance."

Gabriel followed Wilkinson's gaze to the sky. Pulling his coat collar high against the chilling wind, he cupped his hands and blew on them to stave off the cold. As he did, a swirling, shimmering mass of air danced some thirty feet in front of them, creating a near-perfect circular indentation in the snow. There was no accompanying sound, lights or solid structure.

And then all was quiet.

A luminous spot of light, like that of a firefly, appeared some seven feet above the ground. It grew and oozed out, spreading like hot flowing lava until it shaped itself into a doorway and a ramp that extended to the ground. And yet there was nothing solid to be seen behind it.

Wilkinson sucked in a hard breath. "Holy living Christ!"

A smallish figure appeared in the shimmering doorway and descended the short distance to the snow-covered ground. It was Legna.

The lighted doorway and ramp disappeared as if it had been sucked up through a thin straw. The phosphorescence wave then ascended, silently kicking snow outward in a circular arc. Legna ambled toward the men, but stopped half-way. He kicked a toe in the snow as if the substance was foreign to him.

"Don't speak to him unless he addresses you," Gabriel cautioned.

"Not to worry," Wilkinson whispered.

Legna approached. "Please direct me to your late president's former quarters."

"Denver," Gabriel said, "give us a minute?"

Wilkinson shot him a cautionary look.

"It's okay."

Once Wilkinson was out of earshot, Gabriel said to Legna, "This is an abhorrent idea—you need to rethink it. Americans will not accept such a breach of—"

"Hear me clearly. From this moment on the inhabitants of Earth shall do I instruct. Perhaps yet another demonstration is in order, one far more lethal than the first."

"I would hope you wouldn't do that."

"Then inform those who would make such foolish decisions to re-think them. Now then, let us proceed. Instruct this man to remain here."

Passing through the ground floor of the White House, Legna showed little interest in the interior and they proceeded to the second floor without comment where a lone secret agent met them.

"What is your name, Citizen?" Legna questioned.

The apprehensive agent glanced down at Legna then at Gabriel.

"I inquired as to your name?"

"James Carson."

"It is my good fortune to make your acquaintance, Citizen Carson. How many moments have you held this position?"

"Moments?"

"How long have you been in service?"

"Uh, four years."

"Are you with a mate and offspring?"

The question appeared to confuse Carson. "I, uh—yes, I have a family."

"Are they well?"

"Yes, thank you."

"You are to be my squire…" Legna turned to Gabriel. "Squire? Is this terminology, proper?"

"Security attendant will do," Gabriel corrected.

"Citizen Carson, this structure is now the New World Headquarters. Please ensure no others enter this level without my permission." Then to Gabriel, "Make this known to all who labor here. I will take my leave now."

"I'll return first thing in the morning."

"That will not be necessary, Citizen Gabriel. I will seek you out as required. Until then, tend to your duties. Shall we take our leave, Citizen Carson?

With a sudden feeling of helplessness, Gabriel watched as the diminutive alien tagged along behind Carson. The world was now at a dead standstill, bound and gagged by a single alien that had bloodlessly seized jurisdiction over the planet, and there wasn't a thing he could do about it.

The following morning, Legna summarily dismissed President Conrad's civilian and military advisors. Excluded were Gabriel, Alan Cross, their staffs, rank and file administrative support, and those who maintained the White House. Except for fleeting glimpses, no one witnessed Legna's comings and goings to the Oval Office. Agent Carson, standing guard at the portico door, was often the only tip-off that the alien was actually there.

Gabriel made a hurried notation in his journal:

> *Why won't he see any of us face-to-face? What is he doing in there alone? None of this makes sense. It's smacks of an imagined sequence of events bearing no relationship to reality; an outlandish scenario only a Hollywood screenwriter in a cocaine-induced state of non-reality could have conjured up. We wait, for what we do not know.*

Legna wasted little time in issuing a press release confirming his new rules: Governments were to cease all legislative activities including elections, new laws or regulations. Basic government services supporting the daily needs of Earth's citizens were to continue unimpeded. Criminal acts of any kind would be immediately rectified, although the term "rectified" was not clearly defined. The directive ended with: *Be at peace, for we harbor no ill will toward mankind.*

Given the dire position the world found itself in, most displayed unexplainable restraint—or was it unadulterated fear of a scenario so outside human reality that no one knew how to proceed.

If there was any doubt Legna would use force to maintain stability, the Sudan incident confirmed it. As if they were not cognizant of the alien takeover, a long simmering border dispute between Sudan and South Sudan exploded into a military confrontation. It lasted for all of an hour before the political and military leaders on both sides mysteriously vanished and the conflict abruptly ended. With cutting precision, Legna had deftly defined how "infractions" would be rectified.

Air Force One returned President Conrad's remains to his hometown of Rock Hill, Missouri, where the President would be laid to rest. In a sharply worded memo to Legna, Gabriel argued the funeral be televised. The request was denied without comment.

William Jordon Conrad had become a footnote in history.

Planet Earth was now traveling at lightning speed toward an uncertain future. Despite Legna's assurance that they had come in peace an underground counterinsurgency was growing.

From the sanctity of the Oval Office, a single TV camera went live on a wide shot of the presidential desk, an angle that made Legna appear smaller than he was. His charm was on full display, his voice soothing and reassuring. First, he vowed no other Ecaepians would set foot on the planet as long as peace, harmony, and balance were maintained.

"I empathize with your anxiety. Take comfort that the successful resurrection of your planet and its citizens is our only intent. We have come to reverse not only the misjudgments driving your self-destructive characteristics, but that which has caused all mankind to become discordant. I pledge to you the opaque, bleak period of your antiquity will soon end and you will come to know joy."

Legna paused, the camera operator's cue to move in for a close-up. As the lens slowly zoomed in, the alien's comportment changed. His voice dropped an octave, and his message turned apocalyptic.

"Throughout your troubled bloodstained history, you have failed to forge a purposeful, unified society, one that rises above rapacious desires, pettiness, and vengeance. With consistency, you have approached your predicament with short-term applications rather than with cogent, long-term cures. If left unaddressed, these delinquencies will ensure the end of the human race. Mankind must place *self* aside in favor of *all*. Look to your left and to your right. See your fellow man not as adversaries, but as each other's salvation. Your rebirth shall soon begin with the dismantling of formal government entities, which only encourages abuse and corruption by those chosen to govern. If the fundamental principles of right conduct are adhered to, sovereignty is not required beyond that which provides continuity. I realize how difficult a concept this is to accept, for your history has glorified sovereignty and those who would lead. However, the time has come to embrace a new doctrine, a precept that dictates no one need follow and everyone must lead."

Like a laser, his piercing gray eyes remained transfixed on the camera's lens—probing, penetrating.

"The transformation to a peaceful, harmonious existence begins with the dismantling of your hideous weapons of mass destruction. Governments controlling such weapons, as well as the material to make them, are to report their locations to the former American Vice President, Alan Cross. Failure to comply will lead to…" He stopped mid-sentence. His eyes wandered to a silver-framed photo of William and Victoria Conrad, taken at Conrad's inauguration ceremony. "I wish to add that in the brief period I was privileged to know President William Conrad, I held him in high regard. He honored me with his trust. I ask the same of you as you begin a journey of renewal."

The presentation ended—the transition of the human race had officially begun.

Within minutes of Legna's speech, sixty-two-year-old Alan Cross burst into Gabriel's office leaving little doubt of his acrimony.

"Good morning, Alan," Gabriel said, as Cross stomped toward him.

"Your office isn't bugged, is it?"

"I have no idea."

"Did you watch that sawed-off creature's Razzie award-winning performance?"

"Of course."

"I tried to see him—*it*—after the broadcast but was told in no uncertain terms I didn't have access to the Oval."

"No one has been allowed in there," Gabriel said drolly.

"I'm the rightful president of this bloody damn country, and he has me fielding calls from a bunch of brain-dead, foreign leaders and the feckless idiots on Capitol Hill who still believe they have real jobs."

"My phone hasn't stopped either, Alan."

"I'm not buying that bullshit about their grand gesture to save us from ourselves. There's something the bastards want here, and we're in the way."

"We don't know that."

Cross balled his right hand into a tight fist and brought it down hard on the desk—Gabriel flinched. "Jesus H. Christ, who the hell's side are you on?"

"Alan, for god's sake calm down."

"*Do not* tell me to calm down. I refuse to be treated like some adolescent schoolboy. I'd like to march in there and kick the little runt's ass."

"Which you're not going to do unless you have a death wish."

"Then just what the hell do you suggest? Huh? I'm obligated by law to protect the citizens of this country, and by God, that's what the hell I intend to do."

"Alan, stop and think. If they meant to enslave us, Howland Island could have easily been Washington, Paris, Moscow, or London."

"And what makes you think they're not next?"

For one fleeting moment, Gabriel considered unburdening himself with all that he knew by telling Cross what Legna had revealed in that shabby Utah motel room. But he thought better of it—it would only serve to inflame a crisis already out of control.

Cross looked Gabriel hard in the eyes. It was classic, passive-aggressive Cross. "You spent three goddamn days transporting his ass here because you chose not to trust any of us. What the hell do you know that I don't?"

Gabriel sucked in a breath—his eyelids tightened. "Absolutely nothing, Alan."

"I always know when you're hiding something, your eyelids narrow. It's a dead giveaway."

Gabriel tilted his head to one side and rolled his eyes. "Alan, for god's sake!"

"Save the bullshit!" Cross stormed to the door. "You know something the rest of us don't, you and that woman and that goddamn wacky helicopter pilot."

"His name is Skip Galinski, and hers is Dr. Catherine Blake."

"Damn it, Gabriel, what are you not telling me?"

"Nothing."

"Bullshit!" Cross slammed the door behind him so hard it vibrated the walls.

"And a good day to you too, Alan!"

That evening over his third glass of wine, Gabriel sat in his study and wrote in his journal:

> *Communications with Legna are limited to memorandums, a process that continues to exasperate the living hell out of me and everyone else. On the plus side—a complete surprise to those who question his motives—he has shown unexpected compassion for those in need by ordering all nations to release food surpluses and medical supplies. Engineers are being dispersed throughout the world to create clean drinking water where needed. Yet in spite of these acts (are they a diversion?) the silent terror of the unknown continues to burrow deep into the world's consciousness like an invasive parasite.*
>
> *How long can this go on before anarchy erupts?*

27

He rolled one way, then the other, unable to engage in any meaningful sleep. Even though the room was cool, beads of sweat clung to his face, neck, and chest. His tongue was thick and pasty, and a sour taste lingered there like the terrible medicine his mother spoon-fed him as a kid. He licked his lips and swallowed.

The red LED light on the bedside clock glared 2:00 AM. He reviewed in his mind what the upcoming day would bring; the first day he was to meet with Legna since the alien moved into the White House. Swinging his bare feet to the carpeted floor, he ran his hands through his thick brown hair and stared blankly at the wall trying to focus.

Catherine, ever so beautiful, lay in a semi-restless sleep beside him. Occasionally, her face contorted, her eyelids tightened, and a slight moan escaped her throat. In the days that followed their safe arrival in Washington they had shared a few lunches and quiet dinners. Then came that fateful day at the United Nations when the world came to a standstill and everything ceased making sense. It was Catherine who consoled him through the loss of President Conrad.

In contrast to the conflict of personalities that had dominated their bold cross-country escape, Gabriel found his feelings for Catherine changing. Whereas before he had seen a caterpillar, he began to see a beautiful butterfly. Surprising even himself, he verbalized his evolving feelings over one of their quiet dinners, boldly suggesting she spend time at his place. It was more than a risky move, it was downright courageous.

At the suggestion that they cohabitate, Catherine had laughed, giving it a scientific spin as nothing more than the biological laws of attraction between two people who had shared uncertainty and life-threatening danger. Halfway through her clinical and unconvincing explanation of human chemical attraction and its inevitable pitfalls, Gabriel stood, walked to her side of the table, and kissed her. It was a long passionate kiss and brought applause from restaurant patrons. But when they parted, Catherine diverted her eyes.

"What's wrong?" Gabriel asked.

"Please, Gabriel, you're embarrassing me. Sit down."

Gabriel took his seat. "Considering the times we're living in; *time* is not to be wasted. I want you to stay, I'm asking you to stay."

"This is happening way too fast."

"Who says there's supposed to be a defined time period?"

"You know what I mean."

"No, I don't."

"I do have feelings for you, Gabriel, but—"

Gabriel reached across the table and placed a finger to her lips. "In case you haven't noticed, we're operating under a different set of rules. Nothing is ever going to be the same ever again." He rose again, walked around the table, lifted her to her feet and wrapped his arms around her. "The future is a question mark, let's not be guilty of wasting the present."

He kissed her again, and this time she responded.

For the second time, restaurant patrons broke out in enthusiastic applause.

Watching her sleep now, Gabriel marveled at her simple beauty. He could feel this extraordinary woman without touching her. He savored her intoxicating scent from afar. It was beyond understanding, beyond definition. But none of that mattered now, for whatever perilous borders required crossing, they had agreed to cross them together.

He made his way to the guest bathroom and stared in the mirror at his sleep-deprived reflection. Splashing cold water onto his face, he rubbed vigorously, but it did little to improve his mood. In the kitchen, he gulped a cold swig of soda and swished it around his mouth, hoping the carbonation would strip away the grungy taste. Feeling more than a bit melancholy and knowing he would not embrace peaceful slumber anytime soon, he shaved, showered, dressed, and downed a cup of coffee before heading out the door.

It was now 2:35 AM and a cold thirty-four degrees outside. Snowflakes danced and glistened as they floated past street lamps, refracting light in a cascade of muted colors. Not another soul was in sight. Sane people, he knew, were sleeping under warm covers.

In the small park across the street from his building he brushed powdery snow off a forest-green wooden bench and planted himself there. *With the arrival of these bloody aliens,* he mused, *everything we knew, everything we trusted, has been ruthlessly stripped away. What I know for certain is that life-giving blood courses through my veins. I exist in this place and time, but have no idea of why or how the lights and shadows of my life fit into the scheme of things. When I consider the short duration of my life, the minor space I fill, I'm more perplexed than ever. There is no rhyme or reason to any of this. In the end, perhaps the answer isn't an answer at all, but a question; does anything really matter?*

He was pleased with how coherently he had assembled his thoughts.

Will I remember any of this? Your journal Gabriel, next time bring the damn thing with you.

28

He routinely arrived at the West Wing at 6:15 AM, which allowed sufficient time to meet with his team and prepare for President Conrad's arrival at 7:00 AM. Sadly, this morning, and all the mornings to follow, President Conrad would not be there.

As usual, his secretary Betty had a steaming cup of black coffee waiting for him.

"Good morning."

Betty's voice rang hollow in the far reaches of his still-sleepy brain.

"You seem to be functioning on two cylinders this morning."

"I didn't sleep well last night."

"That's become a universal problem." She forced a half-smile and motioned to the coffee. "This will help."

Gabriel took a sip from the steaming cup. "Any immediate fires to put out?"

"Not unless you consider *his royal highness* a fire that requires extinguishing."

"The walls have ears, Betty," Gabriel admonished.

Timidly, Betty's eyes went to her lap. "He asked to see you first thing."

Gabriel glanced at his watch, winked, and whispered, "Short stuff can damn well wait until I get this coffee in me."

Betty forced a nervous smile, then said softly, "Gabriel?"

There was no mistaking the hollow look in her eyes. He understood her unresolved fear, but the only assurance he offered came off sounding lame. "It'll be fine, it'll be fine."

She folded her hands in her lap, but said nothing.

"Listen, I, uh, I'll understand if you choose not to stay."

"Are you staying?"

Gabriel nodded in the affirmative.

"Then when you go, I go." She placed a flat hand on her desk. "Until then, this is *my* desk."

Moved by her loyalty, Gabriel knew that if he did not retreat at that very second his emotions would get the better of him.

In his office, he set his coffee cup down. He expelled an audible breath and planted his elbows firmly on the desk, lowered his head into his hands and held himself there like a small child. "Damn it, damn it, damn it, how in the hell did we get to this place?"

In utter frustration, he balled both fists and brought them down with such force, coffee splashed up and out of the cup. The hot liquid flowed toward him dripping over the edge onto his right leg. He flinched. "Goddamn it!" He quickly brushed a hand over the wet spot. "Shit!"

"What was that? Are you okay?" Betty called over the intercom.

"Nothing!" Gabriel yelled. "Nothing!"

"Well, be sure to call if you're bleeding."

"Thank you for that bit of sarcasm."

"You're welcome."

He snatched several sheets of tissue and patted the wet spot on his leg and dabbed at the desktop. From the bottom right drawer, he withdrew a half-empty pack of Marlboro Lights, lit one, took a long drag and held it as if it were a magical drug that would release him from the bedlam swirling around him.

"Gabriel?"

It was Betty again.

"Yes, mother?"

"The administrator's secretary asked if you had arrived. Are you smoking in there?"

"No," he lied.

"I thought you said you quit those filthy things? You're going to set off the smoke alarm—in the White House, yet! Are you mad?"

"Certifiably." He snubbed the cigarette in his coffee cup and placed it in the drawer next to the pack of cigarettes.

The day following President Conrad's death, Eileen Mosby had replaced Helen Ryan, President Conrad's longtime secretary. Legna had personally selected her, but how, why, or where she had come from remained a mystery. Mosby looked fortyish, was short with close-cropped brown hair, pinched lips, deep-set eyes, and narrow hips like a boy's. Her taste in fashion, or lack thereof, was limited to various shades of grays and blacks. Gabriel had only one occasion in the past week to even say hello, let alone question her.

"The administrator is expecting you, Mr. Ferro," Ms. Mosby said in a halting, slightly high-pitched voice.

"Thank you, Eileen. By the way, where did you work before joining our merry band of—?"

"I was not in government service. The administrator is waiting, Mr. Ferro," she said emphatically and turned away.

Gabriel always experienced a renewed burst of energy when entering the Oval Office. There was an undefined, unexplainable air of mystery about the iconic room that couldn't be characterized in mere words. Even those who held the United States in contempt looked upon this life-altering space with a level of respect if not reservation. Except now it was no longer the Office of the President of the United States, but the official headquarters of an extraterrestrial promising to bring salvation to a troubled civilization.

Legna was seated at the presidential desk absorbed in the document that lay before him. Since human furniture did not accommodate his diminutive stature, the high-backed leather chair had been cranked to its maximum height, placing his midsection even with the desktop but left his feet dangling a foot or so above the floor.

It angered Gabriel that Conrad's personal effects had not been removed. Still in place were treasured photos, a small alabaster bust of Abraham Lincoln and an engraved wooden sign, which read *Do the Right Thing*, prominently displayed on the front edge of the desk.

"It's time we sent the president's personal effects to Mrs. Conrad."

Legna continued reading, his index finger tracing below each line as if written English presented a challenge the spoken word did not.

"I'll see to it." Gabriel shifted uneasily from one foot to the other waiting for Legna's reply, but none came. "It's been a week. Why have you refused to meet with me?"

Without looking up, Legna answered, "I have been consumed."

"What's taking so long?"

Legna's eyes came up to meet Gabriel's. "I find your tone disrespectful."

Gabriel ignored the rebuke. "Surely, you're aware that every last person on Earth is living in suspended animation waiting for some word, any word, regarding their fate."

"Rome, as you humans are so fond of saying, was not built in a day. All will become transparent."

"While we're waiting for *transparency,* may I speak to you concerning Vice President Cross?"

"Mr. Cross has become a nuisance."

"For all his faults, Mr. Cross is the lawful successor to President Conrad. You're treating him as—"

"There are no successors, Gabriel. That is all past."

"With all due respect, I—"

Legna cut him short. "Interesting," he said and closed the document he was reading.

Gabriel eyes went to its blue cover. Even upside down he could make out the silver-embossed italic letters—*The Constitution of the United States.* "That was President Conrad's personal copy."

Legna looked up and his eye immediately went to Gabriel's wet pant leg. "Your clothing?"

"Coffee—I spilled coffee."

"I see," Legna said with indifference. He placed a flat hand on the copy of the Constitution. "If this instrument is indicative of how citizens are governed, it explains your failed society."

"That instrument, as you refer to it, is unique to *our* country."

Legna tapped a long boney finger on the document's cover. "This overly ambitious testimony attempts to create a societal order that cannot possibly succeed."

"But it has for well over 200 years."

"It stresses personal freedom beyond acceptable levels. Social standards, attitudes and conformity are all but impossible to enforce as written here."

"Within reason, that *was* the point," Gabriel said with confidence.

"I fail to grasp your meaning, Gabriel."

"The authors of our constitution saw to it that citizens were free to create a society based on personal liberty while avoiding the kind of acquiescence that imprisons men for having free thoughts." It was a long-winded reply, but he felt he had made his point well.

"Each of us is obligated to forge morally acceptable choices that not only affect one personally but all citizens equally."

Gabriel bowed his head slightly. "I agree."

"Then why does major discord persist within your society? Human history is blighted with intolerance perpetrated by those who disrespect the race, politics and the spiritual beliefs of others." Legna tapped a boney finger on the document. "No doubt these words were well-intentioned. However, it appears the high-minded goals outlined in this pretentious document have never been fully achieved."

"On the contrary," Gabriel retorted. "America created a society of free citizens, free to live as each deems fit, short of crimes against their fellow man. Despite enormous challenges we've succeeded quite well."

He was damned if he would admit it even though he understood all too well the alien's point. Not because the sacrosanct constitution no longer served its stated purpose, but because the historical document's articles were continually challenged, most often by those pursuing self-serving political or financial agendas.

Legna thumped a finger on the document again. "You are too philanthropic with your praise for this instrument. Its words encourage citizens to consider audacity as a right, abrasive speech as equality and anarchy as progress when they are displeased with their leaders."

The right corner of Gabriel's mouth curled into a cynical grin.

"You find my observation amusing?"

"What you just said, it was first spoken by the Greek philosopher Isocrates."

A knowing smile from Legna. "It appears you know your history well."

"I paid attention in school."

Several long seconds ticked away before Legna pushed the document to one side. "No matter, I shall study this instrument further in an attempt to interpret its meaning as you do."

"If I can be of assistance with that noble task, please call on me." Gabriel's voice dripped with sarcasm.

Legna slipped from the chair, ambled to the window and stared at the snow-covered ground. Gabriel waited—more seconds ticked away.

"Have I lost you?" Gabriel quipped. "We were discussing the Constitution."

But Legna's thoughts had moved on. "How do humans reconcile life and death?"

"How do you mean?"

"The ambiguity of consciousness, at least how humans perceive it, is that you are born, live, and expire without ever discerning meaning or interpretation."

"If what you shared with us in that motel room was the truth, then—"

"I assure you, Gabriel, I revealed only the truth."

"I question whether humans are prepared to accept your truth."

Legna turned from the window and took two steps toward Gabriel. "Have you shared this truth with anyone?"

"No."

"Has Catherine?"

"Not as far as I know."

Legna's stare was intense, a stare Gabriel had become all too familiar with. "If you're inside my head again—and I suspect you are—then you know I'm telling you the truth."

"Have you given thought to your mortality?"

"*Ahhh*, we're onto yet another weighty subject. My mortality is as fragile and fleeting as everyone's."

"Come, come, Gabriel," Legna said mockingly. "That is hypocrisy."

"Hypocrisy?"

"Humans have gone to great lengths to create a celestial afterlife to justify physical death, not as an end, but as the beginning. I recall that you said this yourself."

Gabriel inhaled and exhaled hard. "I haven't the foggiest idea where you're going with this."

"It is a simple question, Gabriel. Is your life span sufficient?"

"There's no simple answer. Tomorrow, I could be hit by a bus—end of Gabriel. Listen, what are we talking about here?"

"We are speaking of the duration of your life force."

A wry smile crossed Gabriel's lips. "On this planet, we all end up in ceramic urns; ashes to ashes, dust to dust. And to add insult to injury, most endure tribulation in their final days."

"Sarcasm does not become you," Legna scolded. "Know that all things possess an energy that exists outside the constraints of time and space. In sync with your physical death, your energy dissipates back into the vast, harmonious system from which it came."

"What is your point?"

"Humans identify with their physical structure and believe that when it dies, so does their earthly consciousness. I am not speaking of spiritual concepts, but the actual laws of—" Legna paused—his intensity diminished and his expression softened. "Perhaps we have entered a realm beyond your ability to comprehend."

"Hey, you brought it up."

The alien smiled sardonically and turned back to the window, swung his hands behind his back and intertwined his long fingers. Outside, the overcast sky cast a dullish gray pall across the snow.

"If not for your heroics Gabriel, my mission may have failed, leading to a far more forceful and regrettable intervention."

Frustrated, Gabriel retorted with, "I don't believe that. I think you could have flown the coop anytime you chose. Perhaps it amused you to flee with Catherine, Galinski, and me."

Legna remained silent.

"Okay, no answer to that one. Let's move on. You deceived me, telling me one thing, then stealing it all back in spades at the United Nations. However, misguided their motives, Directors Downing and Benthurst were right, and I was dead wrong."

"It is true that I misled you. For that, I seek your absolution. But we offer no apology for seizing jurisdiction over a race bent on self-destruction."

"Knowing what you told Catherine and me, how can you absolve yourself of responsibility?"

"Save your rhetoric Gabriel, mankind alone is responsible for what they have become." The alien's head joggled left and right in a hopeless gesture. "They have not progressed beyond stone tools and clay tablets."

Gabriel had no quick reply.

"You offer no defense—how disappointing."

"Why do you insist on stuffing us all in the same garbage bag? There are billions of decent, honest, moral people who rail against—"

Before Gabriel could complete his thought, Legna swiftly closed the gap between them. The abrupt move startled him, and he backed away. But Legna was quick, seizing Gabriel's right hand and pulling it tightly to his own chest.

"What are you doing?"

"Imagine you hold a weapon, and you will use it to end my life force."

Gabriel struggled to free himself, but Legna proved to be incredibly strong for his diminutive size.

"When the first human extinguished the life of another, be it from anger, fear, hunger, or jealousy, your race was cursed. It was at that moment a primal creature discovered he could dominate others through brute force."

Gabriel jerked back, but was still unable to free his hand.

"However, your race might justify the taking of life, know that you possess *free will...* you choose to act the way you do. So please save your misplaced verbal posturing for your fellow man."

Yanking hard, Gabriel broke free from Legna's grip. "Enough of your theatrics! If I'm to believe a single word you spoke in that motel room, then the original act of violence—the original sin—began with your kind. It is you who need to end the rhetoric."

Gabriel's assertiveness surprised Legna. He stepped back and fell silent, his head swiveling to the portico door and the snow-covered landscape beyond. "Why have I come to Earth, Gabriel?"

"I ask myself that question every waking hour of every day."

"Please answer without sarcasm."

"I placed my life on the line for you, assured by you that you came in peace. It was a monumental leap of faith on my part."

"We *have* come in peace, yet there are many humans who would cause us misfortune."

"What do you expect? You tell us to continue living our lives like nothing's changed, yet *everything* has changed. Fear is our primary motivation now. Do you understand fear?"

"No others of my kind have set foot on Earth's soil."

Tossing his arms haphazardly in the air, Gabriel bellowed, "Well, that's comforting. Knowing there are hovering ships with God knows how many of you on them is hardly a recipe for a good night's sleep, is it?"

Legna went silent again—pregnant pauses that drove Gabriel crazy. Finally, the alien said, "It is you they need to see—your voice they need to hear."

"What in the living hell are you talking about?"

Legna ambled toward the desk, gently touching Gabriel's arm with the tips of his fingers as he passed. "Hear me." The alien sat, intertwined his fingers and set his hands upon the desk. "I wish you to be at my side, disseminating the strategies that will rehabilitate your planet and bestow new enlightenment on its citizens."

Gabriel pointed an accusing finger. "You mean the brainwashing of the human race for nefarious reasons yet to be revealed." He strode to the door. "Hell, I have no earthly idea who you are, or what your true intentions are. Why should I believe you, let alone help you?"

"In time, you will know all," Legna said easily.

Gabriel's right hand wrapped tightly around the brass doorknob. "Great, until then I refuse to be your human mouthpiece."

"Gabriel, please look at me," Legna commanded.

Gabriel took a breath and cast a defiant stare.

"I would not require that you compromise your principles nor bear false witness to an untruth."

Gabriel's hand slipped from the doorknob and he curled it into a tight fist. "Forget it! I will not succumb to—"

"Gabriel, I wish you to sit."

With rancor rising within him, Gabriel's neck muscles tightened. But he realized his acrimony would not serve him well, not now. *Don't lose it Sparky, don't give him the edge.*

"Please, I requested that you sit."

Drawing in a deep, calming breath, Gabriel strode slowly to one of two facing sofas and slumped down.

The bantam alien approached the opposite sofa. Using his arms to pull himself up, he twisted to one side so that he was now upright with his feet dangling several inches above the floor. He spoke in the quiet, reassuring tone that served him so well. "Your animosity toward me is validated. And yet you accepted my petition to remain at my side."

"We have a saying here: better the devil you know than the one you don't."

Legna's thin lips curled ever so slightly into what Gabriel had come to recognize as a smile.

"I have been truthful; our purpose is to assist Earth's citizens."

"So you say, but is it out of guilt?"

Legna looked away, his gaze straying to nothing in particular. For several long seconds, the rhythmic sound of Conrad's beloved grandfather clock prevailed.

How do I make points with this arrogant midget when I harbor disdain for mankind's inability to see beyond the immediate? How do I make this insufferable creature understand without betraying my own kind? Try scoring a point. "Life on this planet is far more complicated than you realize. If it is your mission to change us—"

"To advance you."

"There are almost nine billion people representing contrasting ethnicities, traditions, and beliefs, all living and functioning within vastly differing economic spheres. Believe me, before this is over, you're going to wish you stayed home."

Legna laughed a deep, throaty laugh. "Come, come, you can do better. Allow your thoughts to flow freely." Legna placed his right hand flat against his chest. "Speak from here, Gabriel."

"Bare my soul, is that what you're asking?"

"It can be quite rewarding."

"For whom?"

If politics had taught Gabriel anything, it was to keep his own counsel, lest his words be used against him. This smug alien was encouraging openness and honesty, but for whose benefit and for what purpose? His mind wandered, and his eyes strayed to the floor. He was distracted by a scuff on the toe of his right shoe. *Hey, where are you? Snap out of it! Focus! Focus!* His eyes came up to meet Legna's. "I hardly require a history lesson from you. I know very well who we are."

"Please, enlighten me."

Gabriel's eyes wandered to the photo of President Conrad and his wife Victoria and he felt a sudden rush of melancholy. This was the man who had shown unwavering confidence in a young, naïve law school graduate; the man who had guided him to the top of the political mountain. He could not fail the late President, not now, not when the very future of the human race hung in the balance.

He searched Legna's face for any sign that might give him an edge. But, alas, the alien's blank expression was impossible to read. He swallowed hard and began.

"We are driven by primal and instinctive urges without regard and often with deep hatred for those outside one's own tribe. I'm not sure that will ever change. Humans are also capable of seeing the good and are inspired to do what is right, but are often predisposed to follow the worst. That's a question psychologist continually ponder. And yet in other ways, evolution has been kind to us. We are gifted with curiosity and imagination, inventiveness and ambition. But we're also tormented by uncontrollable appetites for more and more, far more than we require and nothing, it seems, can stop our forward thrust in that direction." Taking a deep breath, he expelled it slowly. "There, is that what you were hoping to hear?"

"You articulated it very well, Gabriel."

"Oh, I can articulate it all right, but how do you intend to defeat it?

"We have come not to defeat humankind, but to advance it."

"If you have any hope of succeeding, there are billions of non-believers that will require convincing."

Legna brushed a finger lightly over his small chin. "The impoverished will succumb willingly, for they shall be elevated to equal status. The privileged will reject changes that deprive them of the leverage." The smooth gray skin above his eyes arched ever so slightly. "I assure you, they will acquiesce." There was arrogance in his voice, a manipulative conceit that reaffirmed his determination. "All will embrace our way, for we offer a life devoid of avarice and moral weakness." His voice dropped to barely a whisper. "When we depart Earth—and that day shall come—citizens shall look to an unyielding leader who is true to the dynamic new doctrine that will have been promulgated. It is you, Gabriel, you will be the shepherd guiding Earth's citizens to a joyful passage."

To Gabriel's bewilderment, Legna was in effect anointing him, Gabriel Javier Ferro, the kid from a poor barrio in Miami, as the human protagonist who would govern humankind. "Why me, what have I said or done that would lead you to believe I'm the one to impose *your* vision of who *you* think we should be?"

Legna slid from the sofa and ambled to the desk as if Gabriel's protest had fallen on deaf ears. "All will become clear upon your return."

"Return? From where?"

Legna retrieved a manila file folder from the edge of the desk. "You shall visit the Mogen."

"Who?

"The Mogen inhabit Surin Island off the coast of Thailand and Myanmar. They are known as the *Sea Gypsies*."

"I've never heard of them."

Legna extended the folder. Gabriel eyed it like it was laced with poison. He placed it in his lap without opening it.

Legna clambered back up onto the sofa. "I wish you to study the Mogen in their habitat for one of your weeks."

"And just what will I learn from these ... these Sea Gypsies?"

"The wisdom required to lead the triumphant rebirth of the human race."

Curious as to what he might find inside the file, Gabriel opened it. It contained a single sheet of paper.

"Before leaving, please refrain from conducting further research on the Mogen beyond the material provided."

Gabriel closed the file without reading it. "Why?"

"You must experience Mogen life without preconception."

"You want me to do this despite the contempt I've expressed for your deceit?"

Legna slid from the sofa closing the short gap between them. Taking Gabriel's right hand, he clasped it in his and placed his left hand on Gabriel's forearm. "You are true and steady, a man of conviction and courage. These virtues eclipse any reservations I may harbor."

Uncomfortable at the alien's touch, Gabriel withdrew his hand and stood. "This is happening way too fast. I have to sleep on it."

"Sleep?" Legna asked.

"I have to think it out—give it serious thought."

"Yes, I understand."

"I don't think you do. You're asking me to get involved without my knowing the game plan."

"This is not a game, Gabriel."

"Don't play dumb, you know exactly what I mean."

"First, you must visit the Mogen. They will assist you in harnessing the courage required to lead mankind to a joyful transition."

There it was, as clear as a cloudless blue sky; the transition to change the human race was to advance with or without his involvement. If he acquiesced, he would surely be labeled a traitor by his own. If he rebuffed Legna, he would have no further sway—assuming he had any to begin with. "If I do this," he said pointedly, "*if* I do this, the second I have reason to question your motives…" He felt no need to finish the sentence. He stood and walked to the exit and wrapped a hand around the doorknob. "There is a condition. That night in the motel, you revealed the existence of what you called the *Kebun*. I want to go there."

Legna's eyelids narrowed. "The Kebun is no longer accessible."

"I don't believe you."

"You are free to believe whatever you wish, Gabriel."

"If I agree to go halfway around the world to meet some primitive tribe that I've never heard of, I want a side trip to New Guinea. I want to see with my own eyes where, according to you, it all began."

"Why is this relevant?"

"To see what might have been."

"You will only find what was meant to be, but is no more."

"Consider this the first test of our newfound trust."

Legna looked away as he often did as if his consciousness had wandered to a time and space not available to mere humans. His gaze settled on the portico door. Agent Carson, covered shoulder to knee in a winter coat, stood just outside.

"I'm waiting," Gabriel said.

Legna stared at the back of Carson's head. "I have been unable to observe Agent Carson's thoughts. Perhaps he is devoid of them." Slowly, purposely, Legna turned back to Gabriel, his mouth curling into a crooked smile. "You are feeling empowered?"

"Empowered?"

"You are negotiating with me."

Call his bluff and be ready to bolt if he gives you a ration of shit. "The Kebun is part of the deal, or there is no deal."

Gabriel waited patiently for an answer. The grandfather clock was irritating him now with its *tock, tock, tock*, that sounded louder than usual.

Legna finally said, "It shall be, you shall visit the Kebun."

"Thank you." Gabriel's hand tightened around the doorknob, but there was more, much more he wanted answers to.

"Why didn't you intercede earlier? Why have you waited until now?"

"An attempt was made… we were rejected."

"Rejected? When, by whom?"

"In your year 1982, we audited Mankind's progress. What we witnessed was disturbing. In their insatiable hunger for scientific, technological and pecuniary advancement, humans had failed to grasp the simplest of principles; life is dependent on a single, but diverse entity—*the living Earth*. Why, we wondered, were humans wantonly abusing their precious life force? To forestall further erosion of both the species and the planet, an intervention was required." Legna's right hand brushed lightly along his temple. "Your President Ronald Reagan was chosen as the human to be contacted."

"President Reagan?" Gabriel said with surprise. "Why Reagan?"

"We believed him to be sincere in his quest to foster solutions and therefore would be receptive to our guidance. Does the name William Casey resonate?"

"He was the director of the Central Intelligence Agency at the time."

"We knew Mr. Reagan would never be allowed to meet with us directly, so, Mr. Casey was chosen as the intermediary. The gathering took place the 5th day of your month of March in the year 1982 in a remote area of the state of New Mexico." Legna smiled. "You were not yet born." His smile faded. "Mr. Casey's attendants erected a reinforced structure within an existing structure which they referred to as a 'clean room'. We were greeted by men in white protective clothing—hazmat suits they called them—ostensibly to ensure we would not contaminate them."

"Did you share with Mr. Casey what you revealed to President Conrad, Catherine, and I?"

"That would have proven far too labyrinthine for a first contact. Our only mission was to draw attention to the degradation of human society and life-sustaining natural environments. Mr. Casey appeared well versed in those matters. In great detail, he defined the corrective measures being explored. It was painfully clear that none of the solutions would prove adequate."

Legna paused—his gaze wandered off as it often did. "Our offer of assistance came with conditions."

"What conditions?"

"Enlightenment will come in due course. Mr. Casey did not mask his displeasure with our conditions. He would, however, convey them to President Reagan—could we wait two of your days? On the 6th day of your month of March, Mr. Casey met with Citizen Reagan. On the 7th, Mr. Casey returned and presented a handwritten note from the President." Legna paused and lowered his eyes to the floor. "His reply was disturbing."

"What did Reagan say?"

"It is what he did not say that was most revealing."

Gabriel waited, but Legna's attention drifted again.

"You're killing me here." Gabriel groaned. "What did Reagan's note say?"

"You must master patience, Gabriel. Mr. Reagan wrote: *We are very much aware of the enormous challenges facing our civilization and are most grateful for your willingness to assist. However, the terms you propose are beyond our ability to enforce. Therefore, we respectfully request you allow us to confront our future without further interference.*"

"That was it? That's all he said?"

"No doubt it was a decision of political expediency. We were appalled by the fatuity of an ego-driven society that failed to come to grips with an impending apocalypse."

"You could have forced the issue."

Legna sighed. "Our intent was never that of an aggressor, but the benevolent ally."

Gabriel pointed an accusing finger. "How could you justify walking away knowing full well what was on our horizon?"

"I fail to appreciate your tone, Gabriel. Please temper it."

"Okay, okay, but why now? What motivated you to return after all this time?"

"The solutions put forth by your leaders have proven wholly insufficient. The decline of your society and your environment will continue and life on this planet will be extinguished. We cannot allow that."

Reticent to trust Legna, Gabriel's mind raced, analyzing every detail just as President Conrad had taught him: Consider the causes, key factors, potential damage, and possible results. He diverted his eyes. *What is it that I'm missing here? What's below the surface that I'm failing to grasp? What is it that he's not telling me?*

"The healing process commences with your visit to the Mogen."

What's with this Mogen business? Gabriel wondered. *Is there a connection to the Ecaepians? Okay, if he wants me to visit some primitive tribe on some far-flung island, and that's what it takes to stay in the game, then do it.* "This Mogen visit, it's important to you?"

"It is important to humanity's future."

"I never thought of myself as a savior of anything, let alone humanity. But yes, I will visit these Mogen, if that's what you want."

"You do this of your own free will?"

Gabriel's hand gripped the doorknob tightly. "Is it of your free will that I visit the *Kebun*?"

Legna hesitated for a long moment before whispering, "If you insist."

"I insist," Gabriel quickly replied.

Then out of the blue, Legna asked, "How is Miss Catherine?"

"Dr. Blake is spending time here in Washington."

"Please express my desire for her to visit."

"Are you aware Owen Jennings is alive?"

"I am."

"Perhaps you could expedite his recovery. And while you're doing good deeds, authorize Catherine's transfer to the Bethesda medical facility here in Washington."

Neither request seemed to surprise Legna. "This is important to you?"

Gabriel nodded.

"Then it shall be so."

"Thank you." Gabriel knew he had been tossed another bone, but he would take whatever he could get. He turned the doorknob fully.

"Gabriel?"

Gabriel had one foot out the door.

Legna closed the distance between them, and he gently touched Gabriel's arm. "In time, I hope to convince you I played no role in President Conrad's departure." Legna wrapped his long, bony fingers around Gabriel's forearm. "Come to terms with your destiny, young Gabriel Ferro. Prepare mentally and morally to confront the tasks that are demanded of you. Cherish every forward moment, be in awe of the gift of renewal offered freely by each new sunrise, and lead your fellow man to a joyous rebirth."

Legna's smile faded, and his face became a blank page again. Moving across the oval rug, he approached the portico door and stood still and quiet.

The sun was out now, and the snow gleamed bright white again.

29

Gabriel leaned against the wall just outside his office suite. The meeting with Legna had left him physically and emotionally drained. Part of him wanted to believe that Legna was there for no other reason than stated, but the judicious part of him screamed *caution*!

Twenty-nine-year-old Tyler Harney, one of the young, bright bulbs on Gabriel's team, approached.

"Hey Gabriel, you okay?"

"Hi Tyler, yeah, I'm fine."

"I was just coming to see you."

The last thing Gabriel was in the mood for was a conversation. "What's up?"

"This." Tyler held up a single sheet of paper.

Gabriel scanned the sheet of paper. "I didn't send this."

"It came from you-know-who. He wants the annual number of worldwide births and deaths, prisoners incarcerated for murder and the identities of known terrorists and their suspected locations."

"Why does he want this?"

"Beats me, but the number of murderers—jeez, that's an unwieldy task."

"The Bureau of Prisons will have the number."

"But he wants the number for the entire world. Am I supposed to contact every country? My god, I'll be at it for weeks."

"Interpol will have a handle on it."

"*Ahhh*, Interpol. You see, that's why you're the chief of staff, and I'm not. Thanks."

"Tyler, I want to see that report before you turn it in."

"My instructions were to turn it in directly to—"

"I don't care who told you what. Be sure I see it first."

"Okay, yeah, sure."

"Good, anything else?"

Tyler's eyes went to the ceiling. "Why are they up there and not down here? What are they waiting for?"

Having no desire to discuss what he was unable to answer, Gabriel changed the subject. "How's Bonnie doing through all this?"

That brought a beaming smile Tyler's face. "We're four months pregnant today."

"Whoa, that's heavy. Know the sex yet?"

"Oh yeah, it's a girl."

"Wonderful, I hear girls are easier to raise."

"I suppose we'll find out soon enough." Tyler's eyes shot to the ceiling again. "Will the kid have a world to grow up in?"

Despite his misgivings, Gabriel said, "She will, she will—my best to Bonnie."

Gabriel breezed by Betty without a word.

"Well, hello to you too," she said.

Once settled at his desk, he opened the file on the Mogen Tribe. The single sheet read like a page straight out of Wikipedia:

The Mogen—Chao Lei, or people of the sea—are the smallest minority in South East Asia. For centuries, they have inhabited the waters off Thailand, Malaysia, and Borneo in the provinces of Satun, Trang, Krabi, Phuket, Phang Nga, and Ronong and through the Mergui Archipelago of Burma, now called Myanmar. This particular tribe of 128 men, women, and children you will be visiting reside on Surin Island, off the coast of Phuket. The Mogen are not known to be religious in the conventional sense, but are viewed as far more spiritual than traditionally organized faiths. Pay close attention to this detail.

"That's it? That's all the info I get?" Gabriel cursed. "They sound like stone-age, cave-dwelling Neanderthals. Why in the hell is he sending me there?"

One of Legna's earliest actions was to ban any mention of the alien presence either in the mainstream media or the Internet and threatened retaliation against those who did. But this ill-conceived decision only led to rampant underground rumors and misinformation provoking even greater fear and uncertainty. He did, however, allow the Internet to operate freely, ignorant of the fact that on Planet Earth the World Wide Web was the biggest single, wackiest venue for rumors and misinformation.

Established bloggers and social media sites went into instant overdrive.

One far-right militant group, calling themselves "New Knights of the Round Table," created a website advocating for an immediate uprising, ignoring the real possibility that millions might die as the result of an ill-conceived rebellion. Yet another faction, calling themselves "The Believers," believed the aliens were messengers sent by God. The first gatherings of this faux religious group took place in the city of Liege, Belgium, and, numbered a little over 300 defiant souls. As their convoluted message spread through social media, their numbers swelled exponentially. Within days, the crusade had grown worldwide to several million seeking solace in what they hoped would be their salvation.

Despite the craziness, and for reasons known only to him, Legna allowed the Internet to continue unabated.

That evening, Gabriel shared with Catherine his meeting with Legna but was careful to avoid any

Mention of his forthcoming trip to Surin Island and the Kebun. "There wasn't much to it. He mostly rattled on about how they're going to save us."

"Well, he better get moving before there are riots in the streets." And then she became pensive and her gaze went to the floor.

"I know that look, what's wrong?"

"There's something I've been meaning to tell you." Her eyes met his. "I thought I saw something, something that I failed to mention when it happened."

"Well?"

"Just after Legna was shot, his... what I mean is, I wasn't sure of what I saw, so I didn't mention it. But just before he pulled that bullet from his shoulder, I could have sworn his eyes turned black."

"Black! And you didn't tell me this?"

"It was quick, like a blink of an eye."

Gabriel's voice leaped up a decibel. "And you didn't think that was important?"

"Everything was happening so fast, bullets were flying, I just wasn't sure. Then at the UN, you said his eyes went black. That's when I recalled what I thought I had seen on the helicopter."

"And you still didn't mention it?"

"I'm sorry, in all the confusion, I..." She looked away. "I should have said something."

Gabriel blew out a breath. "Okay, what's done is done. It's clear now, when his eyes turn black he accesses powers beyond our understanding and that makes him pretty damn dangerous."

By the time the sun had set the temperature had dropped from forty-seven to thirty-five degrees. A light, meandering snow shower floated to the already packed ground, turning Georgetown traffic into a complex maze of chaos. Gabriel had made dinner reservations at Arico's, his favorite neighborhood restaurant. It was an intimate Italian bistro a block from his apartment. He and Catherine braved the short walk in several inches of white powder. They settled two booths away from a distinguished looking elderly couple in the otherwise empty restaurant.

The white-haired gentleman was speaking loud enough to be heard. "Don't be so apprehensive, Alice. What will be, will be."

His female companion leaned back and folded her arms defiantly across her chest. "You're such a fatalist Peter," she seethed. "We'll end up their slaves for sure." She pushed her plate away. "I want to go home. I want to call the children."

Her companion protested. "Alice, I've not finished my dinner."

"I want to speak with the children, damn it!" The woman scooped up her purse, shimmied out of the booth and walked gingerly toward the exit.

The old man shook his head, sighed and dropped his napkin over his food. "For heaven's sake, Alice!" Leaving several large bills on the table and voicing something Gabriel and Catherine could not hear, he stormed out.

"If you're wondering how people are dealing with this, there's your answer," Catherine whispered to Gabriel. "No one believes a word coming out of Legna's twisted little mouth. All he's offered so far is, *we're nice guys, and you shouldn't be frightened of us.* Yeah, right. And the Easter Bunny lays eggs. Honestly, if I could, I'd strangle him and be done with it. For the love of me, I cannot fathom why the human race has rolled over for these creatures. Are we simply going to allow them free rein over our lives without a fight? For God's sake, our entire belief system has been stripped away."

Vicenzo Arico—a tall, distinguished-looking, mustachioed immigrant from the fishing village of Falcone on Sicily's north coast—approached carrying two plates. Gabriel never ordered from the menu, but always allowed Vicenzo and Chef Franco to surprise him.

Vicenzo beamed. "This evening I have prepared special for you, Chicken Vesuvio. Mangiare."

"It's pretty quiet tonight, Vicenzo."

"*Ah* si, Mr. Ferro, everyone is too frightened. I send the wait staff home. It's just Franco and me." Vicenzo filled Catherine's wine glass, but his hand trembled and some spilled to the white tablecloth, "*Nel buon nome di Cristo!* Uh, scusa, my hand, it is not so steady tonight. *Pardon, signor Ferro, ma vi sono i più vicini a lui ora, che ne sai.*"

"Vicenzo, you know I don't speak Italian."

"Forgive me, Mr. Ferro, but I ask of what you know. You are the closest to this monster now and—"

"Vicenzo, how long have I been coming here?"

"Well over a year, signor."

"So, you know me well?"

"Si, well enough."

"I believe they mean us no harm." Gabriel spoke those words with as much conviction as he could muster.

Vicenzo's expression changed to a half-smile. "Thank you, thank you, *Buon appétito.*" As he scurried off they heard, *"Non importa, è tutto madness! Noi tutti moriremo!"*

"What did he say?" Catherine asked.

"Beats me."

Catherine raised her glass. "Let's just toast to safe times."

He raised his glass and touched it to hers. "To safe times."

He could not take his eyes from her. Her understated allure was like a radiant brightness in the soft light. Her medium-brown hair was swept back in a ponytail, just as was when they first met under dubious circumstances in Arizona. Her eyes, two pools of hazel loveliness, sparkled and her minimal makeup in muted colors enhanced her fresh appearance.

"So, I awoke in the middle of the night and reached for you but came up with nothing but a handful of sheets. I searched the apartment—no Gabriel. Then I peeked out the patio doors, and there you were across the street sitting on a cold, snow-covered bench like some sorrowful, homeless person."

Gabriel poked at his food with disinterest. "When I can't sleep, I get up." He sampled the chicken, but his taste buds were not cooperating.

"You're gonna' poke that chicken to death."

He slid the chicken to the other side of the plate. "This feels kind of odd."

With a straight face, Catherine said, "Then move that chicken back to where it was."

"I was referring to you and me."

"Why would you think us odd?"

"Because when we first met, you despised me."

She laughed. "*Despise* is a strong word. I thought you were another government interloper unable to deal with the most colossal discovery in the history of the human race."

"But I dealt with it, didn't I?"

"Kicking and screaming as I recall. When we entered that vault, your heart was thumping like a bass drum."

"Yeah, well, it's not every day one gets up close and personal with an alien." Gabriel poked at his food again. "What I was really trying to say a second ago is... I find it interesting we're together."

"Ah, we're back to the romance thing. Are you shaking with fear at the thought?"

"Just the opposite."

She feigned wiping at her brow. "Whew, that's a relief,"

"You know what I mean. It's bizarre how people find each other in ways that go against the laws of so-called romance."

"You see, there's your problem, you've bought into the myth. There are no such laws or rules. It was purely a chemical reaction; you wanted to jump my bones, pure and simple."

"I'll have you know sex was the farthest thing from my mind."

She twirled her fork in a circular motion. "But it did cross your mind, cowboy."

Gabriel grinned. "That came later. What came first was your arrogant, stand-offish, I'm-smarter-than-you attitude."

Catherine pushed back and laughed. "And to believe you saw through all that and *still* wanted to jump my bones."

"Hey, don't get too cocky, girl, the jury's still out."

Catherine stabbed at her chicken. "I'm going to see Owen Jennings tomorrow—haven't had the courage up until now. I'm a doctor, I'm supposed to deal with this sort of thing, but I'm too close to him."

"He's still in a coma with many skin grafts ahead of him."

"I'm just thankful he's alive."

They fell silent for several beats before Catherine finally said, "I'm curious about something."

Gabriel chuckled. "You're curious about everything."

"How would you have reacted if you had learned of this whole misadventure along with the rest of the world?"

"I would have bent over, grabbed my ankles, and kissed my ass goodbye." Then, without missing a beat, Gabriel blurted, "I'm going to Thailand."

Surprised, Catherine's head bobbed back. "What's in Thailand, besides Thais?"

"Mogen."

"Am I supposed to know what a Mogen is?"

"It's not a thing. They're a nomadic tribe."

"And you are going there for?"

"To study them in their habitat."

"And?"

"To discover why Legna believes they're near perfect human specimens."

"There's no such animal."

"Legna seems to think these Mogen come close. The trouble is, they don't speak my language or me theirs. They don't even have a written language. Anyway, I leave in the morning."

"In the morning? When were you going to tell me?"

"I'm telling you now. I should be back in six or seven days." Gabriel stared at her for a beat, then leaned across the table and whispered. "Have you shared with anyone what we know?"

"President Conrad made it clear to me in a phone call that if I did, I would spend the rest of my life in a Mexican prison."

"I almost spilled it to Alan Cross. Just the thought of what he would do with that information gives me chills." He lifted his glass and emptied it in a single gulp. "At some point, people have to be told. Something that extraordinary can't be kept secret forever."

"I side with physicist Stephen Hawking." Catherine said with a wry smile. "His theory is, if and when aliens arrived on Earth, they would probably cause the same outcome as what Columbus and the Spanish did for Native Americans. Didn't turn out very well for them, did it?"

The food was of no further interest to Gabriel. He pushed his plate aside and folded his arms across his chest. "I can't decide whether he's Yoda, Hannibal Lector, or the Antichrist."

Catherine raised an eyebrow. "Hannibal Lector gets my vote."

"Yeah, well, Dr. Lector asked if you'd pay him a visit."

"Said the spider to the fly."

"And he's agreed to transfer you to Walter Reed Medical Center."

Catherine placed her hands flat on the table and braced herself as if she was going to leap over in a single bound and pounce. "Without consulting with me first?"

Gabriel shifted uneasily. "I thought you'd be pleased."

"You could have asked first! I'm involved in critical research in San Diego."

"You can do it here."

"But you could have consulted with me first!"

Gabriel closed and opened his eyes and looked away. "Maybe I was afraid you'd say no."

Abruptly, Catherine stood. "Jesus, Gabriel, is that what this is about? You're unsure of where this relationship might or might not be going? For a bright boy, you're pretty dumb when it comes to the female species."

From the back of the room, Vicenzo called out, "Yes, miss, you need something?"

"For god's sake, sit down." Gabriel waved over his shoulder. "Maybe a bit more wine, Vicenzo."

Catherine made a grunting sound and sat. "Look, relationships are difficult even when the stars align perfectly. Some of us have learned through evolution to spot those of the opposite sex who spell trouble. With you, I don't see red flags— *not yet.*" She thumped a stiff finger hard on the table. "I'm *here* because I choose to be *here.* It's because of you I can breathe freely again. It's because of you that I… Jesus, why are men so insecure?"

Gabriel looked diminished like a small boy caught peeing in the bushes.

Catherine reached across the table, took his hand in hers and squeezed it. "I will be here when you get back. Okay?"

For Gabriel, the moment was magical, the feeling of euphoria that comes with the confirmation that someone you deeply care for, cares back. He lifted her hand to his lips and kissed it softly.

Later that evening, lost in each other's warm embrace, their lovemaking was intense. Neither wanted to let go of the other. Their relationship, which had begun so badly, had made a wondrous pivot toward the light.

30

The West Wing staff was told Gabriel would be visiting his ailing mother in Miami and he was not to be contacted under any circumstances. In his absence, they were to report to Alan Cross.

Two Secret Service agents drove Gabriel to Joint Base Andrews in Maryland to begin his trek to the Mogen village on South Surin Island in Indonesia. Legna's instructions were to take nothing but the clothes on his back. Other than the two military pilots, Gabriel would be the only passenger on the unmarked twin-engine Cessna Citation X jet. They would refuel at Moron Air Base in southern Spain, then on to Prince Sultan Air Base in Saudi Arabia to refuel again before embarking on the final leg of their journey; Phuket International Airport on Thailand's West Coast. There, someone would meet him.

The prospect of meeting with the Mogen was not what fueled Gabriel's curiosity. Driving him was the prospect of setting foot in the mysterious *Kebun*, a place that would confirm the tale Legna had shared with him, Catherine, and President Conrad.

While waiting for his flight to depart, he placed a call to his mother. He had called her earlier in the week, but they'd both been too impassioned by the fast-moving events and their conversation had been brief.

"Mama," Gabriel said.

There was a moment of silence before she responded, *"¿Gabriel, mi hijo, estás bien?"*

"I'm fine, mama, honestly. I'm calling to let you know I'll be out of the country for a few days."

"Where are you going?"

"Indonesia, mama, he is sending me to Indonesia on a mission."

"They are evil, Gabriel—*malos*. Why do you stay there? You need to free your-self of them."

"I can't leave, I'm needed here. I'll explain when I see you."

"*Regresa a mi casa en Miami.*"

"Mama, mama, I can't come to Miami. Come to Washington and live with me?"

"No, my son, this is my home, your home. *Permaneceré aqui pase lo que pase.*"

"Mama, *Ven a Washington.*"

Gabriel's words were falling on deaf ears. There was no arguing with this proud, stubborn woman, and that was that. He promised to visit upon his return.

"I love you, mama."

"*Tu Eres mi vida, Gabriel. Que Dios esté contigo,*" she said through tears.

"God be with you too, mama."

Upon arrival at Phuket International Airport, the Cessna Citation taxied to an isolated maintenance hangar on the far side of the airport. Gabriel thanked the crew and disembarked. Standing at the foot of the steps was an Indonesian man dressed casually in khaki pants and a colorful print shirt.

"Mr. Ferro?"

"Yes?"

"I'm Rafi Suharto. Welcome to Thailand." Suharto stood around five feet ten, stocky and solidly built and looked to be in his mid-forties. He extended a beefy hand in greeting. "I'm your guide and translator."

Gabriel was jet-lagged, his back hurt, and he was in a foul mood. Forcing a smile, he gripped Rafi's hand. "Nice to meet you."

"You've become quite famous."

"Not by choice. Call me Gabriel. How far are we going?"

"Down to the Phuket waterfront. From there a boat will take us to South Surin Island."

Phuket, with a population of just over 500,000, was the largest island in Thailand. It was stunningly beautiful, offering tourists from around the world white sandy beaches and clear ocean waters. The expansive oceanfront, dotted with high-end resorts, had risen from the ashes after the devastating destruction of the 2004 Indian Ocean earthquake and tsunami that claimed 280,000 lives.

Suharto drove to Bang Toa Beach where a local fishing trawler was to shuttle them to the Mogen village on nearby Surin Island. However, when they arrived, no boat was waiting.

"The captain will be along soon enough," Rafi assured Gabriel. "Life here passes a bit slower than in Washington. Come on, we'll wait over there."

They settled on a faded-green, wooden bench in the middle of a dock that jutted out thirty feet over the water. After leaving a cold Washington, Gabriel was happy to be soaking up the warm sun.

"How much do you know about the Mogen?" Rafi asked.

"Not much."

"Be prepared for culture shock."

"Right, culture shock is what I need right about now. Tell me what you know."

"Well, unlike those of us who reside in so-called sophisticated societies, the Mogen pay little or no attention to the goings-on in the outside world."

"Lucky them," Gabriel murmured.

"For example, ask a Mogen how old he or she is, and they won't know nor do they care. A simple, natural rhythm rules their daily lives. When it's light they rise when it's dark they sleep. Their understanding of life is equally simple: They are born, they live, and they die."

"That's pretty basic."

"On the other hand, maybe it's just that sophisticated. Unfortunately, their traditions and simple way of life are under attack by an invading industrial world."

"How do I communicate with them?"

"Through me," Rafi said. "Their language, which is pretty minimal, is mostly a stripped-down version of Indonesian Bahasa. They don't use words such as 'when,' 'want,' 'hello,' 'goodbye,' or 'worry,' since such notions hold no significance to life's rhythms."

"Why haven't I heard of these people?"

"They've never been paid much attention. That is, not until the 2004 tsunami hit. They foresaw the arrival of that killer wave when no one else did and took refuge in the nearby mountains. Every last one survived."

"How'd they know the wave was coming?"

"Since they have no written language, they rely on a rich oral history to propagate their myths and legends. One such legend is the *La Boon*. Loosely translated, it refers to a man-eating wave brought on by the angry spirits of their ancestors. The devastating power of the wave symbolizes a purification of nature in the face of polluting humanity. On the morning the tsunami hit, things got really weird. The cicadas went silent, and blackbirds went absolutely mad, and the sea began to recede. To the Mogen, that was the sign that *La Boon* was coming and they took to higher ground."

"Were you here when the wave hit?"

Rafi's eyes glazed over as if the memory of the tsunami was still fresh in his mind. "I was living in Bangkok. I came down with other volunteers the day after the tsunami hit. As far as the eye could see, there was total destruction. Dead bodies were piled upon dead bodies. The living—the walking dead—were frantically searching for survivors." He hesitated for a long moment. "Out of the corner of my eye, about twenty meters from where I stood, I thought I saw a body move—a little girl lying face down on top of four or five other bodies. God almighty, I thought, she's alive. I raced to her and turned her over. She was full of maggots. Their movements had caused her dead body to move."

A blast from a horn cut through the air. The fishing trawler that would take them to Surin Island was nearing the dock.

"Our chariot nears." Rafi stood. "Hey, I didn't mean to bum you out with the story of the little girl."

"I won't be able to get that image out of my head."

"Neither can I. Come on. The captain is waiting."

At the end of the pier, Rafi and an elderly boat captain exchanged a quick greeting in the traditional *Phasa Thai* language. "Toa, meet Mr. Ferro. Mr. Ferro, Toa."

Unsmiling, the old man simply nodded, and Gabriel nodded back.

"Toa here is an old and trusted friend. He makes his living fishing, but occasionally I hire him to shuttle me around the islands. He speaks about a dozen words in English, so don't expect a warm and fuzzy conversation."

Rafi whispered something to the captain. From the small cabin, the old man retrieved a tan, grocery-sized, cloth bag and handed it to Gabriel. It contained a pair of khaki shorts; a yellow, short-sleeve shirt; open-toed sandals; a small tube of toothpaste; a toothbrush; a small, black comb; a white and tan striped towel, and a bar of soap.

Gabriel shot Rafi a questioning look. "Are we going camping?"

"Not exactly. Now, if you'll hand Toa your personal belongings and your passport, we'll be on our way."

"Everything?"

"That's what the lady who booked your trip told me—don't remember her name."

"Mosby?"

"Yeah, that's her."

Gabriel thought it odd that he would be leaving his personal items and his passport with some old man who looked like he might have been a pirate in an earlier life. But since Legna had sanctioned the adventure, he complied, but held back his personal journal.

"What's that?" Rafi asked.

"My journal."

"The captain will hold it."

"It stays with me."

"But—"

Gabriel shot Rafi a hard look. "It stays with me."

"Okay. Do you have a cell phone?"

"What if I need it?"

"You won't."

Reluctantly, Gabriel dug into his pocket and held his phone aloft. "This little gadget connects me to the world, and according to you, we're going to a place that doesn't even have an old-fashioned radio. Terrific, just terrific!"

Gabriel changed his clothes and looked quite laid back in khaki shorts, yellow shirt, and sandals.

The trawler chugged across light choppy waters to the calm, sandy shore of Surin Island as a breathtaking red and blue sunset smeared the far western horizon. Standing at the water's edge and waving enthusiastically, was a balding, bare-chested man who looked to be in his sixties. A green and white print sarong flowed from his ample waist to just above his bare feet.

Rafi said, "That's Rahmat Pramonogkij, the village Headman."

From the shore, Rahmat called out, "Rafi!"

"Rahmat!" Rafi shouted back.

Gabriel tossed Rahmat a timid wave. "You'll explain I'm here to study their ways?"

Rafi chuckled.

"I said something funny?"

"As a personal favor to me, Rahmat has agreed to provide us food and shelter and complete access to the village. Beyond that, it's not in his nature to question why we are here. You are entering a world unto itself. Think of it as their private twilight zone. And uh, Mr. Ferro—"

"Gabriel."

"Gabriel. These people have no clue what an extraterrestrial is. Even if you offered an explanation they wouldn't understand, so keep it simple."

The bow of the small trawler eased to a stop on the soft sandy bottom some twenty feet from shore.

Rafi patted Gabriel's shoulder. "This is as close as the Captain gets."

Bidding the old Captain goodbye, they dropped over the side into ankle-deep water and waded ashore.

"Look Rahmat in the eye, place your hand over your heart and say your first name."

Gabriel's right hand went flat to his chest and he smiled at Rahmat. "Gabriel."

Rahmat smiled back. "*Ah*, Gabriel." He put his hand flat over his heart. "Rahmat."

That was the extent of the conversation. Rahmat led them along a narrow dirt path that zigzagged through a patch of palm trees until they were in sight of the village. The entrance was adorned with four high poles featuring carved faces of supernatural beings.

"What are those?" Gabriel asked.

"They're called *Labongs*—spirit poles," Rafi answered. "The Mogen's believe they protect the village against evil spirits."

Beyond the poles, single-room houses on stilts lined both sides of what passed for the main street, which was nothing more than a 15-foot wide dirt path. The walls and roofs of the structures were fashioned from woven bamboo and layered thatch. Just beyond the seventh house was an open area half the size of a tennis court. Beyond that were more huts.

"That open patch is the village's central gathering place; a community center without a pool and an exercise room. In Indonesian, it's called *tempot pertemuan*."

Rahmat turned down a dirt path short of the village entrance through a small grove of mango and banana trees, past a couple dozen free-roaming goats and chickens and a well-maintained garden of spring onions, sugar peas, eggplant, kale, and cucumbers before coming upon a pristine beach on the north side of the island. A bamboo and thatch hut like those in the village sat some thirty feet back from the water's edge.

"Home sweet home," Rafi said.

Gabriel eyed the hut suspiciously. "We're gonna' stay in that?"

"Best accommodations in the village: a ceremonial retreat for newlyweds on their first night, women give birth there and where elders spend their final days before passing on. They're treating you as an honored guest."

Rahmat bowed his head, "Rafi, Gabriel," and retreated back up the path.

"He never spoke a word beyond our names."

"And what were you expecting him to say?" Rafi laughed and waved a hand toward the ocean, "Enjoy the view."

All that was left of the day's sun spread a vivid apricot hue across the sky. There was a gentle breeze and the fragrant aroma of wild flowers. Gabriel ambled to where the white sand merged with gently lapping waves. In this tranquil setting, the complexities of the industrialized world seemed a millennium away and the corrupting morality of Western civilization nowhere to be found.

He took out his journal and made a quick entry.

Arrived in one piece. Have no idea what to expect. For the moment, this is my Shangri-La… or something very close to it.

The one-room hut offered no amenities other than two woven sleeping pads set upon bare floorboards.

"Not exactly D.C., is it?" Rafi said.

"What do you know of Washington?"

"Ah, Washington," Rafi's smile suggested fond memories. "I spent four groovy years attending college there."

Gabriel laughed. "Groovy?"

"At least that's how I remember it."

Before Gabriel could pursue the conversation further, Rafi yawned, lowered himself to one of the sleeping pads and quickly fell into a deep sleep, leaving Gabriel to wonder just who this mysterious man was.

Reclining on what passed for a mattress, he laid his head on the makeshift pillow of crushed leaves wrapped in orange and white striped cloth. Finally, surrendering to the serene surroundings, he fell into a peaceful slumber, the first he had enjoyed in weeks.

31

The egg yolk yellow sun sliced through the crevices of the bamboo walls, casting sharp, narrow shafts of light across Gabriel's face. He opened his eyes and for one jarring moment had no earthly idea where he was or why he was staring at a thatched roof. To make matters worse, the two-inch thick sleeping mat had exacted a toll on his aching back. He struggled to a sitting position and groaned.

"Damn it!"

Exiting the hut, he was greeted by the warm morning sun, a clear cobalt sky and a whisper of a westerly breeze. Rafi was sitting in the sand several feet from the water's edge.

"What were you cursing about?" Rafi called out.

Gabriel made his way to Rafi. "I've got a bum back."

"Sit, have some breakfast."

Nestled in the sand next to Rafi was a bamboo tray with a container of yellowish liquid, two green, plastic glasses and some fresh, indigenous fruits.

Gabriel dropped to the sand with another groan.

Rafi smiled. "You get used to the bed after a while."

"Don't count on it. And please don't refer to it as a real bed."

Rafi poured a glass of the liquid and handed it to Gabriel. "Compliments of Rahmat—a combination of freshly squeezed fruits."

"Room service." Gabriel took a sip, licked his lips and nodded his approval.

Rafi gazed out over the imposing vistas. "There is magic here. It's hypnotic... spiritual."

"It gets my vote." Gabriel set his glass down and ran his fingers through his tousled brown hair. "But at the moment, I need a shower."

Rafi handed him a towel and a bar of soap and nodded to the ocean. "Have at it."

"Don't mind if I do."

Mindful of his aching back, Gabriel carefully rose to his feet, stripped down to his birthday suit and made his way to the water's edge. He whooped loudly like a kid on his first day at summer camp and waded in up to his waist before completely submerging beneath the gentle waves.

Ten minutes later, with a towel around his shoulders and his hair still wet, he sat on the sand next to Rafi. "Don't suppose you have a hair dryer?"

"For that, we'd need electricity."

Gabriel laughed and vigorously rubbed the towel through his hair.

"Listen, ah, don't take offense, but…"

"I never do."

"You strike me as young to have been President Conrad's chief of staff."

Gabriel nodded toward the sky where an unknown number of alien spacecraft supposedly hovered. "Truth be known, I'm too young for just about everything that's happening."

"So, you spent what, three, four days crossing the country with this creature? That had to be weird. What's he like up close and personal?"

"Before I actually met him, my brain went into overdrive imagining the worst. Truth is, I was downright terror-stricken. But when I came face-to-face with him, he was the complete opposite of the horrifying images bouncing around my gray matter. Standing there was a clear-eyed, sweet-faced, twelve-year-old-looking creature that happened to talk like a super intelligent adult. He's gentle and charming and persuasive when he wants something, yet irritatingly impatient and demanding when he's waiting for your brain to catch up with his."

Rafi shook his head, sucked in a quick breath and blew it out through his nostrils. "This is *so* bizarre!" He waved a hand in the direction of the village. "And this, what's it all about? Why are you here?"

Gabriel grinned. "A journey of enlightenment."

"A what?"

"According to Legna, the elementary lifestyle of the Mogen is the key to mankind's survival."

Rafi glanced over his shoulder toward the village. "Here? Really?"

"I'm supposed to learn from them so I can assist in saving the human race." Gabriel tossed his head back and laughed. "I can't believe I just said that." He wiggled his bare toes. "Want to see me walk on water?"

Failing to acknowledge Gabriel's stab at humor, Rafi frowned. "Have a heart-to-heart with Mr. Alien when you return. Tell him to take his marbles and go play elsewhere else in the universe."

"I'll do that." Gabriel scooped up a handful of sand and allowed the fine grains to slip through his fingers. "Your knowledge of these people—where does it come from?"

"My parents ran a small supply store in Phuket. I would play with Mogen kids when their parents came in to trade their woven baskets for staples like sugar, flour, and salt. Hell, there are people in this village I've known most of my life. When I was 14, my parents sold the store, and we moved to Bangkok to be closer to my mom's aging parents. I come back here from time-to-time to visit."

"So, this is what you do for a living, guide tourists around?"

Rafi grinned. "Not exactly."

"Then what, exactly?"

"After high school, I obtained a U.S. student visa and attended Georgetown University in DC. A month before graduation—I had just turned twenty-three—the agency made me an offer I couldn't refuse."

"The agency?"

"CIA."

Gabriel tossed his head back and laughed. "Yeah, right."

"No, really, I signed on. The agency put me on the fast track for citizenship and the rest, as they say, is history." Rafi raised his shirt. Tucked in his belt on his right side was a Sig Sauer P229 pistol. "Did you really think he was going to send you here without someone at your back?"

The idea that he might be in any danger had never crossed Gabriel's mind.

"Why do you think your aircraft pulled into a hangar on the far side of the airport? And I suppose you didn't notice the two black SUVs parked nearby."

"Why would I need protection?"

"For one, there's a lot of chatter on social media accusing the U.S. of being in bed with these creatures."

"That's pure bullshit."

"But wing-nut radicals don't know that. Be thankful ET thinks enough of you to take precautions."

"Well, that's reassuring. On a lighter note, are you a family man?"

"And then there's that," Rafi said gloomily. "I dated a fellow student at Georgetown—she was from Delaware. We fell in lust and married a day after I graduated CIA training. After two years working at Langley, they reassigned me to the U.S. Embassy in Bangkok. At first, she—Connie—was excited to experience this part of the world. But I was away much of the time and when I was home, I couldn't discuss my work. The marriage lasted five years before she packed up and returned to the States. We have a beautiful daughter about to graduate from Georgetown. I visit her when I can, but not often enough. How about you?"

"Married once for all of two years, no kids. My ex, Linda, is a cable news reporter. We met while she was covering Conrad's second term run for the Senate. Unfortunately, our ambitions outgrew our personal commitment, what with her rising broadcast career and me in the thick of politics. My God, what a self-serving, egotistical thing to say."

Rafi laughed. "We sound like a couple of losers."

As they watched the tide slowly roll in, Fulmar birds, scanning for their next meal, fluttered just above the water's surface, while sand crabs scampered across the beach.

Chief Pramonogkij, flashing a wide smile, came up behind them and called out, "Rafi, Gabriel."

Rafi waved. "Rahmat."

The chief pointed to his eyes. "*Mata*."

Rafi stood. "He wants to show us something."

At a gingerly pace, Rahmat led them through a nearby tropical evergreen forest until they came upon a lone member of the tribe. The small, compact, middle-aged man was running his right hand meticulously over the trunk of a tree.

Rahmat pointed to the man. "Lihat Salama."

"Salama," Rafi called out.

"Rafi," the man answered cheerfully.

"Salama's an old friend."

Gabriel waved. "Hello."

Salama cocked his head and shot Gabriel a questioning look.

"Just point to yourself and say your first name," Rafi instructed.

Gabriel touched a hand to his chest. "Gabriel."

"*Ahhh*, Gabriel," Salama said with a welcoming smile.

That was the extent of the conversation. Salama moved to the next tree, closed his eyes and ran a hand ever so gently over the bark of each as if caressing a child.

Confused, Gabriel asked, "What's he doing?"

"He's selecting a log for a *kabang,* a boat," Rafi explained. "He's feeling the tree's breath. Just as he is part of the whole, he believes the tree is also. The final log he selects will serve as a fishing platform, so his task is to find just the right tree trunk. Once they dig out the selected tree in the shape of a canoe, they immerse it in heated water; that enlarges it. Finally, it'll be grilled over a fire of *tanai* wood; that blackens and toughens the underside and protects it from barnacle damage."

"Pretty amazing."

"These simple people know to protect their resources, so every tree they cut down, they plant two new ones. From this very forest, they frame their huts, use some eighty species of plants for food, and twenty-eight to treat illnesses and not a pharmacy or Home Depot in sight."

Suddenly, an excited "*Ahhh*" escaped Salama's lips. He had found just the right tree.

It had been a day of continuous, eye-opening enlightenments. Now, as the last vestiges of sunlight washed over the village, and in honor of Rafi and Gabriel's visit, the Mogen celebrated with a memorable feast around a roaring fire in the center of the gathering place. The food was plentiful, the villagers warm and friendly and the mood festive and joyful. These unaffected humans appeared to be genuinely at peace with their chosen way of life in a way that Gabriel did not yet fully understand.

That evening, before turning in for the night, Gabriel wrote by candlelight in his journal.

> *What is happening here? How have these gentle, thoughtful souls maintained their unique lifestyle? They appear to be more knowing of life than those of us who live in the industrialized world. There is an enigmatic secret lurking below the surface here that I have yet to discover. I can only hope that whatever it might be, it is revealed to me before my short time among these genial beings ends.*

The next few days flashed by in a succession of quick images, new realizations and rediscovered emotions. Fearing this nirvana would slip away before its deepest mysteries were revealed, Gabriel was determined to savor each precious moment. Friendly tribe members, eager to include Gabriel in their activities, taught him to fish in shallow waters, cook simple but tasty meals using local herbs and weave thin, wet bamboo strips into sturdy baskets. He and Rafi pitched in to build a new hut for a young couple who were about to be married. Joyful hours were spent playing with the ever-smiling, laughing children. And with Rafi's help, Gabriel communicated—kind of—with the elders.

The Mogen spent each day in blissful happiness, reveling in the simplicity of their chosen way. Not once did the Gabriel witness man, woman, or child raise their voice in anger or show the least displeasure to others. Violence was nonexistent; they simply did not understand the concept. From age eight on, each member of the tribe was required to perform daily chores that contributed to the well-being of the community. Meals were festive, communal affairs. And what belonged to one member of this incomparable tribe, belonged to everyone. The operative word here was, *equality,* for all.

Gabriel and Rafi attended the marriage of the couple who would occupy the hut they had helped build. The ceremony was called *the joining of simple souls.* Two new souls—one boy, one girl—were also born that week. Celebrations for both events were worthy of a king's crowning. Villagers gathered around a roaring fire, laughter abounded, food was plentiful and the festivities went on endlessly. There was malleability here, a defined way of life that functioned harmoniously on every level; an elementary life ostensibly more organic and fulfilling than any other Gabriel had encountered. Perhaps on this tiny, isolated island, he speculated, was the blueprint the Ecaepians had planned for mankind.

On the morning they were to leave, Gabriel sat alone on the shore of the Andaman Sea and wrote in his journal.

I awoke this morning and realized these gentle people have discovered simple but rewarding clarity. In this sharply defined place, they have demonstrated an amazing sense of compassion, tolerance, and love for their fellow man and the environment that sustains them. They have instilled in me what I thought I had lost: a renewed understanding and appreciation for my own life.

When the time came for Rafi and Gabriel to depart, the entire village came to the water's edge to see them off, something Rafi said he had never before witnessed.

"You should feel honored," he whispered to Gabriel. "Saying goodbye is not something they do. In their interpretation of the way things work, you're either here, or you're not, and if you're not, they expect to see you back at some point—or maybe not."

Gabriel was struck with wonder, admiration, and humility. As he and Rafi prepared to depart, there were smiles, laughter and uttering's Gabriel did not understand. But the language barrier was of little consequence, for in his heart, he felt their affection and they in return, his.

Rahmat, gracious and kind to a fault, placed a hand Gabriel's arm and smiled broadly. This inspired man was communicating his emotions without uttering a single word. Overcome with a sense of pure joy, Gabriel's eyes welled up.

Turning to his fellow villagers, Rahmat raised his arms high in the air. In unison, the entire tribe called out, "Gabriel."

Rahmat repeated softly, "Gabriel."

Gabriel made a fist and touched it to his heart. "Rahmat."

Rafi whispered, "They sense something special in you, Gabriel."

As the boat departed, Gabriel turned back for one last lingering look at Surin Island, a place he was blessed to visit and was saddened to leave. He retrieved his journal and began scribbling.

How could such a simplistic way of life be so fulfilling? Had we in the Western world skipped blindly past the obvious, racing toward what we believed to be a bigger, better, capitalistic, technology-driven society? If only the world could experience the truth as I have during these precious few days. The wisdom imparted to me by the Mogen will remain an indelible part of my being until I take my final breath. For in ways I do not yet fully understand, I was destined to come to this place as if it had been preordained.

They drove to Phuket International Airport in silence. For Rafi, the trip to Surin Island had been a reaffirmation of his lifelong friendship with the Mogen. For Gabriel, it was joyful discovery, far beyond anything he could have imagined or hoped for. If he had only heard of the Mogen—if he had not seen, touched, smelled, and participated—he would have thought it all a myth. Yet, insulated from an iniquitous humanity, the Mogen held sacred their beliefs of what it really meant to be human.

32

Back at Bangkok International Airport, a man that Gabriel hoped would be there was walking around the Cessna inspecting it.

"Who's that?" Rafi asked.

"Somebody very important." Gabriel slipped from the car and waved. "Hello, Dr. Sanjaya? I'm Gabriel Ferro. I was afraid you wouldn't come."

"I was tempted not to, Mr. Ferro," Sanjaya said in a distinct Indonesian accent. "But since I was escorted here in a black van with heavily tinted windows by two burly men who flashed intimidating credentials. I thought it best to oblige."

Forty-seven-year-old B.D. Sanjaya, one of the foremost archeologist in all of Indonesia, was a man of pleasing proportions with brown hair and brown eyes that complemented his bronze Indonesian complexion.

"On the other hand," Sanjaya continued, "I've yet to come to terms with how a single extraterrestrial commandeered our planet."

"You're not alone," Rafi mumbled.

Gabriel shook Sanjaya's hand vigorously. "Well, I'm grateful that you came." He placed a hand on Rafi's shoulder. "Rafi Suharto, this is Dr. Bada D. Sanjaya."

"Yes, all of Indonesia is familiar with his extraordinary work."

"That's kind of you, Mr. Suharto. I wish you would convey that to my superiors at the National Research Centre back in Jakarta. Often, they believe otherwise."

"I remember the controversy surrounding those skeletal remains you found on... on—"

"Flores Island."

"Yes, just east of Timor," Rafi said. "I visited there on business once."

"Those skeletal remains you refer to, we named them *Homo floresiensis* after the island. But I'm afraid that the controversy, as you referred to it, continues to this day."

"You declared them *'the missing link.'* That in itself was controversial. How did you reach that conclusion?"

"We were able to retrieve a small amount of soft tissue, protein and a tiny amount of DNA to compare the genetics of modern humans with every relative in the evolutionary tree, and lo and behold, we found a deviation."

"What kind of a deviation?" Rafi asked.

Gabriel already knew the answer, but said nothing.

"It gets a bit technical. Let me take you back to a species known as Denisova hominines—Denisovans. They were Paleolithic era members of a species of *Homo* or subspecies of *Homo sapiens*. Back in March 2010, a fragment of a finger bone of a juvenile female was found in the Denisova Cave in the Altai Mountains in Siberia. Analysis of the bone mitochondrial DNA showed it to be far older and genetically distinct from the mtDNAs of Neanderthals and modern humans. It was, for me, the proverbial smoking gun; evidence of a previously undetected species with DNA that did not fit neatly into the human evolutionary tree. The genome of a Neanderthal found in the same cave confirmed that significant inter-breeding had taken place with this previously undefined hominid. That would clearly change the genetic path of the species. So, there can be no question that our early ancestor mated with a species that was neither human nor Neanderthal. Are you with me so far?"

Rafi scratched the back of his head. "Kind of."

Sanjaya continued, "Here's where it gets interesting. The DNA found in that little finger bone matched the DNA of the skeletons we found on Flores Island. Now how do you think that could have occurred many thousands of miles apart? I meant that rhetorically. To this day my answer was and remains… the missing link."

"But as I recall, your conclusions were roundly rejected."

"Thank you for reminding me, Mr. Suharto. The anthropological community was unwilling to accept that *Homo floresiensis* somehow predated the origins of human evolution already established by the unimpeachable, and oftentimes unimaginative, scientific brotherhood. One prominent colleague went so far as to label my findings voodoo science." Then, as if he had no desire to pursue the subject further, he said to Gabriel, "I was told you would be visiting the Mogen. How did that go?"

Gabriel beamed. "An incredible experience—amazing people! Rafi here was my guide and translator."

"May I assume there was a purpose for visiting the Mogen?"

Gabriel ignored the question. "You've made all the arrangements, doctor?"

"Arrangements?" Rafi said with a puzzled look. "What are we talking about here?"

"Mr. Ferro wishes to travel to New Guinea."

"What's in New Guinea?"

Sanjaya's jaw tightened. "A place I'd rather no one visit."

"Now wait just a damn minute. No one informed me of any side trip to New Guinea."

"You'll have to excuse Rafi," Gabriel quipped. "He's CIA—far worse than the Secret Service."

Sanjaya's eyebrows rose in mock surprise. "CIA? What have I gotten myself into?"

"Sorry if you weren't clued in, Rafi," Gabriel apologized, "but I'm cleared to go."

Rafi raised a hand in protest. "Now, hold on here."

Sanjaya stared hard at Gabriel. "Excuse me—Gabriel—may I call you Gabriel? Shortly after their brazen takeover, I was contacted by a woman representing this so-called alien administrator ordering me to vacate the *Golden Garden* and to never speak of it or reveal its location."

"What Golden Garden? What the hell are we talking about?"

Ignoring Rafi, Sanjaya plowed on. "After being told—threatened would be a better word—to never set foot there again, I received a second call ordering me to accompany you there. Can you kindly explain the contradiction?"

Gabriel opened his mouth to speak, but Sanjaya continued.

"Perhaps the more pressing question is why the chief of staff to the late U.S. President has aligned himself with an invading race of extraterrestrials?"

"B. D. —may I call you B.D.? First, considering what you do, I would think you'd find the arrival of extraterrestrials a bit more than simply interesting. Second, do not assume that because I stayed on, that I'm somehow on their side. I'm on the *inside*. There is a distinct difference."

"Well, I'm pleased you cleared that up," Sanjaya scoffed.

"Someone better damn well tell me what the hell is in New Guinea."

"Don't look at me, Mr. Suharto; Mr. Ferro is doing the talking."

Gabriel placed a hand on Rafi's shoulder. "Look, it's too complicated to explain here and now. All you need to know is that Dr. Sanjaya is the only man on the face of this planet who knows the location of a place I must visit."

"Make that three," Sanjaya corrected. "My two assistants, currently missing, also know. It's obvious there is a connection with this site and your alien friends, Mr. Ferro. What is it you are *not* telling us?"

"Yeah," Rafi chimed in.

No response from Gabriel.

Sanjaya sighed in resignation. "Very well, since I value my life, we'll do as your alien has ordered. I'm assuming this fine-looking aircraft will take us to Papua, New Guinea. From there we'll take a single-engine plane to the Mamberamo basin below the Foja Mountains. A helicopter will complete the last leg to the remote eastern province where we get to hike through an extremely uninviting jungle." Sanjaya's mouth twisted into a crooked grin. "Actually, I'm quite surprised that creature failed to provide a sleek spacecraft. Perhaps he feels you require the full human experience."

"To be clear, Dr. Sanjaya, no sleek alien craft was offered. Legna is not my friend and visiting this place was *my* idea, not his."

"Then I'm compelled to ask you again—why?"

"Perhaps neither of you heard me clearly," Rafi said tersely. "This man is my responsibility. He's not going anywhere without me."

"While you two sort this out…" Sanjaya unfolded a newspaper that was tucked under his arm. "Are you aware of what occurred late yesterday?"

"We've had no access to news for a few days," Rafi answered.

Sanjaya held up the newspaper. The portentous headline read, "Russia's Secret Mountain Destroyed."

Rafi's eyes went wide, and he whistled. "What's that all about?"

"Let's see that." Gabriel took the newspaper from Sanjaya and scanned the article while Rafi peered anxiously over his shoulder.

"Considering the imposed news blackout," Sanjaya said, "it's safe to assume they wanted this particular story out there for all to see."

The article read like a doomsday scenario, revealing one of Russia's darkest kept military secrets. Deep within the Urals region in Yamantau Mountain, the Russians maintained an underground complex that concealed enough nuclear missiles to pack a punch 360 times that of Hiroshima. Without advance warning to other governments, they employed their space-reaching bombers to launch twelve nuclear-tipped missiles at what they believed to be an alien craft. As the missiles entered the stratosphere, they suddenly vanished. There were no explosions or other visible signs of destruction or debris—the missiles simply disappeared. Minutes later an orange beam, identical to the one that vaporized Howland Island, descended upon the Russian complex and the entire 400 square-mile site demate-rialized. Some 2,800 Russian soldiers, scientists, and engineers were reported lost. In Moscow, four generals and two high-ranking government officials mysteriously went missing.

"My God," Rafi whispered, "what were the Russians thinking?"

Gabriel shook his head. "Obviously, they weren't."

"This leaves little doubt of the alien's intent to destroy anything and anyone that dares challenge them. If I'm to risk my life, I have a right to know all that you know, Mr. Ferro."

"It's what you know that I want to know, Doctor." Gabriel folded the news-paper and slipped it back under Sanjaya's arm. "Come on, let's get going," Gabriel grumbled and ascended the steps to the aircraft.

33

When they arrived in Papua, New Guinea, the trio purchased a small amount of food supplies and water-resistant boots, which Sanjaya said they would need. Boarding a single engine Cessna 172 Skyhawk at Jackson International Airport, they flew 5,000 feet above sea level, landing on a dirt airstrip in the Mamberamo basin in Papua's remote eastern province. High overhead was the all but impenetrable, mist-shrouded, foreboding Foja Mountains, which rose 7,200 feet at their highest point.

Much to Gabriel's chagrin, the final leg of the journey would be in a twenty-year-old Bell 206 Jet Ranger helicopter piloted by an aging Indonesian man whose leathery, canyon-wrinkled face was contorted into a permanent scowl. He feared the flying relic would drop from the sky at any moment, providing nourishment for the feral beasts that roamed the tangled jungle floor below. Making matters worse, the pilot spoke rapidly in an Indonesian Bahasa dialect that Sanjaya understood, but Rafi did not. Sanjaya made no attempt to translate, so conversations between him and the pilot remained a mystery.

They flew low and fast over the treetops, making it near impossible to see anything through the dense, primeval forest canopy. As they approached the Birds Head Peninsula in Papua's northeast territory, Gabriel began to wonder if an open patch of ground actually existed where the rickety helicopter could land safely.

"You're sure you know the spot?" Gabriel shouted to Sanjaya over the roar of the engine and whirling rotor blades.

Sanjaya simply smiled.

Just over an hour and a half into the flight, the pilot slowed and circled a small, open bog surrounded by a compact forested area which left little room for pilot error.

Sanjaya called out, "That's it."

The grizzled pilot circled several times before hovering over the open plot. Satisfied that he was aligned with his intended destination, he dropped the aircraft down like a theme park thrill ride, causing Gabriel's face to turn ashen white and his stomach to leap to his throat. Down they dropped until the aircraft was about thirty feet above the ground. The old man hovered for several seconds before gently setting the skids safely on the soggy soil.

Wiping at small beads of sweat that had formed on his brow, Gabriel breathed a nervous sigh of relief. "We must be nuts!"

"You're not in Kansas anymore, Mr. Ferro," Sanjaya said whimsically as he exited the aircraft.

As soon as they had unloaded the last of their sparse supplies, the helicopter noisily ascended, flew east over the tree tops, and was out of sight within seconds. They were alone now, surrounded by a formidable wilderness of tall trees, menacing overgrowth and intimating sounds that confirmed the unwelcome presence of wild beasts.

"If there's a hell on earth, this must be it," Rafi groaned.

Sanjaya removed a two-foot machete strapped to his backpack. "Getting this far was the easiest part, gentlemen."

Gabriel swatted at a hungry mosquito attempting to suck a day's ration of blood from his cheek. "Your gonzo pilot didn't waste any time hightailing it out of here."

Sanjaya swung his backpack over his shoulder. "He'll pick us up around noon tomorrow—that is if he can find his way back."

Weary of Sanjaya's continued snarky remarks, Gabriel huffed. "Look, you've been sniping away ever since we met. Why don't you want us to go to this place?"

"The real question Mr. Ferro is, why do *you* want to go there?"

"No," said Rafi to Sanjaya. "The real question is if this place is so damn important, why is it that only you and your two assistants know where it is?"

"You'll learn the answer to your question soon enough."

Gabriel swooped up his backpack. "Let's just get going, okay? Can we do that?"

The tall trees created a canopy that blocked most of the sunlight, making it appear more like oncoming dusk than daylight. They struggled through areas thick with gnarled vegetation. Prickly thorns penetrated their clothing like tiny spears, leaving behind red and purple welts and droplets of blood. Hungry flies and mosquitoes swarmed around them like mini-dive bombers seeking their target. Creepy, crawling things slipped inside their pant legs, gnawing hungrily at exposed flesh. Their boots made sucking sounds as they made their way across the wet, squishy ground, announcing their presence to whatever wild creatures were watching and waiting. As if that were not defeating enough, the relentless heat and humidity seeped through their clothing sapping their strength.

Some forty torturous minutes in, Gabriel stopped and wiped at his brow. Breathing heavily, he pleaded, "Five minutes—just five minutes."

"Five minutes, then we move on," Sanjaya said. "We don't want to be hanging around in here."

Gabriel dropped his backpack to the ground and swiped his handkerchief across his dripping brow and face. His sweat-soaked clothing clung annoyingly to his skin and he scratched at insect bites.

Sanjaya handed him a canteen of water. "Drink, but not too much."

Gabriel took the canteen and chugged like it might be his last.

"Enough," Sanjaya reprimanded.

Gabriel doused his face and neck with a splash of water and handed the canteen to Rafi. "How much further?"

"I warned you this wasn't going to be a walk in the park." Sanjaya seemed to take perverse pleasure in the reminder.

"How far?" Gabriel insisted.

"In this jungle, one never knows."

Gabriel rolled his eyes, leaned against a Montane Oak tree and ran his handkerchief over his face again. "I thought I was in better shape than this."

"That makes two of us," Rafi groaned.

"I wouldn't lean against that tree," Sanjaya warned. "The ants will have you for lunch."

Gabriel quickly moved away from the tree trunk and checked his clothing—there were no ants.

Retrieving a small, white tube of ointment from his backpack, Sanjaya held it out. "Here, both of you, rub this on those insect bites. And stop scratching, or they'll become infected."

Rafi took the ointment first, then passed it to Gabriel.

"Dare I ask again, Mr. Ferro, why you are so determined to make this trek?"

Gabriel shot Sanjaya a hard look, but did not respond.

"You must know what awaits us. Surely the alien took you into his confidence. Let's see now, you've stayed on at his side as his what—his human liaison? Have I got that right?"

"Goddamn it!" Gabriel barked. "What are you getting at?"

"I'm not sure I'm getting at anything, Mr. Ferro, but I do have this nagging feeling you know far more than you're letting on."

Swinging his backpack over his shoulder, Gabriel growled, "Let's go! Let's get this done!" and trudged off through the underbrush.

"Excuse me, Mr. Ferro?" Sanjaya called to him.

Gabriel swung back. "What now?"

Sanjaya pointed in the opposite direction. "It's this way, actually."

Fifty-five minutes later, soaked with sweat and dogged by fatigue, they broke through to a small, fog-shrouded clearing that would have been far too small for the helicopter to land safely.

Exhausted, Gabriel cast a wary eye to the jungle behind them. "How in hell does anything survive in there? How close are we?"

Sanjaya pointed across the clearing. "Through there is what you're searching for."

Gabriel strained to see through the fog, but it was too thick to make out any detail. "I don't see anything."

"Me neither," Rafi echoed.

"You will," Sanjaya said. "You will."

As they trudged forward through the fog, they could feel the temperature changing.

"Is it getting cooler, or is it my imagination?" Gabriel asked.

"And the bloodsucking insects?" Rafi said with surprise. "They're gone!"

Sanjaya grinned. "It gets better."

The fog was slowly dissipating. And although faint at first, they could hear the distinct sound of running water.

Sanjaya was several yards ahead of them, far enough that he was just a shadowy figure in the remaining mist. "That's strange."

"What?" Gabriel asked.

"I don't hear the birds. Wait here."

There was urgency in Sanjaya's voice followed by the quickened squishing of his boots in the spongy peat. He trudged farther into fog until they could no longer see him. Then abruptly, his footsteps stopped. It went eerily silent except for the faint sound of running water.

They waited—several seconds passed—but there was no word from Sanjaya.

Finally, in a high-pitched, agitated voice, Sanjaya called out, "My God!"

Sanjaya's cry had been loud and shrill. Fearing the worst, Gabriel and Rafi lunged through the mist until they came upon Sanjaya standing in a small clearing. His backpack lay on the marshy ground by his left foot. He stood frozen, his spine straight as a rod, his eyes wide and fixed on something ahead.

Gabriel and Rafi followed Sanjaya's stare to a sight that caused them to literally gasp. There across the remaining few yards of mist and marsh, a stunning visual spread before them like a virtual dream, a magnificent Technicolor ® panorama of such magnitude as to be beyond human comprehension. It was as if a magical time machine had transported them to a fantastical world awash in resplendent colors, so intensely saturated, the scene resembled an impressionistic painting. Overwhelmed by the majesty of it all, Gabriel and Rafi at first failed to see what had caused Sanjaya to go numb with horror.

And then it hit them.

Beyond the vibrant Technicolor hues, beyond the expansive, aesthetic beauty, much of the terrain lay in ruins.

Gabriel's mouth gaped. "What in the hell?"

A number of tall Araucaria trees were partially uprooted. Rotting fruit lay fallow below lifeless, knobby-limbed fruit trees. Thick weeds choked the remnants of vast flower beds, some still clinging to life. A picturesque waterfall plunged from one hundred feet into a circular pool that fed a small stream that meandered into the towering forest beyond. On closer inspection, they saw streaks of red mixed with the blue-white water. Three small Papuan forest wallabies lay lifeless, their bodies half in and half out of the pool, crimson blood seeping from their noses, mouths, and ears. The decomposing remnants of Muridae rodents floated in the middle of the pool, their bloated bodies bobbing in the ripples of the plunging waterfall. A dozen or more dead birds bordered the pool.

Suddenly, like a klaxon horn gone wild, a nerve-jangling scream broke above the sound of the waterfall. On the far side of the pool, a brown tree kangaroo crashed wildly through the thicket. At the sight of the two-legged invaders, the animal grunted and angrily raised its head and released another high-pitched, haunting scream, spun around and limped back into the forest, bleating loudly as it retreated.

"What in god's creation?" Sanjaya cried.

Despite the destruction, this grandiose garden in the middle of a brutal jungle had to have been created by intelligent design. Except now it looked as if a thundering horde of Germanic warriors had trampled everything in their path. Twenty-five feet back from the pool, on the edge of the clearing, lay the torn remnants of two canvas tents. Scattered about were papers, magazines, and eating utensils.

As he moved further in, Sanjaya said, barely above a whisper, "This was our base camp." He scooped up a sheet of paper, examined it wistfully then let it slip through his fingers to the ground.

His eyes wide with wonder, Rafi breathed, "Where in the hell are we?"

"The Golden Garden," Sanjaya answered just above a whisper.

"The what?"

With deep sadness, he said, "My Indonesian assistants and I were guided here by the man who discovered it; the chief of the local Kweba tribe. It was as if we had timed-traveled to another dimension. We walked unafraid among the magnificent flowers and endless fruit trees. There were new bird and animal species never before seen by human eyes." He motioned to the pool. "We drank pure crystalline water from this very pool."

Sanjaya fell silent, his eyes scanning the desecration. Suddenly, his head snapped up, and his expression went flat. He took two anxious steps forward, stopped and listened. Except for a slight breeze whistling through the treetops, all was eerily silent again.

Gabriel called to Sanjaya. "Doctor, what is it?"

Sanjaya did not reply. Digging his heels into the soft soil, he took off running past the red-stained pool, past the trampled flower beds and fallen trees, before disappearing into the jungle beyond.

"Dr. Sanjaya!" Gabriel yelled. "Wait!"

But Sanjaya was now out of their sight.

"Come on, Rafi!"

The two men raced through the butchered landscape, catching only fleeting glimpses of Sanjaya as he bolted in and around fallen trees and rotting flower beds.

They rounded the trunk of an uprooted Araucaria tree and found themselves in a large clearing. Sanjaya was down on his knees on the edge of a fifty-foot circle of arid, pale, dusty ground. Dead center of the circle, standing like some macabre monument, was the remnants of a dead apple tree. Its damaged gray limbs were devoid of fruit, and its gray, crooked trunk split halfway to the ground. Ringing the entire parched sphere—precisely spaced like a well-planned orchard—was just about every kind of fruit tree imaginable. The ground was smeared with rotting fruit.

On his knees and bent forward, Sanjaya was weeping.

34

Wide-eyed, Rafi whistled low. "My God, where are we?"

Sanjaya wiped the back of a hand over tear-filled eyes. "This is what Gabriel was seeking. It is, or was, the epicenter of The Golden Garden."

"Holy mother of god! Even in this desiccated state, I've never seen anything so magnificent."

You have no idea." Struggling to his feet, Sanjaya looked longingly at the splintered apple tree. Stuffing his hands into his pockets, his shoulders slumped forward, he began to slowly walk the rim of the circle.

Rafi's shrugged. "B.D., for the love of Christ, what is this place?"

"Whatever you imagine it might have been." Sanjaya stopped and took a deep breath and held it before exhaling slowly. "This jungle falls within the boundaries belonging to the Kweba tribe. Their roots in this forest go back many generations. They're a simple but cultured people whose religion include a healthy dose of superstition. So, you can imagine what Bayu thought when he stumbled in here."

"Bayu?" Gabriel repeated.

"The Kweba tribal chief. The old man savored the peace and solitude of these forests and would often hunt alone for days at a time. But neither he nor any member of his tribe had ever trekked this far from their village. On one of his solo trips, he ventured farther than he ever had and stumbled upon this." Sanjaya sighed and wiped a hand over his face. "Having never experienced such sensory ambiance and total peace and inner calm as he did here, he believed he had stumbled upon God's home on Earth." Fearing less-than-honorable men would discover and exploit what he perceived to be the holiest place on the planet, he told no one, not even his family. But as the years passed, as he saw his life waning, the desire to protect and preserve this extraordinary oasis weighed heavily on him."

"So, he took into his confidence," Gabriel said quietly.

"After reading about my work as an archeologist and preservationist, Bayu sought me out. He wrote me a letter promising to guide me to what he called *God's Magical Land*. But first, I had to swear to never reveal its location." Sanjaya's eyes swept to the lifeless apple tree. "He simply wanted it documented by someone who would protect it from treasure hunters and profiteers. As fate would have it..." His eyes drifted aimlessly across the arid circle "... Bayu died shortly after guiding my assistants and me here."

"How much ground does this place cover?" Gabriel asked.

"Near as I can figure, two square miles." Sanjaya scanned the area as if the destruction that lay before him was nothing more than an optical illusion that would right itself if he blinked. He closed his eyes and ran a hand over his face again before stepping onto the dry circle. The parched soil swirled up around his boots in a mini cloud of dust. "I've been documenting the wonders of this place ever since. Until today, I've kept my promise to never reveal its location, not even to my superiors back in Jakarta." Crouching down, he scooped up a handful of dry soil and squeezed it tightly in his palm before letting it sift through his fingers. His shoulders hunched forward in a gesture of defeat.

Gabriel moved to Sanjaya's side and placed a hand on his shoulder. "I'm sorry."

Sanjaya bounded up, placed his hands flat against Gabriel's chest, and pushed him back a step. "For what, Mr. Ferro, for what?"

Perplexed by Sanjaya's aggression, Gabriel raised his hands in defense. "I'm sorry, I had no idea."

"No idea of what?" Sanjaya poked a stiff finger against Gabriel's chest. "What is the basis for your sudden remorse?"

Gabriel's hands flew up defensively. "Hey, calm down!"

"When I left, this was a magnificent Shangri-La beyond anything we humans could imagine. Now look." He ran a hand through his dark hair and sighed. "My two Indonesian assistants, Reza and Timoty, have inexplicably gone missing from the face of the Earth. Where are they, Mr. Ferro? Perhaps, your alien friend knows." His eyes flashed with rage. "You wouldn't have trekked through that damnable jungle if all this was not somehow tied to *them*." He jabbed hard at Gabriel's chest a second time. "What do you know that I don't?"

Gabriel swatted Sanjaya's hand away. "Stop it!"

Sanjaya's eyes flashed with anger. Balling his right hand into a fist, he swung wildly, landing a stinging blow to Gabriel's jaw and knocking him onto the surface of the parched circle, a cloud of dust swirling up around him.

Rafi rushed forward, gripped Sanjaya's shoulders, and yanked him back. "Hey, hey, what the hell was that for?"

"Ask him." Sanjaya rubbed his aching right hand and stormed off.

Rafi helped Gabriel to his feet. "You okay?"

Shaken, Gabriel rubbed at his left jaw. "Fine, fine. For an archeologist, he packs one hell of a punch."

Sanjaya was now on the far side of the circle. "If I had known what awaited us, I would not have agreed to return, no matter what that deplorable alien threatened."

Gabriel said, "B.D., I'm sorry. How could I have possibly known what we'd find?"

"Oh, well," Sanjaya yelled from across the circle, "that gets you off the hook, doesn't it?"

Gabriel couldn't help but wonder now why Legna allowed him to see this place in its appalling state of ruin.

Rafi, on the other hand, overwhelmed by the wonder that surrounded them, was anxious to investigate further and strolled away in the opposite direction. He had walked no farther than 15 feet when something glimmered brightly beneath the overgrown ground foliage. "Hey, there's something shiny over here. Help me clear this brush." Dropping to his knees, he pulled at thick weeds, but jerked his hand back and squealed, "Ouch!" The tip of his middle finger bleed. "Damn it!" Rafi cried. "Something cut me!"

Sensing the excitement in Rafi's voice, Gabriel joined him and dropped to his knees.

Rafi pulled at dead foliage. "There's something bright under there."

Together they pulled at the dead, tangled vegetation. The more they cleared, the more it became apparent that whatever was there was far bigger than first realized. What they finally uncovered took them by utter surprise.

There, buried beneath the overgrowth was a five by two-foot cobalt blue, metal structure that rose six inches above the ground. A three-by one foot section of its face had been ripped open leaving razor sharp edges. Despite the damage, they could see remnants of words etched a quarter-inch into the surface of its face.

"B.D.," Gabriel shouted, "there's something here!"

Sensing the urgency in Gabriel's voice, Sanjaya made his way to the two men. His face lit up with unbridled recognition. "My god, I forgot about the monolith!"

Rafi's head popped up. "The what?"

Sanjaya dropped to his knees and peered into the jagged hole. "Quick, hand me a flashlight!"

Rummaging through his backpack, Rafi retrieved a small flashlight. But as he handed it to Sanjaya, it slipped from his hand and tumbled through the torn opening.

"In my backpack—there's another light!" Sanjaya barked.

This time, Rafi carefully handed the light to Sanjaya, who pointed its bright beam into the dark abyss.

With high anticipation, Gabriel inched closer. "What do you see?"

Sanjaya shined the light from wall to wall, corner to corner. Finally, turning the flashlight off, he rose to his feet, his face drawn, his eyes transfixed on the black hole. "It's empty."

"Empty?" Gabriel repeated.

"This was impossible to open—trust me, we tried."

Gabriel pointed to the twisted letters. "The writing, do you have any idea what it is?"

"Are you sure you don't already know?" Sanjaya challenged.

"Damn it, B.D., how would I know? If you do, tell us."

Sanjaya took in a long, slow breath and expelled just as slowly. "It's written in *Bahasa pertama yang diketahui*, the first documented language in Indonesia."

Rafi's head bobbed back. "Whoa! Do you know what it says?"

"I was hoping Mr. Ferro might tell us."

"I have no bloody idea…" Gabriel shifted his weight uneasily from one foot to the other. "… but I think you do."

"As a matter-of-fact, Mr. Ferro, I do." With his face drawn and his eyes locked on Gabriel, Sanjaya recited from memory, *"All beings are born free and equal in dignity and rights. They are endowed with reason and conscience and should act toward one another in a spirit of brotherhood."* Sanjaya eyes went briefly to Rafi then to Gabriel. "It's Article One of the United Nations Universal Declaration of Human Rights."

"Holy shit!" Rafi jeered. "What's it doing here?"

Sanjaya's eyes shifted back to the twisted opening. "Perhaps the answer lies in the wording. The UN article reads '*all human beings.*' This inscription reads, '*all beings.*'"

Rafi whistled. "What?"

"Mr. Ferro. When I flashed the light in, there was anticipation in your voice. You expected we'd find something. What?"

Gabriel backed up two steps, pivoted, and walked to the edge of the arid circle, his eyes fixed squarely on the dead apple tree. If there was ever an indelible symbol ingrained into the hearts and minds of millions upon millions of the faithful, that apple tree was it.

"Your silence speaks volumes," Sanjaya called to him.

Gabriel remained silent.

"Okay," Sanjaya began, "I'll go first. Let's see if it takes us anywhere near the truth as you might know it. Look over there."

Sanjaya pointed to two banana trees on the opposite side of the circle. The few remaining clusters of yellow-fleshed fruit still clinging to the tree were mottled black. Neither Gabriel nor Rafi had noticed that between the trees there were two moss-covered mounds approximately five-feet long, two-feet wide, and less than a foot high.

"Thanks to the heavy concentration of peat, we unearthed two well-preserved skeletons—one male, one female. I was able to extract a small amount of DNA." He paused, just enough to heighten the suspense. "It was a perfect DNA match with the hominid remains we unearthed in the Liang Bua Cave on Flores Island. Both contained traces of the Denisova DNA found in that Siberian cave. Care to fill in the blanks, Mr. Ferro?"

With his eyes fixed on the mounds, Gabriel answered, "It doesn't much matter now."

"It damn well does to me," Sanjaya said sharply. "Turn around, look me in the eyes, tell me the truth as you know it."

Gabriel's hands flew up in a hopeless gesture. "How can I explain what I'm still struggling to understand?" The bright sunlight, negotiating its way through the expansive treetops, cast narrow slashes across his face—he blinked several times. Like a magnet pulling at him, his eyes shifted back to the gnarled apple tree. Its limping branches hung low, its exposed roots grasping perilously to the parched earth in a last gasp of life. "I gave my word I would not speak of it."

"You gave your word to whom?" Rafi hissed.

"Legna."

Rafi squawked, "You gave your word to an invading alien?"

Standing on the very spot that Legna had described to him and Catherine in the Utah motel was confirmation the alien had not misled them. In a low voice, he said, "This is, or was, the *Kebun*—the Garden of Eden."

That statement was so audacious, neither Sanjaya nor Rafi reacted. Then, as the words sunk in, Rafi's lips curled in a cynical grin. "And I'm the King of Siam."

"I can only tell you what I was told."

"And you accepted his word as truth?"

"For Christ's sake, man, look around—this has no equal on the planet."

"Come on..." Rafi persisted, "... the biblical Garden of Eden; what happened to Mesopotamia?"

Gabriel pointed to the two burial mounds. "There's your Adam and Eve." He pointed to the apple tree. "There's your apple tree. Every culture has their stories, don't they? Might as well be this one."

"B.D., you're the expert here, are you buying this?"

"Let Gabriel speak."

"This was to be their grand experiment."

"Experiment?" Rafi repeated. "What kind of—"

"Rafi," Sanjaya growled, "let Gabriel explain."

Gabriel turned back to the two earthen mounds. "Fifty beings, created on Ecaep, were transported here."

"Fifty what?"

"Damn it, Rafi, be quiet!" Sanjaya admonished.

As if he was inexplicably drawn to it, Gabriel's eyes switched from the mounds to the dead apple tree. His mind slipped into idle, his thoughts straying back to that fateful night in the Utah motel room when Legna had revealed the unimaginable story he was now about to reveal. "This place—this Garden of Eden—was home to twenty-five females and twenty-five male hybrids. According what Legna, it was an experiment to determine how long it would take somewhat primitive beings to acquire useful knowledge… and would they use that knowledge to create a flourishing society. In the lab, in the embryo stage, their consciousness was tweaked—ego and violence were removed—that was critical to the experiment. I raised the moral implications—accused them of playing god. But then he said something that struck like a lightning bolt. It was only a matter of time, he said, before…" Gabriel went silent, his gaze straying back to the earthen mounds.

"Before what?" Sanjaya asked.

Gabriel turned to Sanjaya, hesitated, then said, "The created one day shall become… the creators."

Rafi hooted. "*Jeeesus*! Did I hear right?"

Sanjaya growled, "Rafi, be quiet!"

"How many times has mankind done something simply because we could and not because we had to or should? How advanced are our own cloning experiments before we too create life?"

Sanjaya asked. "Why didn't they conduct this experiment on their own planet?"

Gabriel waved a hand across the expanse. "Because our environment matched theirs, Earth presented the perfect incubator to conduct the experiment in secret. Here in this safe, grandiose environment, the hybrids were free from the hardships of daily survival, free to focus on the well-being and growth of the colony. But over time, something went wrong with their creations and over time subtle changes began. Since the Ecaepians only checked on the Colony periodically, the changes went unnoticed… until it was too late."

"What kind of changes?" Rafi asked.

"Inexplicably, the males began to demonstrate signs of aggression. Eventually, it led to a struggle for dominance of the colony. Something, it seems, had gone awry in the Ecaepians' petri dish." Gabriel nodded to the earthen mounds. "The male buried there lost the fight. With her mate gone, the female checked out shortly thereafter, presumably of a broken heart. The experiment was deemed a failure and terminated."

"And the surviving members of the colony?" Sanjaya asked.

"Banished to Flores Island to live out their natural lives where you found them. This place was preserved as a shrine—why I have no idea."

Sanjaya walked to the edge of the circle, scooped up parched soil and squeezed it until his fingers turned white. Like a magnet pulling him, his eyes went to the decaying apple tree, the evocative, biblical symbol of good and evil.

"Care to hear the rest?" Gabriel asked.

"Is there some good in this wild tale?" Sanjaya asked.

"You be the judge. Periodically, the Ecaepians' returned to Flores Island to check on the status of the remaining colony. On one of those visits, they found only thirteen colony members remained. They were living in caves surviving off the scraps of the land."

"Why were they allowed to live at all?" Rafi asked.

"Maybe out of guilt, who knows, he failed to explain why. On what would become their last visit to Flores, they were met by the unthinkable: there was a new species of hominids—a dozen or more—much like the original hybrids but far more primitive and were living apart from the colony."

"The slip of a yet another gene," Sanjaya muttered.

Gabriel nodded. "Yes. The Ecaepians rounded them up and relocated them to what became East Africa."

A crooked grin came to Sanjaya's lips. "And the long, arduous, evolving journey of the human race began."

"And the original survivors of the colony?" Rafi asked.

"Left on Flores right where B.D. found those remains."

Sanjaya ambled back to the mangled opening of the monolith and stared into the black hole. "Gabriel, you expected to find something in there. What was it?"

"He said it contained *The Codes* to be gifted to the colony if and when they passed muster."

"The codes to what?"

"I don't know, I asked, but he refused to say—just that they were *The Codes*."

They fell quiet as each man grappled with the implications, wondering if this place, this narrative, was real or just an allegory perpetrated by an advanced alien race bent on a yet-to-be-revealed agenda.

Finally, Sanjaya spoke. "Why did Legna tell you this?"

"I threatened him if he didn't."

"What chip did you have to bargain with?"

Gabriel squatted and scooped up a handful of dry soil. "The only thing I had any control over—his life. I wasn't about to risk mine unless he came clean in that motel room. Was he truthful? Look around, this is not a mirage."

Rafi surveyed the butchered landscape. "So, what do we do now?"

"I think, Gentlemen, we punt," was Sanjaya come back. "If nothing else we know where we all came from… as if that makes me feel any better."

By the time they returned to Sanjaya's waterfall campsite the sun was dipping over the horizon. They would spend the night before navigating the tortuous jungle again and hoping the old pilot and his decrepit helicopter made it back. Little conversation passed between them, for Eden, this once wondrous garden of splendor, was no more.

Sanjaya started a small fire, and they ate the rations they had brought with them. Except for the occasional haunting squeals of nearby animals, the night was still and peaceful, the clear sky twinkling with glittering stars in far off pockets of the universe.

Later, when they had finished eating, Gabriel retrieved his journal. Opening to a blank page, he noted with amusement a tiny dead insect smeared across the lower right corner. He brushed it off and began writing:

If life was an enigma before, it is now more inexplicable than ever.

"What are you writing? "Sanjaya asked.

"A few thoughts before I forget."

"Spell my name right," Rafi dead-panned.

Gabriel smiled and continued writing.

I remember studying the writings of Austrian author Viktor Emil Denverl who wrote: "If there is meaning in life at all, then there must be meaning in suffering." Well, Emil, you were spot on because we humans suffer all right, and nobody, least of all me, knows why. I sit here by this fire in what is left of this once-magnificent Garden of Eden and try to comprehend yet again the significance of life. So many live moment to moment in ignorant bliss and for them, I feel great sadness, for none of what has happened, and none of what is to come, will make sense to them. I know th...

The words were no longer showing up on the page. Gabriel tried again, dragging the pen's tip across the edge of the page. "Shit!"

"What's wrong?" Sanjaya asked.

"My pen! The damn thing is out of ink!"

"I have one in my backpack," Rafi offered.

"Too late, my thoughts are gone."

At first light, they began the treacherous trek through the jungle back to the small, open patch where hopefully the old stone-faced pilot would be waiting to return them to Western civilization. As they slogged across the misty bog, Gabriel turned for one last lingering look at the Kebun—the Golden Garden—before it vanished into the fog of time forever.

The old helicopter pilot was there to meet them and their return trip to Papua's Jackson Airport proved uneventful. Gabriel and Rafi bid goodbye to Sanjaya, who traveled on to his home base in Jakarta.

"It's been real, as they say," Sanjaya said, half-joking. "So, what do we do now?"

"We do nothing, nothing at all," Gabriel answered. "What we've seen has to remain our secret... at least for now."

"You'll keep me informed?"

"As best I can, B.D."

From Papua, the Cessna flew to Rafi's home base in Bangkok.

"Same question.," Rafi said. "You'll keep in touch?"

"Yeah, you do the same."

Rafi shook Gabriel's hand. "I'm a phone call away if I can be of help."

"Thanks, I may take you up on that."

35

Unable to sleep, Gabriel tossed and turned as if the mattress was studded with nails. He rolled onto his back, and that eased the pain in his spine a bit, but not enough for him to lay there. He opened his eyes—the still blades of a ceiling fan came into view. His gaze strayed right to the walnut dresser against the wall and the silver-framed photo of his mother and father hanging above it.

He was home. That brought a smile to his lips.

Catherine slept peacefully beside him. They had talked until just past midnight as he recounted the details of his trip. Mesmerized by his impassioned description of the Mogen and excited to hear of the actual existence of the Kebun, she had listened with rapt interest. But she was disheartened to hear of the Kebun's destruction and disappointed that he had kept his destination a secret.

Eventually, they had fallen asleep in each other arms.

Now at 4:15 AM, he was wide awake with lower back pain and a throbbing headache. He forced himself to a sitting position. Murky facsimiles of the Mogen, Rafi, Sanjaya, and the Golden Garden were now foggy, dreamlike recollections cluttered with tenebrous details that he struggled to assemble into coherent images.

Rising to his feet on weakened legs, he wandered off to the bathroom where he came face-to-face with a week-old beard and dark circles beneath his eyes. Red welts and scratches from insect bites and thorn bushes covered his arms and torso. "Who are you and what the hell are you doing in my bathroom?"

He slipped into the shower, placed his hands flat against the tiled wall and lowered his head. Not a muscle moved for five long minutes as hot water slowly restored some semblance of life to his aching body.

Showered, clean-shaven, coffee cup in hand, he sat in front of his computer, pouring over the scribbled notes he had made during the trip. Several pages held the remnants of the jungle: the salty-smelling stains of sweat; small droplets of dried blood; smudged fingerprints and a few tiny, dead bugs. Trying to keep pace with his cascading thoughts, he finally began typing. His fingers flew across the keyboard in a race to document the trip exactly as it had unfolded, fearing that if he did not, his notes would somehow liquefy and be lost forever.

Considering how the West Wing moved at hyper-speed during normal business hours, it was a bit eerie at 5:45 AM. Only uniformed Secret Service, the cleaning crew, and a few night staffers normally moved about. But this morning there were twice as many uniformed Secret Service agents patrolling the halls while two fully armed Marines stood guard at the entrance to the Oval Office.

At his desk, he punched in his security code and password and his computer sprang to life. There were 107 emails either addressed or copied to him. He scanned through them quickly until he came across one signed by all 535 former members of Congress. Believing they still wielded some influence, they demanded Gabriel withdraw from any further cooperation with Legna. There were emails from foreign leaders urging the U.S. State Department to negotiate with the aliens without articulating what exactly was to be negotiated.

All were knee-jerk proposals that lacked clarity.

But one email in particular caught his eye: a profanity-laden message from Alan Cross to the leader of the U.S. Senate with a cc to Gabriel. Cross was demanding that the now-powerless Congress officially authorize his swearing in as President.

"Alan," Gabriel mumbled, "what the hell are you thinking?" His hands went to the keyboard. "Screw it! If he gets pissed, so be it." He typed: *Alan, what is happening is not theater, not a bluff, but the real thing. At this critical time, we need your learned counsel, not your fits of anger.*

There was a light knock at his door.

"Come," Gabriel called out.

A Secret Service agent who Gabriel did not recognize entered.

"Good morning, sir," the youngish-looking man said timidly.

"Good morning—you're new here."

"Tom Garrett. I was attached to the State Department—this is my first day in the White House."

Garrett handed him a large manila envelope, then quickly withdrew without further comment.

The sealed envelope was simply addressed to *Gabriel Ferro*. Below his name, the words *Top Secret* was stamped in red ink. In the upper left-hand corner was a drawing of an unadorned white dove. Below the dove, it read: *Office of the Administrator*.

Running his letter opener along the sealed flap, he removed a thin 8 by 11-inch blue document with the white dove symbol imprinted on its cover. He opened it to the first page. The word *Strategies* was printed in bold red letters. Flipping to the next page, he read a critique of Earth's exploding population and how it was expediting Earth's dwindling natural resources. If the cataclysmic trends continued unabated, the report stated, man's existence on the planet would end.

"Can't get more apocalyptic than that," Gabriel mused.

He flipped to the next page titled, *Solutions.* Scanning the text, he came to a paragraph that stopped him cold. His jaw dropped. Shooting straight up from up his chair as if an electric eel had attached itself to his bottom, he said aloud, "What the hell! Is he out of his mind?"

"Who's out of whose mind?"

Standing in the doorway was his secretary, Betty.

"What are you doing here?"

"I work here."

"At this hour?"

"I could ask you the same." Besides Legna, Betty had been the only one aware of Gabriel's true itinerary—at least the part that dealt with the Mogen. "Where did you get those welts on your face?"

Gabriel rattled the document above his head. "*This...*" he declared in a forced whisper as if someone might be listening, "... this will guarantee an uprising of unmanageable proportions." He held the document out to her. "See for yourself." He thrust the document toward her. "Second page, third paragraph."

Her eyes scanned down to the third paragraph. It took only a few seconds for her to see what had so inflamed her boss. "This can't be! My god, this can't be!"

"Tell that to his Lord and Master."

She handed the document back.

"This is genocide! He has to be stopped!"

Betty glanced up to the ceiling. "With his ships circling like a pack of hyenas stalking a newborn gazelle, whose gonna' stop him?"

"Me, damn it, me!" Gabriel flung the document to the desk.

"Well, you'll get your chance. You have a meeting with him at 7:30 sharp."

Glancing at his watch, Gabriel sighed and dropped to his chair. "What happened while I was gone?"

"Up until two days ago, nothing much."

"What happened two days ago?"

"He circulated a memo to all West Wing staff proclaiming you his second in command with the full authority of his office. Need I mention that Alan Cross is foaming at the mouth? Did you agree to this?"

Gabriel sucked in a long breath and ran his hands through his hair. "We spoke about it before I left."

"And?"

"And I didn't acknowledge it either way, Betty!"

"Don't raise your voice. Anyway, he seems to think you did."

Gabriel set his elbows on the desktop with a thud and buried his face in his hands. "Jesus!"

"Jesus ain't going to help you now. His Royal Highness believes you're on board 100 percent."

"I said I would consider it if they were truly here on a peaceful mission."

"And when will we know that?"

Gabriel rubbed at his bloodshot eyes. "I need coffee."

"Have you seen your coffee cup?"

He ignored the question, picked up the document and shook it. "And you never saw this piece of crap!"

"I wish I hadn't. I pray you can talk him out of it. How did the trip go?"

"Not now, I wouldn't know where to begin."

"Okay, coffee coming up."

His computer pinged, alerting him to the arrival of an email. It was from Legna informing him that B.D. Sanjaya and Rafi Suharto had been taken into protective custody.

36

At 7:28, Gabriel approached the Oval Office with the dreaded document clutched tightly in hand. Eileen Mosby, the Administrator's new assistant, was busily collating papers.

"Good morning, Eileen," Gabriel said.

"Good morning, Mr. Ferro," Mosby replied without looking up.

"I wish you'd call me Gabriel. We really do go by first names around here."

She fidgeted nervously with the cuff of her long-sleeved gray blouse. "The Administrator has instructed you be addressed as Mr. Ferro."

"Has he now?"

"Yes, sir." Mosby looked up and nodded politely. "The Administrator is expecting you, sir."

Gabriel eyed her closely, looking for that one clue that might give him some insight into this seemingly impassive woman. There was nothing.

Stepping to the entrance of the Oval Office, he straightened his shoulders, smoothed the front of his dark blue suit and mentally cautioned himself to keep his anger in check knowing full well that if he provoked a confrontation with Legna, he would lose.

He knocked lightly before sauntering in.

Legna was standing to the left of a window, peeking around the beige curtain as if hiding from whatever was outside.

"Good morning," Gabriel said softly.

Legna stepped back from the window and said without preamble, "What do they want, Gabriel?"

"Who?"

"Come see."

Puzzled by the alien's behavior, Gabriel moved to Legna's side and peered out the window. He was stunned to see several hundred-people gathered along the black iron fence that surrounded the White House compound. They had not been there when he'd arrived. The crowd stood in silent vigil without protest signs, shouts, or threats.

"What is their purpose?"

Gabriel took a step back. "You."

"They are curious to see me?"

"They're frightened. When humans fear for their safety, they often protest."

Legna peeked around the curtain again. "There are reports of such gatherings elsewhere on the planet. Surely they would not resort to violence."

"I wouldn't count on it," Gabriel sniggered.

"I have done nothing to cause them alarm."

A slight grin came over Gabriel's face. "Forgive me if I find humor in that."

"Humor?"

"You don't get it, do you? Those people out there—people everywhere—they're petrified, living in a vortex of fear, not knowing who you really are, what you want, and worse, how many more of you are you those circling spacecraft."

"All will become clear."

Damn him, he's forever saying that. "When will all be *clear*?"

"When I deem it so." Legna ambled to one of the two facing sofas and crawled up.

"Fear of the unknown is a powerful force. There are hotheads and nut jobs out there that can and will whip those crowds into frenzied feral dogs; if one attacks, they all attack."

"I do not fear them, Gabriel."

"Again, you're missing the point—they fear *you*. Convince them you mean no harm. Show them a gesture of goodwill, instead of dead air."

"Dead air?"

"Your continued silence—it's deafening."

"Please sit, Gabriel. May I have Ms. Mosby provide you with refreshment?"

Despite having cautioned himself to keep calm, Gabriel's acrimony slowly bubbled to the surface. "You're not listening to me."

"But I am Gabriel, I am. Please sit."

Gabriel peered out the window again—the crowd was growing. He turned to Legna and raised the offending document to eye level. "Let's begin with this."

"Yes, yes, we will address such matters."

"I want to address this now."

"I'm beginning to find your audacity offensive, Gabriel."

"Yeah, well, I don't know any other way to make an impression on you." Shaking the document, Gabriel took a few steps forward. "You'll never pull this off, not in a million years."

"Are humans so arrogant, so ego driven, they would reject a transition to ensure the survival of their species?"

Gabriel snapped the document up over his head. "And you believe this to be the answer?"

"Tell me of the Mogen." Legna's tone was level and calm.

"Have you not heard a word I've said?"

"I requested you to sit, Gabriel. Please do so now."

At that charged moment, Gabriel's impulse was to tell Legna in plain English to shove it. But he knew he would be rebuked and whatever headway he hoped to make would be lost in translation. *Hold on, Sparky,* he cautioned himself, *allow your rage to surface, and he will have won. Take a step back—breathe. Use a little savior-faire just as President Conrad taught you.*

As he rounded the desk, his eyes were drawn to the floor. In his absence, the traditional oval rug with its navy-blue background, tan border, and Great Eagle Seal had been replaced. The new rug sported a moss green background accentuated around its outer edge by two white bands set two inches apart. Dead center was a white dove in flight. Not wishing to give Legna the satisfaction, he chose to ignore it. He moved to the sofa and dropped the offending document to the coffee table. "Why did I find the Kebun destroyed? Dr. Sanjaya assured me it was not so when he was last there."

"That is of no concern now."

"Then why was I allowed to go there and see it in that state?"

"As I recall, Gabriel, you insisted."

"But it could have stood as a symbol of hope."

"That is illogical. Hope without meaningful change is nothing more than self-indulgent fantasy."

"You built the Kebun, you destroyed it, you can restore it. Show people what still can be. Is that concept so *alien* to you?"

Gabriel's tone was aggressive—perhaps too aggressive. He anticipated a backlash. Instead, the alien's eyes strayed to the window as if the demonstrations had distressed him after all.

Legna's attention came back to Gabriel. "Now then, we will speak of the Mogen." Legna leaned back, folded his hands, and set them in his lap.

As much as he wanted to flee this room he revered so much, Gabriel reluctantly sat down on the sofa opposite Legna. He brought his hands together and squeezed until his knuckles turned white. *Slow down, slow down. Don't lose it. Play your game, not his.* "Are the Mogen connected in any way to your failed experiment?"

"All humans are a result of that undertaking."

"Yes, but in the case of the Mogen, was there—"

"The Mogen by their very nature are unique humans. Did you not find them so?"

"I did. Their simplistic lifestyle and genuine affection and concern for others is extraordinary. And yes, I agree, we could learn much from them."

Seemingly pleased with Gabriel's response, Legna smiled. "The Mogen have been blessed with a powerful inner spirituality and an unparalleled underlying strength. They revel in the joy of simplicity, not because of circumstance, for they could possess riches if they so desired. Rather, they chose to practice the esoteric truth of what it means to be alive. They respect all as equals and are guardians of the bounty that nurtures all within their caste. These are the very virtues that must be embraced if mankind is to be emancipated."

"As praiseworthy as that is, there's no rewinding the clock, no turning modern society into a Mogen village."

"Oh, but you are wrong, Gabriel. Mankind's innate instinct is to survive. They will respond to our efforts for no other reason than to save themselves."

Gabriel swept up the document and held it high. "And you believe *this* to be the way to accomplish that?"

"It is but one component."

"If you believe you can successfully implement this…" Gabriel tossed the document to the coffee table. "… you're on the wrong planet. Obviously, you have never experienced nine billion people all revolting at the same time." Stabbing a stiff finger against the document, he carped, "This hideous document will guarantee such an uprising."

Legna's gaze wandered aimlessly as it often did. It was irritating, but there was no rushing him; he'd come back to the conversation when he was ready and not before

"It took 200,000 years for human population to reach 1 billion and only 200 years to reach 7 billion. That number now exceeds 9 billion, yet humans remain apathetic to the obvious: Sooner than later there will be too many vying for dwindling resources, yet Mankind remains blind to the warning signs with no clear strategy to stem the impending cataclysm."

Angrily, Gabriel scooped up the document and shook it. "And this is *your* answer—*zero population growth*?" There, he finally said it aloud. He raised the document above his head. "Humans do not respond to draconian rule—they will see this for what it is—*genocide*.

Legna sighed. "You diminish yourself with such imbecilic statements."

Slow down, you're letting your tempter speak for you again. Reason with him. "Slowing population growth will—"

"Suspending and reducing."

"However you label it, it will prove a Herculean task. Bearing and raising children is an intrinsic component of being human. You just can't stop it."

"Humans breed indiscriminately. Do they not?"

It was becoming arduous arguing with a creature whose innocent face resembled that of a twelve-year-old. *How do I get through to him? This zero-population plan is insane.* "For the sake of discussion, what is the number?"

Without skipping a beat, Legna said, "Five billion."

"Five billion! You want to reduce population to five billion? You must be mad!"

Legna settled back against the sofa, folded his hands in his lap and calmly said, "Mankind must accept this challenge or perish—those are the only choices."

Gabriel slumped back. "Was zero population growth one of the conditions presented to President Reagan?"

Legna nodded in the affirmative. "The method was not specified, only that was it was imperative to mankind's survival that child bearing be terminated forthwith."

"Then I understand why he rejected your help."

"It was surely politically motivated—a fatal rush to misjudgment."

Gabriel's eyes strayed to the window where he knew, in the cold light of day, hundreds—maybe thousands by now—of frightened, innocent souls stood oblivious to the machinations that awaited them. How could he in all good conscience be a conspirator to such oppressive alterations? Swallowing hard, he spoke just above a whisper, "I question whether mankind will accept such an extraordinary and primordial course correction now or ever." His eyes went to the floor. "Perhaps, in the end, our fate is extinction."

"You shall comprehend upon our return."

"Our return? From where?"

"Ecaep."

Gabriel's voice cracked. "Your planet?"

"My home, Gabriel, my home. There you shall bear witness to our civilization coexisting in peace, harmony, and balance.

"You're asking me to become a conspirator—to betray my own."

"Not to betray... but to save. In your heart, you are a Mogen, seeking only peace, harmony, and balance for your kind."

"I have no right to make decisions affecting the lives of other humans. It doesn't work that way here. We in public life suggest, guide, but in the end people decide for themselves."

"Listen to me well, Gabriel. Direct all of your resources to the resurrection of your race, and you will free them from their demons. There will come a day when we shall leave, and you shall lead."

Speechless and confused, Gabriel swept up the document and walked to the window. Outside, the growing throngs of laconic bodies stood in silent defiance. At that moment, he wanted to reject Legna and join the crowd. Then he was on the move again toward the door.

"Gabriel?" Legna called after him.

Gabriel stopped and turned back. "I fear our civilization is far too complicated for what you are proposing. If we are incapable of working this out for ourselves, then maybe extinction is our final chapter."

Legna slipped from the sofa and moved to Gabriel's side and placed a reassuring hand on his forearm. "When the Kebun colony failed, we abandoned them. It was a selfish misstep. We cannot, will not, allow failure a second time."

Come on, Gabriel berated himself, *think on your feet. It's clear their plan is going forward with or without you. Play his game, be on the inside.* "If I agree to accompany you to your planet—if such a thing is even possible for a human—I want Catherine to be with us."

Legna didn't appear surprised by Gabriel's request. "Excellent. As a medical professional and scientist, Catherine will be of enormous assistance with the task at hand."

"You know she holds you in contempt."

"I am mindful of her displeasure. I shall endeavor to regain her confidence."

Then Gabriel blurted, "Release Rafi Suharto and Dr. Sanjaya."

A moment's hesitation before Legna said, "It was unwise to have shared what I had revealed to you."

"How do you know I told them?"

Legna simply stared.

"Okay, fine. But they are honorable men and gave me their word they would not speak of it. Release them."

Legna strode across the new oval rug avoiding stepping on the white dove symbol. Circling the desk, he sat and thought for a long moment. "I shall honor your request. However, if either speak of what they know—"

"They won't."

"Very well. Please be prepared to depart tomorrow at sunset."

Legna turned and strolled to a window—the meeting was over.

37

With the offending document clutched tightly in his hand, Gabriel paused in the hall outside his office. Leaning against the wall, he lowered his head, closed his eyes and lingered there for several seconds, hoping against hope that when he opened his eyes, the nightmare will have somehow ended.

"Hey, Gabriel, I heard you were back. How's your mom?"

Gabriel's eyes popped open. Standing there was Tyler Harney, his top research assistant.

"Mom's doing well, thank you, Tyler."

"Good news. Where'd you get that scratch on your face."?

Gabriel's hand went to his cheek. "Ah, fell while trimming mom's bushes in front of her house."

"Hmm," Tyler held up a manila envelope. "Anyway, the report."

"The report?"

"You said I should give you a copy before turning it in."

"Right—the report—thanks."

"Listen, uh… you remember I was to turn it in directly to"

"No one will know I have it—fair enough?"

"Fair enough, Boss."

When Gabriel entered his office suit, Betty was on the phone.

"Hold on, please." She placed the call on hold. "Gabriel, do you know a Rafi Suharto?"

"Why?"

"He's on your secure line—says it's urgent."

Moving swiftly to his office, he dropped the manila envelope on his desk and scooped up the phone. "Rafi, you're out of custody!"

"Yeah, I called Sanjaya, and he's out too."

"I'm sorry, it was Legna's doing."

"What's done is done. Now, secure line or no secure line, let's make this quick. Crowds are amassing all over the world."

"I know, there's a mob circling the White House."

"Insurrections are born out of fear and ignorance. He needs to calm things down."

"Things are happening fast here. He's taking me to his planet."

"What?"

"Ecaep, we're going to Ecaep."

"Is that even safe?"

"I didn't ask."

"Maybe you should have."

"He wants me to witness Ecaepian society firsthand, how they live and… hell, I can't explain what I don't fully understand myself."

"Okay, okay, I just called to give you a contact number in case you need me."

"Gabriel scooped up a pen and a notepad. "Go."

"04-04-77-3. Got that?"

"Yes, yes. Are you in Bangkok?"

"Best I don't answer that. Safe travels, my friend."

The line went dead.

Gabriel dropped to his chair. From the bottom drawer, he retrieved the foul-smelling coffee cup, and the pack of Marlboros and lit one. His eyes went to the envelope Tyler had given him. Tearing at the flap, he removed three double-spaced pages. The first listed annual worldwide deaths as well as new births. Page two listed known terrorists and their suspected locations. The third page was a list of all persons either convicted of or awaiting trial for murder.

"So, this is the first salvo he intends to fire?" he muttered.

Betty's shaking voice came over the intercom. "Gabriel, quick. Turn on CNN!"

"What?"

"Turn on the TV!"

Scooping up the remote, he turned to CNN. The screen was split: to the left was reporter Jim Warren and to his right was an overhead shot of a bare plot of ground. Superimposed on the lower portion of the screen were the words, *Paris, France.*

"Just minutes ago, there were over 100,000 protesters gathered in and around the Eiffel Tower. French authorities received notice from the Administrator's office in Washington D.C. they had only minutes to evacuate the area if they wished to avoid casualties. No further explanation was given. Parisian police quickly dispersed the crowd. Minutes later, a single orange beam descended from the sky and struck the iconic landmark. The Tower simply vanished into thin air as if it had never existed. Amazingly, no casualties have been reported."

Gabriel's face dissolved into a look of horror. "Holy Christ!"

The scene switched to a full-screen helicopter view of where the Eiffel Tower once stood. Then the shot switched back to reporter Warren. He held in his shaking right hand a single sheet of paper.

"I've just been handed this memo. It's from the Administrator's office in Washington, D.C.: *"This regrettable demonstration was necessary to make clear that civil unrest cannot, will not, be tolerated. We have come not to harm, but to assist. Conduct yourselves accordingly."*

"My God!" Gabriel whispered. Turning off the TV, he snuffed the cigarette in the coffee cup, turned to his computer and began composing a memo to Legna:

Your ill-conceived destruction of the Eiffel Tower as a way to reign in the demonstrations was an act of aggression despite your advance warning. Thankfully, no one was injured. You fail to understand, that humans require an outlet to express their frustrations, their fears—demonstrations are that outlet. Your heinous behavior defeats your stated purpose for being here.

He pondered his words. Were they too aggressive? "Screw it," he whispered and hit the print key.

Betty called on the intercom. "Dr. Blake is calling."

"Not now, tell her I'm in a meeting. Check the printer, run it down to the Oval."

The rest of the day zipped by with no response from Legna to his memo, although he called the Oval Office to discuss it, but was told Legna was unavailable.

At 6:30 PM Betty stuck her head in the door. "I'm going home."

"I'm going to Bethesda to check on Jennings."

"Any update?"

"Just that he remains in a coma. I'll see you in the morning."

On his way to Bethesda Medical, his phone rang—it was Catherine. He let the call go to voicemail.

At the hospital, he was surprised at what he was told.

"I thought he was in a coma?"

"He is." The attending physician told him. "And yet, his vital signs have returned to near normal. His burns, as life-threatening as they were, are suddenly and inexplicably healing faster than any patient I've even cared for, and I've been doing this for 21 years. Some would call it a miracle."

That evening, after a late dinner, Gabriel and Catherine sat in the living room doing their best to empty a bottle of Chardonnay, which was now half empty. Before he could tell her, he had checked in on Owen Jennings, she launched into a tirade of the Paris incident.

"Thousands could have been killed." Catherine said. "That bloody creature is insane."

"I sent him a memo telling him how ill-conceived it was."

Catherine smacked her lips. "Oh good, that should scare the living crap out of him."

"I'm not exactly in a position to issue mandates."

Gabriel filled their glasses again fell silent.

"Something bothering, what is it?"

"Now don't go off on me, hear me out. Tomorrow... tomorrow we're traveling to Ecaep."

"Ecaep!" Catherine tossed her head back and laughed.

"No, really, we're going there."

"You're serious? You and Legna? How do you intend to get there?"

"Greyhound?" Gabriel paused and averted his eyes.

"Your hangdog expression tells me there's more."

"I convinced him you should go with us."

Catherine's reaction was explosive. She leaped to her feet. "How's that even possible for a human—and with a deranged alien yet?"

"If it's safe for them, I assume it's safe for us. I thought you'd be ecstatic. When was the last time you, the scientist, had the opportunity to study an alien civilization up close and personal?"

"I remind you that I'm a medical scientist, not a cosmologist."

"Catherine, listen to me. They're here and there isn't a damn thing we can do about it. But, you and me, we're on the *inside.* That's our advantage, our strength, the only card we have to play, and we better play it. You spent the most time with him. Who knows him better than?"

"Alan Jennings and Rod Sandford for two. Lest you forget, Jennings's in the hospital and Sandford and that traitor Daniels and six security guards are dead."

"But he didn't lie about the Kebun—I've seen it and it's real."

"You saw what he wanted you to see."

"No, I saw it, smelled it and held it in my hand. It was real. The way I see it, we're obligated to every soul on Earth to plunge headlong into the mayhem to do whatever we can to—"

"Honestly, your acceptance frightens me."

"I'm being pragmatic. It is what it is until proven otherwise. Come here," he enveloped her in his arms.

At first, she resisted. Then her arms went around him and she laid her head on his chest. Playfully he swayed and pressed his hips against her suggestively.

"You're changing the subject," she mock-scolded.

He nibbled at her neck. "You have a better idea?"

As if her thoughts had suddenly spun on a dime, she pushed back. "By the way—"

"Ah, 'by the way' means change the subject."

"My transfer to the Bethesda Naval Medical Center came through channels. You, sir, are looking at the Administrative Director of Naval Scientific Studies."

"Wow, I'm duly impressed, Madam."

"I can continue my research here."

His lips moved to the crook of her neck. "You never told me what that is?"

"It's classified."

"Excuse me, but I do hold the highest security clearance. Give me a hint."

"Jeez, you're like a spoiled two-year-old."

Gabriel laughed. "Then treat me like one and give in."

She raised her right hand and held her thumb and index finger a quarter of an inch apart. "We're this close to a life-changing procedure."

"For what?"

"If our clinical trials are successful..." Catherine's face lit up like a 100-watt bulb. "We're on the brink of curing just about *everything*!"

"What does *everything* mean?" Gabriel mimicked.

Her eyes were alive with electric excitement. "We can manipulate a gene and instruct it to attack and kill a disease before it spreads." She snapped her fingers. "Poof, gone, never to return."

Gabriel whistled. "Which diseases?"

"Name one! The human genome is packed with at least four million gene switches that reside in bits of DNA. Those little magic switches are key players in controlling how cells, organs, and other tissues behave. Control those switches, and you control the genes. Think of it, free of life-threatening diseases, life expectancy can be extended to god knows how long!"

Gabriel's expression changed from high excitement to cautious reservation."

"Jeez, Gabriel, I thought you'd be doing handstands."

"I'm excited for you, for the world, honestly, I am."

"Then what's with the doomsday look?"

Gabriel averted his eyes."

"What?"

Hesitantly, Gabriel turned back to her. "Does Legna know what you're working on?"

"I don't know... I don't think so."

"There's something I need to share with you."

He was about to burst Catherine's bubble. Her entire research program was on a collision course with Legna's zero-population plan.

38

The following morning, Gabriel awoke in one of his dark moods. Catherine had exploded the night before when he broke the news of zero-population and the rest of their conversation had gone badly.

When he arrived at the West Wing, Betty handed him an envelope from Legna. "My guess is it's not a birthday card."

Once settled at his desk, he opened the envelope to find a single-sentence note: *Do not be apprehensive, for your trip to and from Ecaep will prove both comfortable and safe.*

"Easy for you to say," he said low.

At 6:30 that evening, Gabriel met with his staff and informed them he would be away for several days on a special assignment for Legna. The meeting ended at 6:50 PM.

"Gabriel." Betty's voice came over the intercom. "The gate called. Doctor Blake is on her way in." There was a moment of silence. "Are you smoking in there again? Gabriel Ferro, in spite of who is occupying the Oval Office, this is still the White House."

Like a kid caught with his hand in the cookie jar, Gabriel snubbed the cigarette in the coffee cup and placed it in the bottom right drawer of his desk.

Moments later Catherine entered looking quite sexy in tailored black slacks, an off-white wool sweater, and a knee-length winter coat. Denver Wilkinson, President Conrad's former lead agent, was at her side.

Catherine sniffed the air curiously, but made no mention of the scent of tobacco.

Wilkinson walked quickly to Gabriel's side like a man on an urgent mission. "I'm not sure why, but Legna confided in me, so I know where you're going. Be safe." He shook Gabriel's hand, turned and strode to the door and left.

"Don't mention your research to Legna." Gabriel said to Catherine.

"Do I look dumb as a cat to you? I have no intention of—"

Before she could finish, the door burst open and in stormed an angry-looking Alan Cross.

"Alan," Gabriel said in greeting.

"Don't Alan me, Goddamnit!"

Ignoring Cross' belligerence, Gabriel greeted him with a smile. "Alan, you remember Dr. Catherine Blake."

Shooting a sour look in Catherine's direction, Cross said under his breath, "Yeah."

Catherine smiled. "Nice to see you again, sir."

It was clear from his expression, Cross was angling for a verbal mix-up. "This is not going to fly, Gabriel. I'll be a son of a bitch if I stand by while you play footsie with Mister Hobbit. I'll have the military blow his goddamn brains out."

Considering Cross' provocation, Gabriel responded in as tranquil a voice as he could muster. "If you do, laser beams will rain down from hovering spaceships."

Cross took a threatening step toward Gabriel. "We've been invaded, and so far, all we seem capable of is bending over and taking it in the ass!"

"Have you forgotten Howland Island, the Russian missile base, the Eiffel Tower?"

"That doesn't explain what in the living hell is going on between you and Tinker Bell. On the other hand, maybe it does. Maybe you're kissing that little shit's gray ass to save your own." He glared at Catherine. "And hers."

Cross had crossed the line—it was the final straw for Gabriel. "Listen, you foul-mouthed son of a bitch, don't you dare come in here and accuse me of being a traitor!"

Catherine quickly slipped between the two men. "Whoa, gentlemen, gentlemen, get a grip."

Thrusting a finger Catherine's face, Cross barked, "Lady, stay the hell out of this!"

That infuriated Gabriel, and he swatted at Cross' hand. "Alan, for god's sake, stop. You're making a fool of yourself."

"Maybe you've bought into the bullshit that gnome is peddling, but I haven't. You do what you have to, and I'll do what *I* have to."

Gabriel reached and swiped a hand across Cross' right shoulder.

"What the hell was that for?"

"I thought I saw a chip on your shoulder."

"Very funny." Spinning on his heels, Cross stormed toward the door.

"Alan, don't do anything stupid!"

"The stupidity is coming from you, young man. I heard—you're off again doing his bidding and no one seems to know where or why. Fine, have it your way!" Cross spun around to leave.

"Wait a minute! What do you know about that ill-conceived Russian nuclear missile attack?"

Cross' body visibly stiffened. "Russia does not seek my input, and I do not presume to tell them what to do."

Cross stormed out, slamming the door behind him.

"If he stays true to form, the bull-headed son of a bitch will go off half-cocked, and there's no telling what the fallout will be." Gabriel scooped up the phone, dialed, and waited. "Andy, it's Gabriel. Your boss just breezed out of here after one of his grand hissy fits. Calm him down before we all pay a terrible price."

Despite Legna assurances that the trip would be safe, apprehension and a healthy dose of fear still hungover Gabriel and Catherine like a storm cloud. It was not a question of what might happen, but the inescapable feeling of what *could* happen.

They had been told to rendezvous with Legna in the Oval Office no later than 7:30 PM. When they arrived, Ms. Mosby was not at her desk.

Gabriel shrugged. "Well, that's disappointing,"

"What is?"

"I was hoping to introduce you to a descendant of *Vlad the Impaler*."

Legna was perched high in his chair behind the presidential desk, his head bent forward intently reading a document. Although President Conrad had paid tribute to her and pilot Skip Galinski in this very room, Catherine canvassed the space with a sense of awe. Shifting uneasily from one foot to the other she waited, but there was zero recognition from the alien.

Finally, Catherine said, "The proper thing would be to ask how I've been."

The alien did not reply.

"Something wrong?" Gabriel asked.

The alien's head came up slowly and he leaned back, folded his hands and stared curiously at Catherine as if seeing her for the first time.

From the adjoining office, a second alien entered. Down to the minutest detail, this new entity was an exact duplicate of the one sitting behind the desk.

"Ah, Catherine, it is comforting to see you again. Are you well?"

It was Legna—or so they assumed.

Legna gestured to the alien sitting behind the desk. "Catherine, Gabriel, may I present Citizen Roama."

Gabriel's eyes widened. "What in the—?"

"Citizen Roama is Ms. Mosby. An impressive visual transformation, is it not? When approaching this office, better humans be greeted by someone they perceive as their own, hence Roama in the form of Ms. Mosby. Citizen Roama will occupy this space in my absence, and none will be the wiser."

Gabriel and Catherine stood speechless at the sight of two aliens, so identical, there was no way of telling who was who.

Roama slipped from the chair, bowed his head to Legna and exited to the adjoining office without ever uttering a word.

"It pleases me that you are at my side again, Catherine. Are you ready for your adventure?"

"Curious, if nothing else, I guess."

"Gabriel has advised me of your contempt toward me."

"Gabriel is correct."

"Please, articulate."

With a grim look, Catherine said, "We placed our lives on the line for you and—"

"Willingly, as I recall."

"Because we believed you, or we would not have risked our lives to save yours."

"I was deceitful yes; a necessary tactic for which I wish to make amends." His lips curled into a slight smile. "Without further delay, let us begin our journey."

And with that, Legna proceeded to leave.

Catherine looked to Gabriel with a *here we go* look and whispered, "We must be drunk out of our minds to be doing this."

39

The last vestiges of the day's sun shone as a thin sliver of purple light on the Western. The trio approached the south lawn where the presidential helicopter, the Sikorsky VH-4A, normally landed. It was a brisk forty-one degrees with six inches of loose-packed snow blanketing the ground. All exterior lights had been extinguished. Those needing to be in the complex had been instructed to stay clear of the area.

No one would witness their departure.

Quiet and apprehensive, Gabriel and Catherine gazed at the night sky wondering why they had agreed to a voyage through space that could prove a dangerous, if not a foolish, undertaking.

"I'm not sure we made the right decision," Catherine whispered to Gabriel.

He whispered back, "You can still back out."

Catherine took a deep breath and mock-shook her head. "Not on your life."

Legna stood several feet in front of them. He turned, smiled, and asked, "Are you galvanized?"

The alien's use of euphemisms always amused Gabriel. "More like cautious anticipation."

"Do not fear what is beyond understanding. Embrace the undiscovered, and you shall act with surety." Raising his right arm, he pointed to the sky. "There you will find legions of uncharted dimensions. In time, mankind will travel freely within their boundaries and revel in their majesty."

No sooner had those words escaped the alien's thin lips when a large mass of air shimmered and danced some thirty feet away and scattering the powdery top layer of snow.

"My God!" Catherine gasped as she took a quick step back. "My God!"

Gabriel took her hand and squeezed. "Don't be frightened, I've seen this before."

Whatever was whirling in front of them stopped and all became quiet except for there a slight whistling of the wind. Suddenly, like a flickering firefly, a dime-sized fissure of intense white light appeared out of nowhere some seven feet above the ground. Like a flowing river of hot lava, it splayed out into a doorway and ramp with nothing visible beyond it.

Catherine swallowed hard. "Holy…"

Legna bowed his head slightly and motioned to the light. "After you, Catherine."

Her eyes narrowed to tight slits. "Uh, you first."

"As you wish." Legna stepped on the shimmering ramp and disappeared into what they could only assume was the interior of the unseen craft.

Gabriel inhaled and exhaled quickly and took Catherine's hand. "Like Astronomer Carl Sagan was fond of saying… 'Extraordinary claims require extraordinary evidence.' I think we're about to get it."

Taking Catherine's hand in his, he led her to the ramp. Ever so cautiously he set his right foot on what looked like nothing more than a flat wave of light. But to his relief, it proved to be solid. Guardedly, they continued up the ramp and through the lighted doorway.

The interior of the craft dashed their wildest imagination of what an alien spaceship might look like. The perfectly round interior was devoid of any electronics or anything else for that matter. At twenty-five feet in diameter, it was far smaller than they had imagined. The clinical white interior encased them in a seamless Cyclorama—no beginning, no end, no windows, no flight controls, just an empty space devoid of any character besides the flying white dove emblem embedded in the center of the floor.

Gabriel eyed the space. "Who's gonna fly this thing… and how?"

"A sensory implement will guide us."

"A what? To where?"

Legna offered no further explanation.

Just as mysteriously as it had appeared, the liquid doorway dissolved, leaving no visible sign it had been there. Then, a central section of the floor evaporated before their eyes, and two rows of seats silently rose up on a platform. The seats—clearly designed for someone of Legna's size—were arranged in two half-circles: seven in the first row and six in the second. Except for the red one in the middle of the first row, the seats were covered in a gray, microfiber-like fabric. On the red chair's right arm, a star-shaped light pulsed blue.

Legna motioned to the seats. "You need not fear for your safety. Your anatomy will function as it does so on Earth."

"Radiation," Gabriel asked, "… how is it deflected? What about weightlessness? The atmosphere on your planet? Will we be able to breathe normally?"

"You have many questions."

"Concerns."

"Very well," Legna's arms, palms up, splayed out, "We are safely sheathed within this magnificent instrument. However, I fail to understand how it works. That is, as you humans say, above my pay grade." Legna chortled. "As for Ecaep's atmosphere, it is the same as Earth…" His brow fluted. "… only cleaner. Please, sit wherever you wish." Legna settled in the red chair.

With uneasiness, Catherine took a seat at the far end of the first row. Gabriel sat next to her. Because of the chair's small size, their knees jutted up, and they were elbow to elbow. Gabriel mumbled under his breath and moved one seat over. Instinctively, they searched for safety belts, but found none.

"How does this thing defy gravity?" Catherine asked.

"Ah yes, that I am able to clarify. Silent rotating mechanisms reverse magnetism—spin-stabilized magnetic levitation—the propulsion required to cause centripetal acceleration. Further definition would prove beyond your sphere of knowledge."

Catherine smirked. "From this point on, I think everything will be beyond our sphere of knowledge."

The blue light on Legna's chair turned amber. "We shall take our leave."

Gabriel and Catherine instinctively stiffened in anticipation. But to their befuddlement, there was no movement or sound, just unnerving quiet and stillness.

They waited.

"When do we leave?" Gabriel asked.

"Forgive me, I am a deficient host." Legna rose and strolled to the white metallic wall to their right. He swiped his hand along the wall and a small oval window appeared where there was none. "Come… witness your planet."

Exchanging nervous glances.

"Come, come, it is quite safe."

Catherine reached the window first. Whatever trepidation she had was replaced by sheer wonderment. "Holy mother of God," she murmured.

Gabriel stood behind her and peered over her shoulder. "Jeez, it's magnificent!"

There, down below, was Mother Earth looking like a sparkling jewel cradled ever so delicately in the vast blackness of space. A portion of the planet was in daylight: large swatches of green, brown, and blue dotted the surface. Intricate artistic swirls of scattered clouds covered portions of the sky. Where the sun had already set was equally mesmerizing with a dancing, dazzling display of lights. The heart-stopping sight, a view only a small, brave group of human astronauts had been privileged to witness—but never from this distance—left them mesmerized and speechless.

"I've never seen anything so magnificently beautiful."

"And yet, Catherine," Legna lamented, "it is not so inviting when standing on it."

The light on the arm of the red chair pulsed red. Legna swiped a hand across the window, and the seamless white wall returned. "Please take your seats."

Two minutes later, they experienced a slight jolt followed by a low hissing as if air was being released under great pressure.

"We have arrived."

The entire trip had taken seven minutes.

The glowing door and ramp reappeared.

"We shall disembark."

Following Legna, Gabriel and Catherine stepped gingerly over the lighted ramp as if walking on hot coals. Once they were clear, the door and ramp evaporated.

Turning back, Gabriel was surprised to see the shuttle was now visible. It was matte-gray and perfectly round without markings or windows. He tapped Catherine's shoulder. "Turn around."

"What." Catherine looked back and said low, "Wow!"

They were in a square-room, approximately fifty-by-fifty feet. They assumed they were in the belly of the Mothership. The space was bare and constructed of the same white, plastic-looking material as the shuttle's interior.

Gabriel was brimming with questions, but before he could fire off the first, a faint sucking sound drew their attention. To their right, a section of the wall opened and three entities, mirroring Legna in minute detail down to his clothing, appeared.

"What?" Catherine murmured.

Even though they had witnessed Roama and Legna as identical, this was disorientating. Legna acknowledged the three with a slight nod. Avoiding direct eye contact with either Gabriel or Catherine, the three aliens bowed to Legna.

"My fellow citizens welcome you as honored guests." Amused by their reaction to the identical figures, Legna said, "As you can see, the anatomy of all Ecaepians is self-same. An explanation shall be rendered in due course. Come now, allow me to familiarize you with our vessel."

Totally perplexed, Gabriel and Catherine followed Legna while three identical aliens marched close behind in lockstep. They navigated a corridor that continually veered left, an indication they were following the outer curve of the ship. Catherine worked up enough courage to peer over her shoulder at the three aliens following. Starring straight head, they displayed no interested in the humans before them.

"Our transport is comprised of three cylindrical elevations," Legna explained. "Each serves a specific function. We are on promenade one. Beneath lies the force components that provide thrust control and power support for all onboard functions." He stopped in front of what looked like a pencil-thin gray outline of an arched door, and it snapped in and to the left without making a sound. "Our journey begins with the validation of your well-being. Please enter."

Gabriel peered into the dimly lit room. "What happens in there?"

"An analysis of your anatomy."

"A physical examination?"

"Yes, Citizen Catherine. It will ensure your safe journey to Ecaep—please enter."

Apprehensively, Gabriel looked to Catherine. "This is your purview, doctor. After you."

As Catherine set foot inside, the illumination increased. The source appeared to be coming from the white, metallic walls. The circular space was no approximately 12 feet in diameter. Dead center of the room was a clear, round, Plexiglas-looking tube that extended from floor to ceiling. Inside, two sets of two bright blue strips spaced two feet apart ran top to bottom.

"Please remove your clothing and position yourselves one in front of the other."

Gabriel's brow creased. "Uh… wait a minute."

"The procedure will cause no discomfort. You are familiar with cytology, Catherine?"

"The diagnosis of abnormalities and malignancies."

"If any are found, the corrective measure will resolve imperfections."

"Just like that?" Gabriel glanced at Catherine.

She raised an eyebrow as if to say *we don't seem to have a choice.*

Folded neatly on a small stand to the left of the cylinder were two jumpsuits. They were the same color, design, and material as what the aliens were wearing.

"Upon completion of the process, please change to those."

Legna stepped into the hall and the door silently closed.

"Come on, lose the duds." Catherine began unbuttoning her blouse. "Let's get this over with."

"If you're sure this is safe."

"It's just a body scan, surely more advanced than what we have, but a body scan just the same."

Turning his back to Catherine, Gabriel kicked off his shoes. Freeing his belt buckle, his trousers fell to the floor. Next went his underwear and socks. Last to go was his shirt. He turned slowly to face a nude Catherine. His eyes never leaving hers.

She laughed. "Stop acting like a schoolboy."

"Front or back?" he groused.

"Back."

As they approached the cylinder, a small light flashed blue, and a door slid open. Catherine positioned herself between the second a set of blue strips. Gabriel positioned himself in front.

A spot-on Gabriel's lower right shoulder-blade caught her attention. "What's this? A mole?"

"A birthmark."

"I haven't noticed it before. You should have it removed."

"Can we just get on with this?"

Legna's voice boomed over an unseen speaker. "Please stand perfectly still."

The blue strips lit up like neon bulbs, and they both flinched. A second later two laser-like orange beams shot over their heads, connecting the blue strips then cascaded down through their naked bodies. Catherine's beam stopped briefly at her hip before continuing to her feet, paused for a moment, then returned to the top.

Gabriel's beam stopped just above his waistline and lingered for several seconds before continuing to his feet. Reversing direction, it stopped at the small of his back. A rapid clicking sounding like a dead car battery trying to start preceded what felt like a low charge of electricity. Something was moving along his spine at the L-4, L-5 lumbar position. He felt no discomfort or pain, just a creepy sensation that his lower spine was being manipulated. Finally, the beam proceeded up and disappeared.

Legna's voice came over the speaker again. "You may dress now."

Exiting the tube, Catherine pulled up the smaller of the two jumpsuits up to her waist just as Legna entered. She quickly turned her back to him. "Just a minute, please."

"Citizen Catherine, I assure you I have little interest in your anatomy."

Gabriel pulled his jumpsuit up to his waist. Curious as to what had occurred, he traced a finger along his lower spine. "I felt something moving inside me."

"A posterolateral disc bulge in combination with facet arthropathic was discovered."

"Yeah, an injury some years back."

"It would have led to bilateral neural foramen stenosis. It has been repaired."

"Just like that—I'm cured?"

Ignoring Gabriel, Legna addressed Catherine. "You are a perfect human specimen devoid of defects."

"Thank you. Please bear that in mind." She said playfully to Gabriel. Glancing back at the tube, she whispered. "We desperately need that technology back home."

40

They continued along the curve of the corridor. Other than the three aliens following close behind, no others were in sight. Being in the presence of these identical-looking aliens was unsettling. Even more disconcerting was Legna's silence on the issue.

Catherine nudged Gabriel. "Ask him. It's driving me nuts."

Gabriel placed a finger to his lips and whispered, "Later."

They stopped at a gray door, the first thing they'd encountered that wasn't white. Legna bowed his head to the three aliens, and they nodded back. They spun on their heels and marched down the corridor looking like the Munchkins from the *Wizard of Oz.*

Bemused, Catherine said, "They never once spoke."

The gray door silently slid back and left, revealing a square white box approximately three feet square and six feet tall.

"The lift will take us to level two," Legna said.

The space was just large enough to squeeze into elbow-to-elbow, and Gabriel's hair brushed against the ceiling. The door snapped shut. They waited, but there was no sound or movement. Seconds later, the door opened to another long corridor perpendicular to them. Legna turned to the left. They had not traveled more than twenty feet when Gabriel noticed a series of faint outlines on the right wall. Spaced about twelve feet apart, they looked like arched doorways about two feet wide and five feet high.

"What's behind the doors?"

"Citizen quarters," Legna answered.

"The crew lives here?"

"There is no crew, only citizens."

Fifteen feet farther on, Legna stopped by four additional outlines only these were six feet high. The first door snapped back and to the left and the walls illuminated as they entered.

The small room was molded of the same white material. In the center stood two upright clear tubes, each large enough to accommodate a single human. From top to bottom, the backs of each tube were thickly padded with two straps; one at chest level and the other just above the shin. The only furniture was two human-sized chairs separated by a small end table.

"Your travel sanctuary." Legna said. He tapped a section of the wall to his left. A door snapped open. To their utter surprise, it was a small restroom equipped with a standard commode and a sink. On a shelf to the right of the sink was a bar of soap, toothpaste, and hand towels. "I trust this is agreeable to your needs."

"Yes, impressive." Gabriel pointed to the two upright clear tubes. "What are those for?"

Without explaining, Legna said, "I will return in thirty of your minutes at which time you shall take nourishment."

And with that, Legna left.

Catherine scanned the room curiously. "We've entered the *Twilight Zone*."

"I only counted thirteen other doors before we came to this one," Gabriel said.

"So?"

"There has to be more crew—*citizens*—even if they bunk two to a room."

"Maybe there's more in another section."

"Maybe," he muttered. "Hey, that reminds me—my journal, I need to make notes."

Sheepishly, Catherine looked away.

"You did bring it?"

"I'm sorry, Gabriel. I forgot."

"It was on the dresser in the bedroom."

"With all the excitement, it slipped my mind."

"Shit! Shit!"

"Hey big boy, get a grip."

He grunted and shook his head.

Catherine mocked him by grunting back. Curious to explore further, she entered the compact bathroom and ran her fingers over the wall. "Everything's monotone; white-on-white except for that lone, gray elevator door." She tapped a finger against the wall. "What is this material anyway? I don't think it's plastic like we know plastic."

There was no response from Gabriel.

"Gabriel?" She popped her head out to find him slumped in one of the chairs, elbows on his knees, head planted in his hands. "Hey, what's wrong?"

He slowly lifted his head. "I'm beating myself up for getting you into this."

"Well, stop. I came on my own volition bursting with scientific curiosity and you should be, too."

"I am."

"You have a funny way of showing it, Mr. Ferro."

"I'm searching for the *why*."

"The what?"

"It's always been the *why* with me; why this, why that, ever since I was a kid. It drove my parent's crazy. Being here, I'm more overwhelmed with the *why's* than ever."

"You sure it's not just a case of intense curiosity? An alien spaceship has a tendency to do that."

He feigned a smile. "Your lame jokes aside, since I've seen the *Kebun* with my own eyes, we can assume he was telling the truth about our beginnings. So, when—how—did evolution lead us down the divergent path we've been on? Maybe we're just another hologram like Ms. Mosby created for their amusement."

"Perish the thought."

"There are times I feel like an observer rather than a participant. Sometimes I see a stranger and my neurons switch gears and suddenly I'm a detached observer wondering what *their* lives might be like. Are they happy or sad, wealthy or poor?

Or do they simply exist below the radar waiting for the inevitable, only to realize as they gasp their last breath of polluted air, it was all for naught?" He tapped his temple. "That this super engine we call a brain simply stops and our bodies decay and nothing ever really mattered."

"I would say that makes you eccentric."

"Is that bad?"

"If it controls your life, it is."

Gabriel wiped a hand across his mouth and down over his chin. "Look around, what's the message here—what's the *why*?"

"That in the big picture, we're a pimple on a gnat's ass?"

"That, too."

Catherine tapped at his temple. "But there's more going on in there, what is it?"

"How we humans justify our existence, our very behavior; a pat on the back for something good, lame excuses for our misdeeds. How the hell is humanity, barely capable of dealing with our world, going to handle this?"

"But isn't this the very answer we've been seeking, to know if there are others? Now that we've found the answer, why are you questioning it?"

"But that's my point. I question whether or not we're ready. I've spent the last couple of years working in the West Wing—the 'cockfight arena' as President Conrad called it—witnessing up close billions living out their lives in obscurity and imposed poverty. Then there are those, whether of means or not, contributing zip to anyone or anything other than themselves. How the hell is humanity going to wrap their minds around this?"

"Where are you going with this, Gabriel?"

"Just this: We better damn well get our act together because our insatiable appetite for more and more has become our driving force—more this, more that, more profits, whatever, forcing our basic values to slip to the point of shame." He made a slight snorting sound through his nose. "We were sold a bill of goods, that technology in the hands of the masses would set us free. It hasn't. It's become an addictive pastime, a never-ending stream of digital information, a replacement for our childhood security blankets. I read an article recently that put it this way:

We're living in a warp-speed, toxic, bullying, troll culture where far too many, with their little electronic gadgets, take perverse pleasure in exploiting the shortcomings of others." His voice softened. "I feel contempt for Steve Jobs and Bill Gates and others of that ilk. Sure, they were revolutionaries alright, but they unknowingly contributed more to the declining levels of civic engagement than all before them. What becomes of us when all these awe-inspiring advancements consume us and we no longer set our own course, but blindly accept the course set for us by the few who control it all? Your smartphone is the beginning of artificial intelligence and computers are the unseen battlefield of the future."

"It's called progress, Gabriel. You can't fight progress."

"Yeah, yeah, right. Albert Einstein knew better when he said: *"I fear the day that technology will surpass our human interaction. The world will have a generation of idiots."* All the good stuff we learned as kids has been replaced in the name of the mindless pursuit of things and status. When the hell did we lose our basic moral compass?"

"Long before it became apparent, I'm afraid."

He swallowed hard. "And where has it driven us? To an unhealthy place, that's where. To snap us out of our self-induced dementia would take a distraction of such magnitude, we couldn't possibly ignore it." He tossed his head back and chuckled. "And damned if it hasn't arrived in the form of funny little creatures whose plan is to force-feed us *their* way, *their* reality and I'm betting it doesn't come within a mile of mirroring ours."

"You don't know that for sure."

"Oh really?" He sneered. "Does the name Joseph Campbell mean anything to you?"

"As I recall, he was an author."

"Author, lecturer, mythologist. He died back in 1987. I studied Campbell's writings in college, specifically a course on comparative mythology. He spoke words so profound they've stayed with me all these years like a beautiful poem never to be forgotten: 'We're so engaged in doing things to achieve purpose of outer value that we forget that the inner value, the rapture that is associated with being alive, is what it's all about.'

"That's amazing."

"Yeah, the words are pure and—"

"No, I mean that you still remember it."

"I can never forget it."

"You and your never-ending quotes."

Gabriel grinned and tapped his head. "They're all stored here."

"You should have been born Jewish for all the guilt you carry."

"Not guilt, just plain common sense."

"Look, Gabriel, it's not that I disagree with anything you've said, but I'm a bit more pragmatic. I can't remember a time in my life when there wasn't squalor and disease on patches of earth that nobody cared about, but we're willing to start wars over, ending the lives of millions of soldiers and innocent men, women, and children... and for what? But, here is the difference between you and me—I know my limits. I know what I, as an individual, can and cannot do. Just like everyone in this world, you have to come to grips with the boundaries of your limitations."

"Why?"

"There's that *why* again." She lowered herself to the chair beside him, cupped his hands in hers and gently squeezed. "Your hands are too small to capture all the world's pain."

"And yet I've been asked to, haven't I? Again, it comes down to the *why*. Why me, why have these creatures chosen me to lead? Why are we traveling to another planet to mingle with a civilization that wants to morph us into them?"

Catherine looked deep into Gabriel's eyes. This man who had been the confidant to the most powerful leader in the world and whose compassion and goodness went deeper than any other she had encountered now looked lost and childlike. She cupped his face, pulled him close, and gently kissed him.

41

Thirty minutes later to the second, Legna returned and announced, "You shall consume nourishment now."

They traveled a short distance down the corridor to a door that opened to a rectangular chamber. A white, fifteen-foot table sat in the center; fifteen white chairs; six on either side, one at the far end and two at the other end.

Legna motioned to the two seats at the far end of the table. "Please, be comfortable."

Gabriel and Catherine sat just as an alien—identical to the others—entered and placed white plastic trays in front of them. He stepped back and stood quietly by the door.

The trays contained hamburgers and fries.

Legna spoke. "Is this not a cherished human food?"

"Yes, of course," Catherine answered. "But where did you get it?"

Legna simply smiled. "May you enjoy your sustenance."

"Are other Ecaepians joining us?" Catherine asked.

"We do not consume comestibles."

"Well then, I would say you are missing one of life's great gratifications."

Legna replied, "Which encourages gluttony, does it not?"

She made a playful sweeping motion across her stomach area trying to make a joke of it. "You have me there."

Legna's screwed his face. "What do you mean '*you have me there*'?"

"What I meant was…"

293

Gabriel jumped in. "It must take many crew members to run a ship this size."

"We have no crew, only citizens."

"Yes, citizens, forgive me. How many are there?"

"There are twelve others."

Perplexed, Gabriel's brow furrowed. "Only thirteen citizens control this craft? How many ships are circling?"

"Two."

"How many on the other one?

"The same."

Gabriel sputtered in disbelief. "There's a total of twenty-six citizens on two ships!" He rose to his feet so quickly, he almost lost his balance. "Twenty-six citizens invaded our planet?"

Legna laced his fingers and placed his hands on the table. His face slackened, his eyes narrowed—he looked annoyed. "We did not *invade* your planet." His voice spike up. "We are not a warring race; we did not come to harm. How many times must I make this point?"

In defiance, Gabriel snapped, "Right, tell that to 2,800 dead Russians!"

"I remind you, Citizen Gabriel we were not the offender, humans were. In all societies, there must be consequences for inappropriate actions."

"Inappropriate actions? They perceived a threat and took action to protect themselves."

The alien's voice dropped a full octave. "Our response was appropriate."

"But 2800 people died."

Legna offered no further explanation.

They rode the box lift to level three in silence. Still fuming, Gabriel was unable to wrap his head around the idea that a miniscule number of Ecaepians had entered the realm of Planet Earth and seized control.

When the door opened, they were immediately struck with a dazzling display of multicolored lights. The round room was about twenty feet in diameter. Two Ecaepians were perched in front of control panels and flat-screen displays. Unrecognizable graphs, charts, and symbols covered the wall to their left. To their right, the wall displayed visuals of major cities on Earth: Paris, New York City, London, Moscow, Madrid, Berlin, D.C., Sydney, Tehran, Mexico City, Cairo, Toronto, and Beijing.

Legna scanned the images of the cities and shook his head disapprovingly. "Unauthorized assemblies continue on your planet."

Gabriel looked and nodded. "And I suspect they will grow."

If Legna heard the comment, he chose to ignore it. "Do you have knowledge of the birth of your universe?"

"Many scientists subscribe to the Big Bang Theory," Gabriel answered.

"They are mistaken. Your scientists believe space is rigid and does not exist independently of the object, when in fact how objects interact is what defines space. Nor was the macrocosm a conscious act, but an act over which no entity exerted control."

Neither Gabriel nor Catherine challenged him, for no matter what their personal beliefs or those of human scientists, they would prove hollow against the wisdom, intelligence and knowledge of a civilization millions of years in existence.

Legna silently stared at the images for several moments. Then slowly, his arm went out and up toward the wall. "Behold the majesty of the supreme power."

The room plummeted into darkness. A heart-stopping panorama of the sheer wonder of the immense vastness of space splashed across the walls.

Catherine sucked in a breath. "Oh, my God!"

"You are witness to your ever-expanding universe."

Magnificent vistas of boundless space flashed before them like strokes of a master painter's brush: polychrome nebulae of great swaths of swirling white and blue formed cloud-like formations. Giant discs of intricate, multi-colored gas and dust circled planets and stars. Churning mosaics of deep reds, grays, yellows, and blues, swatches all intertwined with the coal-black backdrop of endless space.

At a loss for words, Gabriel gasped.

Catherine's face beamed with recognition and excitement. "Oh, my God, a black hole?"

"If you were to enter," Legna said, "you would emerge into yet another space-time created by the singularity of the black hole."

"Unbelievable!" Gabriel whispered.

"Earth is but one small, sphere in a wondrous Universe of continuous creation," Legna beamed, "where a myriad of life forms thrives."

What they were witnessing was so incredibly beautiful, so awe-inspiring, Gabriel and Catherine were at a loss for words. The spectacle went on for several minutes before abruptly ending.

"Come now. More will be revealed following your rest period."

Catherine, however, was not quite done with him. "Just a minute, please."

"Yes, Catherine?"

She hesitated.

"You may speak freely."

"Gabriel shared with me your plan to reduce Earth's population."

Legna flashed Gabriel a look of betrayal.

"She has a stake in this too," Gabriel said firmly. "There can be no secrets, otherwise, she's just along for the ride. I assure you this lady will not settle for that."

Catherine took a step toward Legna. "You should know this: Humans will never accept such an oppressive mandate—not now, not ever."

An Ecaepian citizen manning one of the consoles glanced over his shoulder. It marked the first time any of these creatures had reacted to their presence.

Legna admonished the alien with a cutting look. "We shall leave now."

It was not a request, but an order clearly given.

Not a word passed between them until they had returned to Gabriel and Catherine's temporary quarters.

Legna turned to Catherine, his thin lips tight, his eyelids constricted. "We shall *not* converse on such matters in front of citizens."

"That *citizen*," Catherine retorted, "understood every word I said. A breakthrough, considering not one of your *citizens* has spoken to us, let alone made eye contact."

"That is of no concern to you."

Catherine's eyes flashed with belligerence. "Everything on this cockeyed junket is my concern."

Gabriel placed a hand on her arm. "Wait a minute, Catherine."

"Wait, *hell*—zero population growth? If that's your plan, I promise you a violent backlash."

"It does not have to be so, Catherine."

"It *will* be so, *Citizen Legna*. You cannot take away—"

Gabriel interrupted. "Hold on both of you!" And then to Legna. "I didn't sign on to help create authoritarianism and that's where this enterprise appears to be headed."

"I fail to grasp your meaning, Gabriel."

"Human society for the most part functions within the rule of law. That means our citizens have rights and—"

"Citizen Gabriel, does not your Statue of Liberty proclaim... *'Give me your tired, your poor, your huddled masses yearning to breathe free.'*?"

"Damn it, why do you ask me questions you already know the answers to?"

"Because the key component of your diatribe is *for the most part*— you did not say *all*. Is that not a contradiction, an injustice to those who are deprived of equal status?"

"Don't play semantics with me. You know very well what I meant. You're talking about zero births, a radical, unworkable plan at best; go through with this and the resulting rebellion will be beyond anything you could have anticipated."

"Mankind could wage yet another savage war. That would effectively reduce an expanding population, would it not?"

"Damn it, you twist my words."

"It is not possible to have it both ways, Gabriel: survival or extinction, which is it to be?"

It was a rhetorical question and Gabriel was not about to let himself fall prey to Legna's word games. He simply crossed his arms, stood resolutely, and stared.

Legna's facial muscles tightened. "Listen well, for I will not speak of this again. Your planet is a self-regulating organism suffering from a crippling illness brought on by unabated, dare I say ignorant, abuse that has and will continue to have a devastating effect on human life. Deterioration has reached the tipping point. Total desolation is imminent, equaled only by mankind's bewilderment over how to abate it. Business as usual—to quote a human phrase—is no longer an option. Without that first courageous step, there is no future… except of course for the animals and insects who will joyfully reclaim the planet. Might there be questions?"

Catherine, resolute, fired back, "You failed the test."

"Test?"

"You fail to grasp that our society is built upon the concept of *family*. It is within the arms of our families that we first experience unconditional love; a fundamental human emotion. We do not live our lives isolated here…" She tapped a finger hard to her temple. "… but through and *with* our families *here*." She placed a flat hand over her heart. "It remains the one dynamic that must never be stripped from humankind. If our population must be reduced, and I agree wholeheartedly that it does, a method must be found that is supported by all for the good of all."

"She speaks the truth," Gabriel added.

"Perhaps you failed to comprehend my words; propagating yourselves on an already overpopulated planet is purely a selfish act. Abeyance shall be the first step to your survival."

Catherine's brow went up, and she gushed sarcastically, "Perhaps you should return to Ecaep and leave us to solve these problems on our own. Might that be an option?"

"Your impertinence is disrespectful. I cannot allow you to—" He stopped mid-sentence, laced his hands behind his back, and sighed. "Let us approach this from a purely practical perspective, one I believe you can readily comprehend. Gabriel, please answer this question: Is there not an endeavor to store seeds?"

"Seeds?"

"Yes, seeds, they are being stored in the Svalbard Global Seed Bank on the Norwegian Island of Spitsbergen in the Svalbard archipelago."

"Well… yes, there is."

"Catherine?"

"I'm fully aware."

"Then you must know these vital seeds are stored for no other purpose than to prepare for a catastrophic event on such a grand scale it would cause all life-sustaining plants to be extinguished."

"It's a precaution," Gabriel said, "not a foregone conclusion."

"Come, come, you are both aware that such an undertaking is not a mere precaution."

Neither offered an argument.

"Our assistance ensures that such a disastrous day does not fall upon you. For that alone, mankind should be eternally grateful." Then abruptly, he turned his back to them. "We must continue on now."

Both were prepared to argue further, but before they could, the invisible door glided opened. An Ecaepian citizen stood outside, his eyes laser-focused on Legna.

"May I present Citizen Masma? He shall prepare you for our journey."

Masma stood quiet, neither acknowledging them, nor making eye contact.

Catherine, still in angry mode, blurted, "So that's the end of the discussion as decreed by you?"

"I shall seek your counsel when I deem it appropriate, Citizen Catherine."

"Might that be in my lifetime?"

Her snarky remark was leading to yet another pissing match. Trying to avert further confrontation, Gabriel changed the subject. "I have a question; where is *Ecaep* and just how do we get there?"

Catherine shot a glance at Gabriel and fumed. "I'm not finished."

Legna's attention was on Gabriel. "You asked two questions."

Gabriel rolled his eyes. "All right then, *two* questions."

"Which would you prefer I address first?"

"*Ecaep*—where is it?"

Catherine blew a hard breath. "First, reply to *my* question!"

Ignoring Catherine, Legna tapped the blank wall next to the open door three times. What looked like a large schematic diagram containing thousands upon thousands of dots of varying sizes appeared. The larger dots were labeled with algebraic-looking symbols. "Contrary to what benighted humans believed before our arrival, Earth is not the center of the universe."

Breathing fire now, Catherine crossed her arms over her chest.

Legna pointed to a remote section of the wall image. "Ecaep is in the Nantopia galaxy." He tapped the wall to enlarge the area and pointed. "Ecaep is here."

He tapped the wall again, which enlarged the graph even further. Now they could see a sphere clearly labeled *Ecaep*. In relationship to their the sun, the number of planets and their positions within the Nantopia galaxy mirrored those in the Milky Way. Ecaep was smack in the *Goldilocks Zone,* as it was referred on Earth.

"My God, it looks like our Milky Way."

"All life-giving zones and all life within all universes are created equal by the one true force, the *Originator.*"

"The Originator?" Gabriel questioned. "If what you told us in Utah was truthful—"

"I assure you it was."

Catherine said, "Then based on that, we're the consequence of *your* experiment, not this *Originator* you refer to."

Legna's eyes bore into Catherine's. "And for that, you should be eternally grateful." He tapped the wall, and the map vanished. "You shall rest now."

Gabriel arched an eyebrow. "Wait, we have more questions."

"Following your rest period your queries shall be illuminated."

"Wait," Gabriel said. "How long will it take to reach Ecaep?"

Legna placed a reassuring hand on Gabriel's forearm. "Be trustful, and all will be revealed." And with that, he left.

Masma stepped into the room and stoically motioned to the two upright cylinders. "Please enter."

Finally, Gabriel thought, another Ecaepian speaks. But it might just as well have been Legna for the voice was identical in pitch and tone.

Masma motioned to the tubes again. "Please enter."

"What are those for?"

"For your comfort and safety during travel."

"Really? What happens in there?"

"They are for your comfort and safety."

Catherine eyed the tubes warily. "I am not getting into one of those unless I know why."

"You will rest for a brief period. When you become aware again, we will have arrived on Ecaep. You will experience no discomfort."

For no particular reason, Gabriel glanced at his wristwatch; it was 10:44 PM EST.

"Please enter and place your backs to the lining."

With a healthy dose of reservation, they each entered a tube and positioned themselves as instructed. Masma strapped Catherine in first: one strap across her chest, one just above her knees.

"Why are we being strapped in?"

"For your comfort, Citizen Catherine."

Once her straps were secure, Masma moved to Gabriel's tube and strapped him in. As he stepped clear, the doors to both tubes rotated to the closed position. Slowly, the cylinders began to tilt back until both were completely horizontal. Like a magician's illusion of levitation, they were floating two feet above the floor with no visual support structure beneath them.

Catherine turned her head toward Gabriel. He mouthed the words *I love you,* and she mouthed them back. The clear surface of the tubes began a slow transition to a deep shade of blue, and within a few seconds, they lost consciousness.

42

He was tumbling violently, end over end through a vortex whose walls resem-bled stormed-whipped ocean waves. Over and over Gabriel's body spiraled through the meandering twists and turns. And then suddenly, he was ejected into a vast, blue void free-falling down and down until his fall was broken by something soft. To his bewilderment, he had landed on a puffy white, gossamer cloud. Above, the sky was a vibrant periwinkle. Cool, fresh air assaulted his senses with the unmistakable scent of lilacs and a profound sense of tranquility washed over him. Peering over the cloud's edge, he saw nothing but an effervescent, azure vacuum.

Someone called his name—*Gabriel, Gabriel.*

"What? Who is it?"

Gabriel, Gabriel, he heard again before realizing it was none other than his mother's voice. He scanned the cloud, but Isabella was nowhere to be seen. And then, like an aberration, her shimmering figure appeared hovering at the far edge. She looked old and frail. With arms outstretched, she began to sing a lullaby she had sung to him as a child: '*Golden slumber kiss your eyes; smiles await you when you rise. Sleep, pretty baby, do not cry, and I'll sing you a lullaby.*'

"I'm here," Gabriel called to her. "I'm here!"

Isabella's ghostly image floated up into the blue and evaporated.

"Please mom, come back." But she was gone. "What's happening!?"

Laughing voices broke the silence. Where his mother had appeared, now there was an image of two young men walking across the University of Missouri campus. He recognized himself and his roommate, Owen Jennings. Carefree and laughing, the two young men walked among the other students with a youthful bravado. Jennings turned and looked across the cloud and waved, his face beet red and disfigured. He laughed as the image faded away.

Now Gabriel saw himself standing before an altar next to a pretty young woman in a white, flowing dress; it was his wedding day. He and his bride embraced and kissed, but the kiss was short-lived. They began to float away from one another farther and farther until that image, too, faded.

Gabriel closed his eyes and pressed his hands over them. "This isn't real! I'm dreaming!"

He opened his eyes to yet another image. He and his weeping mother were peering into a casket at his beloved father, Javier. Too much makeup had been applied to his face—he looked like a grotesque circus clown. Rosary beads were threaded through his folded hands. His eyes popped open, and he grinned wide, exposing discolored, yellowing teeth. His right hand rose toward Gabriel. The rosary beads slipped to the side of the casket as his image flared and disappeared.

Gabriel laid back on the cloud and screamed. He heard his name called again. Pushing himself to a sitting position, he saw his beloved benefactor, President Conrad, standing by a window in the Oval Office, his shoulders slumped, his hands clasped behind his back. Slowly Conrad turned to Gabriel. "What are you doing on that damn cloud, boy?" Raising a clenched fist, Conrad lunged toward Gabriel, his image wavering like a hot, desert mirage before morphing into five charging Ecaepians.

The one on the far left spoke, *"It was the best of times. It was the worst of times. It was the age of foolishness."*

Then the second in line picked up. *"It was the epoch of belief. It was the epoch of incredulity."*

Gabriel couldn't believe what he was hearing; the Ecaepians were reciting the opening lines of *A Tale of Two Cities.*

The third alien continued. *"It was the season of light. It was the season of darkness."* Then the fourth. *"It was the spring of hope. It was the winter of despair."* Next was the fifth in line. *"We had everything before us, we had nothing before us."* And finally, all five called out in unison, *"We were all going direct to Heaven, we were all going direct the other way."*

303

He panicked and rolled to his right and slipped off the edge of the cloud. With arms flailing aimlessly and legs buckling and unbuckling at the knees, he tumbled over and over into the endless blue nothingness.

"It's a dream! Wake up, wake up!"

If only he could rub his eyes, he knew he'd wake up, but his arms were thrashing about wildly. Finally, straining his facial muscles until he thought they would burst, his eyelids popped open like a soda can. He blinked several times and focused; he was staring into the face of an alien. He tried to move, but could not.

"It is I, Masma," the diminutive creature said and proceeded to free Gabriel from the restraining straps.

Gabriel swiveled his head to Catherine. She was still strapped inside her tube. Her eyes were open, but she looked dazed and confused. "Catherine?"

"She is well. You may stand now." Masma proceeded to Catherine's tube to undo her straps.

Unsteady on his feet at first, Gabriel moved to Catherine's cylinder and guided her out. "Hey."

Catherine smiled. "Hey, yourself."

"How do you feel?"

"Like I just slept 20 hours. What about you?"

"I'm fine." He looked at his watch. It was now 10:50 PM. He tapped at the clear casing cover several times.

Rubbing at her eyes, Catherine asked, "What is it?"

"We entered these contraptions at 10:44. My watch shows 10:50. Here, look for yourself."

"It must have stopped."

"No, it's still running" He held his wrist out to Masma. "Is this right? Where's Legna?"

"Citizen Legna awaits your arrival." Masma stepped out into the hall and waited.

Gabriel whispered to Catherine, "I had one hell of a dream."

"About what?"

"I'll explain later."

Masma delivered them to a circular room on level two whose walls, floor and ceiling were coal black. A narrow shaft of light from an unseen source spilled onto an alien seated in front of a curved video screen covered with unrecognizable symbols.

Gabriel strained to see in the dimly lit room. "Where are we?"

Before Masma could reply, the door slipped open and light spilled in. It was Legna. Masma nodded respectfully and left.

"Are you feeling well?" Legna spoke cheerfully as if what they had just experienced was nothing more than a harmless ride at a theme park.

Catherine responded first. "I'm not sure what happened in that tube, but—"

"When we exited that tube," Gabriel held out his watch, "It was 10:50. When we entered it was 10:44."

"Your time mechanism is free of error," Legna said. "We have arrived at our destination."

"In 6 minutes?"

A low guttural laugh escaped Legna's throat. "As I previously stated, the universe moves in but one direction—forward. There is neither past nor future, only single moments; one fleeting moment advances to the next... we are always moving forward."

"That may be so in your world," Gabriel said, "but in ours, we have memories and I remember dreaming and it lasted more than 6 minutes."

"As I have previously clarified, human memories are but a temporary reality, bridging your past with your present to reinforce a sense of self. Unfortunately, it often leads to contentious altercations over issues no longer relevant. In time, intellectual advancement will render memories unnecessary."

Catherine's left eyebrow raised half an inch. "That may be so, but we humans *learn* from past memories."

"Imagine you no longer require memory of events past, that all exploits occur in moments going forward. You will avert previous missteps, for there is no memory of them. You would be in control of your *present* actions, not reactions to previous events."

Gabriel tapped his watch again. "You still haven't explained what happened in that tube in a mere 6 minutes."

"Very well. Let us refer to the phenomenon as *flash travel*. We do not travel to destinations, but transport them to us. Envision a tunnel to another dimension with each end at separate points in space-time providing a shortcut in real time."

"Space-time tunnels: This theory is known to us," Catherine said.

"And yet, it is only a *theory* on your planet, is it not?"

"Well, yes, but—"

Legna brought the index finger and thumb of his right hand together. "A single moment is frozen between point A and point B. At that moment, the distance between the two becomes zero." He dropped his hand to his side. "I fear further commentary will fail to provide the clarity you seek."

"There you see," Gabriel sneered, "you enjoy patronizing us."

Legna sighed. "I have yet to assimilate your impetuous need to delve into areas that remain beyond your understanding. Curiosity is encouraged, but patience and observation shall be your reward." He paused—his expression softened. "Forgive me, my petulance is inexcusable. I must work on that. Now then, let us advance. Rejoice in new knowledge and it shall bathe you in the clarity you seek."

Legna turned to the alien sitting at the control screen. The alien acknowledged with a bow of his head. He tapped a circular symbol and the overhead light extinguished plunging the room into total darkness.

"*lihatlah perdamaian*." Legna's voice spiked with exhilaration. "Behold Ecaep!"

A momentary burst of blinding white light filled the room. The walls suddenly came alive enveloping them in images of dense forests, hills and valleys, all in an elaborate mosaic of brilliant greens, yellows, reds, browns, and blues thoroughly imbued with deeply saturated Chroma and purity. Majestic forests led to expansive plains populated by great flocks of birds, big and small, swooping in and around complex terrain. Then came waterfalls and small tributaries flowing into streams and rivers, all interacting in a unique pattern of blue, mellifluous, silken threads.

Gabriel and Catherine stood speechless. Mere words could not express the unbridled euphoria they were experiencing from the grandiose images bombarding their senses. To their astonishment, what they saw mirrored much of Earth's topography. And yet, the unfolding spectacle had been cleaner, brighter. It was a hyper-enhanced version of what Gabriel had witnessed in the *Kebun* deep in the Indonesian jungle.

Catherine sucked in a quick breath, reached for Gabriel's hand and cradled it in hers.

A high mountain range resembling Earth's magnificent Rockies rose up before them like a majestic cathedral reaching for the heavens. Over the mountains, they flew, higher and higher until they could see a stunning view of the planet's curvature.

Something very large was taking form on the far horizon. It looked like an enormous white bull's eye, circles within circles, so many that it would have taken the largest land mass on Earth to hold it. Each white circle looked like a solid structure rising up 70 to 80 feet. Bridging each inner circle was thousands of connecting spokes surrounded by swaths of lush green foliage.

Wide-eyed, Gabriel spat out, "What in creation are we seeing?"

Legna's arms splayed out and up. "Jubia City!"

Catherine repeated, "Jubia City?"

"Home to Ecaepian citizens."

"Your entire population lives here? How many?"

"Three and a one-half billion."

Catherine's eyes widened in surprise. "Everyone in one city?"

"Jubia City is a closed-plane curve, circles within circles within circles, each connected by—I believe you call them spokes."

"That's incredible!" Catherine mouthed low.

The images were whizzing by at such high speed that soon they were approaching the center of the bull's eyes. It was dominated by a monolith three-times taller than any of the circular structures and its top angled into a pyramid. To the left of the monolith stood an unremarkable, square, flat-roofed building that resembled a warehouse. In the center of its roof was a large open orb.

"The black tower, what is it?" Gabriel asked.

Legna's narrow lips curled ever so slightly into a smile, but he made no attempt to explain the tower's function.

Before Gabriel or Catherine could question Legna further, the craft lunged forward at such great speed that everything below became a smear of passing white circles and fleeting glimpses of green patches. And then the screen went blank and they were plunged into darkness for a few seconds before the room was once again illuminated.

"We shall descend now."

Gabriel and Catherine were about to set foot on a planet somewhere in deep space in a galaxy they had no idea even existed. They were experiencing the unfettered exhilaration of being the first humans to explore an advanced alien society in a world beyond anything either could have imagined.

43

The lift deposited them in an underground area the size of half a football field. The all-white space was spotlessly clean and devoid of any equipment.

"We are in the area beneath our transport," Legna explained.

There was no way of telling how big the ship might be because it was cradled in a bowl with only a small section actually visible. Four aliens, presumably a service crew, silently breezed past them, entered the lift, and ascended to the small elevator to the hatchway above.

Gabriel took a deep breath and released it slowly.

Legna smiled knowingly. "Did I not clarify that Ecaep's and Earth's atmospheres are indistinguishable?"

Gabriel sucked in another breath. "Just checking."

They followed Legna over the gleaming white floor to a clearly marked outline of a door. As Legna approached, it slid back and to the left. They passed through to a pristine white, oval tunnel large enough to accommodate a full-sized locomotive. The only flat surface was the platform on which they stood; it extended out eight feet.

Legna waved a hand across the expansive tunnel. "We have entered Jubia's portage system in which citizens travel to any desired destination."

The tube ran into infinity in both directions. "There's no track." Gabriel said.

"And you expected one?" Legna answered smugly.

"Why is everything here white?" Catherine asked. "What is that stuff made of?"

"That *stuff* is Tantium and Sulium."

"I'm not familiar with either."

"Forgive me, in your language, Tantium and Sulium are similar in makeup to graphene and polymers. Combined with other materials, the result is what you see. Beyond that, my knowledge of the process is deficient. Our transport approaches."

From their right, a large oval, windowless, white cylinder floating silently on nothing but air, traveled toward them at a high-rate of speed. One hundred feet or so of the tube whizzed by before it stopped. A double-door section snapped back and to the left.

Legna motioned to the opening. "Come."

The interior of the transport resembled the exterior: white walls, floors, and seats all molded as one continuous piece. Three-quarters of the seats were occupied by identical-looking Ecaepians. Other than a few transient glances, they appeared undaunted by Gabriel and Catherine's presence.

"Please be seated," Legna instructed. "We will arrive at our destination shortly."

Still in a state of wonder, Gabriel and Catherine took their seats.

"Where are we going?" Catherine asked.

"Two-thousands of your miles."

"Two thousand! How long will that take?"

Legna smiled, but offered no explanation.

Gabriel looked to Catherine and rolled his eyes. She pursed her lips and rolled hers.

In just under 6 minutes, with no sense of movement or sound, the doorway opened again.

Legna stood. "We have arrived."

"How's that possible?"

Legna touched Gabriel's arm. "You have a saying, I believe; let your thoughts live outside the box."

"*Think* outside the box," Catherine corrected.

"Thank you, Citizen Catherine."

As they stepped clear of the transport, Catherine whispered to Gabriel, "Jesus!"

"What?" Gabriel asked.

"Just *Jesus*, that's all."

Gabriel glanced over his shoulder. Thirty to forty Ecaepians had crowded the door, but no-one was exiting. "What are they waiting for?"

"For us," Legna said.

"To do what?"

"You do test my patience."

Directly in front of them were six side-by-side individual square plexi-glass-looking boxes hugging the wall at ground level. Each was 8 feet deep by10 feet wide. Gabriel looked up and counted 5 stories.

"Come." Legna moved to the box farthest to the left. As he approached, a section of it simply dissolved providing an opening 2 feet wide and just over 5 feet tall."

"What just happened?" Gabriel whispered to Catherine. "It looks like a section just melted."

Legna smiled and entered the box. Catherine and Gabriel had to bend down and slip under the low opening. Once inside, the doorway 'healed' itself.

"More magic," Gabriel said.

The Ecaepians who had held back until they had exited the transport now crowded into the other boxes.

"I didn't see any rails or cables. How does this thing work?"

"This *thing*, Citizen Gabriel, rises on air."

There was a sound no louder than what they would normally hear from an air-conditioning vent and the lift began to rise. Up they glided until they reached the top level. The magical doorway appeared on the opposite side, and they exited into a wide windowless corridor bustling with hundreds of Ecaepians moving in a precise ebb and flow reminiscent of a precision drill team. Not one of the small creatures showed the least interest in the humans who had entered their realm.

"I'm beginning to think we're invisible," Catherine said to Gabriel.

"It wouldn't surprise me if we were."

The hallway was austere and white like all the areas they had encountered. The walls to their left and right featured outlines of doors. Like busy bees, Ecaepians were coming and going and entering and exiting through the doors. Gabriel craned to see in but the doors open and closed too quickly.

"I assume these are living quarters?" Gabriel said.

"There are five levels of citizen shelters in each aureole."

"If there are 3.5 billion living in Jubia City, that requires a lot of… what do you call these—apartments, dormitories?" Catherine asked.

"Citizen dwellings."

Legna finally stopped in front of a door that was taller than the others. It snapped back and to the left. "Your chambers."

Gabriel was the first to enter with Catherine close behind. To their surprise, the space resembled a small, well-equipped, standard hotel room back on Earth, only constructed of the Ecaepians favored white material. Curiously, on the left wall, there was a black area the size of a large bay window. A bed large enough to accommodate one sat against the right wall. At the far end were two gray upholstered chairs separated by a small, white end table. An open door to a corner cubicle led to a small powder room.

"Amazing," Gabriel quipped.

"How so, Citizen Gabriel?"

"Except for the white, this could be a hotel room back home."

"These chambers were designed to accommodate guests larger than ourselves." Legna nodded to the powder room. "With, as you can see, appropriate facilities."

"Do you get many?" Catherine asked.

Legna did not answer, but pointed to a door next to the powder room. "Your chamber adjoins, Catherine." He swiped his hand up the wall, and the room's illumination intensified. "You may set the desired level of luminance as you wish."

Gabriel asked, "Where are we, exactly?"

"Aureole 800."

"Aureole?"

"A halo," Catherine said.

"All aureoles are self-contained habitats—a small community within a large city. Now then, you may wish to rest and refresh yourselves. I shall take my leave."

Without further comment, Legna left.

"And just who was that masked man?" Gabriel cracked. He motioned to the black section of the wall. "He never explained that." He approached, and as he did, the black dissolved revealing a window. "Whoa!" He stepped back. "We got us a window."

Catherine joined him and peered out. "Whoa is right!"

By then night had fallen—the sky was jet black. But outside, five stories down it was as bright as daylight. Magnificent manicured gardens stretched across the space between their aureole and the next. Walkways meandered through over-flowing, rainbow-hued flower beds. Small pools of crystal clear water—some with gushing fountains—dotted the area. They were no roads, vehicles, or places of business. Several hundred Ecaepians strolled about or were gathered in small groups. None seemed to be engaged in face-to-face conversation.

A dithery laugh escaped Catherine. "I would not have believed this if not for my own eyes."

"No one is talking to anyone else."

"Communicating telepathically?"

"Look at them," Gabriel said with amusement, "mirror images of one another. How do they know who's who?"

They stood transfixed as they watched the unparalleled sights assailing them.

"Their technology and science leaves us in the dust," Gabriel said, "and yet it seems somehow all too simple."

"How do you mean?"

"I can't shake the feeling there's something going on here that we don't understand, something beneath the surface that warns me to not accept what I see as reality. President Conrad always said to exercise caution is to show wisdom. If there was ever a time to be vigilant, it's here and now."

Clearly, Ecaepians had transformed a unified body of knowledge into a collective theory of what they believed life should be. But the question remained:

Why had they revamped themselves and their planet in this way? What events had occurred to cause them to re-imagine and re-engineer themselves and their world?

A pulsating sound emanated from the door.

"Legna?" Gabriel called out.

"It is I, Masma."

Carrying two trays, Masma entered and set the trays down. The food looked like cubed white meat of some sort with white rice and two glasses of liquid.

"What might that be?" Catherine asked.

"Is it not what you call chicken nuggets and rice?"

"Yes, Chicken nuggets." Catherine glanced at Gabriel—he grinned. "We were wondering, since Ecaepians do not consume solids, what is your nourishment?

"Your inquiries are to be addressed to Citizen Legna." Masma inched toward the door. "Savor your sustenance, and I wish you a good rest."

"Wait, please, don't leave," Gabriel called to him.

Masma had one foot out the door—he stepped back. "May I make an inquiry?"

"Yes, of course."

"You are the first humans I have come into contact with. I am curious; how are Earth citizens at variance?"

Catherine thought for a moment. "Well, we are diverse in many ways, socially, culturally, our appearance. Why have Ecaepians choose the path they have?"

"It is not for me to articulate, Citizen Catherine."

Realizing engaging Masma in this way would gain them little in the way of information, Gabriel said, "Masma, thank you for the nourishment."

Catherine plowed ahead. "But why are all Ecaepians identical?"

Masma's lips pinched and his eyelids compressed. "Do not confuse our anatomy with a parallelism of thought." He tapped his right temple with his index finger "We are as singular as you."

"But it seems odd that—"

Gabriel jumped in. "Dr. Blake did not mean to suggest—"

"Rest well," Masma said and left.

Gabriel fumed. "Thanks, Catherine."

"For what?"

"You went at him pretty hard. It was a bad strategy."

"Strategy hell, I have questions and opinions too."

"Strong ones it seems."

"Hold on, macho man. If what you want is a demure, opinion-less companion, I can introduce you to some bimbos back on terra-firma who will gladly accommodate."

"All I'm saying is we need to use tact."

"I came on this journey, not as your wing man, but as an equal."

"Agreed, but pushing Masma won't gain us anything. I could see he was put off by your questions."

"Like you don't push Legna's buttons?"

"Jesus, you're bull-headed."

Catherine moved to him and planted a light kiss on his lips.

"What was that for?"

"The only way I know to save you from yourself."

"Very funny. All I'm saying is we remain diplomatic."

"Gabriel, love, it's in your blood to play the Washington two-step of diplomacy. We're not here to negotiate, we're here to uncover what they have in store for us lowly humans."

She was right, and Gabriel knew it. His skill as a negotiator and mediator was not what was required—investigation was. Moving to the window, he peered out at the mysterious world the Ecaepians had created. An entire race had succumbed to extraordinary measures for reasons yet to be fully revealed. And yet, this highly-advanced society appeared to be coexisting in complete social agreement, an achievement that had eluded humanity.

"By the way," Catherine said, "What about that dream you had?"

"Oh, that. It started just after we entered those tubes. It was surreal, I was floating on a cloud."

"A cloud?"

"Yeah, the only cloud in a blue sky and I... oh, hell, I can't explain it."

"And do you have these dreams often?"

"See, now you're making fun of me."

"I would never do that, cowboy."

"Okay, smart guy, out... go to your own room, I'm going to bed."

"Without me?"

"Sorry, bed's too small for two."

"A decision you will soon regret."

"Go—get some sleep. And take your chicken nuggets with you."

Gabriel drifted to sleep, only to awake several times with a start. Each time he swiped the wall and brought up the light to remind himself where he was.

Catherine was restless and couldn't sleep at all. Finally slipping out of bed, she made her way to Gabriel's quarters and crawled into his bed, which was barely large enough for one. Neither said a word. Wrapped tightly in each other's arms for fear one of them might fall to the floor, they finally fell into a deep slumber.

An hour later, a loud noise woke them. At first, the ear-splitting sound failed to register. Realizing it was coming from outside, they rushed to the black wall, tapped it, and stared. Horrific lightning flashes ripped across the dark sky, followed by deep, rolling thunder. Nevertheless, the storm appeared to have little effect on the activities down below. The area was daylight-bright. Countless Ecaepians moved about as if the tempest above was nothing more than a minor disturbance.

"What in the hell?" Gabriel whooped.

The storm was intensifying, yet the heavy precipitation wasn't reaching the ground. Gabriel craned his neck and scanned the sky. "I'll be damned; the rain is bouncing off something up there."

Catherine pressed her face to the window. "Yeah, I see it now."

"It must be a dome."

"Remember how Legna lingered in the rain before we entered that motel room in Utah? He seemed to be mesmerized by it. And he kept touching the condensation on the window and sniffing the tips of his fingers like maybe rain was new to him."

"I'm betting there's a shield of some sort up there," Gabriel said. "Jesus, they've buttoned themselves up in a hermetically sealed bubble."

"Over the entire complex?"

"We're talking about an alien civilization thousands of years old. Who knows what they can and can't do."

"First rule, love: Nothing on this planet has to be anything we understand. We've traveled to the land of OZ. Now the question is, what's behind the curtain?"

The next morning, Gabriel went directly to the window. The sun was just rising over Jubia's outermost circle. Down below mirrored the night before as throngs of Ecaepians milled about.

There was a knock at the door. "It is I, Masma."

Gabriel, still in his underwear, went to the door. "Yes Masma, what is it?"

"I have brought nourishment."

"We're not dressed; can you just leave it?"

"As you wish."

"Masma?"

"Yes, Citizen Gabriel."

"About that storm last night?"

"Yes."

"The, ah, the rain—it never reached the surface."

No response from Masma.

"Masma?"

"Citizen Legna will join you directly. Good day."

Gabriel uttered low, "So much for the art of conversation." He waited a beat before opening the door and retrieving the tray of food. Next to the tray, he found fresh clothing. "Assorted fruit this morning and fresh clothes."

Catherine came to a sitting position. "If they don't eat what we eat, where do they get this stuff?"

"Their friendly neighborhood supermarket?"

Forty-five minutes later, Legna arrived. Gabriel and Catherine were dressed in the clothing that Masma had left, which resembled West Point Cadet uniforms: gray slacks and waist jackets with an inch-high upright-collar that fit tight around the neck.

Legna half-smiled. "Good morning."

Gabriel ran his hands over the waist jacket. "My compliments to your tailor."

"My tailor?"

"Whoever made these outfits, they fit perfectly."

"Why would they not?"

Gabriel raised an eyebrow. "Right, why would they not."

They rode the underground transport in silence, surrounded by stone-faced Ecaepians who paid them no attention as if they were not there.

"Why do your citizens ignore us?" Gabriel asked.

"I have revealed this; it is a form of respect," Legna answered.

"By ignoring us?"

"You are honored guests."

"Back home, we actually *speak* to honored guests. At the very least we acknowledge their presence."

No response from Legna.

"All right, let's switch gears, how about last night's storm?"

"You are curious why the precipitation failed to reach the surface."

"I am."

"An impregnable force field protects citizens from displeasing elements." Legna offered the brief explanation matter-of-factly as if it was normal to live in a sealed environment.

"Don't you need rain?"

Unrecognizable symbols flashed on the ceiling. "Our destination approaches."

Gabriel checked his watch and whispered to Catherine, "However far we've traveled, it took all of 4 minutes."

Without making eye contact, the other Ecaepians allowed them to disembark first.

They rode a box lift to level five and exited to an open area the size of a football field. They were pleasantly surprised to see the walls were pastel blue. The floor was an intricate swirl pattern of blue and white marble with a large white dove emblem embedded dead center. A patch of black, three times the size of the one in their quarters, covered a portion of the right wall.

Legna walked to within 5 feet of the dove emblem and with a theatrical flourish said, "Welcome to *Ramah-Tamah Kamar*. The Gathering Place. It is here that all Ecaepians come to pay homage to our beginnings."

There wasn't an Ecaepian in sight. Except for the black portion of the right wall, there was nothing to even indicate what Legna might be referring to.

"Do you govern from here?"

"Ecaepian Citizens do not engage in formal governance, Citizen Gabriel. We are self-governed."

"How does your system work?"

"An advocate—a *Gubernur*—serves each circlet and answers to a three-citizen *Direktorat* who are charged with adjudicating issues."

"Like?" Gabriel asked.

Legna repeated, "Like?"

"What issues might come up?"

"Perhaps I should be conversing with Catherine. She appears to be less pugnacious."

Gabriel found that amusing, considering some of the contentious conversations that had taken place between Legna and Catherine. "I'm simply trying to understand."

Catherine, on the other hand, smiled, amused at how the two went at each other like boys arguing over who gets to toss the ball next.

Gabriel turned his attention to the black section of the wall. "Might that be another window?" Not waiting for Legna to reply, he ambled over. When he was within 10 feet, the black dissolved and a window appeared. Startled, he stopped cold and took a step back. "Whoa, more magic."

Directly outside was a sight to behold: the enormous, mysterious, black monolith shining like highly polished onyx. Silhouetted against the bright clear sky, the colossal structure looked quite sinister.

"We flew over that." Gabriel noted.

"The *Hitam Menara*, the tower of life."

"The what?"

"All in good time, Gabriel—please come."

As Gabriel backed away, the wall turned black again.

44

They tagged along behind Legna down an alabaster corridor. Considering his small size, Legna's stride was quick and deliberate and a challenge to keep pace with. S*tep, step, step*—he forged on in a military cadence that caused his bantam body to sway from left to right like a fast-moving pendulum. Legna stopped in front of bronze-colored double doors.

"We have arrived. Here we shall meet with Tonora, the chair of the Grand Directorate of Ecaep. Clarification shall be ministered."

As Legna approached the doors, both retracted silently into the wall. The room beyond was an eye-popping yellow: Walls, floor, and ceiling were as bright as a ripe banana.

"Someone with a paint brush went gonzo in there," Gabriel muttered.

Catherine poked his arm. "Behave yourself."

They entered the yellow room with no idea why they were there or what they were about to encounter. Only a few steps in, Gabriel stopped.

"What's the matter?" Catherine asked.

"I don't like the looks of this."

There were twelve rows of white seats on either side of a center aisle. An elevated rostrum was perched at the head of the room where three grim-faced Ecaepians sat. The setup resembled a venue where arguable matters might be reduced to order. On Earth, it would be akin to a courtroom where legal minds plied their trade.

They made their way down the aisle until Legna stopped by the first row of seats.

The Ecaepian sitting in the middle spoke. "Citizen Legna, good day."

Legna bowed his head slightly. It was clear that whoever Tonora was, he commanded great respect.

"Good day to you, Citizen Tonora." Then turning to Gabriel and Catherine, "It is my honor to present Citizen Tonora, Chair of the Grand Directorate of Ecaep and an exalted member of the Universal Council of Unified Planets." Legna made no mention of the two aliens flanking Tonora. "Citizen Tonora, I present Citizens Gabriel Ferro and Catherine Blake."

"Finally, we observe earthlings in the flesh." Tonora's voice was a bit throatier than Legna's. "Better than aging transmissions."

"Transmissions?" Gabriel repeated.

"Electronic signals that endure forever in the vastness of space. I find many from your planet quite amusing. I trust your visit has proven enlightening?"

"Yes, sir."

"There are no 'sirs' here." Tonora corrected. "You shall address me as Citizen Tonora, and I shall address you as Citizen Gabriel and Citizen Catherine. Is this acceptable?"

Gabriel nodded. "Yes, it is. And may I say, I would have never dreamed such an extraordinary adventure possible."

Tonora smiled slightly. "All things are possible."

"I have always believed there were others."

"More than all the grains of sand on Earth's seashores."

"May I ask the purpose of our coming before you this morning in this judicial-like setting."

Tonora's eyes shot to Legna. "Citizen Legna, was the function of this assembly not clarified to Citizen Gabriel? Why does he question me?"

"I assure you Citizen Gabriel is simply inquisitive, and not disrespectful."

Catherine lowered her head and grinned.

The two other "judges" sat stoically, eyes straight ahead.

Clearly this throat, Tonora spoke. "To the purpose of our engagement. We wish to address an unresolved matter. On behalf of all Ecaepians, I extend our belated atonement for our abandonment of human society."

"And yet," Gabriel said decisively, "great harm and suffering resulted. And although I applaud your apology, I have no authority to accept it on behalf of mankind."

Tonora shot a stern look to Legna, then back to Gabriel. "Are you not a rightful official?"

"I served the late President of the United States as his chief of staff. I wield no authority beyond that."

"And yet Citizen Legna has engaged you, has he not?"

"If you mean am I assisting him, yes. I have accepted that role in the hope that good will comes of all this. The question I have for you is, just how do you intend to atone for what you have readily admitted?"

"A fair question, Citizen Gabriel. Humans will come to know peace, harmony, and balance."

"But despite your expressed intentions," Catherine said, "your worship's circle our planet, creating uncertainty, fear, and anxiety, which transform into a desire for retribution."

Tonora expression slackened. "Such retribution would be unwise, for we offer enlightenment, not impairment. To clarify in terms that should resonate; Humans will be extinct in less than one hundred of your years due to unbridled consumption, overpopulation, and environmental destruction. These unfortunate developments have cast a dark shadow, posing challenges beyond your ability to solve." Tonora picked up what looked like an electronic tablet. He studied it for a moment and then read from it. *'The planet looks very, very fragile, like something that we need to take care of...'* These words were spoken many years past by human astronaut Mark Kelly as he circled high above your globe in that little space vehicle you called Spacelab."

"I am familiar with what Mr. Kelly said," Gabriel said flatly.

"And yet, astronaut Kelly's words appear to have fallen on deaf ears, for corrective action has yet to be aggressively pursued. Might it be historical amnesia?"

Gabriel began to comment, but Tonora waved him off.

"No need to amplify, Citizen Gabriel. The fact that these issues remain unresolved is sufficient illumination." Tonora set the tablet down, folded his hands, and placed them on the rostrum. "For reasons we fail to comprehend, the human mindset impedes advancement. Mankind defers to social, political and economic disruption, rather than peace, harmony, and balance."

Gabriel shifted uneasily from one foot to the other and folded his arms across his chest.

Catherine tugged gently at his sleeve.

"What?"

Her eyes went to his arms. Realizing his body language was sending the wrong signal, he lowered his arms to his side. "I readily admit we have yet to overcome dysfunctional behavior that undermines our advancement."

"I find your candor refreshing, but somewhat puzzling. Surely, wise men within your society have come forth with viable solutions."

"There have been many. Unfortunately, the human condition causes men to dissent."

"You are forthright, Citizen Gabriel. It is admirable." Tonora waved a hand. "Do you have a trading note on your person?"

"Trading note?"

"A currency note," Legna prompted.

"Yes, of course." Gabriel dug into his pocket, retrieved his money clip, and removed a twenty-dollar bill.

Tonora said, "Please hold it aloft."

Gabriel raised the bill to eye level.

"Pass it to me."

Legna took the bill from Gabriel and handed it up to Tonora. He turned it one way and then the other, examining it. "This worthless bit of paper is a demoralizing system that encourages deception and greed, allowing an unscrupulous minority to accumulate wealth and undue influence, while others descend into subservient poverty. For capitalism to survive, inequality is fundamental, is it not?"

"Placing value on goods and services is rooted firmly in our history," Gabriel explained. "As far back as when shells, stones, and beads were used as currency. I readily admit it is a complex structure that benefits some more than others."

"It certainly does," Tonora retorted.

"It would require many generations to move humans away from the only economic system they understand."

"It is a demoralizing system, Citizen Gabriel. A society advocating the acquisition of great wealth as a goal cannot survive morally, economically or politically." He waggled a finger. "Why the impoverished often hold elitist capitalists in high esteem is beyond understanding. If a civilization were to be created from a blank slate, they would be well advised to distribute resources equally."

"That has been tried, Citizen Tonora; they called it socialism and communism—both have failed."

"This worthless piece paper is nothing more than a distraction." Tonora tore the bill in half and tossed it aside. "It is meaningless to a fulfilling existence. During your stay, you will discover that all Ecaepians enjoy equality—none rise above any other in stature or position."

Tonora abruptly went silent, his eyes straying to one side of the room and then to the other. Gabriel had witnessed this often with Legna; his attention would wander in the middle of a conversation as if his consciousness had shifted to another place and time entirely.

"Yes," Legna said, "we must be open and honest."

And there it was. They had exchanged thoughts telepathically.

Catherine raised a hand. "Excuse me, may I say something?"

For the first time, Tonora actually smiled. "By all means, Citizen Catherine."

"We understand all that you have said."

"Then we are reconciled."

"With respect, I fear you fail to grasp the multiplicity of our civilization. From the genesis of your experiment in the Kebun, human civilization evolved, developed diverse lifestyles, social statuses, and economic standings. There are 190 separate countries on our planet and as many as 5,000 ethnic groups practicing over nineteen major religions with as many as 300 sub-groups all—"

"Yes, yes, we are aware."

"Then you must also be aware of the enormous obstacles you face attempting to transform an entire society to something they are not."

Tonora's spine straightened, his eyelids constricted, and he grimaced. "Regardless of the challenges, the transformation *will* proceed as planned."

Now it was Gabriel's turn. "Do you really believe you'll snap your fingers, and poof, mankind will morph into what *you* think they should be? I encourage you to think again, sir."

Tonora's torso shot forward until it was up against the podium. "Perhaps you will temper your tone, Citizen Gabriel."

"I meant no offense. I'm trying to explain."

"Then do so without rancor."

"My apologies. What I was trying to say is that from the time of hunter-gatherers, humans have tried and failed to create a truly altruistic society. For reasons I cannot explain, a preliterate social division spawned early on in our history in the form of ethnic tribes. For centuries upon centuries, these tribes preyed upon one another for any number of reasons. Your guiding hand was needed back when your Kebun experiment failed and humanity was spawned. If I understand you correctly, you plan to force upon us extreme changes with or without our cooperation."

Tonora eyed Gabriel for a long moment before dropping the bomb. "Course corrections have already begun."

"What does that mean exactly?"

Tonora said to Legna sharply, "Have they not been enlightened?"

Catherine eyes narrowed and she stared at Legna. "What is he referring to?"

Legna hesitated before saying in a low voice, "Curtailment has begun."

"Curtailment of what?" Gabriel asked.

Rendering a scolding look to Legna, Tonora pushed back against his chair. Several beats passed before he said, "Your planet has been sown. Humans have been rendered barren."

Catherine's jaw dropped and her face went pale. "My God, what have you done?"

Tonora's voice spiked up. "What mankind should have done for themselves."

Gabriel was damned if he would label it as anything other than what it was. "By rendering humans infertile? That is clearly feticide."

Confused by the word feticide, Tonora looked to Legna.

"He accuses us of terminating new life, Citizen Tonora."

"We have done nothing of the sort, Citizen Gabriel." Tonora leaned forward aggressively and his voice spiked up. "Humans are slaves to their most insatiable, animalistic cravings, rendering them incapable of creating peace, harmony, and balance. We, therefore, will do so for you."

Unable to hold back his rising anger, Gabriel took a step forward and raised a clenched fist. "By what authority do you get to decide? You are not judge and jury!"

Tonora folded his arms and said nothing.

Gabriel lowered his fisted hand to his side. "I have a message for you, Citizen Tonora, one that you should listen to carefully. Humans treasure family life above all else. To exclude children is to decimate our society, not save it. I ask you, sir, where is your progeny? We've seen none."

Tonora became visibly agitated and shifted in his seat. "Enough! Further discourse on this subject is of no further significance. Now then—"

Gabriel erupted, "*Now then*, hell! That you deem yourselves as our Savior does not make it so." Almost immediately he realized his mistake and softened his tone. "Your knowledge, your technology, if offered without conditions, is welcome. But to simply replicate Ecaepian life on Earth is not and will not be acceptable, despite how reprehensible you think us to be."

Gabriel's outburst brought a momentary silence as Tonora and Legna traded looks.

Tonora's face contorted into a tight scowl. "I remind you, Citizen Gabriel, that at one-time humans believed their planet to be flat and occupied a fixed position, while other spheres revolved around it. I could navigate your history with more of the same, but my point is made, is it not?" He abruptly stood and the two Ecaepians flanking him followed. "As Chair of the Grand Directorate of Ecaep, and with the consent of the Universal Council of Unified Planets, I have fulfilled the task given me. May the remainder of your stay with us be joyful."

With a cold, determined stare, Gabriel shouted, "Wait a minute! We're not done here!"

Tonora and his two silent associates stepped from the platform and sauntered off through a side door.

They would never see Tonora again.

45

Distraught by what they had endured at the hands of Tonora, Catherine and Gabriel followed Legna back to the Gathering Place in silence. It was still deserted.

Angling for a dust-up, Gabriel lashed out. "What happened back there wasn't a discussion, but a one-sided trial rendering the human race guilty as charged."

Legna calmly replied, "Pity you perceived it as such when in fact it is an opportunity freely given."

"For who?"

"For all mankind, of course."

"Pure damn hogwash! If you are so bent on helping us, there are less drastic ways than sterilizing an entire civilization."

"What you rail against is the method employed to achieve the objective, not the objective. Humans allow their emotions and prejudices to dictate how challenges will be confronted when what is required is absolute resolve. Emotions must be removed from such decisions."

"Call it what it is—murder!"

"I will not dignify your impassioned outburst."

"But you've removed the most important aspect of human life," Catherine argued. "You speak of living with joy, yet this decision will only bring profound sadness."

"As a child learns from its begetters, so shall humans learn from the source that granted them life."

"Granted us life? You granted nothing but pain and suffering."

"Restrain your fervor Citizen Catherine, for nothing shall be gained by—"

Cutting him off, Catherine lashed out. "Okay, try this on for size; if the transformation's path has already been decided, why do you need this man to front your... your coup d'état."

A knowing smile came over Legna's face. "I am familiar with this term; it is beneath you."

Her eyes flashed with rising anger. "Do *not* patronize me. Answer my question! Why do you keep pulling him in?"

"Citizen Gabriel commands the discipline required to lead upon our departure."

"And if he chooses not to?"

"His wishes shall be honored, Citizen Catherine."

Catherine looked to Gabriel expecting him to weigh in, to say something, anything. "Well? You're okay with this?"

Gabriel turned to her. He stared, she stared back waiting for him to say something. Instead, he turned to the black area on the far wall. "That obelisk, you called it the *Hitam Menara*."

Seething, Catherine delivered a stinging rebuke through clenched teeth, "You just changed the damn subject!"

Gabriel crossed the Gathering Place until the coal-colored section dissolved into a window once again. The mysterious tower stood like a dark angel guarding the gates of hell, its pyramid-shaped top jutting toward the cloudless blue sky like a rocket waiting to be launched.

"Exactly what is that?"

"It is not the moment for clarity," Legna said.

"When is the moment for *clarity*?"

Legna turned away. "Come, there are other matters requiring—"

"Wait!" Catherine said sharply. "If this is a trip of discovery, then everything is fair game. Answer Gabriel's question—what is that thing?"

"You test my patience yet again, Citizen Catherine."

"You test mine—we're even."

Legna shook his head disapprovingly. "Humans are a persistent lot."

"We hear that a lot," Gabriel shot back. "I'm not moving until we get an explanation."

Catherine's head bobbed toward Gabriel. "You're looking at one stubborn Cuban. Better explain what that thing is, or we'll be here all day."

Legna breathed in slowly; his exhale sounded like a long sigh. With measured steps, he approached the window, his eyes scanning the black structure from ground level to its peak. There his stare lingered several moments before he finally whispered, "Within lies the nucleus of all that exists, the indomitable force of all universes."

"Gravity, electromagnetism, strong and weak nuclear forces? Which one is this?"

Legna smiled. "You disclose only what you know, Catherine, but fail to imagine what you do not."

"This structure is obviously of major significance, or it wouldn't be sitting prominently dead center of Jubia City," Gabriel rattled off. "So, cut to the chase, take us to the finish line."

Like a clichéd western shootout in a ramshackle town in the middle of a muddy street, the four-foot alien and the six-foot-one sheriff stared each other down.

To Gabriel's surprise, Legna blinked first. Moving closer to the window, the alien said in a calm, controlled voice, "Let us begin with the mystery of dark matter and dark energy. They are the glue that holds galaxies, stars, solar systems, as well our being, intact.

"This we know," Catherine said.

"But only a small fraction of matter is *Tokcolian*."

"Tokcolian?"

"Forgive me, Citizen Gabriel, in your language the translation would be *baryonic* matter."

"Baryonic?" Gabriel questioned.

"Matter composed of protons and neutrons," Catherine explained. "Ordinary matter as distinct from exotic forms."

"How do you know that?"

"I read, I absorb, I learn."

Gabriel was about to zing her back, but Legna spoke. "If I may have your attention. There are four conventionally accepted fundamental interactions and—"

Catherine piped up, "Gravitational, electromagnetic, strong nuclear, and weak nuclear."

"There is yet a fifth force." Despite his initial reluctance to explain the black tower, Legna seemed eager now to share its secret. "After many eons, we discovered that beyond the effect matter has on the amount of gravitational force influencing any given area, it also interacted with itself within galaxies and clusters of galaxies, modifying the predicted mass distributions of dark energy. But the challenge was to understand the nature of what was hidden within those distributions. Which brings us to your inquiry, Gabriel. The tower gathers *Pencipta*."

"Pencipta?"

"The *Originator*."

Finally, there it was, the Originator Legna had previously alluded to, the transcendent intelligence he claimed was the creator and architect of all that existed.

"Within the tower is gathered the eternal essence of all that ever was and all that will ever be—the very author of our being."

"We're well aware of dark energy. But there's no science to support it to be a practical energy source."

Legna cracked a wry smile. "As we all know, Catherine, your science is categorical."

"I was simply pointing out that human science—"

"But your brightest minds have yet to identify the subatomic particles in dark energy. That and that alone is the secret which, once discovered, allowed us to harness its infinite power." He pointed a long bony finger and pointed to the obelisk. "There dark matter is gathered and the force of dark energy separated, collected, and distributed throughout Jubia City." Legna approached the wall until he was standing within a foot of it.

Gabriel and Catherine were speechless at the very idea that within the confines of the black monolithic was an energy source so independently powerful, Legna credited it with being the supreme creator.

Legna drew a breath, held it, and expelled it slowly before speaking just above a whisper. "If dark matter and dark energy were to end, all that exists would end."

"Could that happen?"

Legna left the question unanswered and abruptly turned away. "Come now, your enlightenment continues."

Standing in the shadow of the black tower and the mighty force locked within its walls, Gabriel thought of how insignificant and microscopic Earth and its inhabitants were in comparison.

Catherine came to his side. "Despite his reluctance, he was quick to give in."

"Maybe there's a chink in his armor we can exploit after all."

"Like what?"

He nodded in the direction of the tower. "Build us one of those so we can tap into that energy source. But that crap about *The Originator*, it's just that, crap—a way to explain what they can't explain, just like us with our superstitions, prejudices, all created to make us feel better. Whatever is behind the mystery of our lives, it's not this Originator."

On the far side of the Gathering Place, Legna stopped, stood pole-straight with his arms by his side, his bald head slightly arched back. His eyes were locked on a spot where the wall and ceiling joined some 25 to 30 feet up. With a dramatic, sweeping gesture, he raised his hands with his extended fingers outstretched in line with the top of the wall. With a dramatic flourish, he announced, "Welcome to *Juil Suci*—Jubia's most Sacred Place."

Like a zipper opening, a black, two-inch wide line snaked down from the top of the wall to the floor. Silently, the wall split and silently parted to the left and right like large aircraft hangar doors creating a 20-foot opening. Beyond was the face of the warehouse structure they had seen opposite the black tower during their flyover. There was a 10 by 10-foot opening, which Legna passed through. As he did, the interior illuminated, revealing yet another building tucked away inside the warehouse.

Gabriel and Catherine approached the opening—what they beyond saw stopped them cold.

"God, it's right out of—" Gabriel exhaled without finishing his thought.

The structure was ancient in design. The imposing portico featured three rows of round alabaster columns: eight in the first row, four in the latter two. Two, enormous, bronze-colored doors dominated the entrance. Portions of both doors were covered with intricate engravings. Legna lightly touched the right one, and it glided open.

Other than a quick glance, Gabriel paid little attention to the ornate door engravings as he followed Legna to the interior. Ever the curious scientist, Catherine stopped to examine the designs more closely. What she saw jolted her. There, on the left door, were lines of hieroglyphics like those found in the tombs of Egyptian royalty: static, abstract drawings of tools, birds, snakes, boats and more. She traced a finger lightly over one in the shape of a lion. "What are these doing here?"

With heightened curiosity, she turned to the right door to find astrological symbols representing all 12 zodiac signs. Below those were lines upon lines of what looked like cuneiform, wedge-shaped characters used by the Ancient Akkadians, Assyrians, Babylonians, and Persians. Below that was Bahasa Indonesia, a version of the early Malay language. There were also lines of binary code used in computer processor instructions. And then something else caught her eye. Between the Bahasa and binary code was Albert Einstein's Theory of Relativity: $E=MC^2$.

"Oh, My God!" she said in a forced whisper.

Excited to share with Gabriel what she had found, she dashed ahead to catch up. But once inside, she was so taken by what greeted her, she said nothing of her discovery.

The expansive, cylinder-shaped interior rose to a four-story high hemispherical dome. The only visible light source illuminating the semi-dark interior came from an unglazed Oculus at the dome's center that sent a lustrous shaft of sunlight to the white dove emblem embedded in the gold-hued, granite-like floor. A continuous, luminous, color-coded 3D map covered the circular walls with hills, valleys, flatlands, and great bodies of water. Six regions were highlighted in different colors and were identified as Cota, Frova, Dova, Aroa, Fora, and Gova.

"What is this place?" Catherine's voice echoed throughout the vast rotunda.

Legna stood silent, pensive, his eyes scanning the map from section to section as if seeing it for the first time.

Examining the map, Gabriel asked, "Is that what we flew over?"

"It is." Legna answered.

"I'm confused. You said everyone lives here in Jubia City."

"That is so."

"Then what's out there?"

"At one time, all citizens lived in the six provinces. Upon the completion of Jubia City, they provinces were repurposed."

"In what way?"

"Did you not witness their splendor?"

"Yes, but…" Gabriel glanced at the map again. "You re-engineered an entire planet? How is that even possible?"

"Allow inspiration to propel you beyond perceived limitations, and you will know all that you imagine is possible."

The alien's eyes flitted across the wall map, then up to the Oculus and down to the dove emblem. He ambled across the stone floor and stared at the dover for several moments before arching his head back and gazing up to the dome again. "No society can rise to greatness if segments are impeded, for the very survival of a civilization demands a compelling, unified vision. We once governed with such a vision. For many eons, the six regions, although autonomous, coexisted in great harmony."

His tone was even, his volume low, his delivery slower than usual. "We had reached a period when advancements in science and technology came easily: We prospered, often before the citizenry was prepared for such amelioration. Soon, it consumed us and invaded our cohesiveness, which led to a hunger for more far beyond our needs. Before long, the clouds of life grew dark. Unscrupulous deceivers seeking greater recognition and fortune mislead the multitude into believing that *their* prosperity would flow to the benefit of all."

Slowly, he turned to them, his eyes vacant as if verbalizing such memories caused him anguish.

"Our collective behavior had slowly drifted to a new paradigm that preached: All that brings pleasure is inherently good and right, a deceptive narcotic that disenfranchised those less fortunate. Pernicious coalitions within the six tribes began to compete for what was there. In the name of irrational growth and progress, resources were rapidly depleted as our numbers increased. Our treasured habitat was being plundered by those who cared not for the future."

Like a ghostly parallel dimension playing out for their benefit, Gabriel and Catherine stood in rapt silence, stunned by the unmistakable similarities between Ecaep's past and Earth's present.

"For our society to survive, it was imperative intrinsic barriers be removed if we were to retain a sense of self, but acknowledge the whole. However, it was not to be, for correcting our serpentine course would not come before we had lived many legions."

Suddenly, an inquisitive look came over Gabriel's faced. He turned a quick 360 degrees. "The size, the shape, the dome…" And then like an errant thought connecting with the mind's often elusive memory, recognition struck like a lightning bolt; this building was a duplicate of a magnificent ancient structure he had once visited.

Legna smiled knowingly. "I wondered how long it would take you."

"Damn you, you're in my head again." Gabriel's eyes shot up to the Oculus. "But this can't be!" He laughed nervously. "Except for the absence of ornate altars and interior columns, this could be… the *Pantheon*."

Catherine spun first to her left, then to her right. "The what?"

"I toured it when President Conrad was a senator. We were in Rome attending a trade mission. This structure is a duplicate of the Pantheon!"

"You are privileged to be standing in the original," Legna said, "built on this very spot by Ecaepian ancients many millenniums before your world came into being. It is preserved here as a hallowed reminder of our provenance." Legna clasped his hands behind his back and strolled across the ornate floor. "There were three structures at the Rome location. The first, built by Emperor Marcus Agrippa, was a rectilinear, T-shaped design. It was destroyed by fire. Emperor Domitian resurrected it only to have it struck by lightning, which caused the second fire. Finally, in your year AD 118, Emperor Hadrian commissioned it to be resurrected yet again."

"But how could Hadrian possibly duplicate what he had never seen?"

"Have you omitted from your memory the genesis of mankind?"

Gabriel glowered. "I haven't forgotten who abandoned us."

Legna shot back. "Why must you keep recalling such adverse thoughts?"

"Because that errant slip of a gene caused us to—"

"Hold on, both of you," Catherine scolded. "We're going over ground already explored. Can we get back to Hadrian? Gabriel?"

Gabriel took a breath and nodded.

"Yes, we failed to intercede in mankind's evolution, but remained cognizant of your advancements and from time to time interceded. Emperor Hadrian's rebuilding of the Pantheon is but one minor occurrence. The good Emperor awoke one morning to find detailed renderings by his rest area. Having no idea how they materialized, he simply presented them as his own."

Legna chortled and strolled off again, stopping to stare at sections of the wall map. "Like all societies throughout the universes, early Ecaepians pursued the mysteries of their origins. Charlatans who held sway over the masses preached that a divine deity was the answer. A new paradigm was born that prevailed until we discovered the infinite power of the Originator and the truth was revealed; The universes were a force wholly unto themselves, untouched by a mythical hand. But it was for naught, for such enlightenment failed to protect us from our inherent weaknesses."

Legna swiped a hand across the lower section of the wall. The map was replaced by a series of blank panels. Turning to Gabriel and Catherine with an impassioned expression, he said, "In that unseemly lodging in the area you call Utah, I attested to man's beginnings. I said to you then, and I say to you now, what I reveal I do with great reservation, for it may serve to turn you against us. There can be no trust without truth; I offer truth and seek your trust."

He swiped a hand across the wall again. The first three panels lit up as black and white paintings. The brush strokes were smeared as if the artist intended the primitive-looking scenes to be vague.

"These ambiguous compositions represent testaments authored by our earliest citizens. They have been passed from one begetting to the next through oral history, but speak a true message."

To Gabriel and Catherine's astonishment, the figures in the rough illustrations looked astonishingly human.

"My God, the similarities are—"

Legna finished Gabriel's thought. "Miraculous?"

Catherine's voice cracked. "How can this be?"

"You place far too much mystery in that which you perceive to be foreign."

"But the similarities?"

"All universes consist of particle substances that cannot be separated into simpler substances, thereby ensuring that all there is and all that follows emanates from the same source. Only evolution and environment determine which path civilizations will follow.

Gabriel eyed the painting with disbelief. "I'm speechless."

"However, unlike humans, Ecaepian did not evolve into divergent races; we have no insight as to why." Running a single finger over the back of his left hand, he said soberly, "Despite the absence of diversity, below this veneer all civilizations throughout all universes share analogous beginnings."

Hearing those insightful words, Gabriel recalled how President Conrad had made the same analogy when relating the story of his African ancestor, the slave girl, Atiya.

Legna swiped the wall again, and the remaining panels lit up. Each subsequent illustration was slightly more modern in style and vibrant colors and details were introduced until the last two depicted life in Jubia City. He moved to the fourth panel and swiped at the bottom from left to right. A monitor, stretching five feet across and three feet high, materialized in the middle of the painting. Moving images appeared in color, although the hues bled around the edges like old film stock.

"The citizens of the *Dova* district were the first to rise up against the inequality that had invaded the provinces."

On the right side of the screen, hundreds of demonstrators entered the frame. From the opposite direction, heavily armed soldiers marched in front of, alongside, and behind several armored-like vehicles. The demonstrators began throwing small objects. The soldiers opened fire, and within seconds the groups collided head-on in a brutal, bloody clash.

"Thus, began the struggle for equal standing of all citizens in all six provinces. The uprisings would lead to the eventual collapse of our civilization as we knew it." He abruptly stopped. "Enough!" He swiped a hand, and the screen vanished, and the map reappeared. "It troubles me to revisit such turbulent periods of our antiquity." Stepping back from the wall, he continued. "After many such encounters and much bloodshed, there began a forced period of political and social reconciliation. But it was not to be. Our numbers continued to expand and civil order followed. Conflicting ideologies led to isolated groups unable hear, to see, to compromise. Soon the *Raya Berperang*—the Great War—was upon us, which led to the death of over 800,000 citizens."

Legna's face was drawn, his shoulders stooped, his arms dangling by his side like loosely attached appendages. Drawing in a deep breath, he asked, "Is this not mankind's fate?"

"You know the answer," Gabriel said quietly.

Legna nodded and continued. "A new method of governing was required, one that would unite the six provinces under a single rule. A leader was chosen, a governing body created. But revolutionaries preaching separatism remained. To quell rising dissension, harsh sanctions were imposed, which led to an even greater divide, followed by a devastating second battle. To our credit, the bloodshed was short-lived; we realized such madness would not resolve the crux of what plagued us." Shaking his head in resignation, he continued in a subdued voice. "By then our lives and our planet were in disarray. Natural resources had been plundered, pollution darkened our skies. Changing weather patterns turned sustenance growing land into dusty, barren terrain. Soon famine swept across the land, followed by mass migrations. Ecaepian society was traveling in reverse."

Legna ran a hand over his bald head down to the base of his neck, lingering there for a moment before lowering his hand to his side and sighing. In his tortoise-like speech pattern, he continued. "Several generations would pass before..." He stopped.

The alien regularly used these starts and stops to heighten the listener's curiosity. Each skillfully chosen pause seemed calculated to cause them to pursue *him*. A less interested listener might dismiss it as clever theater, but here in these electrifying surroundings, his audience proved to be more than eager.

Catherine took the bait. "Several generations would pass before what?"

Legna strolled past several panels before turning back and staring with emotionless, vacant eyes that made it impossible to divine fact from fiction. "Allow me to use a word familiar to you: *Apocalypse.*"

"The end?"

"The beginning, Catherine, for the true definition is"

Gabriel spoke up. "From classical Greek, apocalypse translates to *the lifting of the veil* or *the revelation.*"

Legna forced a hesitant smile. "And the veil was lifted, and the unknown became known. The first step was to acknowledge our failings, to accept that both our citizens and our planet were on life support. What followed was an epiphany, a unified effort to restore the fundamental principles we had once held sacred. The first step was to control our surging numbers." He paused for several beats. "To that end, the citizenry was rendered... barren."

He said it all too casually as if it was just the first simple step in whatever process they had conjured up to reinvent themselves using whatever science was at their disposal.

Catherine's brow pressed down, and her lips tightened. Sensing her rising rancor, Gabriel brushed a finger lightly against her hand—a subtle signal they should allow Legna to elaborate. However, the alien's cold reflection had struck her like a blow to the stomach.

"My God, you said that with such dispassion as if it meant nothing."

"It meant *everything,* Catherine, *everything.* The very survival of our society was at stake."

"Just how many of you were there when this... this course correction began?" Gabriel asked.

"Seven billion."

"And..."

"Over time, aided by attrition, the citizenry was reduced to four billion."

The number rendered Gabriel and Catherine speechless.

Seeing their antipathy, Legna said, "Do not be quick to judge. Our solution was benevolent, unlike your wars that kill millions who are labeled collateral damage as if somehow that justified the madness."

Gabriel raised a clenched fist. "Don't you *dare* shift the blame to us."

Legna voice spiked up. "What you may denounce as extreme is not so when faced with unacceptable alternatives. I remind you that Earth's population will soon exceed nine billion. Surely, humans are not so ignorant they fail to comprehend your planet's boundaries. Imagine that you possess the knowledge, science, and technology to correct past missteps and forge a harmonious, balanced society. The reduction of our numbers was the first critical step in that process." Legna turned back to the wall and stood silently as he scanned the map of Ecaep. "But it was not to be. Like humans, our fragility continued unabated."

Catherine blew air hard through her nose. "After all that, you still failed?"

"We failed to harness the congenital defect that plagues all beings—the most uncontrollable and destructive trait: *ego*. It fosters arrogance, selfishness, and a sense of false entitlement. The only logical answer was to divest ourselves of this genetic flaw."

Catherine folded her arms across her chest. "And you viewed that as the final solution?"

"Believe whatever you wish. For Ecaepians, the question was, had we reached a natural limit of our inbred genetics? Could we, through science and technology, create a tolerant and giving society, one that could live in peace, harmony, and balance in concert with its surroundings?"

A light went on in in Gabriel's head and he finally pulled it all together. "Now the pieces fall into place. Those hybrids in the Kebun, they were your genetic guinea pigs to see if you could pull off the switch."

No reply from Legna.

"What was to be gained by playing God?"

"Peace, harmony, and balance."

Gabriel fumed. "That seems to be your standard answer for everything."

No reply from Legna.

"With all your advanced science and super technology, how could a petri dish miscalculation find its way to your Kebun hybrids?"

"An explanation will neither resolve nor advance your understanding."

Bristling, Gabriel shot back. "Let us be the judge of that."

"Very well, if you wish. Catherine, you are aware that code sequences determine the type of protein produced in any given cell?

"I do," Catherine answered. "What's your point?"

"The mechanical properties of DNA act as a *second* layer of information. It was in this less dominate layer that led to the genetic mutation in the Kebun hybrids."

"In other words," Catherine said with steely eyes, "a gene from your past, one that you had not intended to be present, surfaced. Have I got this right?"

"It serves no purpose to further question what is past."

"But now you feel *oh* so sorry for passing that errant gene onto us. How do you intend to rectify the problem? Turn us into you?"

Legna strolled back to the dove emblem and stared. After several moments, he placed a flat hand to the side of his head. "Within this vortex lives a most extraordinary and complex mechanism. It orchestrates the symphony of consciousness that continually stores new knowledge. To achieve the desired objective, modification, extraction, and preservation of each individual's cognitive powers was required."

Catherine looked appalled. "Surely, you're not suggesting what I think?"

"We possessed both the science and the technology to extract one's essence safely and successfully. An avatar was required that would shelter one's essence free from disease and decline." He turned, locking eyes first with Catherine and then Gabriel. "The result stands before you."

The very idea that their embodiment, their *avatar,* had been created and mass-produced in laboratory incubators, that an entire civilization willingly agreed to be transformed as a germ into an embryo, larva into an insect, struck them both as preposterous.

"This is nuts!" Catherine said pointedly. "I find it abominable that you speak so casually about turning an entire civilization into something other than—"

Gabriel raised a hand. "Hold on, this is not helping."

"If I may continue, two clusters of genes linked to cognitive functions were identified in each citizen and isolated. Advanced therapeutic procedures allowed for the enhancement and correction of select areas of the brain."

Catherine snapped, "Just which sections are we talking about?"

"The dormant capability to communicate through thought was awakened. Sectors that controlled hate, violence, greed, bigotry, carnal desires and envy were disarmed. The abridged physical carriage allowed for a lessened impact on the environment and would end forever discrimination and bigotry."

Gabriel sniggered. "While we're playing truth or dare, what about children? We've seen none."

"We are absolute—renewal is unnecessary."

Catherine shot him an incredulous look. "You live indefinitely?"

Legna nodded.

"You would deny new life in favor of your own immortality?"

"Once again you judge before you comprehend the benevolence employed to save a civilization that had lost is way, Catherine."

"And this avatar you created, its flesh and blood, it's real?"

"Am I not apparent?"

Neither Gabriel nor Catherine knew how to react or what to say. The very thought that the Ecaepians willingly underwent drastic alteration to their DNA and physical appearance was beyond comprehension, as was the concept of eternal life.

Finally, Gabriel asked in a barely audible voice, "Is this what is planned for us?"

Legna replied, "It is not."

"It is not, what?"

"You shall be gifted with eternal peace, harmony, and balance. If mankind chooses to go beyond, it will be their choice freely given."

"We have your word on that?"

"You do. The reduction of your numbers has begun. The cleansing of the environment will soon follow. The process of governing will be modified to assure equality for all, the ability to wage war terminated. Upon the successful completion of these undertakings, we shall gift mankind with science and technology to amplify their being."

Was any of this real or an elaborate illusion for unknown, nefarious reasons?

A still skeptical Catherine asked, "Why are you confessing this to us now?"

"Was I not transparent? We wish to atone for our deficiency and ensure the survival of your species."

"I understand the first part—the second may prove difficult for a civilization disparate from yours."

"A civilization doomed to perish if they do not embrace our patronage." Legna abruptly swung around and strolled toward the massive gold doors. Stopping by the inlaid white dove, he pivoted back. "All civilizations face a moment in history that propels or impedes their advancement. On behalf of your fellow citizens, I implore you to seize this moment."

46

As they traversed the corridor to wherever Legna was taking them next, they passed a number of Ecaepians silently going about their business. Neither Legna nor his fellow Ecaepians acknowledged one another.

"They act like zombies," Catherine whispered. And then she stopped cold and listened. "Do you hear that?"

Gabriel listened. "Music."

"Where's it coming from?"

"From behind those double doors over there."

And then they heard a voice begin to sing: *Nessun Dorma! Nessun Dorma! Tu pure, o, Principessa, nella tua fredda stanza....*

"I know those lyrics!" Catherine said with excitement. "I know that voice."

Legna smiled and said, "As well you should. Come."

As the approached the doors, they could hear the singer's voice clearly: *Ma il mio mistero è chiuso in me, il nome mio nessun saprà!*

Legna swiped his hand across the doors and they slid open. Gabriel and Catherine were presented with an unbelievable sight, one they could hardly have imagined would exist on an alien planet.

Some three to four-hundred feet away was a massive screen displaying the image of one of Earth's most revered Tenors: Luciano Pavarotti was singing: *No, no, sulla tua bocca lo dirò quando la luce splenderà! Ed il mio bacio scioglierà il silenzio che ti fa mia!*

Superimposed on the lower right corner of the screen was the familiar PBS logo.

Below where they stood was a half-bowl-shaped venue that plunged down as many as two-hundred rows. What had to be as many as twenty-five to thirty-thousand Ecaepians sat in rapt silence as Pavarotti performed.

Gabriel's mouth gaped, but nothing came out.

Catherine murmured, "Unbelievable!"

Legna smiled wryly. "All electronic transmissions float freely and forever in the vastness of space."

Pavarotti's voice swelled: *Dilegua, o notte Tramontate, stelle!* His ample body stiffened, his face quivered, his eyes wide: *All'alba vincerò! Vincerò! Vincerò!* The great tenor's body visibly shuddered with the last powerful thrust of his voice.

The on-screen PBS audience roared. Pavarotti sucked in a quick breath and held it as if he had achieved the pinnacle of joy. The ever-reserved Ecaepians, on the other hand, applauded politely—thousands of hands striking in perfect controlled unison: *clap, clap, clap.*

Legna was taking pleasure in Gabriel and Catherine stunned reaction. With a twinkle in his eye and a smile on his lips, he declared with a flourish, "On behalf of all Ecaepians, we thank you."

"No one would believe what we just saw!" Gabriel breathed under his breath.

When they returned to their temporary quarters, the sun had sunk low. It had been an unsettling and exhausting day, leaving them with more questions than answers.

"In the new day, we shall return to Earth," Legna told them. "Rest well. Masma will be along presently with nourishment."

He sauntered to the door, but Gabriel was still brimming with questions. "Wait a minute."

Legna did a slow turn.

"What we've witnessed today, an entire civilization that willingly accepted an extreme transformation—"

"Do not presume to judge what is and is not extreme. When mankind is faced with extinction, what you deem extreme will not appear so."

"You have surreptitiously chosen to keep this oppressive plan from our people. They have a right to know."

"Given the fragile human psyche, it was a prudent decision. In due course, your citizens shall be enlightened. Until then, to deflect further anxiety, you must not divulge what you have learned. Rest well, for we return to Earth in the morning."

Legna left without further word.

Catherine tossed her hands up. "Damn it, they're insane!"

Gabriel crossed to the back wall and tapped the black area. He watched as hundreds of Ecaepians roamed below. "What we learned today, the parallel between their past and our present, is frightening."

Catherine said, "the line between what is *being* and what is not has been blurred. I'm beginning to believe what they did wasn't a solution, but a convenience. If my house needs painting, I don't burn it down and build a new one, I paint the damn thing."

"I can't shake the nagging feeling something's going on here we have yet to discover." His head bobbed from side to side. "They're autopsying the human race before it's dead."

"The word autopsy also means an eyewitness observation or a critical analysis."

"Thank you, *Doctor* Blake."

There came a knock at the door, and the center portal opened. "It is I, Masma." He entered holding a tray of food. "Your day was enlightening?"

"Let's just say it was interesting and leave it at that."

"I fail to understand your meaning, Citizen Gabriel."

"What he's trying to say is," Catherine added diplomatically, "we experienced many new things."

"Yeah, and many questions went unanswered—a few you might clarify."

Mama set the tray down. "Please direct your inquiries to Citizen Legna."

And with that Masma promptly left.

"How the hell do we get them to stop calling us *citizen*? Gabriel grumbled. "It's driving me crazy. What's to eat?

Catherine removed the tray's cover. There were hamburgers and French fries. "Again? They must think this is all we eat."

They retired early—each to their own beds—hoping to get a decent night's sleep before returning home in the morning. But that was not to be. They had not been sleeping an hour when loud noises woke them.

Catherine came to Gabriel's door. "What now?"

Gabriel sat up and rubbed his eyes. "It sounds like music."

The musical notes were raw and staccato and very loud. Slipping out of bed, Gabriel went to the window. "You better come see this."

Catherine joined him—she could not believe her eyes. Down below, several hundred Ecaepians appeared to be dancing, their bodies moving in jerky motions in rhythm with the quirkiness of the music. The scene was right out of a Fellini movie.

"They're dancing; oh, my god, they're actually dancing." Catherine laughed. "One-minute Pavarotti, the next grunge rock."

They watched the spectacle in wonder, each trying to assemble a coherent understanding of this odd look-alike society of diminutive aliens.

"What's going on here, Gabriel? What are we missing?"

"If Legna is to be believed," he whispered, "we're witnessing a civilization that decided for whatever screwball reason to transform themselves into an androgynous society of look-alikes as the only way to save their race."

"And how would we know, we haven't been allowed to mingle and meet and converse with any of them. Hell, we haven't been allowed outside its boundaries."

"The future sure as hell isn't what it used to be." Gabriel said.

"What?"

"It's a quote from French poet Paul Valery," Gabriel said, "commenting on the devastated landscape of post-WWI Europe. He wrote, '*The future isn't what it used to be.*' This scene, in fact this whole adventure, reminds me of it."

"How do you remember all that crazy stuff?"

He tapped his temple. "I have razor-sharp gray matter." He turned and crossed to the bed and sat.

"You're thinking again."

"I am indeed."

"What's coursing through your gray matter?"

"You've heard the saying *trust, but verify?*"

Catherine crossed the room and sat next to him. "It's a bit late for that, the process has already begun."

Gabriel brought his hands together and squeezed. "We should welcome their help if what's offered can advance us. But, what we've seen so far is extreme to the tenth degree. I have no interest in you and me looking alike; I like you just the way you are, thank you very much."

"He promised that was not part of their plan."

"And you believed him?"

She shook her head in the negative. "I don't know what to believe."

"You make my point."

She planted a kiss on his lips and laid back on the bed and laughed. "Pavarotti, really? At least they have good taste."

"Move over, Lady, make room, and I'll serenade you in another way more familiar to humans."

Moments later they were making love while the strange music continued outside. They did their best not to tumble off the small bed, but it didn't work. They ended up on the floor laughing like little kids playing with puppies.

47

The return to Earth proved to be as painless and uneventful as the trip to Ecaep. This time, Gabriel did not dream during their comatose state. Masma was returning with them—he would serve as Legna's assistant for however long the aliens would remain on Earth. It was the first time Masma had ventured off his home planet.

At 12:45 PM, the stealth shuttlecraft set down on the White House lawn. Masma was all eyes when he saw the White House. "It is attractive. Are all structures as this one?"

"No," Gabriel said. "This one is special."

"How is it special, Citizen Gabriel?"

"It is very old and the very symbol of American democracy."

"Democracy, yes, I know this word."

Legna bid them a goodnight. "It is my hope your trip proved enlightening."

"In many ways," Gabriel answered.

Without further conversation, Legna and Masma entered the White House.

The following morning, Gabriel awoke before sunrise. Catherine was still sleeping. He kissed her on the forehead before slipping quietly out of bed to shower and shave in the guest bathroom. Skipping breakfast in favor of coffee, he entered his study, opened his journal file, and began typing.

> I'm not sure where to begin. We've just returned from the most incredible, unbelievable trip across the cosmos to exactly where I'm not certain. Before Legna's arrival, I would have thought the entire experience

impossible. Oh, how I would love to sit with our finest scientific minds and relate to them all that Catherine and I experienced with our own eyes. Would I also reveal how the Ecaepians have seeded our planet with whatever it is that has rendered humans infertile? Am I a traitor to my own for not shouting that out to the world? Would they even believe me? They'll realize what has been done soon enough.

A profound change has come over me. How can there not be, considering where I've been and what I've seen? But I am at peace. Strange that I should describe my feelings that way. I should not be at peace; I should be afraid, afraid of what is to come. Unless I want to start another worldwide riot and risk an unwinnable military response, I will keep my silence... at least for now.

When Catherine awoke, she joined him for a light breakfast.

"The White House can damn well do without me for a day. How about we spend it together."

"We have an awful lot to digest."

"Damn it, Catherine," Gabriel said loudly, "they're talking about killing babies!"

"Killings a strong word, zero births to control population is how they're explaining it. And keep your voice down."

"Surely you don't condone any of this?"

"Certainly not, just making clear what happy face Tonora told us. Look, we can't deny we're suffocating from overpopulation. Maybe we need this lifeline."

"Are you so sure it's a lifeline?"

"Then what, Gabriel, what's the answer?"

"Live free or die, isn't that what they say up there in New Hampshire?"

"Okay, tell me this: How do we negotiate our future with an alien hell-bent on transitioning us to something akin to them?"

"I'm working on it." He took a sip of coffee. "I want you there with me. I want us to meet this head on together."

"No, no, cowboy, this is far bigger than me—this is your arena. I can accomplish more through my research."

"Your research is a moot point if they do to us what they've done to themselves."

Catherine pushed back against her chair. "Until we know exactly what they have planned, my research stays on course. I have to distance myself from this... whatever *this* is."

"Like it or not, you're a party to all that is happening."

"Only because you made me one!"

"I do not understand your attitude, Catherine. What are you afraid of?"

"Damn you!" She stood, whipped around, and walked out of the room.

"We need to talk about this!"

"No, we don't!" she called over her shoulder.

"You can't walk away without—oh, the hell with it!"

Considering where Gabriel had been and all that he had witnessed, being back in the cockfight arena was anticlimactic. Besides Denver Wilkinson, Betty Spanning was the only other person privy to where they had traveled. And she was all questions as he entered his office.

"Honestly, I wouldn't know where to begin, Betty. Maybe after I gather my thoughts and regain my sanity."

Tyler Harney, senior staff member, came by. "I'm not going to ask where you've been."

"Smart move, Tyler."

"So, where have you been?"

"How about you just brief me on what took place while I was gone."

"The world is still in a state of shock and denial, and worldwide demonstrations continue unabated. In short, the shit's hit the fan."

"What about Alan Cross? Is he behaving himself?"

"What can I say, Mr. Cross is *Mr. Cross*."

Gabriel frowned. "Right. Gather up the troops around 4:00 for a briefing."

As soon as Tyler left, Gabriel checked in with Bethesda for an update on Owen Jennings.

"Mr. Jennings is conscious and talking," the doctor said. "In fact, he's showing a miraculous recovery."

"Is he up for visitors?"

"In fact, Mr. Ferro, I would encourage it."

His next call was to Rafi Suharto. "Rafi, where are you?"

"You know I'm not going to tell you, right?"

"Listen, I need you here in D.C."

A moment of silence followed. "Why?"

"I can't go into details. I just need you here."

"In what capacity?"

"Does it make a difference? I need to know you're here and available. I'll get Legna to approve it."

"Good luck with that. Call me when you do."

He called the office of former Vice President Alan Cross next. "We need to meet."

"I'm going into a meeting, Gabriel. What's this about?"

"I can't tell you over the phone."

"Okay, it'll be about an hour before I can get away."

"An hour then."

Betty buzzed him. "Gabriel, you're wanted in the Oval Office."

"Jesus!"

As he was leaving, Betty handed him an envelope. "An agent dropped this off."

"Hopefully, it's my dismissal notice."

"You should be so lucky, young man."

It turned out to be a brief memo from lead agent Wilkinson informing Gabriel that threats on his life had increased. As of that day, he would be shadowed by a two-man Secret Service detail.

He tore the note into little pieces and handed it back to Betty. "Trash."

"Care to share?"

"No," he said gruffly and left.

When he arrived at the Oval Office, he expected Ms. Mosby to greet him, but she was nowhere to be seen. He checked his tie and pulled at the hem of his suit jacket like he always did, and reminded himself to check his temper at the door no matter how many times Legna might push his buttons. *Don't let him get to you. You have a plan, such as it is. Stick with it.*

Stepping into the Oval, his eyes went directly to the new rug featuring the flying dove emblem. He wanted to walk across it in muddy shoes.

There were two Ecaepians standing by the window. He assumed one was Legna and the other Masma. One of them turned, strolled to the desk, and addressed Gabriel with a broad smile. "Welcome Citizen Gabriel, are you rested?"

"Yes, thank you."

The second alien spoke, "It is I, Masma."

Gabriel forced a smile. "Good morning."

Masma bowed his head and retired to the adjoining office.

"What's with him?"

"I fail to understand."

"Masma, he left in a hurry."

Without commenting, Legna lifted himself to his chair, which always left his feet dangling a foot above the floor. "I sought your council yesterday, but was informed you were unavailable."

"Catherine and I needed a day of rest after our grand space adventure."

Legna grinned. "Space adventure, indeed. Have you had sufficient time to reflect?"

Gabriel opened his mouth to reply, but hesitated.

"You may speak freely. Directness is honesty, and honesty is trust."

"It was eye-opening—mind-boggling—to witness a society beyond our own… I'm at a loss for words. Your citizens appeared to be…" *Choose your words carefully, Sparky.* "They appeared to be quite content in their chosen lifestyle. However, I fear humans will reject—"

"The path to lasting peace, harmony, and balance is never a straight one. There will be resistance—this is expected and understandable. However, mankind must come to accept that when the transformation is complete, the millenniums of human turmoil will end."

"Yes, so you've made clear. But with all due respect, if you had provided guidance early in our evolution, perhaps this transformation would not be required." It was a snarky remark, one that was risky, but a point he felt important to make. *Okay, you got your licks in. Time to shift gears before you get your ass in a sling—do it now.* "People are most grateful for the clean water and the distribution of nourishment to the poor."

"Why then do they exhibit displeasure. I am informed the demonstrations continue?"

"People are still confused and frightened. Gathering in groups is their way of dealing with the fear and uncertainty—I've told you this."

Legna slipped from the chair and walked slowly to a window and clasped his hands behind his back.

"Surely, you know your arrival was the most monumental event in the history of our world. To learn that intelligent life existed beyond Earth, to have you actually walk among us, well, words can't explain the emotional shock."

Legna said, "We must explore ways to belay their unwarranted fear."

"There is something you can do; restore humanitarian medical assistance for the elderly and terminally ill."

"That would defeat efforts to reduce your numbers." Legna swung around and quickly returned to his chair.

"Surely, you have compassion for—"

"Hear me well, Gabriel. The ill and the elderly will be allowed to expire without intervention; there can be no exceptions. We will not speak of this again. Are there other issues you wish to discuss?"

Gabriel knew not to push it further, for it would prove to be an exercise in futility. Legna's decision—or was it Tonora's—was final. He blew a breath and strolled to a window and stared out.

"Gabriel?"

"Yeah, there's a few other issues." His face drawn with concern, he turned to face Legna. "The world economy is collapsing, stock markets are crashing, and thousands of jobs are being lost. People still have to make a living so they can eat, maintain a shelter, and pay bills."

"A redistribution of resources shall ensure an adequate and equal position for all citizens."

"There are other issues we need to be dealing with. For starters, you cannot shut down governments—not yet. Until there's another system in place, the rule of law must be preserved, or anarchy will rule."

Legna slipped from his chair, ambled to a window and stood silent for several moments before speaking. "No government in your history has yet to endure. Far too many of your leaders use their positions to enrich themselves at the expense of those they serve. Power corrupts, and absolute power corrupts absolutely; is that not what humans are fond of saying? Yet the madness continues. Soon all governments will be dismantled, all borders erased. There will only remain one dominion from which you, Gabriel, shall rule."

There it was again, the offer to crown him the new world leader. He still had no clue why they had chosen him for a position he did not seek nor did he want.

"You have yet to formally accept such authority. I request that you do so now."

Gabriel thought, *this is my opportunity to decline, to tell him to shove it where the sun doesn't shine; not a realistic option—not yet anyway—not if I want to stay in the game.* "I thought I had made my position clear—I'm in. But don't be lulled into believing I won't continue to voice concerns."

"The matter is settled then."

"Many question my continued involvement and have labeled me a traitor. Terrorists, fanatics, and militia groups are gunning for me."

"You received notice from Agent Wilkinson regarding your safety?"

"I did. I would also like a CIA agent by the name of Rafi Suharto transferred here. He's the one who accompanied me to the Mogen Village and the Kebun."

"He was your—I believe you refer to such a person as a body man."

"Yes, and I trust Rafi above all others."

"Trust is essential in all relationships." Legna thought for a moment. "If this is your desire, then it shall be."

"Thank you."

"Is there more?"

"It won't be long before people realize no children are to be born. They'll automatically attribute whatever the cause to you. If you hope to gain their trust, they must be told why this sacrifice is necessary."

"I will take this into consideration. Until then Masma will assist in guiding you through the labyrinth of transformation adjustments."

Gabriel snorted. "Adjustments... is that what we're calling it now?"

"Please go about your duties. I shall summon you when I require your presence."

Legna turned to the window, placed his hands behind his back, and intertwined his fingers signaling the meeting was over.

Alan Cross swept into Gabriel's office looking like he was in one of his pissy moods and ready for a verbal dust-up.

"Alan, nice to see you."

"Where have you been?"

"Surfing."

"Funny. I've had a hell of a morning. Just got off a conference call with China and North Korea trying to get the nuclear weapons report finalized for Mr. Muppet."

"You're still grappling with that?"

"They're on board now, but dealing with them was like trying to reason with Neanderthals." Cross plopped down in a chair, crossed his legs, and glanced at his watch. "What's going on?"

"You and me, that's what going on."

"You and me what?"

"Alan, you've served this country well. You've been a savvy diplomat, able to plow through hard issues when others failed. That's why President Conrad chose you as his running mate."

Cross's eyes narrowed like he was willing them to shoot darts. "Is there a point to be made here, or are you just blowing smoke up my ass?"

"Why are you always so angry and combative?"

Cross sneered. "Excuse me, this is not a confessional, father."

Gabriel thrust his torso forward until his midsection bumped against the desk. "For Christ's sake, Alan, for once give me a straight answer."

It crossed Gabriel's mind that Cross might tell him to screw off and storm out. Instead, Cross sat quietly, the gears clearly turning in his head. "You want a straight answer?"

"Preferably."

"First," Cross began, "I have no confidence in anything these sawed-off space-bastards say or do. So, I blow off steam, so what's the big deal?"

"Alan, Alan, you were an angry son-of-a-bitch before they arrived."

"Because of the fools in the world who can't think beyond the end of their runny red noses; because of the idiots in the former Congress whose only goal in life was to get re-elected and feed off the public troth; because of the fifty states who see themselves as sovereign fiefdoms, and last but not least, people who think democracy is something that's just handed to them on a silver platter and doesn't require their active involvement. Have I stated enough reasons why anyone with half a brain *would* be pissed off?"

Gabriel chuckled. "Point made."

"There's another burr in my saddle."

"Shoot."

"They've crowned *you* the prince of the new world, whatever the hell that is."

"You know I had nothing to do with that."

"Just the same, I assume you've accepted, or you wouldn't still be here." Gabriel began to speak, but Cross waved him off. "No need to explain; it is what it is. Get on with whatever you called me here for."

"Once and for all, I want us to bury the hatchet."

Cross tossed his head back and laughed. "It's been a while since I heard that phrase. Why now?"

"Look, despite our differences, we are both loyal to this country. And except for your non-stop bluster, I've always had the highest respect for your work on behalf of this country."

"Gee, thanks."

"For Christ's sake, Alan, I'm tossing you an olive branch—take it."

Cross went silent for a beat. "You have the floor, young man. Spit it out."

"Like I said, I have the highest regard for—"

"Stop blowing smoke."

"Want something, coffee, whatever?'

"Jesus, Gabriel, get on with it."

"I was gone for a few days."

"No one knew where. Want to share?"

"You have to swear it stays in this room."

"Tough promise to make when I don't know what the hell you're gonna' say."

"I need your solemn word, Alan."

"Solemn word? Heavy stuff—okay, you have it, shoot."

Gabriel took a long breath before diving into the details of the story Legna had told him and Catherine in the Utah motel room.

The look on Cross's face was pure shell shock. "Holy Christ! Are you telling me we're *them*?"

"We, the human race, are the evolutionary result of their experiment that crashed and burned."

Cross sat up straight. "Holy living crap! You believe him?"

"There's more."

Gabriel told of his trip to the Mogen village and the mystical Kebun hidden in the Indonesian jungle.

Cross bounded to his feet. "You actually saw the damn place?"

"I did. Sit down, there's more."

Next came the details of Gabriel and Catherine trip to Ecaep.

Cross tossed his hands up and wailed. "You went to another frigging planet? On a damn spaceship?"

"Correct."

Cross roared. "How in the hell did you do that?"

"The same way they came here."

"In spacesuits?"

Gabriel chuckled. "No, nothing like that."

"And they all look identical?"

"Doctor Blake can corroborate everything I've told you."

For one of the few times in his adult life, Alan Cross was speechless.

"Want to hear the rest?"

"Try me."

Gabriel told how the aliens had set in motion a reduction of the population by rendering all living creatures incapable of reproduction.

Cross folded his hands, set them on his lap, and quietly said, "Jesus!"

"You and me, we have to work together."

"To do what? After what they did to the Russians, we'd be crazy to go up against their weapons."

"I'm not suggesting military action, Alan, that would-be suicide. We have to take them at their word that they're actually here to help. If they're on the level, what can we glean that will benefit us without their turning us into them? Jesus, Alan, we saw a power source that would electrify our entire planet."

"You're suggesting we play chess with players smarter than us."

Gabriel nodded.

Cross put out his right hand. "Okay, we give it the old college try, we bury the hatchet and hope for the best."

Surprised, yet pleased, Gabriel rose and shook Cross's hand.

"Don't let this go to your head."

Gabriel laughed. "Alan, Alan, why do you always have to have the last word."

Cross smiles. "Because I'm older and wiser."

48

Legna had dispatched engineering teams across the globe, bringing clean water and electricity to poverty stricken areas in Ethiopia, Chad, Haiti, Bangladesh, Ghana, Rwanda, India, Afghanistan, Laos, and Cambodia, along with millions of pounds of government food stores. Although these goodwill gestures reinforced his promise to aid mankind, mistrust among the masses continued. People still viewed the alien presence as an invasion and worldwide demonstrations showed no signs of slowing.

The day following their meeting, without advance notice to Gabriel, Legna addressed the world in a TV appearance from the Oval Office at 6 PM EST.

"From the very beginning of your civilization, you have settled conflicts by tribes attacking other tribes. From millennium to millennium, it has led to long periods of self-inflicted suffering. This violent behavior has kept human society from forging a cohesive civilization. Realizing this, it mystifies us as to why you continue to reject our guidance, guidance that will put an end to your despair." He paused while the camera slowly zoomed in for a close-up. His expression, which up until then appeared impassioned, now changed to belligerence. "You shall gain nothing through unruly and infantile declarations. This behavior must cease by midnight tomorrow, or yet another expression of our resolve will fall upon you. Be forewarned, all demonstrations must end."

Gabriel was outraged. Knowing that innocent people would be hurt if Legna were to retaliate, he made several attempts to get through to the Oval Office. His calls were rejected. He tried reaching Masma but was greeted with the same silence.

Calls flooded into both Gabriel and Alan Cross from domestic officials and foreign heads of state seeking guidance and clarification. Gabriel and Cross' advice to all was to engage their security forces in peaceful ways to stop or at least diminish the size of the demonstrations. The alternative, they counseled, could prove to be far worse than the cure.

That evening, emotionally whipped, Gabriel and Catherine dined at Arico's. There were only four other couples present. Three tables away were two Secret Service agents who now shadowed Gabriel's every move.

"You haven't said much about your meeting with Legna yesterday. Why?"

"I pledged my support; I agreed to be the public face of whatever the hell they're planning. It's counterproductive to do otherwise, since they're holding all the cards."

"I'm taking you at word that you're *in*—as you put it—to be on the *inside* and not because you support their insane attempt to reinvent us."

"Haven't I had made that clear?"

"Just checking."

"I told Alan Cross everything, from the Utah hotel encounter to the Mogen, the Kebun, our trip to Ecaep—the whole ball of wax."

"Was that wise? You two have never been best buds and he's a wild card."

"We need him, if for no other reason but to keep him from going off half-cocked."

Catherine snorted. "Good luck with that."

"Beyond that bullheaded exterior lies a seasoned diplomat, although at times you'd never know it. I also convinced Legna to have agent Suharto transferred here."

Catherine glanced at the two Secret Service guys trying their best to be inconspicuous. "What's wrong Curly and Moe over there?"

"Rafi will become my main ears and eyes on the ground."

"So, what happens tomorrow at midnight? They didn't hesitate to demonstrate their weapons before, they won't now."

Gabriel sighed. "I know, I know."

Early the following morning, Gabriel sat at his desk wondering what would happen at midnight.

As the clocked ticked away, he became more desperate to reach Legna. Leaving his office, he made his way to the visitor's lobby and slipped outside and around to the far edge of the Rose Garden. From there he could see the Oval. Legna's body man, Agent Carson, stood guard at the Portico door, confirming Legna was inside. Hurrying back to his office, he placed a call to Ms. Mosby to request a meeting, but was told the Administrator was unavailable.

Two more hours passed and the incoming reports only worsened; rioting and looting were escalating. The animals had been set loose, and there was no stopping them.

He made his way to the Oval and found Mrs. Mosby at her desk. "It is imperative I speak with the Administrator."

"That is not possible, Mr. Ferro."

"I know he's in there."

"I will inform him you were here."

"Thanks for nothing."

He turned on his heels and stormed off, speaking just loud enough for Ms. Mosby to hear him say, "son of a bitch!"

Back in his office, he composed a quick memo warning Legna that if he implemented reprisals at midnight, he would only be adding fuel to an already inflamed populace.

"Betty," he called over the intercom. "Check the printer. Deliver that memo to the Oval pronto."

Gabriel and Catherine had a quiet dinner at home that evening, but not much in the way of conversation passed between them. And when they did speak, it was about anything other than Legna's midnight deadline. His assistant, Tyler Harney, remained on duty at the White House ready to call if anything at all occurred. Following dinner, Catherine disappeared to the guest bedroom, which Gabriel had set up as a home office for her. He retired to his study to write in his journal.

The clock is ticking. I feel like a man on death row waiting for the phone to ring, waiting for a reprieve from the madness swirling around us.

At 11:45 PM he and Catherine gathered in the living room and waited. Midnight came and went then 12:15, 12:30 and still no word. At 12:47 AM, they gave up and went to bed, hoping against all hope Legna had come to his senses. Neither expected to get much sleep; nevertheless, they both fell into a deep slumber almost immediately.

At 5:30 AM Gabriel moaned loudly. He rolled to his left, then to his right and moaned again. Catherine placed a hand on his shoulder. It woke him with a start and he bounded to a sitting position.

"What! What!"

"You were dreaming." She glanced at the bedside clock. "You okay?"

He washed a hand over his face and through his hair. "I dreamt lasers were raining down on the protestors. Jesus, what time is it?"

"3:36."

"Damn it, what's going on?"

"Apparently, nothing or Tyler would have called."

As if on cue, Gabriel's cell phone rang and it jolted them. Turning on the bedside lamp, he scooped up the phone. "Tyler?"

It was Ms. Mosby. The Administrator wished to see him. Could he come immediately.

He rubbed at his face. "What's wrong?"

"I have no idea, Mr. Ferro," Mosby replied dryly. *"The Administrator requires your presence."*

"Okay, okay, give me an hour." He hung up.

"Who was it?"

"The ever-charming Ms. Mosby. His lord and master wants me back at the White House."

Catherine glanced at the bedside clock. "At this hour? What did she say?"

"Just that he wants to see me. Let's check the internet."

A quick search turned up no news of retaliation against the protestors.

"He blinked, damn it, he blinked!"

Thirty minutes after Mosby's call, Gabriel was out the door and into the dark night with a Secret Service detail following.

When Gabriel arrived at the West Wing, he noticed an increased presence of uniformed Secret Service agents as well as two fully armed Marine guards at the entrance to the Oval Office. That was a first.

Ms. Mosby was at her/his desk. "Good morning, Mr. Ferro."

Gabriel nodded. "Should I address you as Ms. Mosby or Roama ... I mean now that we're formally acquainted."

"You are the only one aware, Mr. Ferro. Please refer to me as Ms. Mosby."

Gabriel made a quick sign of the cross over his heart. "Scout's honor. Is his majesty ready for me?"

"Please do not disrespect the Administrator."

"Sorry, my faux pas, I must work on that."

Roama's face tightened in unmistakable disapproval. "You may go in."

"Thank you."

As he approached the door, he made quick eye contact with each of the Marine guards, but neither acknowledged him.

He entered to find one Ecaepian seated at the desk and one standing. He assumed the latter was Masma. He glanced at the portico door: Agent Carson was at his post.

"He needs sleep too, you know."

"Good morning, Citizen Gabriel. As I recall you consume coffee. May I have Ms. Mosby provide it?"

"I'm good."

Legna motioned to the chair next to the right side of the desk. "Please be comfortable."

"The midnight deadline passed. I can only assume you had second thoughts or you wouldn't be calling me in the middle of the night."

"I find humans to be an obstinate race. Without regard for their safety, they carelessly place themselves at great risk, resorting to activities that lead to abominable behavior. What purpose is served?"

Gabriel thought *Here we go waiting for the other shoe to drop.*

"The other shoe to drop—what does this mean?"

"It's an expression." And then he realized he had not verbalized it. "Please, stop that."

Ignoring him, Legna continued. "The imposed deadline passed without incident because I deemed it so. However, it would be a miscalculation for humans to assume we are less determined."

"The citizens of Earth view your presence as an invasion—an act of war: The violence, the looting, the destruction of property; that's how these events play out. How many times must I point that out?"

"That is not justification for such appalling behavior."

"I agree."

"May I offer a solution that can lead to peace, harmony, and balance?"

If Legna preached peace, harmony, and balance one more time, it would be one time too many for Gabriel. It was one thing to fantasize about creating a human utopia; it was entirely another to hope that somehow you could change human behavior.

Legna lifted himself out of the chair, swung his hands behind his back, intertwined his fingers, and sauntered to the nearest window. Gabriel exchanged glances with Masma. He wondered if Masma had an opinion in all of this, and if so, would he express it. He got his answer—Masma diverted his eyes.

"I wish you to address your fellow citizens to clarify our mission. You must speak to their well-being."

Gabriel grimaced. *If I was a marked man before, doing that will surely seal my fate.* "You want me to extend my behind-the-scenes involvement to public spokesperson?"

"I wish you to address your fellow citizens." Legna turned from the window. His eyes constricted and trained on Gabriel's like a piercing ray. "You need not fear for your safety."

"Easy for you to say, but if I make a public statement, I might as well put a target on my back."

"If it is your desire to deny me, then you are free to do so."

So, there it was, Gabriel's option was to accept or refuse; there was to be no fudging, no middle ground. His thoughts went to Catherine. He wanted desperately to reach out to her, to seek her council before committing. And yet he knew what her answer would be: *Stay clear of this. He wants you to do their dirty work. Quick Sparky, think on your feet.*

"Who is Sparky?" Legna asked.

"Damn you!" Gabriel fired back.

Legna let out a low guttural laugh. "Yes, damn me."

"My concern is for the well-being of my fellow citizens. That's all I care about."

Legna crossed the room and took Gabriel's right hand in his and wrapped the long bony fingers of his left hand around Gabriel's forearm. "We share the same concerns, do we not?"

Gabriel withdrew his hand. "Why not allow humans a voice? Engage them in a meaningful dialogue. String together a consortium of leaders who—"

"The same leaders who fail their charges?" Legna sauntered back to the window.

Tell him what he wants to hear, Gabriel's inner voice screamed. *Do it and do it now.* "I will do as you ask as long as I get a seat at the table."

"What does a *seat at the table* mean?"

"From this moment forward, I'm to be informed of every decision every step of the way—every step. Nothing happens without my involvement and input. Agreed?"

Legna nodded. "This I pledge to you. Masma shall meet with you daily and share all that you wish to know. You will, as you have requested, have a seat at the table. Go now, join Masma. Together, you shall create a communication to be delivered this day." Legna turned to the window, his usual way of ending a meeting.

Gabriel and Masma spent the next hour crafting the speech he would deliver to the world. It was a calculated risk, if it backfired, he would be labeled a traitor.

"Will Legna tamper with this?" Gabriel asked.

Masma diverted his eyes. "I do not know."

"Keep in mind, I deliver this at 5:00. I'd like a little practice time before then. Let me know what changes, if any, he makes." Gabriel headed for the door.

"Citizen Gabriel?"

Gabriel turned back.

"May I converse with you further?"

"Sure, what is it?"

"Please, come sit."

"Uh, okay." Gabriel took a seat in front of the desk. "What's on your mind?"

For a long moment, Masma said nothing. He seemed hesitant.

Gabriel chuckled. "That important, huh?"

"I wish you not to make humor."

"Sorry. Go ahead."

"I am to inform you that plans are to be drawn to collect all personal weapons, all military is to be disbanded, and a single governing body is to be created."

Masma rattled it off quickly and waited for Gabriel's response.

"Did I hear you correctly?"

"I believe so."

"Well, now, if Legna thinks the present demonstrations are problematic, he hasn't seen anything yet."

"It is for the good of humankind, is it not?"

"No doubt, but humans will not support anything that encroaches on their freedom. Personal weapons for one falls into that category, especially in this country. As for shutting down military forces and transition to a one-world government, good luck with that."

Masma stood. "I have fulfilled that which was requested of me. Thank you, Citizen Gabriel.

"Hold on, this requires discussing. He can't just—"

"You must speak of your concerns with Citizen Legna."

Gabriel was livid, but held his temper. "Well, okay, I'll do that... I'll do that. Until 5:00 o'clock then. Have a nice day, Citizen Masma."

"I look forward to our future encounters, Citizen Gabriel."

Gabriel wasn't settled back at his desk 5 minutes before Betty buzzed; Rafi Suharto was on the secure line.

"Rafi, where are you?"

"On my way to the States. How the hell did you pull this off?"

"I have friends in high places. I'll have White House credentials prepared for you."

"Bad idea. I can best serve you in the shadows."

"But—"

"No buts, I land in DC later today. After I check in at Langley, let's meet. You have a security team tailing you?"

"A couple of Secret Service guys."

"Find a way to ditch them, and we'll meet. Write down this address. Meet me there at twenty hundred hours."

Gabriel wrote down the address, hung up and lit another cigarette, arguing with himself over whether to tell Alan Cross what he had learned from Masma about Legna's plans. "I better or he'll have a shit-fit."

Cross' reaction was typical Alan Cross. "Are you kidding me? He can't confiscate personal weapons!"

"He can and he will."

"We have a goddamn Constitution in this country and—"

"I've already been down that road with him once," Gabriel said. "We ought to be concerned about shutting down world military forces before we worry about some guy's gun collection."

"This is exactly what I feared; strip the world of their military and take away private weapons and you have the population by the balls. Then create a one-world government, and the next thing you know, we're kissing their ass and doing their bidding."

"Give me more time to get into this, okay?"

"Make it soon all we're all be sucking hind-tit."

At 2:45 PM Betty handed him an envelope from Masma containing the final version of the address he would deliver at 5:00 PM. There were a few changes, but essentially it was what he and Masma had drafted.

At 3:30 PM Catherine checked in, but Gabriel did not take her call. If he told her of his impending television debut, she would try to talk him out of it for sure.

At 4:50 PM he paced nervously outside the Roosevelt room from where his speech would be broadcast live on television, radio, and the Internet.

At 4:55 PM a technician approached him. "On the air in five, Mr. Ferro. Better come inside now."

Gabriel pushed his tie up, pulled at the hem of his jacket, took a deep breath, and entered the Roosevelt room. There was a podium where he could set the written speech in case something went amiss with the TelePrompTer. Taking his position, he blinked a number of times to adjust to the TV lights.

"See the prompter, okay?" the technician asked.

"Yeah."

"Relax, Mr. Ferro, you look nervous."

Gabriel wiped a hand across his brow. "I am nervous, this is a first for me."

"You'll be fine, sir."

At exactly 4:59 PM all programming on television, radio, and the Internet was replaced with a notice—on the radio, it was a voice message—that a major announcement from the office of the Administrator was about to take place.

"Thirty seconds," came a voice from behind the camera. "I'll count down, then use my fingers for the last four seconds and then point to you."

Gabriel cleared his throat, blinked several times and stared into the camera lens like a deer caught in the headlights of an oncoming semi-tractor. A voice from beside the camera broke his reverie.

"In ten, nine, eight, seven, six, five…"

The technician held up his fingers for the last 4 digits and then pointed to him. Gabriel froze as a final thought raced through his mind: *Am I about to lie to the world, or am I trying to save us all from certain retribution?* His eyes went to his printed script.

"Mr. Ferro?" The technician pointed to the camera. "We're live!"

Gabriel cleared his throat again, looked into the prompter, and began.

"My fellow citizens, my name is Gabriel Ferro, chief of staff to the late American President, William Conrad. Many have taken me to task for my continued involvement with the new Administrator. I have done so because I believe the Ecaepians are here for their stated purpose: to save our civilization and our planet from certain extinction. Millions upon millions continue to live in deplorable conditions at a time in our brief history when mankind should have elevated itself beyond the senseless conflicts that keep us from becoming a unified society. The Ecaepians say they have come to free us from that bondage, to assist mankind in its passage to a benevolent civilization that enjoys peace, harmony, and balance. How can we in all good conscience deny ourselves that opportunity?"

He paused, took a sip of water from the glass on the podium, and continued.

"Mankind will be denied lasting peace and prosperity if we allow fear to control our lives. Fear has always opened the door for those who would act in unlawful ways against others. We must not fall victim to such demagoguery. In closing, my message to everyone is clear: Allow the Ecaepians to prove to us their only interest is the enrichment of our lives by broadening our knowledge of ourselves, our planet, and our universe. I ask you—no, I plead with you—for the sake of unity and a brighter, hopeful future, stop the violent demonstrations. Thank you, and I wish you peace."

He was drenched with sweat.

On his way to his office, he received a call on from lead White House Secret Service Agent Denver Wilkinson.

"By the end of your presentation, the threats on your life doubled."

"Great, why don't I paint a target on my back and save them time?"

"I should double your detail."

"No, please don't, Denver."

"But if anything were to happen—"

"I'll be fine with the two that are shadowing me—cross my heart."

His phone rang again; it was Alan Cross. "What happened to our newfound alliance? You could have clued me in before you slit your throat on television."

"There wasn't time, Alan, it all came together quickly. Trust me and just hang in there."

"I'm hanging all right, by my fingernails."

As soon as he was in the safety of his office, he lit a cigarette. Betty, who normally knocked before entering, breezed in with a sour look. "You didn't tell me you were doing that."

"I didn't tell anyone."

"Dr. Blake called twice before you were off the air. She sounded pretty mad. I've taken messages from heads of state, the Joint Chiefs, Congressional members and—"

"Got it, duly noted."

"What do I tell Dr. Blake if she calls again, and you know she will?"

Gabriel thought for a moment. "Tell her I'll be home late."

Betty turned to leave, but swiveled back. "Gabriel, what's going on? Are you really with them now?"

With an impassioned expression, he said softly, "You know better. All I ask is that you trust me."

"I do. In the meantime, I remind you that you'll set off the smoke alarm with that nasty cigarette."

"I had a guy in maintenance disconnect it a week ago."

Betty grimaced, shook her head with disapproval, and left.

At 7:20 PM Gabriel departed the West Wing for his meeting with Rafi. As he approached his Vehicle, he spotted his Secret Service detail ready to shadow him. He approached their vehicle.

"Hi, guys."

"Good evening, Mr. Ferro."

"I don't know your names."

"I'm Remy Bernard," the driver replied. "This is Dex Patterson."

"Remy, Dex, thanks for watching my back."

"That's what we get paid for, Mr. Ferro," Remy said. "That speech you made, did you mean what you said?"

"The part about stopping the demonstrations, yeah; everything else was bullshit. If you repeat that, I'll deny it."

Dex, sitting in the passenger seat, leaned across. "If you're playing both ends against the middle, you're playing with fire."

"I promise not to get burned. Listen, guys, right now I need to take you into my confidence. Follow me if you must, but no one is to know where I'm going, who I'm meeting, or why."

"That's asking a lot, Mr. Ferro," Dex said.

"Look, I don't plan on shooting anyone and I'm not dealing drugs. Let's just say what I am doing needs to be kept quiet for national security reasons—our national security, not theirs. Okay?"

Remy's look went to Dex, who nodded his okay. "Okay, we'll trust you know what you're doing. The who, what, and why stays with us unless you get into trouble. Fair enough?"

"I don't care what Denver Wilkinson says about you two, you're okay in my book."

Remy and Dex laughed.

Gabriel smiled. "And they say Secret Service guys have no sense of humor."

At 7:50 PM Gabriel arrived at 1401 Wilson Boulevard in Arlington, Virginia. The location struck him as familiar like déjà vu all over again. And then it came to him; the Rosalyn Oakhill Office Building once stood on that very spot. It was in the parking garage that Washington Post reporter Bob Woodward met with FBI Special Agent Mark Felt. Thirty years later, in 2005, Felt was identified as *Deep Throat*, Woodward's informant that helped bust open the Nixon/Watergate scandal. The Oakhill Building had since been torn down and replaced with a twenty-eight-story residential tower, a twenty-four-story commercial building and an underground parking garage.

Gabriel entered the garage and parked in space 40D as Rafi instructed—he would be waiting in 32D, the same space where the Woodward/Felt meetings had taken place.

"You have a wicked sense of humor," Gabriel called out as he approached Rafi. "The irony is not lost on me,"

"It struck me this would be appropriate for a surreptitious meeting."

The two men smiled and shook hands. "It's damn good to see you."

"What was with that speech?"

"First, let me give you lots of background to digest."

Gabriel dove into the details of how the population had been rendered sterile, how the old and sick would be allowed to expire without medical assistance, the plan to confiscate personal weapons, disband all military, and consolidate all sovereign borders in favor of a one-world government. He capped it with his journey through space and all he had witnessed on Ecaep.

"God almighty, this is science fiction stuff."

"Unfortunately, it's reality. On Ecaep we witness a civilization unlike anything we could ever imagine—so radically different that—"

"What do they want from us, Gabriel, what?"

"You saw the Kebun, you know the back story. For them, it's *mea culpa* time. The challenge for us is to separate the wheat from the chaff; what will help us without us becoming them."

"You have a plan—does anyone have a plan?"

"Mine is to play nice with Legna. That's why I agreed to my TV debut. And Alan Cross is on-board. There's another alien—Masma—he came back with us—my liaison with now Legna. I think there might be a chink in his armor I can explore."

"Legna has reduced Langley's operations to spying and reporting on protestors."

"Yeah, I know."

"He informed the director all security agencies are to be disbanded and replaced by a single authority. And no doubt all communications are being monitored by who knows how many of their ships floating around up there."

"Now is as good a time to break the news: There's only two ships. Total crew: twenty-six."

"What!"

"Thirteen little aliens on each ship—that's it."

Rafi's whistled. "Holy shit! Who knows this?"

"Me, Alan Cross, Catherine Blake, and now you. If that leaks, military forces will feel their oats and do something stupid. Keep your ear to the ground and inform me of whatever you learn."

"What about you? You're in the middle of the fire."

"For the present, I have Legna's ear, I'm going to play that card for all it's worth. Be my eyes and ears out there. Let me know the minute you hear anything I should know."

At 9:30 PM he arrived home knowing Catherine would be loaded for bear. Her first words were, "What the hell did you do!?"

"Exactly what I had to, otherwise I would've been drop-kicked out of the Oval."

"You could have confided in me *before* you hung yourself out to dry as the official voice of madness!"

"Calm down, you know what I'm up to."

"What I know for sure is that you're playing a dangerous game that could get you killed."

"Listen, damn it—"

She thumped a finger against his chest. "No, you listen, cowboy, we're either together, or we're not."

His frayed emotions unraveled like a strand of pearls spilling across a slick floor. "Damn it, I don't have to answer for my actions!"

Catherine took a step back—she looked betrayed. "Okay, have it your way, macho man." Spinning around, she stormed out of the room.

49

As the week progressed, worldwide demonstrations began to diminish. No one was more surprised than Gabriel that his speech might have had a positive effect. To his dismay, however, he was granted no meetings with Legna. However, his daily get-togethers with Masma and Alan Cross continued as they coordinate electricity, clean water, and food distribution to blighted areas around the world. The complexities associated with Legna orders to collect guns, close down military forces, and make plans for a one-world government was discussed. Yet, the question that loomed the largest was, what would happen when the population learned they had been rendered sterile? Would such a drastic measure be embraced to insure the survival of human civilization, or would there be renewed demonstration leading to reprisals?

Anxious to visit Owen Jennings, Catherine and Gabriel made the trip to the National Naval Medical Center in Bethesda, Maryland.

"I can't explain his miraculous recovery," His doctor reported. "Yesterday, he was still in a coma. This morning he opened his eyes and was completely lucid and hungry and badgering us to remove his head bandages. His skin is regenerating like nothing we've ever encountered. And that gunshot wound to his upper chest? The MRI shows none. Your friend is our miracle patient—one for the textbooks."

As Gabriel and Catherine prepared to enter Jennings' room, a broad smile came over Gabriel's face.

"What are you smiling about?"

"Legna."

"What?"

"I asked him to intervene, but he said Owen's injuries were too severe. But given what this doctor told just told us—" He left it hanging.

Other than a dressing that covered the upper left side of Jennings face, all bandages had been removed. Though some burn scars were still visible, his complexion looked surprisingly good for a man who had been through hell.

"Where have you two been?" Were the first words out of Jennings.

"Playing golf." Catherine gave him a gentle hug and kissed his forehead.

"How about a kiss from you?" Jennings said to Gabriel.

"I'll settle for shaking your hand. God Owen, for a while there we weren't sure you'd make it."

"So, the doctors tell me." Jennings patted a shoulder. "Must have been my angel."

Catherine grinned. "Your angel?"

"I know it sounds nuts, but last night, I sensed something or someone hovering over me in the dark in the middle of the night—couldn't make out who or what. It was like I was dreaming, only it felt real. Something touched my forehead and my pain intensified—my whole body felt like it was on fire. But then the pain subsided. That's all I remember. Then they come in this morning and woke me up and told me… well you can see for yourself. Hell, I must have had a dozen doctors in here trying to figure out how I healed so much in one night. Now they want to study me from head to toe to figure it out. Crazy, huh?"

Gabriel glanced at Catherine with a knowing grin.

"So, enough about me—what's going on? No one here will tell me a damn thing."

"There's plenty of time for that. Just concentrate on getting well so you can get out of here."

"Hey, Cuban Boy, it's me you're talking to, remember? I know when you're hiding something. Pull up a chair and tell me what it is that you don't want me to know."

Gabriel looked to Catherine. She nodded. "He needs to know."

They sat by Owen's bed and Gabriel filled him in on all that had occurred from the moment he, Catherine and Legna had left the Arizona lab. By the time Gabriel finished, the three of them were in tears.

In the days that followed, Gabriel repeatedly requested an audience with Legna. But each day, he received the same answer from the ever-present Ms. Mosby; the Administrator was unavailable. His daily sessions with Masma continued, sometimes with Cross present, sometimes not. Whenever they were alone, Gabriel would seize the opportunity to share with Masma his life: where he was born, his parent's flight to freedom, and tales of his mentor, President Conrad. He expressed his love for Catherine and how their relationship was the next chapter in their life; all in an effort to enlighten Masma to the ways of humans. He encouraged Masma to reciprocate about, but Masma remained reluctant. But, a few days later, when they were alone, Masma finally spoke of how the transformation had rescued a failing Ecaepian society.

"These meetings have allowed you and me to express our thoughts freely, Citizen Masma; for that I am grateful."

"In the Gathering Place, you witnessed our past? Were you not enlightened?"

"I was astounded by the similarities of our beginnings. But if I may speak freely, Dr. Blake and I were struck by the lack of interaction between Ecaepians on a personal, emotional level."

"Emotions are a human condition. We are free of such impediments, as we are of past memories other than those preserved in the Gathering Place."

"Yes, I know, but to know us, to really know us, is to acknowledge that our emotions enrich our lives: kindness, love, and fellowship, as well as the joy we experience sharing our existence with a mate, children, extended family, and friends."

"Despite what you say, Citizen Gabriel, humans experience deep sorrow, fear, hostility, and a certain death. Ecaepians are all free of such impediments."

How the hell do I argue with that? Don't. Play the Washington two-step and stroke him a bit. "From what you have told me, the transition has served Ecaepians well. However, such a transition asks humankind to abandon the only life they know for something they don't."

"It was so with Ecaepians, yet we found the courage to accept the truth. Are you in conflict with our endeavor to bring peace, harmony, and balance to mankind?"

"No, no, not at all. But for the transition to be successful, humans must be engaged in the process; they must be willing participants, not indentured slaves."

"We enslave no one."

"Uh, wrong choice of words. I go back to what I said about emotions; they control every aspect of their daily lives. No doubt they cause us negative experiences as well, but to abrogate them, Well, that's—" Gabriel paused and thought for a moment. "Let me put this another way. Can we convince Citizen Legna that sugar achieves better results than salt?"

"I fail to comprehend."

"Sugar is sweet, salt is bitter. Citizen Legna would be well advised to use a gentle hand to engage humans in a more direct dialogue. Humans don't deal very well with uncertainty."

Masma's eyes strayed as he considered Gabriel's words. "Citizen Legna has been given a formidable task."

"Yes, he has. Perhaps together we might convince him to consider the human emotional factor and how best to deal with it."

Again, Masma's eyes strayed. After a long moment of thought, he said, "Perhaps."

"Then together we will pursue this with Citizen Legna?"

"If this pleases you, Citizen Gabriel."

"It does, Citizen Masma."

"Then I shall seek Citizen Legna's council on your behalf."

"Thank you."

Gabriel returned to his office hoping that maybe he had gained an ally in Masma, unless Masma was playing him as Legna so often did.

Gabriel's clandestine meetings with Rafi continued as well, but little to report. As hard as the CIA and NSA tried, it proved impossible to break through whatever communications might be taking place between the hovering Ecaepian spacecraft and the Oval Office.

"If we're caught doing it," Rafi said, "I hate to think of what he might do."

"Maybe" Gabriel answered, "he's aware and amused by our futile attempts."

"Does he amuse easily?"

"I think he enjoys toying with us."

People around the world began to settle into their daily routines as best they could despite the uncertainty of what the future might hold. Adults went to work, and kids went to school only to return to the relative safety of their homes. Attendance at entertainment and sports venues dropped drastically.

The second and third week came and went without new decrees from the Oval Office. But at the end of the month, the proverbial shit hit the fan when worldwide 10,964,310 babies were born—normal for that period—without a single new pregnancy reported. Over five million women less than four months pregnant began to mysteriously miscarry. It did not help that many religious leaders preached that it was the apocalyptic chaos predicted in the Book of Revelations come true. Conspiracy theorists flooded the Internet charging the aliens with systematic genocide against mankind. People were urged to organize and to rise up in retaliation.

Legna ordered the Internet shut down. No further reports were to be issued from any public source without authorization from the Administrator's office.

Early one morning, Gabriel heard Alan Cross's voice booming just outside his office. "Good morning, Betty, how the hell are you?"

"Fine, thank you, Mr. Cross."

Cross swooped into Gabriel's office in his usual whirlwind fashion.

"Slow down, Alan, slow down."

"I only have one speed, young man." Cross slumped into a chair. "People have to be told what's happening. Jesus, not a single word of warning of what just might be the vilest thing the aliens could have done. For God's sake, have they no compassion?"

"Emotions don't enter into their decision making, remember?"

"You need to set up a face-to-face, we need to confront him head on."

"With all due respect, we don't need you storming in there making threats."

Cross ran his fingers over his heart. "Won't happen, scout's honor. But damn it, people are entitled to know what the hell is being done to them."

"Maybe I can get Masma to run interference."

Cross popped to his feet. "Do it quick before we have a full-scale revolution on our hands." Just as he had entered, Cross flew out the door like a man on a mission. "So long, Betty."

"Good day to you, Mr. Cross."

"Gabriel," Betty called over the intercom, "it's time for your meeting with Masma."

"Call him, see if he'll come here."

"Good luck with that."

Several minutes passed before Betty came back with an answer. "No dice, he won't come here."

"I didn't think so."

Gabriel went to Masma's office next to the Oval Office and was greeted with a smile and a cheerful, "Welcome, Citizen Gabriel."

"The cat's out of the bag."

"The animal is where?"

"People are not stupid. Unless they are told what's happening and why, there'll be an insurgency leading to more bloodshed. It's imperative you set up a meeting for Alan Cross and me before this day is out."

Masma's forehead crinkled. "I do not dictate to the Administrator." And then his eyes strayed—his thoughts had drifted elsewhere.

Shit, where the hell do they go when they drift off in the middle of a conversation? It's exasperating! "Still with me, Citizen Masma?"

Masma's head swiveled back. "I am here."

"To uproot people and spin them around 180 degrees without an explanation is to—"

"Have you not informed me of the difficulty of achieving consensus among humans?"

"That's all the more reason this be done with their full cooperation."

"Is such unanimity possible?"

"You and I spoke of this; people must be engaged in the process."

"Do they not comprehend we are here to help?"

"How can they if these things are done behind their backs? There has to be trust, and trust can only be gained through honest disclosure, not authoritative pronouncements after the fact. If that sounds familiar, it's words straight from Legna's own mouth."

"Citizen Legna understands such changes are troublesome to humans."

"All the more reason to be open and honest."

Masma stare was intense. Gabriel quickly diverted his eyes, afraid Masma was capable of invading his thoughts as Legna could. *A little late to think of that now. Calm down, getting pissed is not going to get you there.* "May I ask you a question?"

"Yes, Citizen Gabriel."

"Are you happy?"

Masma brow crinkled again. "Please define happiness."

"What makes one person happy may not apply to another. So, no, I cannot define happiness. An individual knows it when they feel it."

"As I have related, we are not burdened with emotional distractions, but skilled in the ways of *Jelasnya*—translucency of the mind, a lucidity which provides a path to heightened enlightenment." Masma's eyes strayed, and he was silent again. After several moments, he stood. "Very well, I shall seek Legna's counsel in this matter. Good day to you."

"You're back already?" Betty said as Gabriel entered.

"They seem to enjoy ending meetings abruptly."

At his desk, Gabriel retrieved his cigarette. Leaning back, he placed his feet up on his desk and reflected. *If I were a betting man, I'd wager Masma is more understanding of the fear and despair they've inflicted. Maybe he can get this point across to the almighty Administrator... or maybe not.*

An hour later Masma called; Legna would grant them an audience at three that very afternoon.

Gabriel breathed a sigh of relief, told Betty to notify Cross, and called Rafi for an update.

"The natives know something's up, how can they not?" Rafi said. "For Christ's sake, no new pregnancies and thousands of spontaneous Miscarriages? Do they think all humans are stupid?"

Gabriel blew a breath. "Me and Alan Cross have a meeting with Legna at three. Maybe he'll listen to reason."

"Nothing but nothing is going to stop renewed mass demonstrations. Count on it."

At 2:45 PM Cross blew into Gabriel's office like the proverbial bull in a china shop. It was the perfect metaphor for his entrances, which could be intimidating to the point of distraction. His expression telegraphed he was, as usual, loaded for bear. Slumping down in a chair, he crossed one leg over the other, folded his hands, and set them in his lap.

"First things first." Gabriel held out a single sheet of paper. "Read it."

Cross glanced at the single page on EPA stationary. It was a report titled *Current AGI Index.* The EPA regularly issued the AGI, the Air Quality Index, as a measurement of air quality specifically for carbon monoxide, sulfur dioxide, and nitrogen dioxide.

"That report was issued late this morning," Gabriel said. "Two weeks ago, the index was 157. In EPA language that meant people would begin to experience adverse health effects, and for those in the sensitive groups, it could be serious. This latest report states it's dropped, from 157 to 115. Not perfect but a hell-of-a-lot safer."

"You're about to tell me *they* did this?"

"Jesus, Alan, he told us they would improve air quality—there's the proof. I don't know how they did it, but they did, and it has to get out to the world."

Cross studied the report again. "This doesn't deflect from they've done."

"I agree, but at least it's a positive. I just don't want us to go into this meeting with an *attitude.* That'll get us nowhere—a little sugar might."

"So help me, if that little son-of-a-bitch tries to—"

"Alan, you're doing it already. Swallow hard, calm down. Look at the good they've done with power, clean water, food supplies, and now the atmosphere."

"You sound like a convert."

"Cut the bullshit, Alan." Gabriel glanced at his watch; it was 2:47 PM. "We better amble on down there."

It was 2:59 when they reached the Oval Office. Ms. Mosby's greeting was short and direct. "You may go in."

Legna was seated, and Masma was standing beside him. They were deeply immersed in a document and neither acknowledged their arrival.

Gabriel whispered to Cross, "The one standing is Masma."

"How the hell do you tell them apart?"

Masma's gaze went to Cross; he had heard the comment. Without he nodded in greeting and withdrew to the adjoining office.

Legna stood and came around to greet them. "Citizen Cross, Citizen Gabriel, it is good to see you. Please, be comfortable."

Cross dove right in. "Thirty days without a single pregnancy reported and thousands of miscarriages do not go unnoticed."

"Please, citizens, sit."

Cross glanced at Gabriel as if to say *the bastard ignored what I said.*

They sat on one sofa and waited for Legna to crawl up on the other.

"You haven't exactly pulled the wool over anyone's eyes."

Gabriel rolled his eyes and thought, *Damn it, Alan, that's not sugar!*

"Pulled the wool over the eyes? What is this meaning, Citizen Cross?"

"You haven't *fooled* anyone."

"Let us begin with the location of nuclear weapons and the materials to create them. I have yet to receive your report."

Cross cleared his throat. "We're still working on that."

"And?"

"Well…" Cross shifted his weight "… we have recorded the location of all active weapons, but are still gathering information about the materials to produce more: highly enriched uranium, Oak Ridge alloy, plutonium, and—"

"Yes, yes, I am familiar with these elements as well as the location of both the weapons and the elements you speak of."

Cross's face tightened. "Then why did you ask for a report?"

"As a test."

"A test?"

"To see if those in possession of such weapons would comply voluntarily. Apparently, they have not."

Cross's spine stiffened and his face flushed. "A bloody damn test?"

Legna waved a hand dismissively. "It is of no further concern the devices have been rendered useless. Trust is the basis for a propitious relationship, Mr. Cross. Without trust, deceit flourishes, does it not?"

"That dog hunts both ways."

If Legna understood the jab, he ignored it. "You have reviewed the testimony referencing Earth's air quality?"

"We have," Gabriel answered.

"As I promised, the cleansing of your atmosphere has begun."

Gabriel forced a half-smile. "We are most grateful."

Cross leaned forward aggressively. "Frankly, I find your seemingly altruistic gestures misleading. You offer this assistance yet pursue the deliberate and systematic extermination of our future society."

"Your boorish description aside, do you not view the reduction of Earth's population as a worthy cause?"

"Not if it means killing innocent babies."

"Come, come, Citizen Cross, such harsh rhetoric is not conducive to harmony. No human is being butchered, hanged, electrocuted, or beheaded; tactics all too often employed by your own. Despite your condemnation, our method will create a proper balance without harm."

"That's a matter of opinion. What about the terminally ill and the elderly?"

"They shall pass quietly."

"Without medical assistance."

"The methods employed are humane and shall assist in bringing Earth into proper balance."

"Humane by whose standards?"

Now it was Gabriel who argued. "Then people have every right to know what is being done and why."

"The *why* should be obvious—to avoid the extinction of human society. However, I will entertain your thought."

Is he actually seeking our opinion? Put him to the test now—do it. "People are entitled to know why they are being asked to make these sacrifices."

"Is the 'why' not clear? How many times must it be clarified?"

"Telling us is not the same as informing the masses."

Cross blew out a hard breath. "Tell me this much, when balance is achieved, will all this be reversed?"

Legna diverted his eyes.

"Shall I repeat the question?"

"It is not permanent—it will terminate in one of your years."

"Then, damn it, why not tell them that?"

Cross was inching ever closer to an argument that would only inflame Legna, so Gabriel jumped in. "You once told me our civilization was but a blink of an eye in time. That makes us intergalactic babes in the woods."

"Babes in the woods?" Legna repeated.

"We're still evolving and are entitled to be in control of that own journey just as Ecaepian decided on theirs."

"To achieve a supreme level of consciousness, mankind must embrace our benevolence as an opportunity freely given, one that may never come their way again." Legna slipped from the sofa and ambled to a window and intertwined his hands behind his back. "Citizen Gabriel, you have plighted, have you not?"

"I have, Citizen Legna."

"And you, Citizen Cross?"

Gabriel looked to Cross. *Damn it, Alan, say yes, say yes!*

Cross answered, "Yes, I stand with Gabriel."

"Then there is no discordance among us."

Legna strolled back to the desk and sat.

"We still owe the public an explanation about zero births," Cross said resolutely.

Legna's look shifted to Gabriel.

Gabriel shook his head. "No way, I'm not making another televised speech."

"Very well, I shall honor your conviction. Converse with Masma. A written explanation is to be circulated, endorsed by you both."

Wow, Gabriel thought, *did he just give us a big wet kiss? One for our team. e H*

"There is yet another matter I wish you to oversee." Then he went silent for what felt like an eternity. "The weather is turning. Your sun warms the Earth. Soon a new season will arrive." Without skipping a beat, he dropped a bomb. In a soft, hushed voice, he said, "As Masma had informed you, citizens are to relinquish their weapons. I wish you to present a proposal to accomplish this task."

Cross leaped to his feet and whooped, "Whoa! You're moving a little fast. First zero births and now the confiscation of personal weapons? That will cause—"

Legna turned swiftly and cut Cross short with a contemptuous wave of his hand. "I will not entertain further discussion. If there is opposition, it will be dealt with."

Now Gabriel was on his feet. "Your actions will be seen as a hostile act."

Legna moved swiftly across the room and planted himself three feet in front of them and said forcefully, "There is little need for weapons in a peaceful, harmonious society. I leave the method by which this task is to be achieved to you both. When created, present your proposal to Masma."

Legna returned to the window. "So pleased you could join me this fine day. Peace, harmony and balance be with you."

As they left, Cross stole a glance at Ms. Mosby, who sat stone-faced at her desk. She smiled, but it looked more like a smirk.

Cross waited until they were out of ear range of Mosby. "I can't stand to be in the presence of that little shit."

"That little shit, if he's telling the truth, can do for us what we've failed to do for ourselves, however painful that might prove in the short run. The trick is reining him in from his heavy-handed pronouncements like all he has to do is snap his fingers and '*it shall be so*.'"

"With every bone in my body, I don't trust a word that comes out of his little mouth."

I'll set up a meeting with Masma and we'll draft that announcement."

They paused at Gabriel's office door.

"Tell me Alan, why have you chosen to stay? Legna said there would be no recrimination if either of us left."

"Easy question, easy answer: I took an oath to the American people. I intend to keep it. Just one point keeps me up at night. Those ships up there, they could have extracted him from the Arizona site easily. Yet, he chose to go on the run with you and Blake. Why?"

"I've asked myself the same question a dozen times."

50

As Gabriel entered his suite, Betty grabbed his arm and whispered, "Hold on Sparky, you have a visitor."

"Why are you whispering?"

She nodded toward his office. "See for yourself."

"I'm not up for more surprises."

"This one you'll like."

Entering his office, Gabriel saw a man studying his framed University of Missouri graduation certificate hanging on the wall behind his desk.

"Impressive as hell. I have one of those too."

"Owen?"

Owen Jennings turned and greeted Gabriel with a wide smile. "In the flesh."

"My God! Who let you out of jail?"

"Don't sound so disappointed, Cuban boy."

Gabriel encircled Jennings in a hug, then inspected him from head-to-toe. By some miracle, Jennings looked extraordinarily fit. Only a few lingering scars remained on the right side of his face. "You look wonderful."

"I'm officially an out-patient; twice weekly checkups and no surgeries."

Gabriel hugged Jennings again.

"I'm just so damn happy to see you healthy again. Back in Arizona, when we heard those helicopters circling overhead…" His words trailed off at the memory. Moving to his desk, he retrieved the pack of Marlboros from the drawer.

"Are you allowed to smoke in here?"

"I had the smoke detector disconnected."

"That'll get you a prison term. Toss one over." Jennings lit the cigarette, took a long drag, held it, and expelled it slowly. "After what I've been through these can't kill me."

"What happened after we left?"

Jennings gaze strayed across the room as the memory flooded back. "Once they confirmed Legna wasn't there, they herded us into the first floor and shot everyone... the guards, Rod, even Daniels—me last."

"Daniels? They shot their own guy?"

"Scorched earth—no witnesses. I remained conscious, but played dead. They must have set a ton of charges because there was one hell of a loud explosion one second and the next I was flying through the air. That's all I remember."

"The place was incinerated. The search team found you in the woods."

"So, they tell me. I didn't ask her at the hospital, but what is Blake doing here, I thought she would have returned to San Diego?"

"Catherine and I have become a couple."

"A couple of what?'

"Housemates."

Jennings laughed. "What? You two were like fire and water."

"Suppose I'll let Catherine fill in the blanks. You'll come to dinner?"

Jennings hesitated and took a long drag on his cigarette. "Not just yet, give me a few days. I need to get my head straight, you know. So much has happened"

"No rush—when you're ready. Where are you staying?"

"Would you believe one block from your place—an agency safe house in a high-rise condo."

"Give me a phone number and address."

"Did you not understand it's a *secret* CIA safe house?"

"Cut the bullshit and write it down."

"Okay, but if you go to prison, I won't bring you cigarettes." He scribbled a phone number and address on a slip of paper and handed it to Gabriel. "Please don't share that."

"Do I look like a dumbass to you?"

"Sometimes."

At 6:30 PM, Gabriel arrived home with a large pizza in hand. "Pizza man," he called out.

No answer.

"Anybody home?"

Still no reply.

He set the pizza on the kitchen counter and moved on to the bedroom. Catherine was curled up under the covers sleeping soundly on her side. She stirred and opened her eyes, "How long have you been standing there?"

"Just now—brought a pizza."

"Good, I had nothing planned."

"Why are you sleeping at this hour?"

"Just a bit tired—been feeling that way for the past week. Probably a bug. I'm seeing a doctor day after tomorrow."

"But you are a doctor, dear girl."

"Ha, ha."

"Seriously, are you okay?"

"I've just been a bit tired lately."

"Come, have some pizza, you'll feel better."

"What's on it?

"Fried farts and buttermilk. Come on, I have news."

She stretched and yawned. "Get out of here, I have to pee."

Minutes later they were sitting at the kitchen bar eating a cheese and pepperoni pizza.

"*Mmm*, very good. Arico's?"

"Where else?" Gabriel replied.

"So, what's your news Legna's a transvestite?"

"Don't talk with your mouth full. And just this one time, we will not speak of the almighty World Administrator."

"Then what?"

"Owen surprised me at the office today."

Catherine dropped her pizza to her plate "Holy—how!?"

"They released him. He's officially an out-patient—check-ups twice a week."

"My God, that's wonderful."

"He'll come to dinner in a couple of days. I broke the news that we were together."

"And?"

"His first reaction was—What? Mr. Oil and Ms. Water?"

Catherine laughed.

"But he couldn't be happier. Are you sure you're feeling okay?"

"Stop already, I'm fine."

For the rest of the meal, they engaged in small talk—nothing about Legna, nothing that would stress either of them more than they already were. Later, they watched a re-run of director Ridley Scott's 2000 movie, "Gladiator."

The following morning, Gabriel and Alan Cross met in Masma's office to draft the announcement regarding the mass sterilizations. In less an hour, they agreed on a draft and sent it to Legna for his approval.

"I fear the repercussions when this bomb drops," Cross droned. "If my name is to be attached, I want to be informed of what changes Legna makes *before* it goes out."

"Yes, Citizen Cross," Masma said.

With the meeting concluded, Cross left to attend to other matters, but Gabriel lingered.

"We have become friends?" he said to Masma. "What I mean is, during our brief time together we've developed a level of trust."

"We have."

"Then we can speak openly?"

Masma nodded. "You wish to know if our chosen path has proven to be all we anticipated?"

"Well, yes… but only if you're comfortable sharing it with me."

Masma strolled to the only window in his small office. He swung his hands behind his back and intertwined his fingers just as Legna so often did. They could have been interchangeable, and none would be the wiser.

"The weather is turning agreeable."

That's exactly what Legna said just yesterday. Do they share the same thoughts too?

"You are fortunate to experience seasons."

"Yes, we are. Which reminds me, while we were on Ecaep there was a storm. Catherine and I became aware of a—"

"The dome is for our safety and comfort," Masma said softly.

Damn it, he knows what I'm going to say. "Safety from what?"

"The elements."

Gabriel decided not to push Masma on the subject and shifted to another question, one he considered far more important. "Has the transformation amplified your life as you had hoped?"

Masma slowly turned, his eyes set, his narrow lips tight. Several beats passed before he finally spoke. "All life forms throughout the universes are identical at the moment of birth, replicated unerringly from one galaxy to another; it is the way of the Originator. But the Originator does not direct the path each civilization chooses to pursue. Many are misguided and falter until they are beyond redemption."

"Yes, I understand all too well. It is the same here; we make choices, and we live with the results good or bad."

Masma turned back to the window and joined his hands behind him again.

"Now we are faced with new choices, without a doubt the most critical in our brief history. How we make those choices depends on Legna."

"How do you mean?"

"He has demonstrated great empathy for our citizens with the distribution of water and food and the cleansing of the atmosphere. However, if those gestures prove to be deceptive in any way... I'm sorry, deceptive is the wrong word, what I meant was—"

"You must trust, Citizen Gabriel."

Gabriel closed his eyes. *I think you blew it again, Ferro. Choose your words carefully.*

Masma took a long, slow, breath and expelled it just as slowly. He spoke haltingly barely above a whisper. "Long before the Great Transformation... my life mirrored yours in so many ways."

What did he just say? I thought they had no memory of their past? Okay, be cool, don't question it, let him talk.

"I was authored by parents as were you... educated as were you. In time, I chose a mate, and together we sired a male offspring." He stopped again as if recalling such memories caused him great anguish. "Our descendant..." His eyes strayed to the floor. "... perished in the Great War. Unable to accept this loss... my mate passed on."

Is he speaking to me or to himself—he looks distressed.

Wistfully, Masma continued. "Our society had lost its way... selfishly indulging in our primal impulses... until we were confronted with extinction if we did not champion change."

The phone rang and it startled Masma. It rang twice more time before he scurried to the desk and answer and listened intently without responding then hung up. "Citizen Legna has sanctioned the draft with modifications. He wishes it disseminated at the one o'clock hour this day. I bid you good day."

"But you were explaining your—"

"I wish you not to repeat what I revealed."

"I wouldn't do that."

"I bid you good day, Citizen Gabriel."

Masma turned back to the window. The meeting had ended. Gabriel knew not to push Masma further.

Back in his office, Gabriel drummed his fingers nervously on the desk waiting for Masma to call about any changes Legna may have made in the news release. It was already 12:55 PM.

"Damn it, where's that bloody release?"

"Gabriel," Betty announced over the intercom. "Mr. Cross is on the line."

Gabriel scooped up the phone. "No, I haven't seen the final draft."

"Goddamn that little runt," Cross cursed. "Well, it's too damn late now."

"Turn on your TV; we'll hear it together."

Over the intercom, Gabriel called to Betty. "You're welcome to watch the announcement with me."

"As long as you're not smoking."

Betty entered. "Where do you put the butts?"

"I eat them. Be quiet and sit."

The TV screen was blank. He checked his watch again: 1:02 PM.

"They're late."

A show card appeared on the screen that read: *An important message from the office of the World Administrator.* Five seconds later the screen went blank again. Finally, soft, soothing music began, and text crawled up and back like the opening credits of a Superman movie.

Gabriel groaned. "Whose bright idea was that?"

A deep male voice narrated as the text traveled over the screen: *To our fellow citizens: The rapid expansion of our population has exceeded the Earth's ability to support. Natural resources continue to dwindle at an alarming rate placing our very survival in peril. It is paramount that new life be suspended until our numbers have been reduced to manageable levels. What is underway is but a small sacrifice to ensure the survival of our species. We empathize with the hardship this casts upon our society, but the moratorium will ensure the future of our civilization. That and that alone should be our objective. Thank you, and may we all revel in peace, harmony, and balance.*

It was signed, *Gabriel Ferro and Alan Cross.*

The screen went black for two seconds before the message began all over again.

With a somber look, Betty asked, "You wrote that?"

"Hell, no!" Gabriel slammed a flat hand to the desk. "The son-of-a-bitch pulled a switch. That's not the way we presented it!"

Betty abruptly stood. "You should immediately distance yourself from that message."

"Right, I'll go on TV and disavow everything, in which case I'm toast." He was up on his feet. "No calls, no visitors!"

Betty mumbled something he didn't understand and left.

Within an hour, the calls were stacking up from bombastic military types advocating a military response. Some of the messages were from members of Congress—even though they were officially out of business—and more than a few from irate religious leaders suggesting the devil incarnate occupied the Oval Office.

Gabriel ignored them all.

Alan Cross stormed in just long enough to vent his anger. "Goddamn it, that's not what we wrote! What the hell do we do about it?"

"We do nothing. For the foreseeable future, no new life is going to be born on this planet, period."

"The shit is going to hit the proverbial fan at the speed of light." And with that Cross stormed out.

At four o'clock Betty stuck her head in the door. "You have a call."

"I said no calls."

"It's your friend Rafi—he needs to speak with you, *now*."

Gabriel scooped up the phone. "Rafi, you heard?"

"Who wrote that piece of crap?"

"Legna—what are you hearing?"

"I thought the Internet was down?"

"I thought so too?"

"Well, it's not. Social media's humming like a high-performance race engine."

"Cross and I and Masma tried to soften the tone of the message."

"Well, from where I sit, you failed." There was a pregnant pause before Rafi asked, "Who the hell is Masma?"

"One of them."

"There's more of them down here?"

"Three, total; the rest are on those ships."

"Okay, okay meet me at eight, same place. We need to talk."

"I'll be there."

Gabriel called Owen Jennings.

Five rings later Jennings answered, "Cuban Boy, what's up?"

"Where are you?"

"Langley."

"Can I pick you up at 7:30 PM? There's someone you need to meet."

"Who?"

"Don't want to say. I'll pick you up in front of your place."

He hung up and almost immediately Betty buzzed him.

He grunted, "This better be good."

"It's Catherine."

"Oh, okay." He punched up the blinking line. "Hey beautiful, what's up?"

"That announcement was pure puke!"

"That's a colorful way to put it."

"Gabriel, there is going to be one hell-of-a fallout."

"Tell me something I don't know. Is this why you called?"

"No, meet me later at Arico's."

"I have a 7:30 appointment."

"Then meet me at six."

"I can't be late for the appointment."

"Just be there at six."

The line went dead.

At 6:07 PM Gabriel parked in the garage below his condo. He decided to walk to Arico's since it was just a block away—it would clear his clouded brain before meeting Catherine. As soon as he hit the street, his Secret Service guys waved to him.

"Thought you were going home?" Remy Bernard said.

"I'm walking over to Arico's."

"Hop in, we'll drive you."

"I'd rather walk, see you there."

And off he went with the Secret Service SUV driving slowly alongside.

It was 6:16 PM when he arrived at Arico's. There were two couples at one table, and two others at another. Catherine was sitting in a booth on the far right.

"I thought we agreed on six?" Catherine said through clenched teeth.

"Lest you forget, the world is in a state of flux and I'm in the middle of the flux."

"I remind you you're there by choice."

"You're in a bit of a snit; what's wrong?"

"That news release, you should have told Legna to go straight to hell."

"I did, right after I polished his shoes and made him a hot cup of peppermint tea."

She pushed back against her chair, breathed in, and exhaled. "Sorry."

"Let's have it, what's eating you?"

"Nothing's *eating* me."

"Then what?"

"I saw the doctor's today—an acquaintance at Bethesda."

"What is it? The flu, dead brain cells, what?"

Vicenzo Arico, the restaurant's owner, approached. "Buona Sera, Mr. Ferro, Dr. Blake—come stai questa sera?"

"I think you asked me how we're doing."

"Si, your Italian is getting molto meglio, Mr. Ferro. The world is getting molto passo."

"Vicenzo, tonight we don't discuss bad things."

"Ah si, you are right. Do you wish to hear the specials this evening?"

"No, there's something I'd like Franco to fix."

"Sir, what is that, Mr. Ferro?"

"Something very simple my mother used to make. Drain the spaghetti and place it in a bowl, add some salt and pepper, several pats of butter, lots of olive oil, a handful of Parmesan, and a small amount of crushed red pepper. That's it." He looked at Catherine for her approval.

"Sounds good to me—go easy on the pepper flakes, please."

"Si, Senora."

"And a Caprese salad."

"Capris, si, an excellent choice with your pasta. Wine?

"Not for me," Catherine quickly said.

"Pinot Grigio for me."

"Gracie." And off to the kitchen Vicenzo went.

"No wine?"

"Not tonight."

"So, tell me what the doctor said?"

"Not to drink wine." She placed her napkin on the table and rose. "I have to go to the restroom."

"Wait a minute, you didn't finish."

"I'll be right back."

Vicenzo arrived with the Caprese salad. "Senora?"

"Restroom."

"Ah, si."

Vicenzo placed the sliced tomato, fresh mozzarella, and basil salad in the middle of the table, then stood there like something was on his mind.

"If it's about the aliens, we will not speak of them tonight."

"No signore, I wish to express la mia grande fiducia in—"

"I don't understand."

"Mi scusi… I wish to express my great confidence in you. I know you will do what is right."

"Thank you, Vicenzo. I appreciate that."

"Bon apatite."

Vicenzo left just as Catherine returned.

"Feel better?" Gabriel asked.

"Better."

"So, what did the doctor say?"

She hesitated and looked away.

"What?"

Slowly, her eyes came back to him. "You recall our last night on Ecaep?"

"A first for humans—should be in the Guinness Book of Records."

Her eyes locked onto his like a laser locking onto its intended target. "I'm expecting."

If he understood the implications, he certainly didn't show it; his only reaction was no reaction. Then the gears in his brain began turning faster and faster. Pushing forward against the table, his voice jumped up two octaves. "Jesus, you're expecting! How?"

"Surely, your father explained the process."

"Holy!"

Catherine placed a finger to her lips. "Lower your voice. According to the doctor, I conceived about the time we played space fornicators."

"But it could have also been when we returned home."

"Then, presumably I would have been subjected to whatever is floating around in the atmosphere, so I would *not* have conceived, but I did."

"Holy shit! You're sure?"

"One hundred percent."

He sucked in a sharp, deep breath, then stupidly said, "But you're barely pregnant."

"Gabriel, darling, you either are, or you aren't."

He pushed back against the chair. "I don't know what to say."

"Try uttering the word *happy.*"

"Yes, yes, *happy,* yes!"

He scanned the other guests wondering if they had overheard their conversation. No one was paying them any attention, except one guy in a blue blazer sitting with two women and another man four tables away.

Catherine leaned in close. "You should know right up front that—"

Gabriel's attention had strayed.

"What?"

"Are you listening to me?"

He tilted his head in the man's direction. "That guy—the one in the blue blazer—he keeps looking over here."

"You're paranoid."

"Sorry, what were you saying?"

"I want this baby; their zero-birth policy be damned. No one—*no one*—is going to take it from me. So help me God, I'll march into the White House and kill the bastard myself."

Vicenzo approached with their dinner. "Chef Franco says this is one of his favorite dishes too; simple but *fántastico.*"

Still reeling from Catherine's news, Gabriel forced a smile. "Thank Franco for fixing it."

As soon as Vicenzo was out of range, Catherine leaned forward and whispered, "Let's not talk here. We'll discuss it at home."

"I have that meeting."

"With who?"

Gabriel reached across the table and took her hand in his and squeezed. "This will be okay, I promise."

She smiled a hesitant smile and squeezed his hand back. "I love you."

"Right here, right now, I want to hold you, to kiss you."

The man in the blue blazer who had been stealing glances, approached. He stood about six feet tall, had thinning hair, and was a bit beefy around the waist. "Are you Gabriel Ferro?"

"I am, and you would be?"

"Somebody who thinks you should be tarred and feathered."

Gabriel grinned. "I didn't catch your name?"

"I didn't offer it."

"Whoever you are," Catherine scoffed, "you're being rude."

"Perhaps I could buy you a drink," Gabriel said with a smile, "but only if you'll rejoin your friends. In fact, let me buy a round for your table."

"You're in league with those aliens," the man snarled. "You're an insult to the human race and the memory of President Conrad."

Gabriel exhaled through his nose. "Listen, do us both a favor and go back to your table, okay?"

The man's brow drew down in a sullen, angry manner. "And you should stick it where the sun doesn't shine, traitor."

Gabriel's eyes went to Catherine—she looked horrified. He looked up at the guy with tightened eyes. "Not sure I heard right—what was that last part?"

"Gabriel," Catherine cautioned.

"I said it in plain English—you're a traitor."

Before the interloper could take another breath, Gabriel was on his feet, knocking over his chair in the process. Balling his right hand into a tight fist, he slugged the guy squarely on the jaw—it hit with a sickening thud. The stunned man's eyes splayed wide. He teetered, then fell to the floor like a sack of manure. In unison, the restaurant patrons gasped.

Mortified, Catherine pushed back from the table.

"Ouch!" Gabriel rubbed his hand. "Damn it, that hurt!"

The guy lay moaning on the floor in a fetal position.

Gabriel knelt down on one knee beside him. "You okay, fella? I bet that was worse than having a tooth pulled without Novocain. Come on, big guy, up you go."

He slipped his hands under the disoriented man's armpits and helped him to his feet. "There you go. Be careful, don't fall, seeing stars, are we?"

Gabriel guided him back to his table and sat him down. So stunned were the man's companions, not one uttered a word.

"I believe this gentleman belongs to one of you. He'll wake up in the morning with a headache, but he'll be fine—maybe a little bruised around the chin, even a loose tooth or two." Then turning to the other dinner guests, he announced, "It's all over everyone, enjoy your meals."

Gabriel rubbed his aching hand and returned to his table. "I can't believe I just did that."

"Jeez, me neither." Catherine gulped. "What possessed you?"

"My Miami upbringing."

Vicenzo quickstepped to their table. "I heard what he said, I'm so sorry, Mr. Ferro."

"Everything's under control, Vicenzo, just don't serve him another drink."

Visibly shaken, Vicenzo half-bowed and returned to the kitchen. "I am so dis-piace questo è successo, pazienza con alcune di queste persone. Vino della casa." He pointed to the offending man who still looked dazed. "Per tutti tranne lui."

"Translation?" Catherine asked.

"Only the last part; *wine on the house, except for that guy*—I think." He reached for Catherine's hand and wrapped it in his. "Let's not allow this to ruin your news."

"Do you have to go to this meeting?"

"Yeah, sorry."

"Promise not to hit anyone else tonight?"

He grinned, withdrew his hand from hers and rubbed his knuckles. "For the record, my hand hurts like hell."

51

Jennings was standing by the curb when Gabriel arrived. He slipped into the passenger seat.

"How're the accommodations?" Gabriel asked.

"Adequate for the CIA." Jennings noticed Gabriel's hand. "Your right hand, it looks red and swollen."

"A force that thought it was unmovable was met by a movable one."

"Huh?"

"Long story."

"Where are we going?"

"To meet a friend."

When they arrived, the nearest empty space Gabriel could find in the parking garage was number 47.

Jennings glanced over his shoulder. "A black SUV tailed us. Secret Service or FBI?"

"Oh crap, I forgot—Secret Service."

"Wow, you've gone up in the world."

"Not by choice."

Rafi was leaning up against his SUV in space 36. His eyes narrowed at the sight of Jennings.

"Sorry, I didn't give you a heads ups. Rafi Suharto, say hello to Owen Jennings."

Rafi eyed Jennings suspiciously and shook his hand.

"You two belong to the same brotherhood. Owen is also CIA."

A look of recognition came over Rafi's face. "Wait, you're *the* Owen Jennings?"

Jennings smiled. "There could be others."

"It's an honor to meet you, Mr. Jennings. You're a legend within the agency."

"Call me Owen. And the term 'legend' is reserved for dead agents. Gabriel shared with me your unbelievable Indonesian adventure."

Rafi's brow raised. "It was like slipping into another dimension."

Since Jennings had never been identified publicly as the one in charge of Legna's Arizona internment, Gabriel thought it best to keep it that way. "Owen and I were college roommates. I trust him and wanted him in on this. Okay with you?"

"I welcome a fellow agent."

Gabriel asked, "What's so important?"

"That news release," Rafi said. "All it did was stir up an already disturbed bee's nest. From the reports coming in, the demonstrations are growing fast. You have to find a way to turn this around, and quick."

"You assume Legna listens to me."

"If not you, Gabriel, who? You have to appeal to him or there are going to be a lot of people hurt and killed."

Jennings asked, "The demonstrators look to be well organized. Who's doing the organizing?"

"A self-proclaimed anti-alien groups in Europe—hackers who know how to use the Internet, communicating via shadow sites and changing IP addresses faster than we can track them. I'm surprised the aliens don't shut them down."

Jennings said, "Maybe they want them to keep operating. Gives people an outlet to blow off steam."

Rafi countered, "Except people get killed in the process."

"You think the alien's give a damn about that?" Jennings scoffed.

"Except," Gabriel interjected, "Legna's threatened retaliation if the demonstrations don't stop. Look at what happened to the Eiffel Tower."

"That was purely for show. He's says the demonstrations have to stop, but it's not necessarily what he means."

"I don't follow."

"Maybe it's a tactic, a distraction while he forges on with his agenda. Let the public blow off steam, let them act out like animals. So, some people will die, so what? It fits right in with his 'reduce the population' efforts. My guess is, he doesn't give a rat's ass about the demonstrations, only what he was sent here to do."

"Whew... if that's true," Gabriel said, "then Rafi's right, we have to find a way stop it."

"Now you're thinking."

Suddenly, a loud, sharp crack echoed throughout the vast garage and the driver's side window of Rafi's SUV exploded into sharp shards of glass.

"What the hell was that!" Gabriel wailed.

"Get down!" Rafi ordered.

They dropped to the cement floor just as two more shots rang out. One bore into the hood, the other deflected off the wall into the back of the SUV.

In a forced whisper, Gabriel hissed, "What the hell!"

Rafi grabbed Jennings arm. "Do you have your weapon with you?"

"No, damn it!"

"Crawl behind the vehicle."

On their hands and knees, they scrambled to the rear of the SUV. With his revolver in hand, Rafi rose up until his eyes were level with the left rear tail light just as another shot rang out. It whizzed inches past his head, ricochet off the wall into the SUV rear window, leaving a splintered mark three-inches round.

Rafi had seen the gun flash—it was coming from space 44. He fired twice in that direction only to have a volley of rounds returned. "It's a semi-automatic, maybe two."

Jennings whipped out his cell phone and was about to call for help when they heard the sound of an engine revving and it was traveling fast. Then the sound of screeching wheels followed by brakes being applied hard. Doors were opening, followed by rapid gunfire. Now shots were coming from two locations, yet none of the fire was directed at them. Overlapping gunfire rang out for about a minute before all went dead quiet.

Gabriel's entire body was oscillating,

"Stay down!" Rafi cautioned.

He inched up just high enough to see two men in dark suits, weapons drawn, rushing toward them. He raised his gun and took aim.

"Mr. Ferro!" a voice called out.

Gabriel rose to his knees and was elated to see Remy and Dex trotting toward them. Grabbing Rafi's raised arm, he yelped, "Wait, don't shoot!"

"Everybody all right?" Dex yelled out.

"They're Secret Service!" Gabriel bounded to his feet. "God, am I relieved to see you two. What just happened?"

Remy eyed Rafi's weapon. "Would you put that away, sir?"

Rafi obliged and holstered his gun.

Dex eagle-eyed Jennings and Rafi. "May I ask who you two are?"

"They're CIA," Gabriel said.

"Can we see identification?"

Rafi and Jennings flashed their IDs. Remy carefully examined them, looked the two men over, and passed them back. "Thank you, gentlemen. Those two back there were most likely hunting you, Mr. Ferro. They're both dead."

Gabriel breathed a sigh. "Who are they?"

"Don't know yet." Holstering his weapon, Dex said, "We going to have to make a report."

"I trust you have ways of working this out without involving us."

"Look, Mr. Ferro," Remy said, "you can't be making these clandestine night runs without taking us into your confidence. We're not clueless, we realize you're in the middle of it."

Silence while Dex and Remy exchanged glances again.

"No more night runs without us knowing who and where."

Gabriel crossed his heart. "Scout's honor, Remy, honest."

"All right, let's get you guys out of here before someone stumbles in. We'll leave those two back there. The DC cops will find them and chalk it up as a drug deal gone bad. Let's get you all home."

Jennings said, "Agent Suharto can drop me off."

"Fine. Mr. Ferro, your keys—you'll go with me. Dex will follow in your car."

Still shaking, Gabriel handed Dex his keys. "Never a dull moment."

52

Catherine was curled up on the sofa reading a medical journal when Gabriel arrived home.

"How'd your mysterious meeting go?"

Gabriel gave her a quick forced smile. "Fine, just fine."

He whizzed past her to the kitchen. His hands were trembling, and he felt sick to his stomach. Grabbing the end of the counter to steady himself, he took several deep breaths. He grabbed a glass and placed it under the refrigerator ice dispenser. A couple of cubes missed and fell to the floor. "Goddamn it!"

Scooping up the fallen cubes, he flung them in the sink. Retrieving a bottle of whiskey from a nearby cabinet, he poured an inch into the glass, raised it, and muttered, "To would-be assassins and the good guys who saved us."

In one continuous swallow, he emptied the glass. The second time around, he poured two inches and downed it in one gulp.

Catherine came in as he was fixing a third. "Why are your knees scuffed?"

"What?"

She pointed to his knees.

"Oh, I must have rubbed up against the car." He took a sip of the whiskey.

"That's your third."

"How would you know; you were in the other room?"

"There's nothing wrong with my hearing. I heard you pour. I've never seen you drink like this."

"Like what?" he snapped.

"Hey, don't bite my head off. What happened out there tonight?"

"Nothing." He placed the now empty glass on the counter and turned to her. "You said you loved me."

"I do."

"Say it."

"Gabriel, what's wrong?"

"Just say it."

"Okay... I love you."

"And I love *you*. That makes us a mutual admiration society of two, right?"

"Okay... yes."

"Then marry me."

"Whoa, what brought that on?"

"Mutual admiration societies should seal the deal."

"Come, you're not making sense. What's wrong?"

"Nothing makes sense—not a goddamn thing." He poured another shot of whiskey. "The whole friggin' world doesn't make sense." He took a gulp from the glass and turned to her. "Before the grand entrance of Legna and crew, a survey was taken of senior college students who were about to graduate and enter the big, bad world on the next chapter in their lives." His speech was slightly slurred now.

"Where did that come from?"

"Just listen. These hopped-up, raring-to-go, about to be ex-student were asked what their most important life goals were. Around 60 percent of the little shits said, getting rich. The remaining 40 percent said they wanted to become famous."

"Fascinating but discouraging facts to be sure. Why are you telling me this?"

"Because the ungrateful little bastards believe those are the most important goals in achieving a successful life. When did the world pivot to the bullshit that replaced common sense?"

"Are we going there again?"

Through slurred speech, he blurted, "Where's that mean, pray tell?"

"Your penchant for taking on the sins of the world like you alone are responsible."

He emptied the glass in one gulp.

"Gabriel! Slow down with that stuff."

"You and me, and now a child on the way—that's what's important, that's what this short-lived thing we call life is all about, nothing more, nothing less; it begins with family, and it ends with family. Everything in between is pure bullshit. So, let's try this again for the West Coast."

He set the glass on the counter and warbled down on one knee.

"Oh, for heaven's sake, get up."

"Catherine Blake—Jesus, I don't even know your middle name."

"It's Justine, and I'm not amused by whatever you think you're doing."

"Catherine Justine Blake, doctor extraordinaire, mother of our soon-to-be-born child, will you take this slightly inebriated man to be your lawful wedded husband?"

She placed her hands on his shoulders. "Gabriel, for God's sake, get up."

"I know, I know, you're angry because I'm proposing without a ring. Okay, tomorrow, we'll shop for a proper ring."

"If you don't get up this minute, I'll push you over and leave you lying on the floor."

"I'm not getting up until you accept my proposal."

"Oh, I give up!" She spun on her heels and stormed into the living room.

"Why are you making this so difficult, Catherine Justine Blake?" Placing a hand on the counter to steady himself, he rose to his feet and took off after her.

She was standing by the glass sliding doors, arms crossed over her chest.

"I'm sorry, I royally screwed that up. I never said that I wasn't an asshole."

"You are."

He grinned. "And don't think you're the only one who knows."

"Something happened out there tonight, what was it?"

He came up behind her and attempted to put his hands around her waist. She pulled away.

"Where were you? What happened?"

He hung his head low and lied, "I hit a dog—a *big* one.'"

She turned to face him. "A dog?"

"Damn thing ran out in front of me and *bam*, I hit him. I stopped, but he was dead, no identification. I left him by the side of the road. It really tore me up. I've never caused anything in this world to die by my hand."

"Are you telling me the truth?

He crossed his heart. "Scouts honor."

Catherine reached for him. "Come here, you big idiot." She wrapped her arms around him. "That was a sloppy proposal at best."

"But, I meant it—marry me."

"With all that's happening?"

"All the more reason not to waste the present. I'm thirty-eight, I've been through one marriage that crashed and burned. Now, I'm standing in front of the one person who means more to me than any other. She's going to have a child… our child. So, the only sensible thing to do is to face the future together. No matter what it holds, I want to see this life through with you."

Her arms tightened around his waist.

"I'm going to take that as a yes, *Justine*."

She laid her head gently on his chest and squeezed him tight. "Yes, Gabriel Javier Ferro."

"Tomorrow then—tomorrow, we get married." He lifted her head. Her eyes were tearing. "Those better be tears of joy, girl."

She wiped away a tear and smiled. "You're like a fart in a whirlwind, you know that."

"I hear that a lot." He placed a hand flat against her stomach and kissed her passionately. "My fiery Cuban mother will have a conniption when she hears we got hitched and she wasn't present. Wait 'till she finds out she's going to be a grandmother."

"Then fly her here, or we could go to her. What's a couple of days' delay?"

"Under the circumstances, maybe a lifetime; we need to do this tomorrow."

Catherine breathed out a sigh. "Okay, okay, tomorrow, but you'll catch hell from your mother."

"I'll be first in line to get a marriage license." He kissed her again. Then, feeling a bit dizzy from too much booze too quick, he placed a hand on his forehead. "I need to go to bed. Big day tomorrow. See you in the morning."

He stumbled off to the bedroom. Later, when she checked on him, he was sleeping peacefully but fully clothed. She removed his shoes, pulled the blanket over him, and kissed him on the forehead.

When Gabriel awoke in the morning, he was surprised to find he was fully clothed and under the covers. Catherine was sleeping peacefully beside him. Slipping out of bed, he headed for the guest bathroom and stood and stared into the mirror. The incident of the night before came flooding back like a horrific dream. "You could have gotten yourself killed. How would that had served anything?"

After showering, shaving, and fixing a cup of coffee, he skipped breakfast, slipped back into the master bedroom, and retrieved his best dark suit and a blue striped tie from the closet. Once dressed, he headed to his study to write in his journal:

> *I thought I understood how fragile and immediate life was until last night when I came close to being just another dead statistic. My life could have ended in a parking garage if not for a couple of bad shooters and my Secret Service angels. If things had gone badly, I would have left the love of my life to raise our child alone. I am a lucky man. I will marry this wonderful woman today. I will do all in my power to protect her, our baby, and whatever I am able to do for the rest of the world.*
>
> *That last part sounds pretty damn pretentious.*
>
> *Now I have to find a way to tell my mother I'm married and she's going to be a grandmother. But she'll forgive me... she always does.*

In the kitchen, he scribbled a quick message and propped it up against the coffee maker:

413

I'll be back around ten, the note read, *and we'll be off to find an officiant to perform a civil wedding ceremony. You are the brightest star in my universe. Love you.*

He was first in line to obtain a marriage license at the Moultrie Courthouse on Indiana Avenue. At 9:50 AM, he returned to the condo, marriage license in hand, along with a bouquet of red and yellow roses. Catherine, looking absolutely stunning in an off-the-shoulder, ankle-length, white, chiffon evening dress, was ready and waiting. He presented her with the roses.

"Aww, thank you, they're beautiful… you romantic, you."

"My God, you look absolutely stunning."

Her face stretched into a wide smile. "I bought this dress with no idea when I'd get to wear it."

"Trust me, you should wear it as often as possible."

"So where is all this happening?"

"And ruin the surprise?"

It was all happening in a dizzying whirlwind.

Driving from Georgetown into Washington proper, they turned east on Constitution Avenue, past the White House, south on Second Street NE, and right on First Avenue NE, stopping at the foot of the steps leading to the sixteen imposing golden marble columns that framed the magnificent edifice of the United States Supreme Court.

The look on Catherine's face was priceless. "You have got to be kidding!"

Gabriel cracked a wry smile. "One of the perks of the job."

Catherine cupped her face in her hands and giggled. "I'm not believing any of this!"

They made their way up the steps to the front door to find it securely locked.

"As with any locked door," Gabriel said, "we knock."

And knock Gabriel did. A few seconds later, the door swung open.

A young man who looked to be in his late twenties greeted them. "Good morning, Mr. Ferro. I'm Danny Gilman, junior law clerk to Chief Justice Harold Cunningham. Please come join us."

Blown away by the very idea they could be married in the Supreme Court, Catherine beamed.

Neither of them had ever been inside the Court. They marveled at the Spanish ivory vein marble that lined the walls, and the four towering columns behind the elevated platform where nine esteemed judges in black robes passed judgment on legal issues that set a precedent for present and future generations.

"Please make yourselves comfortable anywhere you like," Gilman said. "Chief Justice Cunningham will be along shortly."

No sooner had they settled when Owen Jennings walked in dressed to the nines like he had not recently been a candidate for a funeral.

"Oh, my God, Owen!" Catherine cried. Her voice reverberated off the walls.

"Well, somebody's got to be best man," Jennings said with a laugh.

Catherine quick-paced over and flew into his arms.

"Now that's what I call a damn sexy greeting,"

"Look at you! You look fantastic."

"I owe it all to my makeup lady. And may I say that you look ravishing."

Arm in arm they marched back to Gabriel.

"Good morning, Cuban boy."

"Good morning, Charlie Stud."

The two men hugged, and Gabriel whispered in his ear. "You got them?"

"Of course."

"Let me see."

"No, you'll marry the lady first." Jennings's eyes roamed the iconic room with awe. "Couldn't you have found a more intimate venue?"

The main door opened again and in walked Gabriel's secretary, Betty, grinning from ear-to-ear. "Good morning, Sparky."

"Well, if it isn't Betty Spanning, surrogate mother to yours truly and loyal servant for more years than either of us want to admit."

"Where'd you get this loyal servant thing?" Betty joked. "I'm the actual brains of the outfit."

"Catherine, you should have a maid of honor. Betty volunteered."

Catherine beamed. "Thank you, Betty, thank you."

"Wouldn't have missed it for all the aliens in the world. When he called me at six this morning, I thought he was joking; he's been known to do that. Mr. Jennings, so good to see you again."

"Hi, Betty, pleased to see you're still putting up with this guy."

"It's not easy, but the responsibility has fallen to me." Betty took Catherine arm. "Come on, some girl-talk before I let you marry this guy."

Jennings whispered to Gabriel, "About last night, are you okay?"

"I don't know if it's possible to be okay after someone tries to kill you, but it happened, it's over, life moves on. That reminds me—I'll be right back."

Gabriel trotted to the front door and disappeared.

"Where's he going?" Catherine asked.

"Maybe he got cold feet," Jennings wisecracked.

"Not funny, Owen!"

Outside, Gabriel approached his security detail whose black SUV was parked at the foot of the Supreme Court steps.

"Come on, join us."

"Uh, thanks, but—" Remy said.

"No buts, it's your job to protect me. Park this battle wagon and get your asses inside."

Remy said to Dex, "it is our job to watch over him, right? Let go."

Back inside, Gabriel was making introductions all around when a voice called out from a side chamber.

"Gabriel, good to see you on this very special day." It was Chief Justice Harold Cunningham followed by his law clerk Danny. "It's been a while, how have you been, young man?"

"Fine, Chief Justice."

"I've known this troublemaker ever since his days as Chief of Staff to then Senator William Conrad, a man who I counted as one of my closest friends. I sure miss my him. Now then, despite what's going on with this unpleasant alien business, this is supposed to be a most happy day. Shall we proceed?"

Jennings took his place next to Gabriel, and Betty stood beside Catherine. Dex and Remy stood close behind.

"I've had Danny prepare cards from which you may read from. There's one for me, considering I don't do this sort of thing on a regular basis."

Danny handed each of them an index card.

"This place," Cunningham began reading, "although not usually a venue for weddings, has been duly sanctioned according to the law for the celebration of a marriage. This sacred ceremony will unite Catherine Blake—do you have a middle name?

"Justine."

"Catherine Justine Blake and Gabriel..."

"Javier."

"Catherine Justine Blake and Gabriel Javier Ferro in marriage. We celebrate with them and for them. I am going to ask you each to declare that you know of no legal reason why you may not be joined together in marriage; Gabriel, you first."

From the card, Gabriel read: "I do solemnly declare that I know not of any lawful impediment why I, Gabriel, Javier Ferro, may not be joined in marriage to Catherine Justine Blake."

Justice Cunningham nodded to Catherine.

"I solemnly declare that I know not of any lawful impediment why I, Catherine Justine Blake, may not be joined in marriage to Gabriel Javier Ferro."

"Gabriel, Javier Ferro, do you take Catherine Justine Blake to be your lawful wedded wife, to be loving, faithful, and loyal to her for the rest of your life together?"

"I do."

"Catherine Justine Blake, do you take Gabriel, Javier Farrow to be your lawful wedded husband, to be loving, faithful and loyal to him for the rest of your life together?"

"I do."

"You may now exchange rings as a binding symbol of your love."

Jennings stood silent.

"Owen?" Gabriel whispered

"Oh, right, it's my turn."

From his right pocket, Jennings retrieved and handed Catherine's ring to Gabriel. The engagement-wedding ring combination was fashioned from white gold with a large, round cut diamond on the engagement ring and sixteen side-stone cuts on the matching wedding ring. When Catherine saw it, she took a quick breath and beamed.

Gabriel read from the card. "I give you these rings as a symbol of our love. All that I am, I give to you; all that I have, I share with you." He then slipped the rings on Catherine's finger.

Jennings passed a wedding ring to Catherine. It too was white gold.

"I give you this ring as a symbol of our love. All that I am, I give to you, all that I have, I share with you." She slipped the ring onto Gabriel's finger.

"Today is a new beginning," the Justice read from his card, "May you have many happy years together, and may all your hopes and dreams be fulfilled. Above all, may you always believe in each other, and may the warmth of your love enriches not only your lives but the lives of all those around you. It gives me great pleasure to tell you both, you are now legally husband and wife. From the sanctity of this great institution, I am privileged to be the first to offer my congratulations."

Gabriel and Catherine locked in a passionate kiss. The small gathering applauded.

Jennings tapped Gabriel's shoulder. "Hey, Cuban Boy, slow down—save some for later."

"And now it's off to Sofie's Cuban restaurant for some excellent food and serious drinking," Gabriel announced. "Justice Cunningham, I hope you and Danny will join us."

"The Court is not in session today, young man, so it will be our pleasure, but only if you promise to swap stories about our dear friend, President Conrad."

Gabriel invited Remy and Dex to join them.

Remy said, "If we get caught partying, it's curtains for us,"

"How about I have some food and a piece of cake sent out?"

"That we can do," Dex replied.

"Guys, thank you for last night."

"That's why we make the big bucks. Now get on with your celebration."

At Sofie's, the revelry began in earnest with many jokes, much laughter, and plenty of good Cuban food alongside pitchers of sangria. Catherine entertained everyone with a rather long version of how She and Gabriel had been oil and water when they first met.

"My first impression was that he was such a political dork. Later, when we were running for our lives, he decided he sort of liked me."

"Truth is, she was insufferably arrogant."

Betty laughed. "So, there you have it, straight from both horse's mouth. Does this marriage have a ghost of a chance?"

"At least through the end of the day," Jennings added.

"Chief Justice," Gabriel said, "we will forever be grateful for your kindness."

"Just for today, can we drop the Chief Justice tag? I encourage Danny here to call me Harold from time to time to remind me that all men put their pants on the same way, one leg at a time; that's the ultimate equalizer."

"He's telling the truth," Danny confirmed, "although, God forbid someone should overhear me calling him by his first name."

"Besides, as the proposed next leader of the world, I should be calling you *Mr. Ferro*," Cunningham added with a grin.

The group fell silent.

"Oops, sorry, that was inappropriate. I didn't mean it the way it came out."

"Not at all, sir," Gabriel said. "I find it amusing myself." Gabriel leaned in and spoke low, "For whatever reason—one I have yet to understand—they believe I'm their guy. I assure you, I'm not."

Cunningham whispered, "Can we trust anything they say, Gabriel?"

"Some, but I'm conflicted. Human society is ill-prepared for all they're proposing."

"But why, why do they care a plug nickel about this far-flung, tiny planet?"

Only three people at the table knew the truth, and Gabriel was reticent to reveal the genesis of the human race and that was the way it had to remain. "I have no answer for that."

Justice Cunningham took a sip of sangria and leaned back. "The Court has been notified by this so-called New World Administrator that we are to be disbanded—that the Constitution of the United States will no longer require clarification and legal disputes will no longer be settled before nine justices. However, this alien has requested—that's a polite way of putting it—the nine of us become regional administrators once they morph the world into one big happy family. Good luck with that."

Just then Remy Bernard rushed up to their table like a man on an urgent mission. "Mr. Ferro, sorry to interrupt—can I speak with you for a moment?"

Gabriel stood. "Excuse me, everyone."

With a sinking feeling, Gabriel followed Remy out of hearing range of the others.

"Your CIA friend Rafi Suharto is on my phone. He says it's urgent otherwise they wouldn't have put it through to me."

"Okay."

Remy handed Gabriel his cell phone. "Rafi what's up?"

"Jesus, Gabriel, where have you been? I've been calling you for the past hour."

"My phone's been off. What's up?"

"In just the last hour, demonstrations and riots have broken out over this zero-birth thing. China is reporting five hundred dead in Beijing alone. Thousand, maybe millions, are gathering in New York, Chicago, Dallas, and L.A."

"Damn it," Gabriel cursed, "the broadcast announcement failed."

"Ya' think! The demonstrators are calling the zero-birth pronouncement systematic genocide."

"Jesus, Rafi, if that were the alien's intent, they have ways of accomplishing it a lot faster and easier."

"From your lips to whoever's ears, my friend. Fear has once again whipped up the populace and this time, there's no stopping them. If Jennings theory was right and Legna cares less about the demonstrations, right about now he wishes he did."

"I'm not sure what I can do to stop it."

"March your ass into the Oval and tell that little son of a bitch that this is his problem to fix. And keep your damn phone on, will ya'!"

Gabriel passed the phone back to Remy just as Dex came running into the building. "We have to leave now."

"What?"

"Thousands have gathered in Lafayette Square. Best we get you back to the White House while we can, Mr. Ferro!"

"Remy, for God's sake, I just got married!"

"Want to stay married? Best you come with us."

Gabriel's head whipped toward the table where Catherine and guests were chatting. "What about them?"

Four more Secret Service agents rushed in and went directly to the others.

"That's why those guys are here," Remy said. "We have to get to the White House before the crowds surround it completely and we can't get in."

Gabriel spun around—his eyes went straight to Catherine. She could see the alarm on his face. She stood and moved toward him—he took a step toward her.

Dex caught his arm and pulled him back. "No, sir, no time."

As Remy and Dex marched him toward the door, the last thing Gabriel heard was Catherine calling his name.

53

Six Secret Service SUVs were lined up at the curb like a military caravan ready to engage in battle. Remy and Dex hustled Gabriel into the second vehicle.

"Buckle up," Remy instructed.

The driver spoke into his communications device. "The package is on-board. Acknowledge."

He listened for a moment. "Copy." Then to Dex and Remy, "We're off."

And with that, they sped off, one SUV in front of Gabriel's vehicle and a second behind, lights flashing and sirens screaming.

They traveled south on Nineteenth Street, then left on Pennsylvania Avenue. As they approached the White House, they could see Lafayette Square was already glutted with thousands of protestors. Several dozen police in full riot gear held them at bay while uniformed Secret Service lined the inside of the White House fence.

With tires screeching, the driver took a hard right onto the White House grounds and gunned it the entrance to the West Wing lobby.

"The package has been delivered," the driver said into his communications device. He waited for a reply, but none came. "Acknowledge."

Still no reply.

"Something's up," the driver said with urgency. "Get him inside."

Inside the West Wing lobby, an agent met them. "There's a complete communications blackout: phones, Internet, TV, no satellites, nothing. We're to take him directly to the Oval."

"Listen, damn it, I left my wife, my secretary, a friend, and the Chief Justice of the United States Supreme Court and one of his law clerks back there."

"They're in safe hands, Mr. Ferro. We need to go."

Hustling Gabriel across the lobby, they swung left down the hall, then right to the Oval Office. Ms. Mosby was at her desk with her/his usual sour look. "The Administrator awaits your arrival, Mr. Ferro."

At the door to the Oval Office, Remy Bernard whispered, "Good luck in there."

Gabriel forced a smile, nodded, took a deep breath, walked past the two Marine guards, and entered without knocking.

Legna and Masma were sitting on opposite sofas. After the tumult that ensued in getting him there, the sanctity of the Oval was like walking into a vacuum. If a pin dropped, it would have sounded like a hammer slamming onto an anvil. Legna rose and meandered to a window and stood silent.

Gabriel waited.

Finally, Legna spoke. "You coupled with Citizen Catherine this day."

How the hell does he know? "I beg your pardon?"

"Come, come, Gabriel, your conscious being betrays you."

Gabriel blew a hard breath. "Why do we bother conversing when you can invade my thoughts at will?"

Legna swung his hands to his back and intertwined his fingers. "I wish you and Citizen Catherine peace, harmony, and balance."

And I wish you'd stay out of my head and mind your own damn business.

Legna's head swiveled from left to right. "Surrounding this iconic structure, foolishness reigns."

Gabriel looked to Masma, but Masma's eyes were on Legna like a dog watches his master.

"I question whether these primitives possess the ability to see past the fog of their lives."

"For all your wisdom, you're often quite naïve."

Legna's head whipped to Gabriel. "Your words are offensive."

"You say you're here to resurrect a troubled civilization, yet you continue to deny the very real emotions humans experience every minute of every day."

"You would speak to me in that tone?"

"I speak of the human condition, which you refuse to acknowledge. So, as a reminder: we laugh when there is joy, cry when we are sad, display anger, surprise, anticipation, and most of all, love, but at the moment, mostly fear. Since you don't experience any of the above, you will never connect with those people out there."

"Your words are not conducive to harmony."

"Well, we have a choice here, don't we? Either I speak the truth, or I simply remain subservient to your will; which is it to be?"

After a moment's hesitation, Legna said, "I wish you to speak the truth."

"Good, here's a bit of truth. Those people gathered in Lafayette Park and around the world are frightened of you, your weapons, and your plans for them. And yet they still assemble at great personal risk. This is how humans react when backed up against a wall, and this time, with zero pregnancies and spontaneous aborting, you've backed them up against the ultimate wall. They understand they're out-gunned, but they bravely stand against what they perceive to be tyranny. And even if they did believe you you're here to make their lives better, maybe they have zero interest in what it is you're offering."

Legna ambled casually across the room until he was a few feet from Gabriel and stared.

Gabriel stared back. "Go ahead, get inside my head. I don't give a damn anymore."

He waited to be rebuked for his strident candor, but to his surprise, Legna's tone softened. "It is my wish that citizens cease this spectacle of defiance. We have no desire to give rise to measures that would cause them harm." Then came another one of his infamous pauses before he said, "What would you have me do?"

Legna's unexpected softening caught Gabriel unprepared. *Seize the moment, Cuban boy, or it may not come your way anytime soon.* "Try sugar instead of salt." He turned to Masma. "Perhaps you would like to weigh in here."

Masma lowered his head in silence.

"Speak freely, Citizen Masma." Legna made it sound like an order.

Masma hesitated. "Perhaps we have yet to fully engage humans. We ask much of them... perhaps we have failed to earn their trust."

Legna strolled back to the window and for several moments stood quietly. "What would you have me do?"

"Explain the reasoning behind the transformation, "Gabriel said. "Explain why it's critical to human survival."

"And if they continue to reject us?"

"Then you will have lost... and you should return home."

"That is not an option."

Select your next words carefully. Don't go off half-cocked and piss him off again. "I said I would support your efforts, not because you deem it so, but because I believe some good can come of it. Nonetheless, I pledge that support only if no one is harmed, either by their own doing or yours. Take seriously what I said; If you fail to gain their confidence, then you should return to Ecaep."

Masma rose and approached Legna. "Perhaps, Citizen Legna, a message directly from you."

"He's right," Gabriel said. "You, not me, must reach out, not as the invader they perceive you to be, but as a benevolent visitor who wishes to enrich their lives."

Legna's eyes slowly came to Gabriel. "Very well, I shall heed your counsel and address humans this very day."

Whew, how did that happen? Seize the opportunity, move in for the kill. "May I see your message beforehand?"

"I think not," Legna said with finality. "I wish you and Citizen Catherine great joy."

Close, but no cigar, he's only giving you so much rope. With Masma's help, we won a small victory. Gabriel made eye contact with Masma who smiled and bowed his head ever so slightly. Gabriel smiled and nodded back.

"Citizen Gabriel?"

"Yes?"

"Earth's atmosphere is fully restored this day."

That alone was such a monumental accomplishment, it took Gabriel a few beats before it sank in. "We might never have accomplished such a feat on our own. Thank you. Be sure to include that in your presentation."

Traveling down the hall to his office, Gabriel's first thought was of Catherine's safety. He reached for his cell phone, then remembered all communications had been silenced. "Damn it."

He was surprised to find Betty at her desk. "You're back?"

"Since I live alone, the Secret Service thought I'd be safer here."

"Catherine—the others?"

"Catherine's home under guard, Mr. Jennings returned to Langley, Justice Cunningham and his law clerk are back at the Supreme Court."

"The madness continues."

"Ah, one more thing." She lowered her voice to just above a whisper and pointed to his office door. "The late, great Vice President of the United States is parked in there."

Alan Cross sat stiff-backed in front of Gabriel's desk.

"Welcome to hell," Cross said with a throaty huff.

"Have you seen Lafayette Square?" Gabriel said as he rounded his desk and sat.

"Damn hard to miss. Does the term 'under siege' ring a bell? All communications are down thanks to Legna. We have no way of evaluating the big picture." Cross shifted in the chair. "One of my staffers saw a plethora of Secret Service guys whisk you into the Oval."

"I was out of the building. The Lord and Master summoned me."

"Hopefully to apologize for that asinine announcement that's turned the world into an angry, armed militia."

Gabriel retrieved his pack of Marlboros and lit one.

"What went on in the Oval?"

"He'll try to soothe the savage beast with a personal appeal for calm and unity."

"And if that doesn't work?"

"It better work because there's no way these creatures are going to be deterred. They're committed, period, end of discussion. There is some good news: as of today, our atmosphere is as pure as a newborn's lungs."

"Bravo for our team."

"No small feat, Alan. We couldn't have achieved that in a lifetime and certainly not in yours or mine. As for zero-population, we have to face the ugly fact that we are crawling all over one another like ants and we have no idea what to do about it short of another world war or a pandemic that wipes out millions the hard way. So, as difficult as it is to accept, they did for us what we refused to do for ourselves. Now for the bad stuff: Humans will never submit to living in a commune listening to Pavarotti concerts."

Cross sighed. "I hope you have an idea how do stop the bad stuff because I don't."

"Legna listens to reason—I saw that this morning. But his hands may be tied because his marching orders come directly from this Tonora character."

"The 'judge' on Ecaep?"

"The Chair of the Grand Directorate of Ecaep, whatever the hell that is. I'm a hundred-percent certain he's calling the shots."

"So, what's that make Legna?"

"The engineer who's been instructed where to drive the train because we were too dumb to steer the train for ourselves."

Betty interrupted via the intercom. "Communications are back up."

"It's about damn time." Gabriel booted his computer and turned on the TV. "Let's see what's going on."

On the screen was a show card that read: *Please stand by for an important message.* Five seconds later the message changed: *At 5:00 PM EST the Administrator will address the world. Please tune into your television, Internet, radio, and other devices.*

The image switched back to the first card, held for five seconds, then changed to the second.

Gabriel blew a breath and grumbled, "Five o'clock tells the story."

Cross placed his hands on the chair's arms and pushed himself up. "Until five then."

"Alan... I got married today."

Cross was already at the door, stopped and turned back. "You did what?"

"You heard me."

"Who's the unlucky lady."

"Dr. Blake."

Cross shook his head. "Congratulations... *I think.*" And with that, he left.

As soon as Cross was out the door, Gabriel called Catherine.

She answered her cell phone on the first ring. "Gabriel!"

"This is one hell of a way to begin a marriage. You okay?"

"I'm still shaking from the whiz-bang ride home. Two Secret Service agents are parked outside our door."

"I want to come home and wrap my arms around you... preferably in bed to consummate our union."

"You do recall I'm already pregnant?"

"No, really?"

"Come home, Gabriel."

"I'm locked in here until Legna gives that speech."

"What speech?"

"At 5 o'clock, he's addressing the world. Be in front of the TV. I'll be home as soon as I can,"

"I love you, Gabriel, be safe."

"I love you, Mrs. Ferro."

"Hmm, who is this Mrs. Ferro you refer to?"

His next call was to his mother. He was dreading having to tell her that she was not present for her only child's wedding. Considering how fast things were happening, he wanted her to join him and Catherine in Washington, but convincing Isabella to leave her beloved home would be difficult. Maybe now that he was married with a child on the way, she would reconsider.

The phone rang seven times before he heard his mother's voice. "Thank you for calling. I'm out at the moment, so please leave a name and number or call back. Thank you."

Knowing a message would only confuse and anger her, he hung up and retrieved the Marlboro pack from its hiding place in the bottom right drawer.

Betty popped in. "Put those nasty things away."

He lit one, took a defiant puff, and blew smoke in her direction.

"Go on, put it out."

Like a child scorned, he retrieved the coffee cup from the bottom drawer.

"Notice that it's clean?"

"What?"

"Your cup. If you insist on using it as an ashtray, it deserves a cleaning from time to time. Go home. You need to be with Catherine."

"I need to be here for Legna's announcement."

"No, you need to be with your new bride who was hauled out of a restaurant by a couple of burly Secret Service agents shortly after her wedding. Are you dense?"

"Betty, I—"

"Don't Betty me. Does the TV at your house work?"

"Of course, but—"

"Stop with the *buts* already, go home. Be with Catherine. I'll call you if anything requires your royal presence."

As reports continued to stream in, it began to look like every last soul on the planet had joined in the revolt. The FBI, CIA, and Homeland Security were receiving reports of at least 145 million on the march in big cities and small towns across America alone. Dispatches from Europe were reporting the same. It was total madness as some unruly demonstrators ransacked private establishments and looted whatever they could.

It was a grab for anything and everything in a terrifying expression of both outrage and fear.

Gabriel was about to get into his car when Remy Bernard called to him, "Going someplace?"

"Home."

"I'll drive you. Dex will follow in your car." Remy held up Gabriel's car keys. "I still have them, remember?"

"Guys, I'm perfectly capable of driving myself."

"And I'm the Tooth Fairy," Remy shot back. "Come on, you'll enjoy the conversation—I'll tell you all about my kids and how they're making me nuts."

When Gabriel arrived home, he found two agents sitting in folding chairs. He recognized them as two of the men who rushed past him at Sofie's.

"Gentlemen," he said.

"Congratulations on your wedding, Mr. Ferro. Sorry we broke up the party," one of the agents said.

"Can I get you anything?"

"Your wife was kind enough make us coffee."

The term *"your wife"* brought a smile to his lips. "Let us know if you need anything."

The apartment was quiet. He passed through the living room to the kitchen, but still no Catherine. He went to the master bedroom and found her under the covers. Not wanting to wake her, he backed out quietly and closed the door and made his way to his study, opened his laptop to his journal file, and began typing:

> *I got married to a wonderful lady this tumultuous day. I wish it could have taken place when the world was not about to collapse under its own weight. The rioting and the looting are disgraceful no matter what the cause or the motivation. Why have we always reacted violently? Why? God knows we have every right to be frightened, but the craziness won't advance us one iota. A lot is riding on what Legna says at five. My best guess is...*

"Gabriel?" Catherine was standing on the far side of the living room dressed in a robe. Her uncombed hair was to her shoulders. "I didn't hear you come in."

He stood. "I didn't want to wake you."

Catherine's eyes welled up, and she began to cry. Walking quickly to her, he enveloped her in his arms, their bodies melting into one, afraid to move, afraid to let go. Gabriel's lips went to her ear, her neck, and finally to her lips in a passionate kiss.

"I dreamt they took you back to Ecaep, and I never saw you again."

"Hey, hey, no more bad dreams. Besides, what self-respecting Ecaepian would marry me?"

A soft laugh from Catherine as she wiped away tears. She wiggled the fingers on her left hand to flash her engagement and wedding band. "Have I told you how beautiful these rings are?"

"I went online in the middle of the night to a D.C. jeweler and chose them. Owen picked them up on his way to the Supreme Court."

"Thank you, Mr. Ferro."

"You're welcome, Mrs. Ferro." He kissed her gently on the forehead.

"I was so bummed out by the scramble at Sofie's, I went to bed after we spoke and promptly fell asleep. What's going on?"

"There's violent demonstrations everywhere. Thousands injured and hundreds are dead; the burning, destruction, and looting are completely out of control. It's worldwide Marshall Law out there."

"My God."

He glanced at his watch. It was 4:50 PM. "Legna's addressing the world at five in an attempt to soothe the savage beast."

Catherine placed a flat hand to her stomach and held it there.

Gabriel placed his hand gently over hers. "It's going to be okay."

"I love you for saying that, but you don't have a crystal ball."

He pulled her in close. "It *will* be okay."

"I will be forever grateful that we found one another."

"Ditto." Over her shoulder, he checked her watch. "It's almost time."

Gabriel turned on the TV and they sat on the sofa. The screen still read: *At 5:00 PM EST the Administrator will address the world. Please tune into your television, Internet, radio, and other devices.*

They sat quietly, not speaking, waiting with trepidation for what would surely prove to be a turning point for the human race one way or another. Finally, the screen changed to a live shot of Legna sitting behind the Oval Office desk. His gaze was slightly to the right of the camera waiting for his cue to begin.

"He looks apprehensive—a first for him," Gabriel commented.

Finally receiving his cue, Legna's eyes went to the camera. *"I wish everyone peace, harmony, and balance.*

Gabriel grumbled. "Does the vast majority even understand what that means?"

Catherine put a finger to her lips. "*Shh!*"

Given the continuing abhorrent behavior, I find it necessary to personally address you yet again. For the well-being of everyone, the unwarranted demonstrations will not be tolerated. Why citizens continue to attack one another is beyond comprehension."

"Jesus!" Gabriel yelled and jumped to his feet. Balling his right hand into a tight fist, he shrieked, "I told you *sugar*, not salt! Just hit them over the head with a bat, why don't you!"

"Be quiet, sit down," Catherine admonished.

He shook his fist at the TV, grunted like an angry bear, and settled on the sofa.

"I recognize and sympathize with your anxiety, but your emotional response is unproductive. The destruction of vast amounts of life-sustaining terrain, the unending depletion of natural resources, tribes who confront one another in battle, and the expansion of vast urban settlements to shelter your exploding population, has plunged your planet into a geological disaster of epic proportions."

Gabriel leaped to his feet again. "He's whipping them into a frenzy!"

"Gabriel, sit down!"

"Ah, the hell with it!"

"We mean you no harm. We have come to assist all mankind in securing your future, a more peaceful and joyful future. Your rulers have consistently failed you, this you know. Yet you continue to sanction the offenders who supplant your interests. We shall not fail you. I say to you, look forward to the future, a future of peace, harmony, and balance."

Legna paused as the camera moved in for a close-up. His expression softened; he was actually trying to smile.

"Here comes the charm."

"It is paramount to your very survival that your numbers be brought under control. This you know. We are not without empathy and are cognizant of the anguish this has caused. The steps instituted on your behalf are but a small sacrifice to achieve a joyful future."

"That's it!" Gabriel hawked. "That's all he is going to say about that?"

Legna continued. *"Sustenance, access to clean water, and electricity are now available to those in need, and this day you may celebrate the cleansing of your atmosphere. I now seek your cooperation in ending the violent demonstrations, not because they bring harm to us, but to each of you. Let us join hands to create a harmonious society that lives in peace, harmony, and balance. May joy be with you."*

Every TV screen in the world switched to Director Robert Wise's 1965 Academy Award winning film, *The Sound of Music.*

"What in the world?" Catherine said. "The Sound of Music?"

"Rah, rah, life is good, all will be well, thank you, Julie Andrews!" Gabriel stood and shouted. "Shut the damn thing off!"

Catherine turned the TV off, pulled her legs up, and curled them under her.

Gabriel was on his feet and pacing.

"It won't solve anything to get angry."

"Let me vent for a couple of minutes, then I'll fix you something to eat."

"I'm not hungry."

"You're eating for two. Come on."

In the kitchen, Gabriel whipped together eggs and milk. "Voilà, scrambled eggs, the extent of my culinary expertise."

"You can't just stew over what just occurred." She tapped her temple. "Not good for the gray matter."

"That's why I'm fixing scrambled eggs."

Gabriel's cell phone rang. Retrieving it from his pants pocket, he saw it was his assistant.

"Yes, Tyler."

"That speech was a big dud."

"Tell me something I don't know."

"Reports flooding in confirm the demonstrations haven't abated one bit."

"It just happened; give it a chance."

"There's something else. That report I prepared on murders and terrorists?"

"What about it?"

"Everyone on the list is missing—gone without a trace."

"And we're just learning this? Gone where?"

"Just gone."

"Jesus!"

"What is it, Gabriel?" Catherine asked.

Gabriel held up a hand signaling her to wait. "There has to be an explanation, Tyler."

"Look to the aliens, and I think we'll find one."

Gabriel blew out a breath. "Okay, keep me posted."

"Okay, boss. Congratulations on the wedding—Betty spread the word."

"Thanks." Gabriel set his phone on the counter and stared at it like it was an explosive device about to go off.

"What's wrong now?"

"Tyler—the demonstrations aren't slowing." He chose not to mention the disappearance of convicted murderers and terrorists. "First things first—toast?"

"Okay—one slice, no butter."

"Only odd people eat dry toast."

"Skip Galinski is odd; I'm eccentric."

Gabriel popped three slices of bread into the toaster, then melted butter in a frying pan, dropped the eggs in, and stirred them around with a spatula.

"I want to talk about the baby. I never wanted anything so desperately in my life."

"I told you it'll be okay. Stop working yourself into a lather."

"Minutes ago, you were reassuring me. Now you sound iffy."

Gabriel set the spatula down. "Whoa, wait a minute, I'm on your side, remember?"

He was about to be introduced to the mood swings of a pregnant woman. Catherine slipped off the counter stool and stormed off.

"Where are you going?"

He found Catherine in the bedroom sitting on the edge of the bed crying.

"Hey, hey." He went to her and hugged and rocked her. "I want this baby just as much as you do. It's just that I fear for the kid's future."

"Why now, why is this all happening now? I just want to go off to your island— what's it called?"

"Surin, Surin Island."

"We could live on the beach and raise our child there."

"If only we could."

Catherine sniffed the air. "Is something burning?"

"Oh crap, the eggs!"

They made a mad dash to the kitchen to find smoke rising from the frying pan.

"Damn it!" Gabriel wrapped a hand towel around pan's handle and dumped the burnt eggs in the sink.

Catherine broke out laughing. "So much for scrambled eggs."

"We're lucky the bloody smoke alarm didn't go off." Gabriel spied the toast that had popped up. "We still have dry toast."

"No thanks."

Gabriel tossed his head back and laughed, "Want to watch the rest of *The Sound of Music*?"

54

Just before dawn, Gabriel woke to find Catherine gone. He thought she might be up and making coffee. Then came the unmistakable sound of vomiting. Flinging off the covers, he raced to the bathroom door and knocked.

"Just a minute," Catherine called out.

"You okay?"

"I said just a minute!"

The toilet flushed, the sink ran, and then silence. After a couple of minutes, she opened the door and greeted Gabriel with a lopsided smile. "Welcome to morning sickness." She was still in her nightgown, her eyes were wet, and her complexion pale.

"Oh."

"What do you mean, *oh*?" she quipped. "What do you know about morning sickness?"

"I guess I'm about to learn."

"I think not… unless men get pregnant."

She trudged across the room and crawled into bed. "I'm calling in sick."

"Good idea. You'll be okay?"

"Please go to work, I'll be fine, really."

"I'll shower and shave in the guest bath."

"Capital idea."

"Is there anything I can do for you?"

She pulled the covers over her head. "Go to work—bye now."

"I'll call you later."

There was no reply.

Once showered, shaved, and dressed, he went to his study, opened his laptop, and began typing an entry:

So, round two begins. The unknown remains: Will Legna's condescending speech do any good? Two steps forward, one back.

By seven he was out the door and navigating Georgetown traffic. He spotted his security team in his rearview mirror. "Don't they ever sleep?"

At 7:30 AM, he entered his office suite. Tyler Harney was sitting across from Betty.

"Good morning you two."

"I thought I better brief you first thing."

"Come on. Want coffee?"

"I'm good."

"I'll have my usual."

"It's on your desk," Betty said.

"How is it you know to have coffee ready when I walk through that door?"

"The guard in reception calls me when you come through the door."

Gabriel made a growling sound, and he and Tyler entered his office.

"So, what's up, Tyler?"

"Well, the Internet went down again about an hour ago—all other communications remain in service. Reports coming in indicate the speech may have done some good after all because the demonstrations have decreased."

Gabriel responded cynically, "Either people were tired and went home, or they realize they're up against an unmovable force?"

"Whatever the reason, crowds have diminished in Asia, Africa, North America and Australia." Tyler added drolly, "There never was any in Antarctica."

Skipping over Tyler's lame joke, Gabriel said, "That leaves Europe."

"Well, there's the rub. If anything, they've increased."

"Damn it!"

"Either people in Europe failed to get the message or chose to ignore it."

Tyler's expression turned dark.

"I take it there's more?"

"People are disappearing: ring leaders, looters, anyone committing a violent act. Right before people's eyes *poof*, they're gone; several hundred so far, maybe more. Maybe that's what's causing some to go."

Gabriel reached into his bottom drawer to grab the pack of Marlboro's.

"I heard you had the smoke detector removed."

"Cripes, does the whole building know? Anything else?"

"I think that's enough; wouldn't you say?"

"All right, keep me posted. How's Bonnie?"

"Still very pregnant." Tyler took a long breath. "God, if we lose this baby…"

"You won't because women over four months are in the safe zone."

"Yeah, well, just the same." Tyler stood. "Congratulations again on your wedding."

As soon as Tyler left, Gabriel propped his feet up on the desk. The wheels in his brain were turning, turning, analyzing all that had happened, trying to make sense of it all. *Perhaps the human race isn't real at all, but a holographic vision to be toyed with and tossed aside when the players get tired and move on. Jesus, where do I get these wacky thoughts?*

He snubbed the cigarette in the coffee cup and reached for the intercom. "Betty, check with the effervescent Ms. Mosby. See if Masma is available to meet with me now… here in my office."

"We've already been through this—he won't come to you, and I have no interest coming face-to-face with one of *them*."

"Just do it, please."

"If *it* should agree, I may take an early lunch."

A couple of minutes had passed before Betty buzzed him. "The answer is yes, he can see you, but no, he won't come here; you have to go there."

"Buzz him back. He needs to come here."

Betty buzzed again. "The answer is still no."

"Okay, so be it."

"Are you going there?"

"Absolutely not."

Suddenly, Betty went silent.

"Betty, are you still there?"

"Oh, my! Oh, my!" She sounded like she was in distress.

Gabriel sat up straight. "What's wrong?"

Then the sound of a familiar voice.

"You are Citizen Betty? I am very pleased to greet you. I am Citizen Masma."

There was no reply from Betty. The door opened and Masma walked in and did a quick scan of the office. "Your task area is pleasing."

"Thank you. What changed your mind?"

"I relayed your request to Citizen Legna. He was cool with it."

"Cool?"

"Is not *cool* a proper term in your lexicon?"

"Yes, yes, it is—*cool*—yes."

"May I recline?"

"Of course, can I have Betty bring you anything?"

Masma took a seat and thought for a moment. "Do you possess Sprite *®*?"

"Sprite?"

"Since tasting this refreshment, I have become fond of it. Upon our return to Ecaep, I shall take quantities with me."

"Yes, of course, Sprite." He buzzed Betty. "Betty, Citizen Masma would like a Sprite."

No answer from Betty.

"Betty?"

"Uh, yeah, okay—Sprite."

"It'll only be a moment, Citizen Masma."

"You may address me as Masma. May I address you as Gabriel?"

"Yes, of course."

"I have a Sprite," Betty said brusquely over the intercom.

"Thank you, bring it in."

Silence.

"Betty?"

"Would you mind coming out?"

Gabriel frowned and sighed. "Please excuse me."

Betty was standing on the other side of the door. She grimaced and handed the Sprite and a glass to Gabriel. With a "harrumph", she returned to her desk.

"Here you go." Gabriel handed the soda and glass to Masma.

"Thank you." Masma poured a small amount into the glass, took a sip, and smiled. "For what reason have you summoned me?"

"Well, to begin with, I have come to know you as a kind and gentle soul."

"I do not have a soul, Citizen Gabriel."

"A gentle *being* then."

"All Ecaepians are gentle beings."

Masma took a sip of the Sprite and licked his thin lips to show his approval.

"I was hoping we could get together to, uh, to speak of other things."

"Other things?"

"Like your perception of our world. What is your opinion of us humans?"

"To enlighten me, Citizen Legna has provided some... forgive me, I fail to recall what those round, silver discs are."

"DVDs?

"Yes, DVDs. I found one quite joyful. It was a television program called a *A Capital Fourth Celebration*."

"It is an annual event held each year across the street on the National Mall."

"Another was most disturbing: *The History of World War II*."

"A most unfortunate period in our history."

"There is an absence of unity and understanding amongst your tribes. Why might that be, Gabriel?"

"Men far brighter than I have struggled with that issue for many, many centuries."

Masma sipped the Sprite. "During your visit to Ecaep, did not you and Dr. Blake find it difficult to comprehend our transformation?"

"I admit we did. But perhaps if I knew more…"

"You have previously queried me."

"I just thought that you and I had gained a level of trust and could speak openly as we did in your office."

Masma sipped more Sprite.

Several moments of awkward silence had passed before Gabriel asked, "Perhaps you could clarify Legna's role. I feel I am entitled to know who all the players are. Since I'm involved, I don't wish to be cast in the role of the human scapegoat."

"Scapegoat?"

"Wrong choice of words. What I meant was, I don't want to carry the Ecaepian message to my fellow citizens unless I am fully invested. In for a penny, in for a pound, as the saying goes."

It was clear from his static expression, Masma had no idea what that meant. "Have you not expressed your concerns to Citizen Legna?"

"Not in so many words."

"How many words are required?"

"It's just an expression, Masma."

"Yes, I see. To your question, the Administrator dispenses the wishes of the Chair of the Grand Directorate."

"That would be Tonora?"

Masma acknowledged with a nod.

"Do you have elections to select a Chair of the Grand Directorate?

"Only Tonora can be the Grand Directorate."

"Why is that?"

"From the beginning of the Transference, Tonora has been the Grand Directorate."

441

Gabriel had little doubt that Masma was clueless as to why Tonora was their leader other than Tonora had been so for as long as he could recall.

"Look, I'm going to be straight with you—uh, honest."

"Honesty is good."

"There is much that can be done to advance our society; Legna has already demonstrated that."

"Your acknowledgment pleases me."

"However, the populace has yet to accept what I have."

"Why might that be, Gabriel?"

"Fear causes people to be less responsible for their actions; they can easily become an angry mob. It is in our DNA."

"Then your DNA is faulty."

"As was yours at one time."

"This is so."

"What period of time passed before your transformation was complete?"

"There is no past or future, only moments leading to the next."

"Yes, Legna made that point. He also said Ecaepians do not possess a memory of the past, yet you expressed yours to me."

Masma looked fixedly at Gabriel for several beats before his gaze wandered.

Damn it, I pushed him too far!

Masma's gaze came back. "I cannot articulate why I retain past events. It is not supposed to be."

"Does Citizen Legna know of your memories?"

Masma looked away. "He does not."

"Would he be upset if he knew?"

"I wish him not to know."

"I would never say anything."

"I am appreciative."

"Perhaps having memories is a good thing."

"Why might that be?"

"Well, I can only explain it from a human perspective. There are memories of past events that we treasure and many we don't. But whether good or bad, memories influence how we recall our lives. To cause our memories to be lost would strip away a link that makes us human. Do you understand?"

"I comprehend."

"Legna is moving swiftly, and it frightens our citizens. He must be made to understand that."

"I hold no persuasion over Citizen Legna."

"But if the process could be slowed a bit it would allow our citizens time to appreciate the good that has already done as well as that which can be done in the future."

Mama took the last sip of his soda and placed the glass on the desk. "If you wish, I will alert Citizen Legna to your concerns."

"Perhaps we could begin with the confiscation of personal weapons. There are over 360,000,000 personal weapons in this country alone and—"

Masma abruptly stood and he left without further word.

With a smug smile, Gabriel muttered, "I just may have gotten through to my little alien friend—maybe."

The intercom sounded. "Agent Wilkinson is calling on your secure line."

"Thank you." He punched up the line. "You're calling on my secure line—must be trouble."

"First, congratulations on your wedding."

"Thanks, Denver."

"I wanted to update you on your little incident in the parking garage the other night."

"Oh crap, you heard."

"The two would-be assassins were members of a Michigan militia group that goes by the name Acirema Etihw."

"I can't even pronounce that?"

"Spell it backwards."

Gabriel thought for a moment before his brain ejected an answer. "Jesus!"

"Do us and yourself a favor; stay out of parking garages late at night, and keep your detail in the loop, okay."

"Okay."

"You don't sound like you mean it."

"Okay, okay, I mean it."

On the way home, Gabriel stopped for a pack of cigarettes and takeout Chinese. It was 6:30 PM when he strolled in the door. He set the food out and called Catherine.

She entered and sniffed the food. "I'm not really hungry."

"What's wrong?"

"I'm tired, that's all. I think I'll lay down for a while." She placed her hands on either side of his face and kissed him. "I love you, Mr. Ferro."

"I love you, Mrs. Ferro."

"Call your mother."

"In the morning when my head's clear."

"You said that yesterday."

As soon as Catherine had fallen asleep, Gabriel went to his study to make a journal entry. Unsure of what it was he wanted to say, he stared at the computer screen for a full thirty seconds before typing:

> *My intuition is on the blink, my thoughts no longer clear. I'm reminded of what Mark Twain wrote: "Drag your thoughts away from your troubles... by the ears, by the heels, or any other way you can manage it." Well, Mr. Twain, this time we may not be able to drag our thoughts away from our troubles. We are facing the penultimate moment in human history, and how we deal with it will determine whether we get to hang around for a few more centuries. Question mark, question mark, question mark.*

At 5:30 AM the following morning, Catherine experienced yet another bout of morning sickness. Naively, Gabriel asked what he could do to relieve her suffering.

"Nothing. It stops in twelve to fourteen weeks. I'm going to shower and go to the lab."

"You're sure?"

"Relax, I'm fine."

"Okay, you're the doctor."

"Best you remember that, young man. Don't forget to call your mother."

At 7:45 AM Gabriel was in his office working on his second cup of coffee when Betty buzzed him.

"*Citizen Masma,*" she intoned with emphasis on his name, "has requested your presence in *his* office adjoining the throne room."

"Be nice, Betty."

"They can pave the roads with gold, and I still wouldn't warm up to them."

It was only a short walk to Masma's office: down the hall, through the private dining room, and into what had been the presidential private study. He tapped the door lightly and entered.

"Good morning, Masma."

"Good morning, Gabriel, you are well?"

"Yes, thank you."

"Do you wish refreshment?"

"I'm good."

Masma smiled. "I know you are good, but would you like refreshment?"

Gabriel took a seat facing Masma's desk. "Did you just make a joke?"

"I did. Was it proper?"

"Yes, and it was funny."

"I have conversed with Citizen Legna. He respects your learned opinion in all matters."

"I appreciate that, Masma." *I think I just got an "atta boy,"*

"Citizen Legna directed I communicate his compassion for your stated concerns. He deems it appropriate that the surrender of personal weapons be temporarily suspended along with the dismantling of sovereign borders. It is only provisional until Citizen Legna deems otherwise."

Realizing he had won a major concession, Gabriel responded with a bit of sugar. "Citizen Legna is very wise. Please convey my gratitude… to you for presenting these matters to him."

Masma bowed his head.

"I'll inform Mr. Cross." Gabriel stood. "Well then, I'll be off."

"There is more. Although the demonstrations are waning, it is not so in the area called Europe—criminals and… hooligans?"

"Yes, hooligans."

"Criminals and hooligans are acting with impunity. Citizen Legna is concerned that authorities may be in support of the marauders. He wishes you to personally conduct an investigation. Peaceful assemblies are appropriate if citizens express their solicitude with civility."

"Surely Citizen Legna appreciates that the Ecaepian presence represents the greatest unknown in the history of the human race and—"

"Citizen Legna fails to comprehend mankind's inability to overcome such fears. We mean you no harm."

"It would take many moments to fully explain the human psyche."

"This we have come to know. I am always pleased to meet with you, Gabriel."

"Please thank the Administrator for his learned counsel."

Gabriel smiled and left. In the hallway, he balled his right hand into a fist, raised it above his head, and whispered, "Yes!"

The meeting had confirmed he could reason with Masma, and through him, appeal to Legna. Or maybe he was giving himself too much credit. Maybe Legna finally understood he could not control an independent-minded human race by issuing ultimatums.

He breezed into his office suite with a smile and planted a kiss on Betty's forehead.

"Excuse me, have you been drinking?"

"I'm drunk on power. Any messages?"

Betty handed him a small stack of pink phone slips. Scanning through them quickly, he stopped at one he did not recognize. "Who's Rosa Fernandez?"

"I have no idea. She said it was important and you should call."

"Hmm... okay, thanks."

Once at his desk, he went through the messages again until he came to the one from Rosa Fernandez. It was a 305-area code—Miami. He dialed and waited—it rang seven times. He was about to hang up when a man answered.

"Hello?"

"May I speak with Rosa Fernandez?"

"Who's calling?"

"Gabriel Ferro."

"Oh, oh, right... hold on. Rosa! It's for you!"

A woman's voice called out, "Who is it?"

The man's voice dropped to a whisper, "It's Gabriel."

Gabriel heard the woman say, "Oh God!" She fumbled with the phone, then dropped it. "Hijo de puta! Hello, this is Rosa."

"Mrs. Fernandez, I'm Gabriel Ferro, you called."

"Oh, Dios Mio! So sorry for what I said."

"That's okay, what can I do for you?"

"I am friends with your mother."

Here it comes, he thought, *she wants a favor."*

"Mr. Ferro, I am so sorry to tell you..." The woman sniffled like she might be crying.

"... your mother passed away last night."

Rosa's words failed to register. "I beg your pardon?"

Su madre, que murió—ella murió."

This time Rosa's words came through like a knife to his heart.

Gabriel was too distraught to speak directly with anyone, so he asked Betty to inform Alan Cross and the Administrator's office of his mother's passing; He would return in two days' time.

At 1:00 PM that same day, he and Catherine boarded a Delta flight out of Reagan National Airport to Miami. Not wanting to be to be recognized, he wore a Miami Marlins ball cap and dark sunglasses. When they arrived at Miami International, Rosa and Jose Fernandez were there to greet them and drove them directly to the Ferro family home on SW Eighteenth Court in Coral Way.

During the drive, Rosa explained how she and Isabella had met at the neighborhood Catholic Church and had forged a friendship. Yesterday, the two women had planned an early luncheon, but when Rosa arrived to pick Isabella up, she was nowhere to be found. Concerned, Rosa peeked in windows, working her way around the house until she reached Isabella's bedroom. Isabella was lying on the bed and did not respond to Rosa's urgent knocks on the window. Rosa called 911. When the EMS attendants arrived, they broke through the locked front door. All attempts to revive Isabella failed—she had passed away of unknown causes during the night.

With Catherine at his side, and Rosa and Jose close behind, he entered his boyhood home. It had been six months since he last set foot there. His mother had complained he did not come home often enough, but with his responsibilities in the White House, he had told her, more frequent visits were impossible. As often as he invited her to Washington, she refused. She had never flown before, and wasn't about to start now. Isabella was stubborn in that way.

He wished now he had visited more often.

He found the house eerily quiet now. Pausing in the living room, he examined the many framed photos on the six-foot long, cherry wood side-table that sat against the wall opposite the sofa. They represented a photographic history of his family from the time he was a child.

In the kitchen, the faint aroma of the last meal his mother had cooked still lingered. He glanced briefly into his old bedroom and smiled, for it remained the same as when he had left for college. Finally, he reached his mother's room. The bed had not been made, and that bothered him. He pulled the bedspread up over the pillows. Sitting on the edge of the bed, he placed a flat hand on the spot where his mother had died. He thought it still felt warm. And then it hit him hard; his mother's passing defined an end of place, order, and time. Dropping his head to his hands, he began to weep uncontrollably.

Catherine went to him and put her arms around him.

"I should have called her more often. I was so caught up in my work, my dedication to President Conrad and all that he hoped to accomplish. I pleaded with her to move in with me right after you and I made it back to Washington. She refused, she wanted to stay here in her home."

Catherine gently rocked him as he wept.

Two hours later they arrived at the funeral home and were ushered into the preparation room. The harsh odor of chemicals assaulted their senses and Gabriel recoiled.

"Are you okay, Mr. Ferro?" the funeral director asked.

The cold room sent a shiver through him. "Yes… thank you."

In the middle of the room were two side by side stainless steel tables. A crisp, white sheet covered the one to the left. The funeral director nodded to Gabriel. Gabriel nodded back. Slowly, the man removed the sheet exposing Isabella's head. The initial visual impact was so emotionally overpowering, it caused Gabriel to suck in a quick breath as he approached the table slowly. Trembling, he reaching under the sheet and took his mother's hand in his—it was cold. With tears streaming down his face, he bent down and kissed her forehead. His tears fell to her cheek.

Isabella had left specific instructions with her attorney how her funeral was to be handled. There was to be no mass, only a final blessing by her parish priest. Cremation was to take place soon thereafter.

Following the brief service, her attorney presented Gabriel with her will; she had left everything to him. He instructed the attorney to liquidate all assets with the proceeds to be donated to a Cuban charity in both his parents' names.

Gabriel couldn't bring himself to spend the night in his family home, so they stayed in a nearby hotel. The next day, after receiving Isabella's ashes, they boarded a charter fishing boat that had been arranged by Jose. In the blue-green waters not far from the very spot where Isabella and Javier Ferro had first set foot in America, Gabriel spread his mother's ashes.

It was all over just that quick.

"We rise from childhood to adulthood, to our deaths, and all that happens in between," Gabriel said to Catherine, "and yet it ends with little fanfare. In the end, I fear nothing much matters other than our families and our memories."

Later, they joined Rosa and Jose for a quick lunch at a small Cuban restaurant not far from Gabriel's old neighborhood.

"I hope you don't find this disrespectful in your time of sorrow," Jose said, "but these aliens—"

"No need to apologize, Jose. Please know and trust that I and others are doing all in our power to—"

Jose raised a hand. "You need not explain, I understand. God be with you— safe travels home."

They arrived at Reagan National at 5:30 that afternoon. As their cab weaved its way through bumper-to-bumper traffic, Gabriel called Betty.

"I wish there were words that would express how saddened I am for you."

"Thank you, Betty. She passed peacefully in her sleep. Bring me up to speed."

"Agent Wilkinson called, the demonstrations appear to be winding down."

"At least there's some good news. Look, we're both emotionally and physically exhausted—I may or may not be in tomorrow. I'll let you know."

"Get some rest… my best to Catherine."

Once home, they skipped dinner and retired early. In the middle of the night, Catherine woke to the sound of Gabriel crying. She draped an arm around him and held him until he finally fell to sleep again.

In the morning, they ate a light breakfast followed by a long walk. It was windy, and a gray sky promised inclement weather. They roamed their Georgetown neighborhood arm-in-arm for nearly an hour without a word spoken.

55

The following two weeks were unnervingly quiet, but a welcome relief. Spirits were broken, and the will to fight on had taken a toll on everyone's sanity. People had resigned to their fate without fully understanding the consequences. The leaders who had been so instrumental in organizing the worldwide protests were gone, to where no one knew; they had simply vanished.

Gabriel's daily meetings with Masma were reduced to two or three per week consisting mostly of Masma's ongoing explanation of the finer points of Ecaepian life. Gabriel was careful to keep unfavorable thoughts to himself by pretending to be the eager student. However, his continued denial of access to Legna weighed heavily on him. Had he committed an unspeakable offense that caused him to be out of the loop? He could only wait and wonder.

Gabriel and Cross continued to meet daily, and although the confiscation of personal weapons and the dismembering of sovereign borders had been delayed, Legna directed them to continue to pursue strategies to accomplish both. But, they knew full-well that people—especially in America—would never comply with such odious orders as the seizing of personal weapons and the erasing of sovereign borders. Although surprisingly, Gabriel found the latter somewhat appealing. If successfully implemented, he believed, a one-world government could once and for all bring all tribes together as a single, unified species.

At the end of the second month of the zero-population policy, statistics began trickling in. As expected, no new pregnancies were reported. Worldwide births totaled 219 thousand, normal for a two-month period. Not normal, was the over 64 thousand spontaneous miscarriages. Including the sick and elderly that may have survived with medical intervention, deaths totaled just over 9.7 million. Efforts to reduced population was having a pronounced effect.

The one shining spot in an otherwise upside-down world was that Catherine's morning sickness had abated. But her pregnancy would soon become obvious and began to cause her anxiety and she was often quick to lose her temper.

"I have to believe no any danger." She told Gabriel.

"I'll sleep easier when it's over."

Dumb choice of words and Gabriel instantly realized it.

She snapped, "Over?"

"When the baby is born."

"Aren't you the one who's gone out of his way to assure me all will be hunky-dory? Do I sense a sudden wavering in confidence?"

"No."

"That's not what I just heard."

"Sorry, it's not what I meant!"

She abruptly shot up from the chair. "We are not having this conversation!" And with that, she stormed off to the bedroom.

"What conversation?"

No answer from Catherine

Damn it, what she needed was your assurances, not your concerns He chided himself. *Best to keep your trap shut, because at the moment it's full of shoe.*

He went to his study with the intention of adding to his journal, but stared at the computer like it was his enemy—or at least one of them. Finally sitting, he powered up the laptop and opened the journal file. He sat still for the longest time, fixated on the title page: *The Thoughts, Musing, and Memories of Gabriel Javier Ferro.*

"Ha, thoughts, musing, and memories, my ass; I have nothing to say of any importance that will change a damn thing—zero, zip, nada." He slammed the laptop cover down hard and stood. "Who in the hell would want to read this crap anyway?"

"Good morning, how's Catherine?" Betty asked when he arrived in the morning.

He was about to tell her Catherine's morning sickness had stopped when he caught himself. "Ah, busy as usual in the lab."

"Hopefully, training gray squirrels to attack extraterrestrials."

Gabriel chuckled. "I'm ready for a strong cup of coffee."

Once settled at his desk, he checked his emails. There were several from generals at the Pentagon pushing for retaliation against aliens.

Gabriel shook his head. "These assholes think their emails are somehow exempt from alien snooping."

"There's so many assholes in the world, which ones are you talking about?"

Alan Cross stood in the doorway looking like one of the generals Gabriel had just dissed.

"The military geniuses who seem to forget the alien weapons make ours look like peashooters. I suspect they suffer memory loss of what the alien weapons have already done."

Cross took a seat. "They'll all be looking for new careers when he shuts down the military. Not a pretty thought."

"Not to change the subject, before long Legna's going to ask to see our plan for collecting personal weapons. To use a phrase my father was fond of, we're pissing in the wind on that one. But, Legna is fond of telling me a society that enjoys peace, harmony, and balance, weapons are not required."

"And I would agree if we lived in a society that cherished peace, harmony, and balance. In case you haven't noticed, son, Mother Earth is populated by humans. We react to danger, hazard, peril, and jeopardy badly." He stood. "Alright, I'm out of here, just wanted to shoot the breeze before whatever ruins my day."

"You optimist, you."

No sooner had Cross left, Betty buzzed him. "Your wife is on the line."

"Oh." Scooping up the phone, he spoke in his most cheerful voice. "Hey, love."

"How's your day going?"

"Smooth as a baby's ass. How's it with you?"

"Complicated as usual. I miss you, how about lunch?"

"I can't get away, how about dinner out?"

"Okay, but not Arico's—something different. I'm hungry for a steak at Bourbon's."

"It's a date. Pick you up around six. Feeling okay?"

"Smooth as a baby's ass."

At 6:45 PM, Gabriel and Catherine were sitting in a booth at Bourbon's Steakhouse on Pennsylvania Avenue in Georgetown a few miles west of downtown Washington. He marveled at how radiant she looked.

"Gabriel, you're staring."

"Because you look absolutely incredibly beautiful."

She smiled. "You know exactly what to say to a pregnant lady, sir."

"My mother taught me to be a gentleman."

"Bon appetite," the waiter said as he set their plates down.

Gabriel barely got his first bite of his steak when his cell phone rang. "Can you believe this?" He retrieved his phone, but the display did not identify the caller. "This better be good whoever you are."

As he listened, Catherine saw his expression go cold, and his shoulders slump.

"Yes," he said and hung up.

"What?"

Not wanting to alarm her, he chuckled. "The Wicked Witch of the West."

"Mosby?"

"Legna wants to see me."

"Now, at this hour?"

"Our friendly neighborhood alien has no sense of time, remember? Let's finish our meal. When I get there, I get there. Now then, about how extraordinary you look."

"Oh, stop already and eat!"

An hour later he dropped Catherine off and asked if she would stay up until he returned.

"I'll try. If I fall asleep, wake me."

"You're on." He reached across and kissed her. "And yes, you look absolutely stunning."

"You do lay on the charm rather thick."

Thirty minutes later, Gabriel drove onto the White House grounds via the Northwest Appointment Gate, parked and walked the short distance to the West Wing entrance. There, a uniformed agent greeted him.

"Working late, Mr. Ferro?"

"These aliens have no sense of time."

The security man frowned and whispered, "Or decency, it seems."

Gabriel sidled up to the man. "On that, we agree."

He gave the agent a friendly pat on the shoulder and made his way to the Oval. Ms. Mosby was at her desk.

"You may go in, Mr. Ferro."

He was surprised to Alan Cross there—not a good sign.

"Citizen Gabriel." Legna's voice was a full octave lower than usual. "Please, sit."

Gabriel took a seat on the sofa next to Cross. "What's so important to interrupt dinner with my wife?" No response from Legna. "Alan?"

"I guess we'll find out together."

Legna walked to the Portico door and stood silent for several moments. Then in a voice barely above a whisper, he said, "I have been informed our sworn enemy, the Sumina, from the galaxy Nortanis, have entered your galaxy."

Gabriel's back went straight. "Who?"

"Barbarians who know no limit to their savagery, who willingly risk the lives of others for self-enrichment. To know the Sumina is to know their psychopathic behavior knows no bounds. We have engaged them many times endeavoring to end their despicable pillaging of lessor civilizations. They confront us here where they believe us to be vulnerable."

Cross popped to his feet. "What do we do about it?"

Legna reply was swift, "*You* do nothing, Citizen Cross. Please sit."

"Don't Citizen Cross me! These, these—what did you call them?"

"Sumina."

"They're your enemy, not ours. Why are we being placed in jeopardy?"

"I requested you to sit—please do so now."

Cross scowled and remained standing.

Ignoring Cross' belligerence, Legna continued, "The citizens of Earth are in no immediate danger."

Cross spit out, "Define immediate."

"We shall seek mediation."

"And if that fails?"

"If they were to attack, they would target this city for they know I am here."

Gabriel's brow went up—his eyes widened. "So, it's you they want?"

"I have led forces against them."

Cross grimaced. "Huh! That answers that question."

Legna said, "It is imperative you be protected."

"Yes, yes," Cross exclaimed, "we have to alert our military immediately."

"I speak of Citizen Gabriel."

"Me?"

"You have been chosen to lead."

Cross plopped down on the sofa and glared at Gabriel.

"This was never my doing, Alan. I never sought it."

"Allow your wisdom and your courage to guide you, Citizen Gabriel," Legna said. "Citizen Cross, your wisdom is required as well. Will you stand at Citizen Gabriel's side?"

Cross hesitated, his eyes flitting between Legna and Gabriel. "My only interest is protecting the people of Earth." He placed a hand on Gabriel's arm. "If by pledging my support to Gabriel accomplishes that, then so be it."

"Then we are one," Legna said.

Gabriel's mind went into full panic mode. His thoughts whirled with all that could go wrong, the many who would die if the Sumina were to attack. And then there was Betty, Tyler, Rafi, Jennings, Galinski, and B.D. Sanjaya. *God, this is not happening, I'm not prepared for this. Catherine and the baby and....*

"I will arrange for them to be with you."

Angrily, Gabriel shot back, "Stay the hell out of my head!"

Cross was on his feet again. "And mine too!" He walked to a window, and stared out blankly.

"It is only a precaution, but if the Sumina were to attack, it would be best if you were not in harm's way."

"Where is out of harm's way?"

Without skipping a beat, Legna responded, "Surin Island."

Cross spun around from the window. "Where?"

"I told you about Surin Island, Alan."

"Yeah, yeah." Cross snapped. "And what makes you think it would be safe there?"

Masma, who up until then had remained silent, spoke, "The Sumina will express no interest in such an isolated area."

That sent Gabriel's mind reeling again. "Why would we expose the Mogen to this?"

Neither Legna nor Masma commented.

"Well?"

"If it is your decision to decline sanctuary, your wishes shall be respected."

Gabriel looked to Cross—Cross shook his head. "If you're looking to me for a solution, I'm all out."

Then Legna dropped the other shoe. "If the Sumina besiege Ecaep, I will be recalled."

Cross quick-paced to within a few feet of Legna. "Did I hear, right? You'd leave?"

"Masma will remain, as will one of our ships."

"Jesus!" Cross strode back to the sofa and plopped down next to Gabriel.

Legna made his way to his desk and lifted himself to the chair, swiveled and stared out the Portico door.

At least, Gabriel thought, Legna's solution would offer some modicum of safety for Catherine and the baby.

Legna swiveled back. "As we speak, Catherine is on her way."

Damn him, he wasn't even looking at me, and he's in my head again. "You were that sure of me?"

It became pin-drop quiet. Neither Gabriel nor Cross knew how to react or provide an alternative solution.

"Return to your domicile, Citizen Cross and gather your belongings."

Gabriel stood. "Meet me in my office when you get back, Alan."

Cross grumbled something unintelligible and stormed out.

"Citizen Gabriel," Legna called as Gabriel reached the door, "a moment please. You need not fear for your offspring for all is well."

Gabriel froze—his face turned ashen pale. *Damn it, he knows Catherine pregnant!* Unsmiling, he nodded, backed his way to the door, and left.

With a contemptuous look, Catherine was sitting beside Betty's desk. A small suitcase was on the floor beside her. "You better have a good explanation."

Gabriel sat next to her and kissed her on the forehead.

"It's going to take more than that, Gabriel Ferro. The Secret Service ordered me to toss a few essentials in a bag without telling me why then drove me here at ninety miles an hour through DC traffic with sirens and lights blazing."

"Listen carefully, don't say a word because time is short."

He recounted what Legna had told him and Cross. The more he explained, the more the hysteria was rising on Catherine and Betty's faces.

"It's just a precautionary move—Legna is dealing with it."

"Precautionary?" Catherine exclaimed. "You don't move halfway around the world to some island as a precaution unless—"

Betty's voice pitched-up a full octave. "Tell me again, you're going where?"

"Surin Island. I've been there; you'll like it."

"Me?"

"Yes, you. Toss some things in a bag and get back here."

"Wait a minute, I'm not going anywhere."

"Yes, you are. Now, go home, pack something, and get back here—go!"

"But Gabriel—"

"Go!"

"All right, all right." Betty made it as far as the door before turning back with a look of dread.

"Go now!"

Catherine placed her hands on her abdomen. "Gabriel… the baby."

"Legna knows."

"Oh, God, no!"

"No, no, it's fine, he assured me all would be well… really."

"And you trust him?"

"Do we have a choice?"

Catherine buried her head in her hands and began to cry.

56

As soon Betty and Cross returned, the four of them made their way to the Oval Office. Ms. Mosby was at her desk. For the first time since Gabriel had met her, she actually tried to smile.

"Citizen Masma awaits your arrival on the south lawn. I wish you well, citizens."

There was urgency in their steps as they made their way to where the alien shuttle would take them to the distant Surin Island. To Gabriel's surprise, Owen Jennings was already there. Masma at his side.

"Owen!" Gabriel called to his friend.

Jennings motioned to Masma. "In the flesh thanks to a call from him."

"You know what this is all about?" Gabriel asked Jennings.

"I have informed Citizen Jennings," Masma said.

"Owen, you remember Betty."

"Considering the circumstances, it's good to see you again, Betty."

Cross offered his hand. "Alan Cross."

Jennings took Cross' outstretched hand. "Mr. Vice President, a pleasure."

"Former vice president, now lackey to a bloody damn alien. Call me Alan, please."

Gabriel said to Masma, "Do you want to explain our transportation, or do I?"

"You may do so, Citizen Gabriel."

"Any second now something you won't be able to see is going to land a few feet from here. Just follow Catherine and me and you'll be fine."

Betty raised an eyebrow. "Why won't we see it?"

"Suddenly, everything loose on the ground in front of them began to swirl up and out. Then all was still for several seconds before the dime-sized fissure of white light appeared and shaped itself into a doorway and ramp.

Cross' mouth flapped open. "Holy mother of God."

Jennings, and Betty, gasped and took a step back.

"Follow us." Gabriel took Catherine's hand in his and proceeded toward the ramp.

Betty looked at the shimmering light with misgivings. "Follow you where?"

"Come on," Gabriel assured her, "It's safe.

Cross was the first to follow.

"Give me your hand." Jennings offered his to Betty.

Inside the craft, the thirteen seats were already in position. Overwhelmed that they were actually on an alien craft, no one breathed a word.

"Please take a seat," Masma instructed.

With trepidation, they did as Masma asked and waited for further instructions, but Masma offered none. With no windows, sound, or a sense of movement, it was impossible to determine when they might leave or when they would arrive at their destination.

Nine anxious minutes later, the magic door and ramp reappeared.

"What just happened?" Alan Cross asked.

Masma was the first to stand. "We have arrived."

"How's that possible?"

"All things are possible, Citizen Cross."

They exited the craft and found themselves on a wide, sandy beach, the same beach Gabriel had set foot on when he first visited the island with Rafi.

With a flourish, Masma announced, "Welcome to South Surin Island, Indonesia."

The sky was a luminous blue, the sun bright and warm, the sandy beach a welcome reprieve—a far cry from the threat they had left behind. If it were not for the circumstances that forced them to flee, this was an island paradise to be savored.

"Gabriel!" a voice called out. Jogging down the path from the direction of the Mogen village was Rafi Suharto flanked by Secret Service agents Dex Patterson and Remy Bernard.

"My God, Rafi, Dex, Remy, how did you get here?"

"Same way you did—Ecaepian Airlines."

"Wherever you go, Mr. Ferro," Remy said, "we go."

"I'm damn happy to see you." Gabriel made quick introductions all around before asking Rafi, "Does Rahmat understand what's going on?"

"Ur, no, that's a bridge yet to be crossed. Dex and Remy will take you down to the beach. Follow the path to the right before you get to the village—you know where it is."

"Why all the mystery… I want to see Rahmat."

"Go to the beach first, you'll understand." He nodded to Masma. "Keep what's his name under wraps."

"Citizen Masma," Masma corrected.

"Right, got it, now go before someone from the village spots you."

And with that Rafi sped back up the path to the village, leaving Dex and Remy to lead the group to the north beach.

With cautious anticipation, the group followed Dex and Remy up the path. Twenty-five yards short of the village proper, they turned into a narrow but well-worn dirt path that wound its way through a grove of mango and banana trees, a few goats, and a dozen or so chickens, then past a garden of spring onions, sugar peas, eggplant, kale, and cucumbers to a dense tropical forest of ironwood and gum trees that led to the vast blue Andaman Sea.

"Whoa," Jennings said when he saw the Sea.

"Jeez," Betty added, "we've landed in paradise."

"Maybe, maybe not," Alan Cross grumbled.

A man was making his way up the path toward them. At first, Gabriel thought it might be one of the villagers, but the guy was dressed in western clothing, not the traditional sarong worn by both the Mogen men and women.

"So, what have you dragged me into this time?" the man called out.

It was none other than B.D. Sanjaya, the very man who had guided Gabriel and Rafi through the intimidating Indonesian jungle to the secret *Kebun*.

"I don't believe this!" Gabriel quickstepped to Sanjaya and wrapped his arms around him.

"It wasn't enough that we trudged through that bloody jungle, now this?" Sanjaya nodded to Masma. "Imagine my reaction when he showed up insisting I join him on his invisible transport."

Gabriel introduced Sanjaya with a short commentary on their provocative jungle exploits.

Sanjaya said, "Has Rafi explained the beach?"

"No, what?"

"You're in for a few surprises."

"More than a few," Dex added with a crooked smile.

As they neared the sandy beach, Gabriel spied the hut he and Rafi had shared. The thick growth of palm trees and high brush cover to their right kept a portion of the beach from view. But, as they passed, an astonishing sight presented itself.

Back along the tree line, approximately one hundred fifty feet from the lapping waves, sat a row of single-room structures that had not existed when Gabriel had last set foot there. There were ten huts in all that precisely mirrored the woven bamboo and thatched-roof hut Gabriel and Rafi had occupied.

Gabriel stopped dead in his tracks. "What the hell! Where did they come from?"

Masma said, "Citizen Legna has addressed your needs,"

"But how did they get here?"

"Do not attempt to define what is beyond your understanding." Masma pointed to the hut Gabriel and Rafi had occupied. "I shall dwell there." He pointed to the first new hut. "Citizen Gabriel and Citizen Catherine there, your agent persons in the next. The rest may choose whichever dwelling that suits them, except dwellings five and six."

Flummoxed by the sight of the huts, Gabriel whistled. "I don't believe this."

"Hey," a voiced called from the fifth hut, "what's all the noise? Can't an old man take a quiet nap in peace?"

Incredibly, it was Skip Galinski. Then two heads popped out from the next hut. It was Gabriel's aide, Tyler Harney and his very pregnant wife, Bonnie who smiled and waved.

Masma whispered to Gabriel, "Citizen Legna deemed it befitting your confidants be with you during this period of disquiet."

Galinski removed the ever-present cigar from his mouth and made his way barefooted across the white, sandy beach, breezed past Gabriel, and hugged Catherine. "It's damn good to see you, Missy."

"Same here, you old coot." She laughed and kissed him on the cheek. "And don't call me *Missy.*"

"Where have you been? I tried contacting you," Gabriel asked.

"I went off in a different space for a while," Galinski answered, "needed to get my head straight after our little adventure—now we're told the damn planet may be invaded."

Rafi came trotting down the path and onto the beach. "Well?"

"Everyone's here—I'm speechless."

"The villagers are bummed out over these huts. Not one of them will set foot down here believing evil spirits have invaded their island. I told Rahmat you were here. He's anxious to see you—wants to know if you can explain this."

"I'm anxious to see him, but how will I ever make him understand?"

"Don't try," Rafi said. "They won't understand the concept of aliens."

"Who's this Rahmat character?" Cross asked.

"Rahmat Pramonagkij, the tribal chief. Nothing happens on this island without his knowledge and blessing—except of course these huts."

"Masma, you better explain how these huts got here before I see Rahmat."

"Do not be concerned with such matters. May I suggest everyone retire to their chosen domicile."

"Good idea," Rafi said.

Gabriel took Catherine hand. "I'll be along in a minute. Get some rest."

With much apprehension and a million unanswered questions, the group made their way to the primitive-looking huts.

As they all meandered toward the huts, Betty tossed a hand in the air. "Call if you need anything, Gabriel. Oh, I forgot, no phone service."

As soon as everyone was out of range, Gabriel said Masma, "Are you in touch with Legna?"

"I have communicated with Citizen Legna… discourse with the Sumina continues."

"Care to elaborate?"

"Maybe it wasn't the best idea to bring us here." Gabriel pointed to the huts. "I want an explanation how those got there."

"You will find an explanation difficult to comprehend."

"Try me."

"Very well." Masma pointed to the original hut. "This structure was profiled to arbitrate its size and materials." He turned to the new huts. "The result is what you see. Has my commentary been satisfactory?"

"Not even close."

"If I explained they were forged in another dimension and placed here, would you comprehend?"

"Another dimension?"

"There, you see, Gabriel, you make my point."

As desperate as Gabriel was for an earthly explanation, it was clear he wasn't about to get one. "Hopefully, when we leave, the Mogen won't tear them down."

"That would be irrational, would it not?"

"Never mind. What about talks between Citizen Legna and the Sumina?"

"I will keep you informed." Masma ambled off toward his hut. "Be well, Gabriel."

"You'll let me know when you hear from Legna?" Gabriel called out.

Masma raised an arm over his head and jiggled his fingers—his version of a wave.

"We need food and water, ya' know."

The bantam figure disappeared into his hut.

"So much for that."

He entered his hut and found Catherine perched in a chair fashioned out of bamboo and sipping a bottle of water. "Welcome to paradise, or some version thereof."

Gabriel spied something on the floor. "What in the world is that?"

"Looks like a mattress to me."

It was an honest-to-goodness queen mattress and real pillows; a far cry from the grass-filled sleeping mats he and Rafi had slept on. Stacked next to the mattress were several cases of bottled water and boxes of energy bars.

Catherine pointed to candles on a small bamboo side table. "Our only source of light."

He motioned to a small closed-in cubicle next to the bed. "And that?"

"See for yourself."

He swung the door open, and his eyes popped. Incredibly, it was a powder room sporting a commode and a small, oval sink along with soap, towels and various toiletries. "I don't believe this."

"Believe it."

"How in the hell did they pull this off?"

"Ecaepian magic, but no shower," Catherine bemoaned.

Gabriel ran a hand through his hair and blew a breath. "I need to think. I'm going for a walk on the beach, want to come?

"You go."

The low sun stained the western sky a bright orange. Sand crabs scurried about, and Ruddy Turnstone birds hovered just above the waves in pursuit of a quick meal. Gabriel slipped off his shoes and socks, rolled his pant legs up to just below his knees, and waded into the water until the waves lapped at his calves. There he lingered trying to concentrate on nothing more than the bucolic surroundings. But his thoughts wandered back to the quandary they were facing.

He said wistfully just above a whisper. "What have I got us into?"

"You're talking to yourself, kid."

Gabriel spun around to find Galinski standing nearby. "Jeez, Skip, don't sneak up like that."

"I heard what you said. Beating yourself up won't do anyone much good."

"You're all here because of me."

"We're here *thanks* to you because this Legna character decide we, your friends, needed to be protected from those bandits chasing *them*."

"Is that supposed to make me feel better?"

"Whatever. Now, if I leave you alone on this beach, promise not to talk to yourself?"

Gabriel grinned and nodded.

"Good, see you in the morning, partner."

When he returned to the hut, Catherine was sleeping and had left a single candle burning by the bed.

He removed his cloth, slipped into bed beside her, and blew out the candle. Laying there in the dark, his thoughts flitted from one to concern to the other until he finally slept

He was startled awake by what sounded like a cowbell. Popping to a sitting position, he rubbed at his eyes and could see sunlight squeezing through cracks in the thatch walls.

Catherine rolled onto her side. "What was that?"

"Damned if I know unless there are cows on the beach."

"Cows?"

Rising and slipping on his pants, he walked to the door and peered out. There was no one in sight. But, nestled in the sand about fifty feet away, a table had been set up. "Come see."

By the time Catherine joined him, the others had also stuck their heads out.

From the next hut, Dex called to Gabriel. "What's that?"

"I have no idea." Gabriel called back.

One by one, the group made their way across the sand to where a low table had been set. It was laden with fresh juice, an assortment of fresh fruits, and brown flatbread flecked with what looked like sesame seeds.

"Where the hell did this come from?" Alan Cross asked.

467

Gabriel looked up and down the beach. "Where's Rafi?"

"Right here," Rafi called out as he came off the dirt path from the village. "The Mogen hope you enjoy breakfast."

"The Mogen did this?" Betty exclaimed.

Skip Galinski wailed, "Well, I'll be damned!"

Tyler Harney beamed. "I don't care who's responsible, let's just be thankful."

While the others dug into the food, Rafi motioned Ruben to step away. "I met with Rahmat early this morning. Despite his bewilderment why we're here, he's genuinely concerned for our welfare. They brought the food, rang the bell, and left."

"God love them."

"He believes these huts are the work of *Satan*—the devil. Rahmat may be a simple man who lives a simple life, but he's also a wise and curious soul. So, I took a chance and explained why we are here and who Masma is and where he's from."

"Wow, how did he react?"

"I'm not sure how much he understood. I told Masma was a living, breathing being just like us and that he should meet with him and welcome him as he has us. To my surprise, he agreed, but insisted on meeting with you first."

"I don't understand half of it myself, how do I explain it to him?"

"Just tell him the truth as you know it."

"Easier said than done. When does this meeting take place?"

"After lunch on the path away from the village."

"Unless you're there to translate, how do I communicate?"

"You two made a connection; you won't need words."

"How do you say, *old friend*?"

"*Taman lama.*"

"*Taman lama*—got it. Now we need Masma to agree."

"I'll talk to him. Right now, let's eat."

At the table eating, Cross grumbled, "Don't these people drink coffee."

"In fact, they don't," Rafi answered. "They drink tea made from the leaves of the Camellia plant. Very popular in Indonesia."

"Tomorrow we order tea then."

"And a few beers," Remy chimed in.

"And a good bottle of chardonnay," Jennings joked.

"For heaven's sake, listen to you guys." Betty made a sweeping motion toward the sea. "Is all this not sufficient reward?"

"Keep reminding yourself *why* we're here, Betty," Cross said. "A bottle or two of chardonnay couldn't hurt."

Masma made an appearance at the door to his hut, but did not join them. Rafi and Gabriel went to him and proposed the meeting with Rahmat.

"If you insure my safety, then it shall be."

"Okay then. Any word from Citizen Legna?"

"I await further communication. Until our meeting with Citizen Rahmat, I bid you good day." And with that Masma turned and entered his hut.

As they were returning to the beach, Rafi said to Gabriel, "He knows more than he's telling."

At 2:00 that afternoon, Gabriel, Rafi, and Masma made their way up the path to where Rahmat had agreed to meet. Half way up, Rafi stopped. "Go, Gabriel, we'll give you time alone with him. Whistle when you're ready for us."

Rahmat Pramonagkij, was an affable man in his mid-sixties. Despite the language barrier, he and Gabriel had struck up a friendship during Gabriel's previous visit. When the time had came for Gabriel and Rafi to leave, the entire village warmly embraced Gabriel and Rahmat invited him to return one day. This was that day, and Gabriel was looking forward to seeing his friend.

Rahmat was sitting in a chair beside the path. He was dressed in a blue and white striped sarong that flowed from his waist to his flip-flop covered feet. His salt and pepper hair—mostly salt— flowed to just above his shoulders. Four chairs had been set up around a small table whose irregular top was fashioned from a large tree trunk. Atop it was four glasses and a small pitcher of yellowish liquid.

At the sight of Gabriel, Rahmat rose quickly and smiled broadly. Placing a closed fist over his heart, he called out, "Gabriel."

Gabriel placed his hand over his heart. "Rahmat, *team lama.*"

"*Gabriel, Saya jade silken militant team lama Saya sewali lag.*"

Having no idea what Rahmat said, Gabriel assumed it was nothing short of a warm welcome. The chief motioned to a chair and poured the yellow liquid into a glass and offered it to Gabriel who smiled and sipped it.

"Good, very good."

"*Hal in denga subacute bear Baha Saya mandamus cembalo. Anda tolah teraweber.*"

From Gabriel's expression, Rahmat could see he had not understood. Touching Gabriel's arm, he said in halting English, "It-is-with-joy-I-welcome-your-return."

Gabriel beamed. "Your English, it is very good."

Rahmat smiled and nodded enthusiastically. "*Yak yam, Saya Bela jar.*"

The two men chatted easily, even though neither totally understood the other. Occasionally, Rahmat would say a word or two in English. Otherwise, they relied on hand and facial gestures.

Ten minutes had passed when Gabriel asked if Rafi and Masma could join them. "Rafi, Masma?"

Rahmat nodded his approval. Gabriel whistled, which seemed to confuse Rahmat until he saw Rafi and Masma approaching. As gracious as he was, at the sight of the diminutive alien, Rahmat's eyes bloomed. He rose to his feet and took a step back.

"*Rahmat,*" Rafi called out as they approached, "*team Saya ad yang taut. Memperpanjang persahabatan Anda untuk Masma, karena Anda harus kami.*" (There is nothing to fear, extend your warm friendship to Masma as you have with us.)

Rahmat stared wide-eyed in wonder at the sight of Masma. "*Apa yang harus saya sebut makhluk ini?*"

Rafi motioned to Masma. "*Aadalah nama adalah, Masma.*"

"Masma," Rahmat repeated with a look of bewilderment.

Masma smiled and bowed his head in respect to the tribal chief. "Rahmat."

Still unable to comprehend a creature from another world, Rahmat guardedly invited them to sit and poured Rafi and Masma a glass of the yellow liquid.

With his eyes locked on Masma, he said, "*Jus buah.*"

Then Masma knocked them off their feet with, "*Ni adalah kehormatan besar saya, Pak, untuk membuat persahabatan Anda.*"

Rahmat's face lit up like a spotlight. "*Dia berbicara kepada saya dalam Bahasa!*"

"What did you say?" Gabriel asked with excited anticipation.

Masma smiled. "I was honored to make his acquaintance."

The very idea that Masma could converse with Rahmat in his native language was all it took to win Rahmat's trust. An instant connection had been made, a common bond gained through simple communication that allowed Rahmat to see Masma as Rafi had said; a living, breathing being just like them.

Masma and Rahmat continued to converse as if Rafi and Gabriel were not present. But before long Rahmat's expression turned serious. His eyes flitted quickly from Gabriel to Rafi and finally to Masma. "*Bagaimana gubuk muncul di pantai? Apakah mereka ditempatkan di sana oleh setan?*"

Rafi translated. "Rahmat is asking for an explanation how the huts on the beach appeared from nowhere?

Masma attempted to explain, but although Rahmat listened intently, he failed to grasp the complex explanation. He shook his head and waved his hands in the air. "*Apa yang Anda katakan tidak masuk akal.*"

Rafi touched Gabriel's arm. "He says it makes no sense."

Rahmat pointed in the direction of the beach. "*Aku Skipihat gubuk jadi saya menerima mereka ada. Tapi aku tidak mengerti sihir, jadi kita tidak akan berbicara tentang mereka lebih lanjut.*"

"He sees the huts; therefore, he accepts they are there. However, because he does not understand the magic that created them, he wishes not to speak of them further."

Masma nodded and changed the subject. Rahmat listened intently, never taking his eyes from Masma. Suddenly, he slapped his knee and began laughing.

"What does he find funny?" Gabriel asked Rafi.

"Masma told him about his life on Ecaep. For some reason, Rahmat finds it amusing."

Then it was Rahmat's turn to explain Mogen life to Masma. Masma took it all in, occasionally smiling and nodding his understanding.

"This human possesses great wisdom," Masma said of Rahmat. "He treasures his life and the lives of his villagers and the bountiful nature which provides for their needs. There is much that humans can learn from the learned Mogen."

Rahmat placed his hand over his heart. "Miasma."

Mama seemed confused by the gesture.

"He has accepted you as a friend," Rafi said. "You must do the same in return."

Mama placed his hand flat against his chest. "Rahmat."

And then Rahmat suggested something they had not anticipated: Would their group join him and several village elders on the beach that evening to share a meal?

As soon as Rafi translated, Gabriel couldn't agree fast enough. "Tell him we would be honored. Masma?"

"I too would be honored."

When the meeting ended, Rafi accompanied Rahmat to the village to seek the participation of the elders while Gabriel and Masma waited on the path until Rafi returned.

"It wasn't an easy sell," Rafi said, "but the elders agreed. This meeting of divergent cultures will be one for the record books."

56

At 6:00 PM, Rahmat arrived on the beach with three middle-aged village elders whose names were Chula, Kai, and Chanra. They brought with them a large, covered pot of food. The one called Chula set several bamboo pole torches in the sand while Kai spread woven mats for everyone to sit on. It was all very formal for the usually informal Mogen.

Rafi was the first to arrive, followed minutes later by the others—all but Masma—he remained in his hut. Rafi explained to the Mogen that Masma did not consume solids, but would join them following the meal. The Mogen found it odd that anyone did not consume solids unless they were ill.

Dinner was a chicken stew with eggplant, sugar peas, and kale. There was also a local brew the Mogen called *palm wine*, made from a mixture of the fermented sap of palm tree flowers, sugar cane, and red rice grain.

As they dined, everyone chatted easily while Rafi tried to keep up with translations.

"Am I missing something here?" Cross whispered to Rafi. "Not one question about Masma. Aren't they curious?"

"Sure they are," Rafi whispered back, "but they refrain from questioning what they don't fully understand. It's just their way."

As the sun hit the horizon, Elder Chanra lit the torches. Here in this idyllic setting, if for only a few precious moments in time, they savored the camaraderie and the tranquility of their surroundings. Perhaps it was the consumption of palm wine that had turned the assemblage into a sanguine gathering.

Masma finally made his appearance at the door of his hut.

Skip Galinski was the first to spot him. "Well now, this ought to be interesting."

All eyes pivoted to Masma. The conviviality came to an abrupt stop as the Mogen elders bolted to their feet. Their body language and expressions betrayed their fear at the very sight of this small, childlike alien creature.

Rahmat spoke to them in a low, calm voice. *"Jangan takut, saudara-saudara saya. Kita harus menunjukkan pengunjung ini dari jauh hormat kami."*

Chula, Kai, and Chanra dutifully sat down.

"Rafi," Catherine asked, "what did he tell them?"

"Not to fear what they fail to understand, but to show this honored visitor their respect."

Making his way down the steps, Masma crossed the fifty feet of sand, stopping within five feet of where everyone sat.

Rafi stood and introduced Masma to the elders. *"Mari kita menyambut Citizen Masma yang bergabung dengan kami sebagai teman baru kami."* (Let us welcome Citizen Masma who joins us as a new friend.)

Masma directed his greeting to the Mogen men. *"Ini adalah kehormatan saya akan diterima oleh orang-orang Mogen ... Rahmat, Chula, Kai and Chanra."*

The elders, wondering how this being knew their names and language, looked positively stunned.

Chula said excitedly, *"Dia berbicara di lidah kita!"* (He speaks our tongue!)

Wide-eyed with disbelief, the elders chatted to one another like children discovering ice cream for the first time. Rahmat had not told them that Masma spoke their tongue, preferring instead they discover this for themselves. Taking great pleasure in their childlike wonder, Masma's smile radiated like a proud parent.

Rafi motioned to a mat in the sand that had been reserved for Masma. The alien lowered himself and folded his hands. With a nod of respect to the ladies, Masma said, "Good evening, Citizen Catherine, Citizen Betty, and Citizen Bonnie." He nodded to Bonnie. "Your ovum flourishes with life."

It was an odd way to refer to the impending birth of her child.

"Um, thank you," Bonnie said smiling.

"Do you know of its gender?"

"No." She replied.

"Do you wish me to inform you?"

"Uh, no thanks, it's more fun if it is a surprise?"

Then Masma turned to Catherine. In a flash, she realized he was about to comment on her pregnancy. No one knew that she was expecting and that's the way she wanted it to remain. Her eyelids compressed to slits as she shook her head ever so slightly. Masma immediately understood and remained silent.

Rahmat filled a glass with palm wine and presented it to Masma who inspected it before thanking Rahmat. "*Terima kasih, Citizen Rahmat.*"

There was a moment of elevated anticipation as Masma took a small sip from the glass. He smiled and downed a gulp to show his approval.

Pleased by Masma reaction, Elder Kai said exuberantly, "*Ahhh, ia menikmati santan ... baik, baik!*"

Rahmat, Chula, and Chanra clapped enthusiastically, while the others, not knowing what had been said, joined in nonetheless.

Masma was relishing the attention and raised his glass in a salute. "*Terima kasih, terima kasih*—Thank you." He then surprised his hosts by telling of how Ecaepians held the Mogen in high esteem.

Chula asked inquisitively, "*Anda tahu dari suku kami?*"

"*Ya kita tahu Mogen baik, Citizen Chula.*" Masma said. (Yes, we know the Mogen well, Citizen Chula.)

With an inquisitive expression, Chula looked to Rahmat. "*Bagaimana ia bisa tahu dari kita? Bagaimana ini mungkin?*"

"He doesn't understand how the Ecaepians know of the Mogen," Rafi said.

Masma continued in their tongue, "*We honor the Mogen way. You have wisely chosen to reject the trappings sought by others, preferring to hold in high honor the simple joy of living. We applaud the Mogen. Your fellow humans could learn much from your ways.*"

Masma's generous explanation removed any remaining fears the Mogen may have had of this alien creature. They began firing off question after question:

How was it possible that other worlds existed beyond they inhabited? How was he able to travel safely through the heaven and the stars? What was the purpose of his visit? And finally, how had the new huts magically appeared?

Masma patiently answered each question as best as he could, although they looked perplexed when it came to how the huts had materialized. Masma laughed, made elaborate hand gestures, and generally seemed to be enjoying himself in a way Gabriel had not previously witnessed. The gathering became a jovial love fest between three divergent cultures that had come together on a warm, breezy night on a sandy beach in a far-flung corner of the planet. No one appeared to be in a hurry to bring the evening to an end. But as the hour grew late, Tyler and Bonnie bid everyone a good night.

Betty was next. "I think I'll turn in, too."

"Hey, I'll walk you home."

"Not necessary, Sparky. I can find my way."

"I don't know, Betty, you are after all, of a certain age."

"You see what I mean? The boy needs to be spanked from time to time. All right, junior, walk me home."

Betty slipped her shoes off, and she and Gabriel walked quietly across the sand.

"You okay?" Gabriel finally asked.

"Just tired."

"Is that all?"

Betty stopped and turned to him. "This doesn't pass the smell test. If it looks like a duck and quacks like a duck, it's a duck."

"Just what duck are we talking about?"

Betty motioned to Masma who remained in deep conversation with the Mogen. "I don't see any good coming from their being here. This is our planet; they should let us be. In the meantime, I'll settle for a hug and try to get some rest."

Gabriel took her in his arms and held her tight. "Thank you."

"For what?"

"For being you, for looking after me."

"If I don't, who will, Sparky?" She planted a kiss on his cheek and went on her way.

When he returned to the group, the conversation was still going strong. Fascinated with Masma and curious to know more, the Mogen continued firing off questions, taking great delight in Masma's elaborate answers.

Finally, Rahmat announced they would take their leave for the evening. Enthusiastically shaking hands with everyone, including Masma, Rahmat and the Elders bid everyone a good night. The four men could be heard chatting excitedly as they made their way along the dark path to the village.

Dex and Remy wandered off to the water's edge. They had not sooner got there when Dex pointed to the sky above the trees and called out, "Hey, what the hell was that?"

It got everyone's attention at the table, but they were too close to the tree line to see what Dex was pointing to.

Now it was Remy who thrust a hand to the sky. "Holy smoke!"

"What are the boys yelling about?" Jennings said dismissively.

Sanjaya, sensing the urgency in Dex and Remy's shouts, rose from his mat and headed toward them. "Be right back."

When he reached Dex and Remy, he looked to the night sky where they were pointing, but he saw nothing unusual.

Remy pointed again. "Right there, it looked like a narrow beam of light."

"Yeah," Dex added, "an orange-bluish beam that shot down in a perfectly straight, defined line."

"I don't see anything," Sanjaya said. "Could have been a meteor."

"Meteors leave trails—this didn't—and it disappeared in a blink of an eye."

Sanjaya watched and waited, but nothing happened. "Well, there's nothing up there now. I'm going back."

Just as Sanjaya was about to leave, Dex wailed, "Shit! There it is again!"

Sanjaya swung back too late—whatever was there was gone. But a second later, it happened again: an orange-blue line streaked across the sky to Earth. It had lasted no longer than a second or two.

"Holy God, what was that!" Sanjaya all but choked on his words.

Masma sprang to his feet and ordered. "I wish you to return to your domiciles immediately."

"What?" Gabriel responded.

"You must return to your domiciles."

Sanjaya came trotting back. "That wasn't a shooting star; that was a laser beam."

Cross repeated, "Laser beam?"

"The Sumina have discharged their weapons. Please, you must go now."

With no further explanation, Masma walked quickly to his hut.

"Hey, wait a minute!" Gabriel called after him.

"I will communicate with you soon," Masma yelled back and disappeared into his hut.

Remy, Dex, and Sanjaya came running back.

Dex said excitedly, "We sure as hell saw something."

"The Sumina are attacking—Masma wants us back in our huts."

"What the hell good is that going to do?" Galinski wailed.

"Let's go, the party's over." Gabriel took Catherine's arm and nudged her. "Come on. Dex, Remy, check to see everything's okay with Betty and the Harney's.

An hour went by, then two, then three and there was no further word from Masma.

"I'm going to his hut." Gabriel said to Catherine.

"There's nothing anything of us can do. Let's just try to get some rest."

"How can we sleep?"

"Easy, close your eyes and think good thoughts. Masma will come when he has something to report."

Despite what was happening, Catherine drifted off almost immediately. Gabriel, on the other hand, lay there for almost an hour before finally drifting off.

In the morning, a ray bleeding through the narrow slits in the thatched walls slashed across his eyes, and he awoke with a start.

"Jesus! What time is it?" He glanced at his watch. "Five to seven!"

Rolling out of bed, he rushed to the door and peered out. Rahmat and Chula were on the beach setting the table for breakfast. Rahmat waved, and Gabriel waved back.

Catherine was awake now. "Who are you waving at?"

"They have no idea what's happening. Come see."

She made her way to the door and peered out. "They need to be told, Gabriel."

"Hell no, let them live in peace… without our problems becoming theirs."

"But our problems could become theirs."

At the far end of the beach, Masma made an appearance at the door of his hut.

"Masma," Rahmat called out.

Masma waved. "*Warganegara Rahmat. Warganegara Chula.*"

"I'll be back," Gabriel said.

"Put your pants on first."

Minutes later, fully dressed, Gabriel was out the door and hurriedly crossing the beach to where Masma, Rahmat, and Chula were chatting like old friends.

"Citizen Gabriel," Masma said in greeting.

With a forced smile, Gabriel said, "Good morning." He bowed his head slightly to Rahmat and Chula.

"*Selamat pagi, Gabriel.*" Rahmat smiled. "*Hari yang menyenangkan untuk Anda.*"

Masma translated. "He wished you a pleasant good morning."

"Yes, yes… and to you too, Rahmat, Chula."

"*Kami telah membawa jus segar dan buah-buahan dan flatbread. Menikmati.*"

"He wishes you to enjoy the morning nourishment."

"How do you say thank you?"

"*Terima kasih.*"

Bowing his head slightly, Gabriel repeated, "*Terima kasih.*"

The Mogen men smiled and retreated to the village.

"Are you rested, Citizen Gabriel?"

"Don't *Citizen Gabriel* me. How could you let us go through the night without a single word?"

"You are posturing?"

"If you mean am I upset, yeah."

"Come." He led Gabriel to the water's edge away from any of the others who might overhear.

"Have you been in communications with Legna?"

"An assault commenced between our ships and the Sumina."

"As well as our planet—three people witnessed it, remember!"

"Citizen Legna directs us to remain until further enlightenment."

Gabriel's tone turned strident. "That enlightenment better damn well come sooner than later! How much damage was done last night?"

Masma's face tightened. "Impassioned emotions will do little to advance our status. At Citizen Legna's direction, we shall remain here until our return is free from peril." Masma turned and headed for his hut.

"Where the hell are you going?"

Masma did a slow turn and stared."

"Ur, sorry, I apologize for my outburst."

"Your expression of regret is acknowledged."

Masma walked off and disappeared into his hut.

"Damn it!" Gabriel grumped. He lingered a while along the luminous blue water's edge. The sea looked warm and inviting. He was tempted to doff his clothes, forget all the bullshit, and go for a swim.

The others were making their way to the breakfast table.

Galinski waved. "You're up early."

Gabriel waved and smiled but said nothing of his conversation with Masma.

"Any word?"

"Nothing yet."

At 12:45 PM, Rahmat and Chula showed up again, this time with lunch. Rahmat rang the cow bell and promptly he and Chula left.

One by one, heads popped out of the huts. Everyone was curious to know what Legna knew of the previous night's frightening event.

"Nothing yet." Rafi said.

They ate mostly in silence, then returned to their huts. No one appeared on the beach again until Rahmat, Chula and Kai returned at 6:30 PM with the evening meal: whole roasted chickens, flatbread, a medley of roasted vegetables, and two pitchers of palm wine.

When the meal almost over, Masma appeared and made his way slowly across the sand.

Jennings was the first to spot him. "I don't like the look on his face."

Masma stopped 10 feet short of where the group sat.

He said nothing—they waited.

Unsmiling, Gabriel asked, "Do you have news."

"I wish to inform you that our citizens have driven the Sumina from your galaxy."

Betty was up on her feet. "Oh, thank God!"

Sighs of relief and everyone applauded.

"Citizen Legna has deemed it safe for your return at sunrise. I bid you a good evening."

He turned and scurried across the sand and disappeared into his hut as quickly as he had appeared.

"So," Cross said, "the unanswered question is, what exactly are we going back to?"

Bonnie was on the verge of tears. "Why didn't he elaborate? We're not children!"

Catherine took Bonnie's hand in hers. "It must be okay, or they wouldn't be sending back us."

"She's right, Bonnie," Jennings added.

Bonnie persisted. "And our families? What about them? Are they okay?"

No one spoke.

Suddenly, Galinski sprang to his feet and began removing his shirt.

"Skip?" Gabriel said, "What are you doing?"

"Going for a swim."

Bonnie looked horrified. "Mr. Galinski—Skip—how can you think of swimming at a time like this?"

"I am not spending my time worrying about what I don't know. God knows if I will ever get back to this magnificent island." And off he went, running across the warm sand and tearing off the rest of his clothes. "Hi ho Silver and away!"

By the time he reached the oncoming surf, he was buck naked.

"There, ladies and gentleman," Cross said with a laugh, "is a sight I hope never to see again."

When everyone had retired to their huts, Rafi and Gabriel made their way to the village to inform Rahmat they would be leaving in the morning.

Rahmat looked saddened at the news. "*Kenapa kamu pergi? Dapatkah Anda tidak tinggal lagi?*"

"He asked why."

Gabriel shrugged. "Make something up."

"Here goes nothing. *Anda begitu baik untuk Gabriel ketika ia mengunjungi dia ingin teman-temannya untuk bertemu orang-orang Mogen indah.*" (You were kind and welcoming to Gabriel when he and I visited. He wished for his friends and Masma to meet and get to know the Mogen people. But now we must return to our homes.)

"Tell him that when we depart, we're leaving the huts as a gift. We trust that pleases them."

"They may just tear them down, Gabriel."

"Tell him anyway."

"*Pondok akan tetap sebagai hadiah kepada orang-orang Mogen.*" (The new huts will remain as a gift to the Mogen people.

Rahmat looked dubious.

"Just as I thought. *Mereka tidak jahat, Rahmat teman saya, mereka adalah baik. Ini adalah cara kami berterima kasih kepada Mogen untuk kebaikan dan persahabatan mereka.*" (The new huts are not evil magic, Rahmat, they are good. It

THE AUTOPSY OF PLANET EARTH

is our way of thanking the Mogen for their kindness, their friendship, and their hospitality.)

Rahmat thought for a moment. *"Pada hehalf orang Mogen, saya ucapkan terima kasih."*

"On behalf of his tribe, he thanks us and bids us safe travels."

In an unexpected move, Rahmat embraced Gabriel. *"Silakan kembali satu hari, Gabriel. Anda adalah Mogen sekarang."*

"He said you are of the Mogen now. You are his brother and must promise to return one day soon."

"Tell him I will."

"Katakan padanya aku saudaranya dan aku akan kembali."

Rahmat placed a fist over his heart. Gabriel did the same. With deep sadness, Rahmat turned and walked away without looking back.

57

Shortly after sunrise, they all boarded the invisible Ecaepian shuttle. Even though they knew the drill, it was still disconcerting to walk up a ramp and through a door of wavering light.

Their first stop was Jakarta, Sanjaya home base.

"It's been real," was his parting words. "Let's stay in touch."

Next, they whisked Skip Galinski to Colorado and dropped him off next to his beloved Huey helicopter.

Catherine hugged him. "Take care of yourself, you old coot."

"Want to go for a ride in a helicopter ride, Missy?" Galinski pulled her close and whispered, "Take care of that fella of yours."

Their final destination was Washington, D.C. As they approached, Masma moved to the white wall and created an instant window. "Come," he beckoned.

Gabriel was first. Peering out the portal, his face expressed horror. "Holy mother of God!"

Catherine was the first to join him. She moaned loudly, "Oh, no!"

Now the others crowded around. They stood speechless.

The Capital dome looked like it had melted and collapsed in on itself.

Betty stepped back. Her hand went to her mouth, and her eyes welled up.

"Your city was the only one the Sumina attacked before our citizens retaliated and drove them away."

Seconds later they were over the White House. It lay in ruins, its roof looking like it too melted and collapsed on the floors below. But by some miracle, the nearby West Wing complex remained intact.

"Is there more destruction?" Gabriel said just above a whisper.

"There is not," Masma answered.

Seconds later the craft set down near the Rose Garden.

Betty was the first to step off. When she came face-to-face with the remains of what once was the iconic White House, she sucked in a quick breath and began to cry.

The others stood in stunned silence—there were no words to express the emotions they were experiencing.

"Citizen Legna wishes you and Citizen Cross to join him," Masma said to Gabriel.

"Dex, Remy, will you see Catherine home?" Gabriel kissed her. "I'll join you as soon as I can."

"I love you," she whispered.

He turned to the Harney's. "Tyler, Bonnie, go home, get some rest."

"I can stay if you need me."

"No Tyler, take Bonnie home."

A visibly shaken Jennings said to Gabriel, "Call me if you need me."

"Yeah, me too," Rafi added.

Gabriel, Cross, Masma, Dex, and Remy made their way to Oval Office cloister door. Agent Carson was there.

Gabriel greeted him stoically, "Good morning, Jim."

"Sorry, you had to come back to this, Mr. Ferro. It's a sad day for America—for the world."

Gabriel placed a reassuring hand on Carson's arm.

In the Oval Office, Legna was standing by a window, shoulders hunched forward, hands folded behind him. They waited patiently for him to speak. After several moments of silence, Legna asked, "All is well, Citizen Masma?"

"Yes, Citizen Legna."

Without making eye contact, Legna strolled to the desk and lifted himself to his chair. "The Mogen are well?"

"It was an honor to have been among these gentle humans." Masma replied. "They are wise in many ways."

"Yes, in many ways." Legna's eyes shifted to Gabriel and Cross. "You have viewed the plunder?"

Cross frowned. "It was kind of hard to miss."

"The incursion was directed at *us* by an enemy that wished *us* harm. I have apologies to all humans."

Cross shot back, "Yeah, that'll do it alright."

"We have driven the Sumina from your galaxy. They will not return. We shall not discuss this further." He slipped from the chair and strolled to a window.

"What about casualties?" Gabriel asked.

"Suspecting the Sumina would target this city because of my presence, all government structures were evacuated as a precaution. No one was harmed."

Gabriel looked to Cross and blew a sigh of relief.

"These deplorable Sumina seek vengeance against Ecaep. I have been directed to return."

Gabriel's jaw dropped and his brow shot up. "You're leaving?"

"Citizen Masma shall remain as will one of our vessels."

"Wait a minute!" Cross challenged, "You're flying the coop and leaving us in limbo?"

"The threat to your planet has passed."

"Maybe from *your* Sumina friends," Gabriel lamented, "but not from the horrible mess you're leaving behind."

Legna pivoted and took several quick steps closer to Gabriel and Cross. "I will not tolerate impertinence. Hear me well, in my absence, Citizen Masma will ensure that you carry out what has begun. My temporary absence is not to be revealed."

It was an unmistakable threat.

Gabriel's eyes went to Masma, but as usual, Masma's expression remained in neutral when in Legna's presence.

"The transformation is to be realized," Legna continued. "You, Citizen Gabriel, shall carry on as World Governor and Citizen Cross as Vice Governor."

"Whoa, wait just a minute," Gabriel protested. "We're not prepared to—"

Legna sliced a quick hand through the air. "Enough! Accept your destiny, Citizen Gabriel." His look shifted quickly to Cross. "… or someone else will."

"Wait just a damn minute," said Cross. "I will not allow you to pit us against one another. Furthermore, the titles of World Governor and Vice Governor smack of a couple of dictators! We'll have none of that."

"Not dictators… protectors."

"That's not the way it will be perceived."

"You have pledged to me your willingness to guide your fellow man to a life of peace, harmony, and balance. Given the eons of strife and turmoil created by a society which knows no limit to their asininity, it would be foolhardy to reject our assistance."

Cross took a threatening step forward. "Now you listen to me, you little—"

Gabriel wrapped a hand around Alan's arm and squeezed. "Alan, wait." To Legna, he said, "For the sake of argument, assuming we agree, exactly what do these titles entail?"

"You shall act with full authority."

Cross sneered, "To carry out *your* orders."

"I issue no orders, only enhancements."

"Okay, enhancements. Now it's your turn to listen."

"Please, Citizen Gabriel, articulate freely."

"To put this in plain English, your PR remains sorely deficient. I've tried to make you understand, but it has yet to sink in. You have failed to *articulate* in terms people comprehend. All they see is that you've caused them to be infertile, and people are dropping like flies without proper medical care. What do you think is going to happen when you try to take away their guns and strip them of their sovereignty? Have past demonstrations taught you nothing?"

"I have been forthcoming."

"To me, to Alan maybe, but not to those who count—the people. Imagine you are us and we are you. Along comes this alien race, one you had no idea even existed, and you're told your way of life is over; now it's to mirror *ours*."

Gabriel waited for what he expected would be another denouncement from Legna. But to his and Cross' surprise, Legna's expression visibly softened.

A chink in his armor. I can see it in his eyes, Gabriel thought. *Exploit it, move in for the kill.* "All people see is a race of aliens who want to enslave them."

"That is absurd, we wish to enslave no one."

"But, despite what you profess, that's what it looks. For God's sake, we know population growth has to be controlled, we're not stupid. But the remedy you've chosen is problematic for any number of reasons."

"You rail at what has already commenced. Once this objective has been achieved, the process shall be reversed."

Cross erupted. "Damn it, if people had been told this in the beginning, the sacrifice they are being asked to endure might have been more palatable!"

Legna seemed puzzled, as if he had not considered the consequences of what the public perceived to be a heinous act. He strolled to the portico door and stared past Agent Carson. After a long pause, he said quietly, "Perhaps I have misjudged.

Go, Gabriel, jump in, use some sugar before Cross gets into a contentious face-off with Legna. "Mankind has stumbled all too often in ways that negatively affect our lives. With your guidance, our society can transition to a life of peace, harmony, and balance."

Legna nodded his approval.

"However, to be fully on-board, citizens must be unified. That in itself is no small task, as I hope you've discovered. But, success *can* be achieved if people are informed of the how's and why's— 'why' is the key ingredient."

Legna stood pensive for several moments. "In the new day, you shall affirm your positions of authority. You, Citizen Gabriel, will occupy this office. Citizen Cross shall remain in his present quarters. Citizen Masma will occupy the adjoining office. His presence will convice all that I remain." He took several slow steps closer to the Portico door. Agent Carson, sensing someone there, quickly looked away when he realized it was Legna. "There is another matter to attend to, one that shall unify all tribes as we have on Ecaep—we have discussed this. Begin the process of establishing a single governing body."

"That will prove difficult," Gabriel shot back. "Too many races, cultures, and customs, economies and—it's just not doable."

"All righteous efforts are doable; you shall begin without further delay."

Legna's tone was peppered with unmistakable threats. He moved to a window and placed his hands behind his back, signaling the meeting had come to an end.

Back in Gabriel's office, Cross took a seat and stuck out a hand. "Toss me one of those cancer sticks."

Gabriel placed his soiled coffee cup on the desk and passed Cross a cigarette.

"We got to get the word fast that the birth freeze will end. That might calm things."

"Don't bet on it." Cross took a drag off his cigarette. "Maybe the bigger challenge is this one-government idea. Jesus, we can hardly govern our own country, let alone the entire frigging world."

"On the bright side, think of the technology, science, and medical advances they can provide faster than we could ever achieve on our own. If we can stop fighting each other long enough to see the forest for the trees, everyone benefits. Problem is, how do we get *everyone* on board?"

"Why do I get the feeling this one-world thing appeals to you."

"We've tried everything else—so far nothing has worked. Even the Albert Einstein was a proponent of a world government."

Cross laughed cynically. "You think for one second sovereign nations will willingly give up their sovereignty? In case you haven't noticed, sovereignty and nationalism are still big around the world. And if you believe megalomaniac politicians will surrender their power and offshore bank accounts, there's a hallucinogenic chemical in your cigarette. We've never collectively met common challenges; why would we start now?"

"But you make my point, Alan. We've failed to create a global community, one that recognizes all of humanity and not just individual tribes. It requires a different mindset, a coming together for the common good. There could be an enormous upside to a central governing body if it treats every last living soul equally."

Cross laughed.

"What's funny?"

"You, sir, sound like a Bolshevik."

"Should I take that as a compliment?"

"Let's just say it will be a monumental feat to pull off. Besides, I don't trust these alien creatures to limit their ambitions, and neither do you. We could be nothing more than their latest experiment. You do remember their first one, right? It failed. Frankly, I'm surprised you're even entertaining such a wacky idea."

"I can only tell you what Legna told me."

"Do these aliens not understand how the economy works on planet Earth? How the hell would a single governing body work?"

"A sustaining economy will be created."

"Ah ha, more fancy, but vague language."

"On Ecaep everyone provides a useful service. In exchange, they receive all they require equally: housing, clothing, food and all other essentials. There's no economy as we know it—no stores or malls, no cars, trucks, nothing except distributions center where individuals get what they need."

"That's the purest damn form of socialism, and it sounds boring as hell! You'd be stripping away any incentive to get out of bed in the morning."

"You mean the wealthy and the privileged and the crooks will never go for it."

Cross leaned forward. "Let me get this straight. What you're suggesting is—"

"It is not a suggestion Alan; it's what they're bent on implementing."

"But—"

"There are no buts, *this* is the plan. The only thing that will put the brakes on this runaway train is if they just give up and go home, and that isn't likely."

"And you think this one-world bullshit idea is the answer?"

"I wouldn't want for us what I witnessed on Ecaep, but some variation could work here."

Cross shook his head. "You will never get everyone to agree."

Cross's concerns were legitimate. But, a one-world government held enough appeal that Gabriel believed it deserved consideration as a possible solution.

"Alan, we both know human civilization is in deep trouble—has been for eons. We're so damn polarized, so tribal in our mentality that little gets done—there's no forward movement anymore; three steps forward, two back—sometimes three. We're mired in fear, hate, racism—you name it, and we're guilty of it. Let's consider what the aliens are offering, not as a threat, but as an opportunity."

"Be sure to let me know when Comrade Lenin is resurrected." Cross doused his cigarette in the coffee cup. "For all our troubles, I can't see humans adapting such a radical makeover—not willingly anyway."

The door swung open, and Betty entered. "Sorry to interrupt, but I thought you would want to see this." She handed Gabriel a note and left.

Gabriel scanned it. "It's from the FBI Director. The demonstrations have tapered off to almost zero. It seems our fellow humans are going home."

"At last some good news." Cross stood. "I'm going to my office to ponder—maybe even take a nap. Be sure to let me know when it's time to dance around the Maypole."

"Cynic!"

"Damn right," Cross tossed over his shoulder as he left.

For most of the day, Gabriel worked on several drafts of a release that he hoped would ease the trauma of the zero-population effort. Dissatisfied with each, he abandoned his efforts—his mind was too clouded.

Catherine's well-being was at the apex of his thoughts. *Go home, take care of personal business. This stuff can wait.*

At four in the afternoon, he informed Betty he was leaving for the day.

"I was wondering when you would show concern for your wife."

"There's a bar of soap in my top right drawer. Use it to wash out your mouth."

"Huh, you wish. Send Catherine my best."

"Will do."

Outside, Gabriel stood and gazed upon the crumbled remains of the White House with deep sadness. It would never return to the iconic symbol of democracy, he thought, never again.

Driving home, he vented his frustration on the road, driving way too fast and weaving in and out of the heavy traffic like a man on a mission. In the garage below his condo, he was approached Dex and Remy.

"Don't do that again!" Remy scolded.

"Right boss, got it!" he squawked and stormed off.

He found Catherine in the master bedroom sleeping peacefully and decided not to wake her. Making his way to his study, he opened his laptop to his journal and began typing an entry.

The frigging madness continues.

He backspaced and removed the word *frigging*, leaned back, and stared at the screen—his thoughts had slipped away. Several moments passed before another rational thought entered his mind.

> *I'm either in this all the way, or I am not—there is no middle ground. Can I steer this train in the right direction or will it steer me? The real question to be answered: Am I up for the task?*

His mind blanked again. Too much was flooding his consciousness—he found it impossible to concentrate. "Screw it!"

He hit save and closed the laptop.

"Screw what?"

Catherine's voice startled him. He twisted in his chair—she was standing by the doors to his study.

"Hey, sorry if I woke you."

"You didn't."

"How are you feeling?"

"Fair enough for a pregnant lady who just returned home on a spacecraft."

"Hungry?"

"Yeah, I could eat something."

They munched on grilled cheese sandwiches and potato chips in the kitchen, eating quietly until Catherine couldn't stand it any longer.

"It's good that I'm a patient woman because you're a man of few words."

Gabriel grunted. "He's leaving."

"Oh, the master speaks. To where?"

"The Sumina are threatening Ecaep—he has to return."

"Just peachy, and where does that leave us?"

"Whistling in the wind."

"Be serious. The devastating photos of the White House and Capital are all over the news. My God!"

Gabriel placed his sandwich down. "Like Betty is fond of saying, *God* ain't going to help us now."

He picked up the sandwich and nibbled. He was stalling for time, looking for a way to break the news. *Just tell her, get it over with.* "Today Legna crowned me World Governor and Alan Cross, Vice Governor."

"Of what?"

"The world, love, the world."

Catherine set her sandwich down. "So, he's finally made it official."

"What's that supposed to mean?"

"It was only a matter of time before he fully engaged you in their reckless retooling of the human race."

He opened his mouth to respond, but she raised a hand.

"It's all a con, Gabriel. Legna knows full well if he continues to be the face behind this insane transformation, humans will continue to fight him." Her right arm shot up. "But, surprise, surprise, hang a human face out there—one that people might actually trust—and, ladies and gentleman, you have a game changer."

"You do understand this is going forward with or without me."

"I do."

"Well then, what's your problem? Maybe Alan and I can steer it."

"When is the last time a boy scout saved the bloody world?"

"You're not giving me credit for trying."

"Lest you forget, we observed their world up close and personal. From what I witnessed, they missed creating a utopia by a mile."

"Come on, that's too simplistic." He took another bite of the sandwich and sipped his drink.

"You're missing the point, Gabriel. Just as they exercised *their* free choice—assuming they did—I want—no, I insist—the same for us." She thumped a stiff finger against her chest. "*We* get to choose our social and political order, not *them*." Taking his hand in hers, she squeezed hard. "Listen to me. By allowing yourself to be placed front and center, you become the poster boy for their insane plan."

Her comment stung. Jerking his hand free, Gabriel stood. "I guess we'll just have to agree to disagree."

"Oh hell, it wasn't my intention to piss you off!"

Gabriel stormed from the room in a huff.

"Where are you going?"

"Crazy, according to you!"

"Damn it, you can't walk out every time we disagree on something."

She slipped from the stool and trotted after him.

Gabriel was standing by the glass sliding doors in the living room, staring out at the overcast sky.

"Stop pouting—turn around and talk to me."

Begrudgingly, he turned to her.

"Talk to me, Gabriel."

He strolled to his study and retrieved a pack of cigarettes and a lighter stashed on a shelf behind a book.

"You've never smoked in the house."

"There's a first time for everything." He lit the cigarette, sucked in a long drag, and expelled it slowly. "If I retreat now, I'm just another angry spectator like the misdirected anger, frustration, and fear that's out there now, none of which is going to get us anywhere."

"And you think by becoming World Governor, you can turn all it around?"

"Are you suggesting I shouldn't try?" He shook his head forcefully. "That is not an option."

Quickly closing the gap between them, she removed the cigarette from his hand. "Where's the ashtray?"

With a bemused look, he retrieved a square, glass ashtray from the bookcase and handed it to her.

"Why do you hide this stuff? It's your house? And in case you forgot; a pregnant lady lives here now and you don't smoke around her."

He grinned sheepishly. "I stand corrected."

"And well you should."

She always knew what to say to gently disarm him.

Gabriel pulled her close. They stood wrapped in each other's arms, both knowing the new day was bound to bring more anguish to an already fractured society.

58

Gabriel arrived at the White House compound just after sunrise the following morning. He was so used to his day in and day out routine, he failed to notice what should have been completely obvious. By some miracle of miracles, the White House, a pile of rubble the day before, was now fully restored.

"What in the hell?" he muttered. "That's impossible! It's a mirage!"

Quickly entering the West Wing visiting center, he approached a guard. "Did I see what I thought I saw?"

"Yes, sir, Mr. Ferro," the guard answered with a wide smile.

"But how?"

"Damned if anyone knows. No one saw or heard a thing."

Gabriel quick-paced down the hall to where Ms. Mosby should have been on guard at her desk—she was not. He hurried to his office.

"You saw?" Betty said.

"Jeez, I almost missed it! Let's hope it's not another one of his holograms."

"If they can create huts with indoor plumbing on a far-flung island, recreating the White House must have been a piece of cake."

Gabriel scratched the back of his head. "We're living in a nightmare."

"Your presence is requested in the Oval. I've also been informed we're moving there—is this correct?"

"Yes."

"Care to explain?"

"Not this second, Betty."

"Coffee?"

"When I get back."

The door swung open almost smacking Gabriel in the face. It was lead White House Agent Denver Wilkinson. "Oh, sorry, Gabriel, almost got ya."

"Whatever it is, Denver, I'm in a hurry."

"You saw?"

"Almost missed it when I drove in."

"Incredible! I'm just happy its restored, whatever the voodoo magic behind it."

"Yeah… gotta go, we'll catch up later."

"This can't wait, come on."

They entered Gabriel's office. Wilkinson foreboding expression spelled trouble. "Close the door."

"That important, huh?"

"I was called to the Oval at 4:30 this morning and informed of your new position by the man himself. I was also instructed to move you and Dr. Blake upstairs."

"Whoa, wait a minute! We're not moving in here."

"With all due respect, it's not your call."

"Wrong, it is my call. Besides, Legna and Masma are camping out there."

"Now's a good a time to tell you, Legna informed me he was leaving temporarily to fight the good fight back home and your safety was in our hands. Masma's moving to one of the bedrooms on the third floor—guess you won't be playing billiards up there. Expect movers in the morning. Tonight, your condo gets another agent outside your door and three on the street.""

"Catherine will go ballistic."

"It's for her safety too."

"I'm not going to do it. If my safety is a concern, you figure it out."

Gabriel stormed off, leaving Wilkinson in a quandary.

Gabriel went to the Oval Office to meet with Masma. Ms. Mosby remained missing in action. Without knocking, he entered. Agent Carson was at his post outside the portico door. The poor guy had no idea the alien he was guarding was Masma, not Legna.

Masma was perched on a sofa as if he anticipated Gabriel's entrance exactly when it would occur. Unsmiling, he said, "Good day, Citizen Gabriel."

"Begin by explaining how the main structure is no longer a pile of rubble." Gabriel took a seat on the opposite sofa and crossed his arms and legs. "So?"

"It will surely perplex you."

"Give it the old college try."

"As you wish. Anticipating the Sumina might target this structure, one of our hovering craft audited the interior and exterior properties. As you have witnessed, those attributes have been restored."

"Is it real?"

"As real as were the domiciles on Surin Island."

"My God, is there no end to what you people can do?"

"You people?" Masma feigned a look of displeasure. "I often find the human reaction to what they observe as ambiguous, however unintentional."

"You talk funny at times, too."

Masma looked unsure of Gabriel's meaning. Then just as quickly, he smiled, tossed his hands up and began laughing robustly. "I am familiarizing with your humor."

"Great… progress. What about the Capital building?"

Masma shook his head. "No audit was taken."

Gabriel closed his eyes and sighed.

"Citizen Legna has departed and shall return in one of your weeks, perhaps sooner if the Sumina display forbearance."

"And Ms. Mosby—Roama? Where is he—she?"

"There are no he's or she's, only Citizens. Citizen Roama is with Citizen Legna."

"And how do we explain my moving into this office?"

Masma rose and strolled to a window and laced his hands behind his back. "

"The Secret Service has suggested I move into the family quarters."

"In honor of your esteemed position and for your safety."

"They're moving you to the third floor. Are you good with that?"

"I am good, as you say."

"Well, just the same, I have refused."

"Why might that be?"

"The optics stink—looks like I sold out."

Masma stared for a moment as if he had not understood Gabriel's meaning. Without further comment, he went to the door of his adjoining office and left.

Gabriel approached the presidential desk and ran the tips of the fingers over its surface as he had often watched President Conrad do. As he lowered himself into the leather chair, he could not shake the feeling that he had no business being there. He was dreading the announcement of his new position, knowing world leaders would charge both him and Cross to be in support of the alien agenda.

Conspiracy theories would abound.

There was a knock and agent Wilkinson entered.

"I'm not moving in upstairs, so don't ask."

"From now on you won't be driving yourself. Wherever you go, you'll travel in a three-vehicle caravan. Dr. Ferro will be transported to and from her laboratory by a three-man security team."

"That'll go over like a lead balloon."

"You need to take this seriously. There are fanatics out there who wouldn't think twice about doing you in."

"Yeah? Them and who else?"

"Listen to me, Gabriel, take this seriously."

At home that evening, Gabriel waited until they had finished dinner before breaking the news.

"Are you in a good mood?

Catherine raised an eyebrow. "That sounds ominous. Why?"

A moment of hesitation. "As of tomorrow morning, we no longer drive."

"What are you talking about?"

"I get a three-vehicle escort, and you get your own SUV with three Secret Service agents."

"Like hell! What if I don't want it?"

"Then I'll have to find a live-in girlfriend who will."

"A pregnant one, I hope."

"We're not being offered a choice in the matter."

"The choice is always ours, you just have to make the right one."

"Legna left instruction that we were to move into the White House quarters."

"Damn it, this is madness! I'm pregnant for God's sake!"

"I noticed."

"Well?"

"A well is a hole in the ground," he said playfully.

"Save your humor for another day," she said and breezed out of the room.

"Not to worry, I nixed the idea."

"Damn right, I'm not moving into the White House under any circumstances."

"Then we're in agreement."

"For once."

59

At 3:05 in the morning, Gabriel was unable to sleep. His thought shifted from one problem to the other without supplying solutions. Afraid he might wake Catherine, he went to the guest bedroom to sleep there. At 5:30 AM, still unable to sleep, he gave up, rolled out of bed, and made himself coffee, then showered, shaved, dressed.

His instructions from Wilkinson were to notify the Secret Service office in the White House when he was ready to leave, which he did at 6:30 AM. At 7:00 AM, sitting curbside on Wisconsin Avenue were three black SUV's. He would ride in the middle one accompanied by Dex and Remy.

"So, from now on I have to deal with you two first thing in the morning?" Gabriel said.

"Lucky you." Was Remy's deadpan reply.

When he arrived at the Oval Office, Betty was at her new desk.

"Good morning."

"As soon as I confirm it's a good morning, I'll let you know."

Betty squinted her eyes. "I feel strange sitting here."

Gabriel thrust a finger toward the Oval Office door. "How do you think I feel in there? Tell me we have our own coffee maker."

"We have our own coffee maker. A cup's coming up."

Entering the Oval, he stopped in the middle of the oval rug, placed his feet on the flying dove logo, and scraped them back and forth. "I've been dying to do that."

Moving to the desk, he ran his fingertips lightly on its top and lowered himself to the chair. There he sat for a full thirty seconds without moving. "I don't belong here," he said aloud.

"Neither of us do." Betty stood at the door with a cup of coffee in hand. "Drink this and ponder your future, young man. And there will be no smoking in here, or there'll be hell to pay." She set his coffee on the desk but didn't leave.

"Okay, what's eating you?"

"They're using you and Mr. Cross to sell their scam."

"You sound like Catherine."

"Maybe you should listen to her. Damn it, boy, you have a new wife and a baby on the way and—"

"What? How do you know about the baby?"

"Catherine needed someone to share it with so she told me while we were on Surin Island." Betty moved to the chair beside the desk and sat. "Listen to me, Sparky, you and I have survived through far too battled for me not to tell you what I'm about to tell you. You're in the danger zone, and it's a no-win position. Do you really believe the world will thank you for putting yourself out there? If you do, you're tilting at windmills. Before this is over, some nut is liable to take a shot at you. Where does that leave your wife and child? Have you come to grips with that?"

"I think of it every waking minute of every day."

"Okay, I said what I had to say." Betty stood and sauntered to the door. She paused there for just a second before turning back. "You know I love you like a son, right?"

Gabriel nodded.

"Okay then."

Gabriel's first official act as World Governor was to appoint Tyler Harney as his Chief of Staff.

Tyler gushed, "I can't thank you enough for your confidence, Gabriel... I mean Governor."

"Cut the governor crap."

"I don't mean to question it, but… we're doing the right thing, aren't we?"

"Tyler, you've always trusted me?"

"I have."

"Then trust me now. Three steps forward, one back; repeat until it's three steps forward and none back."

An hour later Gabriel, Alan Cross and Masma were gathered in the Oval to draft a statement. Gabriel refused to make another television appearance so it would go out as a news release.

"We can't use language that could be misinterpreted as anything less than the truth." Gabriel argued.

Cross nodded. "I agree—the truth—at least as we understand it now."

Masma held up a sheet of paper. "Citizen Legna's instructions were quite specific. I have his notes."

Gabriel said tersely, "With all due respect, he's not writing this, we are."

An hour later they had a draft they agreed on—sort of.

"What do you think, Alan?"

"I don't know, something's missing."

"Maybe we should add language about the one-world concept."

"No, no," Cross argued. "Way too soon."

Masma spoke. "But Citizen Legna has deemed it to be."

"No, better we dole it out in small doses."

"Alan, read what we have."

'The destructive attack on America's Capital was perpetrated by an alien civilization known as the Sumina who chose to pursue their revenge against the Ecaepians here on our planet. Thankfully, the Sumina have been driven from our galaxy by the Ecaepians and will not return.

Now we must join together as one community that embraces peace, harmony, and balance for all. I, along with former American Vice President Alan Cross, have accepted the positions of World Governor and Vice Governor to achieve this goal with Ecaepian guidance.

We apologize for the lack of transparency regarding the moratorium on new births. It has placed a prodigious emotional burden on our society. We must not allow raw emotions to thwart our resolve to ensure the survival of our race. The moratorium is temporary and will in the near future be reversed. Until then, this sacrifice, as distressing as it may be, is critical to our survival.

Finally, with regard to the miraculous resurrection of the iconic symbol of democracy, the American White House, a video will be posted on YouTube that sheds light on the Ecaepian technology that made this possible. It is but one exciting example of what the future holds as we continue to learn and advance.

In closing, we seek your support in rejecting those who chose violence over peace, anarchy over democracy, fear over compassion. Let us now move forward as a united civilization.'

It was signed Gabriel Javier Ferro, World Governor.

There was a long moment of silence.

"Whatta' think, Alan?"

"I think we could write it six different ways and never get it right. It is what it is, let's release it."

"Masma?"

"I shall defer to you and Mr. Cross."

"Okay, we'll release this at 5:00 this afternoon to be repeated hourly in every time zone around the world."

Cross shook his head. "The shit hits the fan at 5:00."

Just as Cross had predicted, the shit did hit the fan. The number of threats against Gabriel and Cross spiked twofold. They labeled traitors to the human race.

Gabriel, Cross, and Masma continued to meet daily while awaiting Legna's return. But the news was the same each passing day; Legna and Tonora were in communications with the Sumina who remained within striking distance of Ecaep.

At 4:00 PM on Friday, Gabriel decided to call it a day intending to spend a long, quiet weekend with Catherine.

"Betty," he called over the intercom. "Let Agent Wilkinson know I'm ready to check out of this birdcage for the weekend. You do the same—go home."

"That's a deal."

Ten minutes later, Gabriel's three-vehicle caravan was ready and waiting.

"Let's get this parade on the road," Gabriel said to Dex and Remy.

Dex was at the wheel, Remy in the front passenger seat next to him. They drove out of the White House complex bumper-to-bumper and headed west on Pennsylvania Avenue. Rounding Washington Circle, they continued on Pennsylvania Avenue to M Street NW, then right on Wisconsin Avenue. As they approached the intersection of Volta Place NW, they heard what sounded like a car backfiring off to their left. In that split-second, Dex swiveled his head left just in time to see a projectile racing through the air toward them. If it was intended for their vehicle, it missed and struck the front end of the third vehicle, lifting it two feet off the ground. Instinctively, Dex hit the brakes just as the third SUV came down and hit their right rear spinning them sideways and forcing them to a stop in the middle of the road. The third SUV, totally engulfed in flames, slid sideways into the right curb and flipped over on its side.

The entire incident happened in a matter of seconds.

"Gabriel!" Remy yelled. "On the floor now! Dex, back to base!"

The two agents in the lead vehicle, weapons drawn, were out and running toward the burning SUV.

Dex slammed the gas pedal to the floor. The SUV leaped forward, tires screeching, lights blinking, siren blaring as they raced back down Wisconsin Avenue.

Remy was calling for backup.

As they approached Washington Circle, two DC police patrol cars were already waiting to join them. One took the lead, the other the rear. Nine minutes later, the caravan pulled through the Northwest Appointment Gate onto the White House compound to the main house. Gabriel was rushed inside and taken directly to the family quarters.

"Make yourself comfortable," Remy said with a sullen look. "This is your new home now."

Gabriel was shaking. "My wife?"

"She's on her way."

Gabriel, shaking badly, collapsed in a chair and buried his head in his hands.

Remy came to him and placed a hand on his shoulder. "Are you okay?"

Gabriel lifted his head. "What the hell happened?"

"We were attacked, that's all I know right now."

Ten minutes later Catherine walked in with a Secret Service escort. Neither she nor Gabriel spoke, but went into each other's arms and just held on.

With her head pressed to Gabriel's chest, she said, "Are you okay?"

"Shaken."

"My God, you could have been killed."

Catherine hugged him tight and began to cry.

Gabriel lifted her head back and wiped a tear from her cheek. "Hey, hey, I'm here all in one piece."

A sullen Denver Wilkinson breezed in.

"Denver!" Gabriel said. "What the hell happened out there?"

"Someone took a shot at you with a shoulder mounted rocket launcher. They got away."

"Holy—! All I remember is the SUV behind us exploding and Remy telling me to hit the floor. What about those agents?"

Denver bowed his head and went silent.

"Oh, dear Lord."

"Your personal belonging will be here tonight. Make a list of anything we forget. Neither of you leaves this floor without an escort."

"What about Alan Cross?"

"Security has been doubled at Number One Observatory Circle. Mr. Cross has been briefed on your status—said he'd call when you get settled. When something this traumatic happens, it usually takes a while for it to sink in. I suggest you both try to get some rest. I'll check on you in the morning."

Wilkinson turned and walked off.

Gabriel called to him. "Denver, wait!"

Gabriel caught up with Wilkinson and whispered, "There's something you need to know."

Wilkinson leaned close to Gabriel and said low, "Catherine's pregnant."

"How did you know?"

"I have eyes, Gabriel, she's beginning to show. You're both safe here, so don't worry." Wilkinson patted Gabriel's arm. "I'll send up the head butler to help you get settled tonight. Chief Usher Benjamin will be up in the morning to brief you on everything you need to know about living in what President Conrad called—"

"The Birdcage."

"You remember. Get some sleep—see you in the morning."

Gabriel and Wilkinson shook hands, and Gabriel returned to Catherine's side. She wrapped her arms around him and buried her face in his chest again.

And that's how Gabriel and Catherine Ferro came to be the newest residents of the White House.

They spent the weekend getting settled as best they could considering the circumstances that had forced them there. Neither spoke of the attempt on Gabriel life—it was just too painful. Denver stopped by a couple of times to see how they were doing, but was unable to provide details of who may have been behind the attack on Gabriel's life.

Monday morning, Gabriel, Cross, and Masma gathered in the Oval Office, but Masma was unable or unwilling—they weren't sure—to update Legna's status.

"I am truly sorry for what occurred, Gabriel. If Citizen Legna were present, those responsible would be no more."

"Thank you, Masma. I was the lucky one. Two agents lost their lives."

"It is hateful, yes?"

"Yes," Cross said.

"I do not comprehend hate."

"Neither do we, neither do we," Cross offered. "How long are we going to wait?"

"For what, Mr. Cross?"

"For Legna. We can't remain in limbo forever. You understand limbo?"

Masma's face tightened. "I am not clueless, Mr. Cross."

Masma rose to his feet, looked fixedly at Cross, and left.

Cross sighed. "Well, that didn't go too well."

"I think you pissed him off."

"I think you're right."

For the rest of the day, Gabriel and Cross found themselves mired in contentious conversations with anxious military leaders and foreign heads of state seeking clarity on what could be expected next and when. They refrained from revealing Legna's departure, fearing it would only send a world already teetering on the edge into a tailspin of further uncertainty.

Cross made a joke of it. "You think any of them believed us?"

"Would you if positions were reversed?"

"Hell, no three times."

The following morning, Tuesday, Masma was uncharacteristically tardy for their meeting. Finally, a half-hour later, he strolled in with a hound-dog expression. "I have news."

Gabriel rolled his eyes. "From your expression, it can't be good."

Masma stopped on the edge of the oval rug and stared at the flying dove logo. Slowly, his head came up. "Our Citizens have been recalled."

Cross's eyelids constricted. "What's that mean?"

"The remaining ship has returned to Ecaep."

Cross jumped to his feet and his mouth flapped open. "What? Why?"

"The Sumina have engaged and have penetrated Jubia's shield."

Now it was Gabriel who sprang to his feet. "I thought the damn thing was impregnable!"

Masma diverted his eyes to the dove logo.

Cross's tone turned strident. "What if the Sumina return? Who protects us?"

"The Sumina's discord is not with humans—they shall not return."

"Are you in communication with Legna?"

"Communication was via the ship that remained. In its absence, I am no longer in contact."

Gabriel tapped hard at his temple. "What the hell became of your ability to communicate through this?"

Sheepishly, Masma replied, "Separation prevents such communication." He ambled to a window and stood quietly.

Frustrated, Cross tossed his hands up. "Great, just goddamn great! What the hell do we do now?"

Masma turned to them, began to say something, hesitated, then quick-paced across the room and left.

Cross's eyes narrowed, "I think our little alien knows more than he's sharing."

The following week zipped by with no further word from Legna. The more they queried Masma, the more he withdrew. The world remained just where it was; in a state of limbo.

Gabriel was also facing problems on the home-front. Catherine's expanding waistline was becoming more evident each passing week. She constantly fretted over what would happen when she could no longer disguise the obvious. What if someone did the math and realized that, while other women aborted during the same period, she had not? She began dressing in ways that would disguise her pregnancy. And her moods had become unpredictable, often lashing out at Gabriel for no reason, only to apologize when she had calmed. Gabriel was concerned that her anxiety would have an adverse effect on her and the baby's health. He encouraged her to take a leave of absence from her work, and she readily agreed. With her husband's demanding schedule, she was needed at his side; that was the excuse she gave her staff at Bethesda.

Three more anxious weeks zipped by with no further word from Legna. What had taken place on Ecaep? Had the Ecaepians lost their battle with the Sumina? For Gabriel and Cross, the uncertainty and anxiety continued to mount each passing day.

With no new directives coming from the White House, and with demonstrations mostly under control, the public began to settle into a welcomed grace period, although they had no idea what was occurring behind the scenes. Gabriel and Cross feared the welcome moratorium would not last.

It was time to level with the world and disclose the truth.

Gabriel confronted Masma.

"If Legna doesn't return, and that's beginning to look doubtful, people have a right to know."

Masma response was swift. "This will prove unwise, Gabriel, for it will only foster further misgivings."

"But that's just my point. If Legna doesn't return, what then? As it is, there's been an irrevocable adverse impact on human life. Nothing will ever be normal on this planet again."

"My presence leads all to believe the Administrator remains. To reveal otherwise would foster further anxiety, will it not?"

"We're damned if we do, and damned if we don't."

They sat quietly, stealing quick glances as if one or the other was about to speak, but neither did.

Gabriel considered their options; none struck him as promising. "He's not coming back. You know it, I know it."

Masma said nothing.

"We need to take the bull by the horns."

"Bull? Horns."

"Take steps to set this runaway train on a path to the truth."

"Truth is, as you say, in the eye of the beholder, is it not?"

"This time, everyone needs to accept the same truth. That's always proved difficult for us opinionated humans." He thought for a moment. "Let me speak with Cross. Whatever we decide, you'll be the first to know."

As soon as Masma departed, Gabriel met with Cross and presented his thoughts.

Cross' reaction was swift. "That's a risky role of the dice."

"Have a better idea?"

"Yeah, we forget this whole damn thing and move to Surin Island and live out our lives on the beach in one of those huts."

Gabriel blew a breath. "Tempting."

"If we do this and Legna returns, our asses won't be worth the pants that cover them."

"We can't leave things the way they are. Let's at least try to get everyone's life back on track."

Cross laughed. "Jesus, you're one stubborn Cuban. If Legna returns, I'll tell him this was your idea, not mine."

Gabriel snorted and shook his head. "He's not coming back."

"Just the same, we'd be putting our eggs in one dangerous basket."

"Don't sweat the small stuff, old man. Let's take the first step in making the inhabitants of this planet whole again. Let's get Masma in here."

"Okay, but he's never going to go for it."

"He has no authority to do diddly-shit on his own. This is our decision, you and me, Alan."

"Who knew you could be this devious?"

"My parents."

Cross went to the door to Masma office and invited him to join them. He entered with a forlorn expression looking like he had lost his best friend. He sat quietly and listened as Gabriel and Cross presented their plan..

Cross asked, "Well, what do you think?"

Masma did not hesitate. "Citizen Legna would disapprove of such an initiative."

"Citizen Legna is not here, we are, me and the World Governor here—we're in charge now."

"Your *charge*," Masma said forcefully, "is to carry forward the transformation as promulgated by Citizen Legna."

"There's not going to be a *transformation*... unless *you* have the authority to enforce it."

Masma's gaze went to the floor.

Cross sneered. "I didn't think so."

"I must refrain from any involvement in this ill-advised decision. I bid you a good day."

Masma scurried from the room.

"I think we pissed him off again."

"It would be better if he was with us on this."

"Gabriel, Gabriel, he's on their side, remember? Forget it—ain't going to happen."

"If we do this, how do we explain him?"

"By revealing who he really is. With Legna's rush to skedaddle, he was inadvertently left behind; he has no authority, he's not a threat. That's what story we put out there."

Later, Gabriel placed a call to Owen Jennings informing him what he and Cross were about to do.

"You're out of your mind. If your plan backfires, your nuts will be cut off."

"Thank you for that distasteful thought. Anyway, we'll see, won't we?"

He called Rafi next.

"Are you crazy? What if Legna returns? What then? He'll castrate you both!"

"Do you and Jennings coordinate responses?"

That evening he briefed Catherine.

"You can't do this," she warned.

"Why not?"

"I could give you a litany of reasons, all of which lead to your demise if Legna returns."

"Catherine, if he was coming back, it would have happened by now."

"And Masma? What does he say?"

"What do you expect him to say? He's against it. But he has no authority, he is—was—Legna's clerk."

Catherine huffed. "So that's it, you're going ahead with this?"

"Consider it done."

Two days later, Gabriel and Cross were ready to roll out what they hoped would put an end to the uncertainty and fear that continued to percolate throughout the world. The unknown element; Legna's possible return.

It was a risk they were willing to take.

A news release went out stating that Citizen Legna had returned to Ecaep to combat the Sumina and would not be returning to Earth. The transformation of the human race would not go forward now or in the future. Governments were free to return to full autonomy without fear of reprisals. In America, the United States Congress would be recalled. Gabriel Ferro and Alan Cross would no longer hold the titles of World Governor and Vice-Governor. With the approval of Congress, they would retain the titles of President and Vice-President until democratic elections could be held.

That was the entire message; nothing further needed to be said.

Worldwide reaction was immediate—there was a unified sigh of relief.

With the Capitol destroyed, the John F. Kennedy Center for the Performing Arts was pressed into service as the United States Congress's temporary home. Their first official act was to confirm Gabriel and Cross as interim President and Vice-President, the first time in the history of the country that a President and Vice President were appointed without an election, with the exception of Gerald R. Ford, then Vice-President, who stepped in when President Richard Nixon resigned in 1974.

Their second act was to order the rebuilding of the Capital building.

As Catherine's pregnancy progressed, she withdrew more and more. Although she was nearing the finish line, she was unable to shake the dreaded thought that like others, she would not make it to term. Gabriel reassurances did little to curb her rising depression. Since taking leave from her work, she spent her days mostly reading or sleeping. With Gabriel's demanding schedule trying to right the world again, they shared few evening meals together, and when they did, she showed little interest in his activities. He had to find a way to pull her out of it. What she needed, he decided, was a social occasion—an evening with friends. So, without consulting her, Gabriel invited Rafi, Jennings, and Betty to dinner in the White House quarters.

Catherine's reaction was negative. "I wish you had discussed this with me first."

"It'll be fun; you haven't seen them since Surin island."

"And what about Rafi and Owen? Neither of them knows I'm pregnant."

"What's the big deal, anyway? They're our friends, they'll be happy for us."

"I'm just not in the mood to socialize, okay? Can you respect that?"

"No, it's not okay. I'm doing this for *you*."

"Don't do me any favors, Mr. President."

She stormed out of the room.

"Damn her!" Gabriel grumbled. "I'm going ahead with it, whether she likes it or not."

On the appointed evening, while waiting for Catherine to make an appearance, Gabriel conducted a tour of the family quarters.

Rafi was impressed. "I had no idea it was so well appointed."

"For as long as I've worked in the White House," Betty chimed in, "I've never been up here."

Jennings joked, "All I can say is, I knew you when, Cuban Boy."

"Now that the world has been righted again, maybe we can get back to normal."

Jennings offered an opinion. "Afraid not, Betty. How many more are out there, and will they come and try to change us—or worse?"

Catherine, looking radiant, finally made her entrance. And although she had not gained much weight, her pregnancy was obvious. Rafi and Jennings's eyes immediately went to her midsection.

"Oops!" Jennings said.

"Oops is right," Catherine said with a smile." She hugged each of them, then placed a hand on her stomach. "I can see you boys have questions. This child wasn't conceived on this planet, which exempted me from the horrible effects of whatever they did. Enough said about that, no more questions. Let's eat."

They dined on baked children, yellow rice, fried plantains, Sangria, and flan for dessert.

Following the meal, Betty was the first to make a toast. "Here's to happiness."

Rafi stood and raised his glass. "Here's to the future, here's to us, here's to the blessed birth of your child."

"I think of the joy this baby will bring," Catherine said, "and yet it's purely a selfish act, isn't it? We have no right to bring a child into this world. Even before the aliens arrived—and now with them gone—the world was and remains an unsettled, dangerous place."

Gabriel reached for her hand. "Don't go there."

She pulled her hand away. "I question whether human civilization will ever get their act together or will it be business as usual."

"We can only hope the alien presence brought a new dynamic into our lives."

"Do you really believe that, Owen, or is it what you *hope*?"

There followed a long silence.

Catherine pushed her chair back and stood. "Sorry to be the party-pooper. I'm a bit tired, so you'll forgive me if I bid you guys a good night. Thank you for coming. I love you all."

She kissed Gabriel on the cheek and left the room.

Gabriel tried to smooth it over. "Sorry guys, her emotions have been on overdrive."

Betty stood. "You boys talk about whatever it is boys talk about. I'm going to sit with Catherine for a while."

As soon as Betty was out of earshot, the conversation turned to world events.

"Catherine has a point." Rafi began, "Will we go back to our old ways, or have we learned anything from the experience?"

Jennings offered, "The question is, how do we get everyone on the same wavelength?"

"If we don't, we're doomed."

"Hey," Gabriel added, "we have a cleaned-up atmosphere, millions now have clean water, electricity, and food. For that, we should be grateful."

Jennings snickered. "Yeah, but from here on in, it's up to us, isn't it? Forgive my pessimism, but I have my doubts."

And that's the way the conversation went until Betty returned. "The lady of the house is sleeping peacefully. It's time this party ended and let Mr. President here get some rest too."

Rafi and Jennings thanked Gabriel for the evening and departed. Betty held back.

"She's going to be fine, Sparky. You just be there for her."

"I will… and stop calling me Sparky."

"Not a chance." Betty kissed him on the cheek and hugged him.

It saddened Gabriel to think Masma would be stranded on Earth forever, shunned by humans as an outcast, an anomaly in conflict with nature. Masma had mostly kept to himself squirreled away in his third-floor room. Gabriel extended an olive branch in the form of a written invitation for them to meet. Masma refused. But one morning, while Gabriel was nursing his third cup of coffee, Betty buzzed with an unexpected announcement.

"Citizen Masma is here and wishes to see you."

"Uh… yes, send him in."

Masma entered carrying a silver case that was slightly larger than a cigar box.

"Good day, Citizen Gabriel. You are well?"

"I am. It's good to see you."

"And Citizen Catherine?"

"Catherine is well, yes."

Masma ambled across the room and placed the silver box on the desk. The cover was embossed with the flying dove logo. Next to it was a small, opaque, glass square slightly larger than a postage stamp. He placed a flat hand atop the box. "Citizen Legna deemed the contents of this vessel be presented to you if he did not return."

"What does it contain?"

"The *Book of Codes*."

"Sorry, you've lost me."

"Within this box lies the answers to the mysteries all beings seek. You and you alone are to open it when you determine mankind is prepared." He pointed to the small opaque area. "It will only respond to your thumbprint."

"And if I decide not to open it?"

"It is for you to decide, Gabriel."

Masma carefully lifted the box and began to leave.

"Wait, where are you taking it?"

"I wished only to make you aware of its existence. If you resolve to open it, you will inform me." Masma motioned to the adjoining office. "May I occupy my space again?"

"Yes, of course." And then a thought flashed through his mind—his eyes lit up. "Wait."

"Yes, Gabriel."

"The box, by any chance does it have a connection with what was in that buried structure in the Kebun?"

Masma hesitated, his eyes straying. Then, slowly, deliberately, his look came back to Gabriel. "It is the same."

With the silver box clutched in his hands, Masma left, leaving Gabriel in a quandary.

60

As time passed, people returned to the familiar rhythms that mirrored life on Earth prior to the alien arrival. The intrusion by the Ecaepians was fast-becoming social fodder over colorful drinks and a good meal—at least for those who could afford it. On the plus side, Catherine remained the bright spot in Gabriel's life. She was almost full-term now and the picture of glowing health. And Bonnie Harney had given birth to a healthy, seven-pound baby boy. Tyler showed up for work each morning beaming like a spotlight.

But along with the bright spots came some darkness. The age-old tribal mentality, deeply embedded in human DNA, had begun to surface again as if the alien incursion had never occurred. Major crimes and minor infractions were on the upswing; corruption, economic disparity and racial injustice were back with a vengeance. The pent-up anxiety that had endured during Legna's short reign was being unleashed in the ugliest ways possible as if Emperor Gaius Julius Caesar Augustus Germanicus, better known as the infamous *Caligula,* had returned from the dead to orchestrate the *to hell with it* attitude. Coming face-to-face with an alien race had destroyed an entire belief system, leaving the human race in complete disarray.

One morning Masma showed up at the Oval Office. His melancholy expression telegraphed his vexation.

"Good morning," Gabriel said, "You've been missing in action again."

"Your colloquialisms continue to amuse me."

Gabriel smiled. "Happy to oblige."

Masma took a seat next to the desk and folded his hands in his lap. "You have been well?"

"As well as can be expected. If I had to speculate, I'd say we're losing the battle again."

"Your citizens have returned to their previous ways."

"Yeah, well… if you have any ideas, please share them with me."

"I do not." And then he went silent and he looked dispirited.

Gabriel waited as the seconds ticked away. "What's wrong?"

"We have become comrades, have we not?"

"I would like to believe we are."

"Comrades are trustworthy allies?"

"Yes."

Another long pause before Masma spoke again. "Many challenges face human society."

"This is true. For us to forge a better future, it will take the collective will of everyone for the good of everyone—that's proving to be no easy task."

"We too faced tests of will," Masma said solemnly. "It was not until we acknowledged our deficiencies was our passage to peace, harmony, and balance achieved."

Gabriel forced a slender smile. "Legna promised to lead us to the promised land."

"The *promised land*, yes, I comprehend this metaphor. To achieve such an awakening, you must heighten your senses and coalesce what you know to be true here"—he touched a finger to his temple, then placed his hand flat against his upper chest— "with what you feel here. Only then shall you act with courage."

It was not lost on Gabriel that Masma had expressed an emotion by touching his heart—Ecaepians were supposedly free of all emotions.

Masma eyes flitted about the room; he was off in his own space again, first glancing left, then right before coming back to Gabriel. "I have learned much from humans." Masma stood and ambled to a window and stood quietly just as Legna and President Conrad often did when weighing their thoughts. "I have witnessed much here, both good and bad. There is more good than bad—I am certain of that."

"It is true—most people are good. But all too often rogue voices spread hate and dissension."

"This I have witnessed."

"Good always rises to the surface, though. It takes time, but in the end, good always defeats bad. I have faith that it will once again."

Masma turned from the window, his face drawn, his eyes soulful. "We must travel to the Kebun."

"What?"

"You and I, we must visit the Kebun."

"Why? What purpose would it serve to return? It was destroyed."

"I wish you not to question me further, but to trust. You must not disclose this to anyone, not even Catherine."

"At least tell me why?"

Ignoring Gabriel, the alien moved to the oval rug and stared at the embedded dove. "With the departure of our ships, the shuttle is no longer at my disposal— transport must be arranged." He marched to the door to the adjoining office. "I will await your instructions."

"Wait a minute," Gabriel called after him. "Trudging through that jungle is difficult at best, and I—"

"Do not be concerned with such matters. I seek your trust in this matter." Masma disappeared into his office.

Bewildered, Gabriel rounded up Alan Cross and related Masma's puzzling request to visit the Kebun.

"You said it was destroyed when you were there."

"It was, it is, but he was adamant we go."

Cross thought for a moment. "Well, if it's that important to him, *we* better go see why."

"He made no mention of you going."

"It's not negotiable, Gabriel, you are not going alone. When does he want to go?"

"Immediately. I need to arrange transportation."

Cross grinned. "I told you, he knows more than he was sharing."

Gabriel requested Dex and Remy spirit him, Cross and Masma out of the White House compound without anyone knowing, including Denver Wilkinson.

Remy balked. "You're asking us to break every rule in the book without telling us why. It *will* get us fired."

"Not unless I say so, I'm still president."

"From your lips to Denver's ears."

"Just trust me on this one."

"On one condition."

"Name it."

"Dex and me are still charged with your security. Wherever you're going, we go—Mr. President."

"Only if you stop calling me Mr. President."

Gabriel's primary concern was for Catherine. He hated the thought that she might have the baby while he was gone—she was that close to her due date. He explained—almost apologetically—he would be away for two days on a highly classified, but safe mission and Betty would keep a close eye on her.

"Surely, you can confide in your wife?"

"Sorry love, maybe when I get back if it's no longer classified."

"Gabriel, love, you're a politician, not a spy—what in the hell are you doing?"

"My job."

"And what if I was to have this baby while you're gone?"

"You wouldn't dare."

"I just might for spite." She put her arms around him and kissed him. "Whatever it is you're doing, please be safe."

He instructed Betty that in an emergency he could be contacted through the U.S. military command at Don Muang Royal Thai Air Force Base in Thailand.

"You're going to Thailand?"

"Yeah, and it's classified, so mum's the word. If you have to reach me, ask for Howard Littlefield. Alan Cross is Howard Beale. We're traveling under those names."

"With a pregnant wife at home, you're off playing James Bond in Thailand."

"I'm *not* playing spy."

"Whatever you're up to, please be safe."

In the dark hours of the following morning, Dex and Remy drove off the White House grounds in a Secret Service SUV with Gabriel, Cross, and Masma crouched on the floor. Once clear of the seventeenth street gate, they rose to their seats.

"When I write my memoirs, this will be the opening chapter," Cross said.

Gabriel smirked, "Better wait to be sure we survive this."

Masma placed a hand on Gabriel's arm. "You are in no danger."

At Joint Base Andrews in Maryland, they boarded an unmarked Boeing C-32. No one was present except the two-man flight crew already on-board. There was a closed-off section in the rear for use by traveling diplomats. There Gabriel, Cross, and Masma would remain for the duration of the flight since the pilots had no idea who their passengers were.

Travel to Papua, New Guinea's Rodson Airport would take twenty-two hours with a refueling stop along the way. The U.S. military maintained a small presence at the Royal Thai Air Force Base north of Bangkok. Cross had arranged for one of their helicopter to meet them at Rodson, which would take them deep into the forbidding Indonesian jungle.

Upon their arrival at Rodson, Gabriel spied the helicopter and chuckled. "Déjà vu all over again." Waiting for them was a vintage Bell UH-1 Iroquois. "The last leg of our escape from the Arizona site was in Skip Galinski's Huey."

"Too bad Skip won't be our pilot." Cross said.

The first order of business was getting the two US military pilots past the shock of coming face-to-face with Masma. Once that was achieved, Cross cautioned they were on a highly classified mission and were never to speak of what they might hear or see. He handed them the coordinates Masma has provided, which the pilot entered into his GPS system.

They flew east past the Mamberamo basin along the mist-shrouded Foja Mountains to the primeval forest that blanketed the Birds Head Peninsula. When GPS indicated they had arrived at their destination, they slowed and made a wide circle over the dense jungle below.

"GPS says we're over the exact spot, but there's heavy ground fog down there," the pilot cautioned.

"Do not be concerned." Masma told the pilot.

"But, we'll be landing in the blind."

"Do not be concerned." Masma repeated.

"Okay, but braces yourselves just in case."

"In case of what?" Gabriel asked.

"We land in the trees."

The pilot descended ever so slowly into the fog bank. Gabriel and Cross braced themselves until the skids settled safely on the ground. Outside, the fog was so thick they were barely able to see beyond two or three feet.

Cross pressed his face to the window. "How do we find our way through that soup?"

Masma ignored him, slid the side door open, and set foot on the damp, spongy soil. "Come, citizens."

"Dex, Remy, you and the pilots stay with the helicopter." Cross ordered.

Having no clue why they were there or what might be beyond the fog, Dex cautioned, "Ur, sir, is that a good idea?"

"None of you are to leave this aircraft."

"In that case, we need to remain in contact." Remy handed Cross a small device that resembled a wireless Bluetooth earphone. "Insert this in your ear. Its voice activated."

Gabriel and Cross cautiously followed Masma into the thick mist. It was eerily silent except for the squishy sound each time they took a step in the soft, spongy ground. As they advanced, the suspended globules of moisture began to diminish and the faint sound of cascading water and chirping birds could be heard in the distance.

Cross stopped. "What's that?"

Gabriel whispered, "The waterfall! How can we be this close so soon?"

"We berthed closer than your previous visit." Masma said. "Does this not please you?"

"Until you explain why you've brought us here, nothing pleases me."

They continued on, and as they did, the mist began to dissipate, the air cooled, and sunlight streaked through the treetops until they standing in a small open area completely free of the fog.

Directly in front of them was the Kebun.

"God almighty!" Cross wailed. "What in the hell!"

The Kebun—the Golden Garden, as Dr. Sanjaya had dubbed it—was fully restored to its original magnificence.

Gabriel did a doubletake. "What in the hell is right!"

Rows of artfully positioned multi-colored flower beds bloomed as far as the eye could see. Colorful birds of every imaginable variety chirped in a melodious chorus. Clear, clean water flowed from a waterfall into the pool below and into a meandering stream to the forest beyond.

A shiver ran through a speechless Alan Cross. "It's magnificent!"

Masma waved a hand across the area. "Behold the Kebun as it was in the beginning."

Eyes wide, Gabriel looked on with disbelief. "This was destroyed when I was here. How? Why?"

"Citizen Tonora deemed the Kebun to be gifted to humans upon completion of the transformation to peace, harmony, and balance. It was restored prior to Citizen Legna's departure. Come now."

Left speechless by the grandeur of the restored Kebun, they followed Masma past the waterfall along a row of tall Araucaria trees and vast flower gardens before passing through mango and banana tree groves laden with ripe fruit. Once clear of the orchard, they came upon an open, circular space, approximately fifty feet in diameter and completely covered in yellow, red, and purple flowers. Dead center of the circle was an apple tree; its branches heavy with ripe fruit. Ringing the perimeter of the circle was every kind of fruit tree imaginable.

Gabriel pointed to the apple tree. "That was dead when I was here—the ground was brown and arid."

"It is the tree of life," Masma said. "It represents all that is good within the universes."

Cross could not restrain his elation. "Please tell me I'm not dreaming."

"You are not, Citizen Cross."

Gabriel remembered the curious cobalt blue structure buried nearby. Quickly pivoting, he went to it to find the face of it had been fully restored.

Cross joined him. "What is that thing? That writing, what language is it?"

"I shall read it to you." Stepping closer, Masma began, "*All beings are born free and equal in dignity and rights. They are endowed with reason and conscience and should act toward one another in a spirit of brotherhood.*"

Cross' face lit up with recognition. "Dear God, that article One of the United Nations Universal Declaration of Human Rights!"

"With one exception," Gabriel said. "The United Nations' version reads, '*all human beings.*' This inscription reads, '*all beings.*'"

"Unbelievable!" Cross breathed.

"Come now," Masma began to leave.

Cross shook a hand at the buried monolith. "Wait, what's in there?"

"All that mankind wishes to know."

"What?" Cross looked to Gabriel. "What's he talking about?"

Gabriel shrugged and lied. "Beats me."

They followed Masma to the far side of the circle where Masma stopped by a dirt path that led into the surrounding forest.

"This path wasn't here," Gabriel observed.

"No, it was not. Come."

The path was a maze of twists and turns snaking through the jungle past wild tropical vegetation and manicured flower beds. Masma stopped short of where the path ended and the open area began. He stood silent and hesitant.

"What's wrong?" Gabriel asked.

Masma looked beyond the path to the open area, hesitated, then turned to Gabriel. "I am of you now?"

Gabriel immediately understood the question. Masma was seeking his assurance, for he knew to be stranded on Earth, he would always be treated as an oddity. Gabriel spoke softly, "Yes, Masma, you are with us now."

"We have spoken of the virtue of truth, for truth is the foundation of all alliances. And yet, truth can often be deceiving." His eyes went to the end of the path. "Perhaps this truth will turn you against me." He took the few remaining steps into the open area. "Come."

Gabriel and Cross followed. Masma motioned to his right.

What they saw stopped them cold.

A large area of the primeval forest had been cleared and leveled. In its place was an enormous flat-roofed warehouse-like building that rose up two stories. Its footprint was at least the width and length of one-and-a-half football fields. It was hugged by the surrounding Araucaria trees, allowing the edifice's forest-green color to blend in with its surrounding. There was a narrow dirt path leading to it.

Cross gasped. "What in the hell is that?"

"My God!" Gabriel whooped.

Masma ambled along the path to the building and placed a single finger on it. A section snapped back and to the left, revealing a dark entrance. He stepped into the coal-black void.

Speechless, Gabriel and Cross followed and the doorway snapped shut behind them. Immediately, they were bathed in an intense blue light. Then, unexpectedly, the air was sucked out and within seconds they were in a complete vacuum and gasping for breath. Five to six seconds later the process was reversed—fresh air gushed in, and they were able to breathe freely again.

Cross croaked, "What just happened?"

"You have been cleansed," Masma said.

In front of Masma, a door snapped back to the left, but all they saw was a blue haze. Masma stepped through the opening.

Neither Gabriel nor Cross followed.

"Come, you will not be harmed."

Cross whispered to Gabriel, "This is your gig—you first."

Gabriel stepped in and Cross followed. Whatever was there was hidden in thick blue fog. To the right of the door, mounted on the wall, was a lighted square panel. Masma tapped it. Six symbols appeared. He touched the one that resembled an eye. The blue fog began to slowly dissipate and the enormous interior came into view. Directly in front of them was a six-foot wide aisle running to the far end of the building, so far away they were unable to determine where it might end. On both sides of the isle were pallets, as many as 30 in a row back to each wall and stacked eight high to the ceiling. Each pallet held six black, circular tubes, five-feet high and two feet in diameter.

Masma placed a finger on a symbol that resembled the Egyptian hieroglyphic character *Ankh,* the symbol for life.

Thousands upon thousands of the black tubes lit up.

Gabriel and Cross gasped at what greeted them.

For as far as they could see, every cylinder contained fully-formed human-like fetuses suspended in a yellowish liquid, only they were gray. Their heads were bowed forward, their legs arched to their midsections. Their eyes were closed and their hands were joined in front.

They were exact replicas of Ecaepians.

Cross made a quick sucking sound and took a step back. "Jesus fucking Christ!"

Gabriel said nothing. He moved slowly forward down the aisle with his eyes sweeping left and right from one pallet to the next.

"Gabriel?" Cross called.

Gabriel stopped, his head bowed, and he whispered in resignation, "So this was the plan after all."

Masma went to Gabriel's side and placed a hand on his arm. "It was to be the final phase in the transformation. These were the first; there were many millions more to come."

Gabriel pivoted to Cross.

Cross blew a breath and nodded. "I heard."

"Legna lied to me. He said this was not to be our fate."

"It was a mistruth, for if you knew…" Masma's voice trailed off. "As virtuous as our intentions were, if we had pursued this, it would have proved a misstep, a regrettable transgression against human civilization."

Gabriel approached a pallet to his right until he was 2 feet away. He stared at the gray body floating in yellow liquid. It could have easily been Legna or Masma, or any Ecaepian he had come into contact with. He turned to Masma, his eyes tight, his brow crimped. "Are they real, are you real?"

Masma spoke softly. "I am real."

Gabriel swept a hand across the rows of pallets. "How is this possible? How do you create life on this massive scale—like cranking out canned beans on a robotic production line?"

"Unlike humans, we harbor no emotional attachment to our carriage."

"And why would you, it's bogus, synthetic." Cross thumped a finger hard against his temple. "Is what's in here made up too?"

"You are angered with me, Mr. Cross?"

"I am angry at everyone one of you. Answer my question."

"My consciousness remains as it was, retrieved and recorded on a neural sensor and inserted at the base of the cranium. It is attached to the plexus, as is yours."

"You have a microchip for a damn brain? Jesus, we're dealing with a race of androids!"

Masma was angered by Cross' verbal attack. "It is *my* brain, Mr. Cross, as it was, as it shall always be."

"Modified in the process, so I was told." Gabriel said.

"To insure peace, harmony, and balance."

Cross shook a fist at Masma. "If I hear peace, harmony, and balance one more time, so help me I will—"

"Hold on, Alan." Gabriel stepped closer to Masma. "Why have you chosen to reveal all this now?"

"I fear Ecaep has been vanquished—Citizen Legna shall not return."

"There's your answer!" Cross bellowed. "He's looking to save his ass."

"Alan, let him speak."

"If I am to be acknowledged," Masma said softly, "I must prove myself worthy. Although I have not coalesced with many humans, our time on Surin Island provided intimate enlightenment. There I observed your freedom of thought, your jurisdiction over your lives." With a look of anguish, Masma bowed his head. "It was never our intent to harm, but to guide, to advance. I know now we were misguided, for Humankind evolution must be from intervention."

Cross approached a pallet and stared at a body floating in yellow liquid. He took in a long breath and expelled it slowly. "No one must ever know this place, these creatures, ever existed. It has to be destroyed." He spun around to Gabriel. "We need to do it now, we need to get a few bombers in here, pronto!"

"Wait a minute, let's not make snap decisions." Gabriel waved a hand across the pallets. "This maybe, but not what's out there—we need to preserve that."

"None of it is real, it's all a fantasy. It all has to go."

"Perhaps Mr. Cross is right, Gabriel. It is not mankind's reality, it can never be."

Gabriel took a breath and slowly scanned the thousands of floating bodies. "How do we do it?"

"Until they replace you, you're still the Commander in Chief."

"I can't just call in an air strike."

"The hell you can't."

They made a hasty retreat from the macabre scene in the warehouse, down the dirt path, around the apple tree, through the fruit groves, and finally to the waterfall. There, Gabriel stopped.

"What is it?" Cross asked.

"Do we dare destroy this extraordinary place?"

"It's nothing more than a theme park, a deception. Let's go, we're wasting time."

They made their way to the helicopter and Cross barked, "Captain, can you patch me through to CENTCOM?"

"CENTCOM?" Dex questioned.

"Can you, captain?"

"Uh, yes sir," the pilot answered.

"It needs to be on a secure line."

"Yes, sir, we can request that."

"Then do it now." Cross turned to Gabriel. "As Commander in Chief, you're the only one who can issue an order to have this place flattened."

"Whoa, what are we talking about here?" Remy chimed in.

"Gentlemen," Cross said through clenched teeth, "you are to ask no questions. You are to forget for the rest of your natural lives we were ever here. Follow the orders of your Commander in Chief. Have I made myself clear?"

"Yes, sir," they collectively answered.

"Good, now Captain, get me a patch to CENTCOM pronto."

Five minutes later they were on a secure line with the commanding general of the U.S. Central Command at MacDill Air Force Base in Tampa, Florida.

"General, this is Vice-President Alan Cross. I'm here with President Ferro."

"Yes, sir."

"Write down these coordinates: -2.561854,138.290913."

There was a long period of silence while presumably someone at CENTCOM scrambled to check the coordinates.

The CENTCOM Commander's voice crackled over the line, "To confirm sir, the coordinates are 1-3-7-8 kilometers from Papua New Guinea in the Birds Head Peninsula."

"Correct, General. Now listen carefully. This is a priority national security issue, which means as of this moment it is classified at the highest level. Do you understand?"

"Yes, sir."

"Where is the nearest U.S. base to those coordinates with heavy bombing capabilities?"

"Ah, that would be Kadena Air Base in Okinawa, sir."

"The president is authorizing the bombing of those coordinates as soon as you can get aircraft in the air."

There was no immediate response from CENTCOM.

"Did you hear me, General?"

Another pregnant pause before the commander replied, "That's in a friendly territory, sir."

"We are aware of that."

"May I speak with the president again, sir."

"I'm right here, general, go ahead."

"Mr. President, I will require your security code?"

Gabriel carried with him a secret code that only he, as President and Commander in Chief, would know. Once the code was verified, Cross took over again.

"General, how soon can you carry out these orders?"

"The aircraft can be there within a couple of hours, sir."

"Get it done, commander, get it done now."

Another long pause before the General answered. "Uh … yes, sir, but—"

"No buts, General, get it done."

The communications ended.

Dex and Remy looked baffled.

Remy spoke up. "Ahhh, it would best to get back to base before the fireworks go off."

"Right, take us home, captain," Cross ordered. "And a reminder, the president, vice president, his Secret Service agents, and our alien friend here was never aboard this aircraft."

As the helicopter lifted, Gabriel pressed his face to the window for one last glimpse. But the heavy fog-shrouded his view. There was no hint that somewhere in the fog below was a magnificent Garden of Eden.

As they touched down in Papua, the pilot received a message that confused him. "There's a call coming through for Howard Littlefield."

At the sound of his code name, Gabriel's face turned ashen white. "That's me."

Dex shook his head and smiled at Gabriel. "Howard Littlefield?"

The co-pilot handed Gabriel headsets. "Here, sir, put these on."

Gabriel slipped them on. "This is Howard Littlefield."

"Hold please for a priority call," a male voice said.

There was a moment of silence just long enough for Gabriel to feel sweat forming on his brow.

"Are you there?" a voice said.

"Betty? Betty, what's wrong?"

"Catherine had the good sense to call me. I took her to the hospital."

Gabriel's voice cracked. "Good God, is she okay?"

"Catherine's fine. Your daughter made her grand entrance weighing in at six pounds, four ounces and she's just perfect. But I think your wife is very angry with you."

Gabriel's face splayed into a wide smile and his eyes welled up.

"Are you still there?"

"Yes, Betty, I'm here."

"I suggest you get your Cuban butt back here, pronto."

"I'm on my way. Tell the good lady I love her." He slipped the headphones off. "Son of a bitch, I'm a father—a daughter!"

"Congratulations," said Cross.

There was a round of applause from Dex, Remy and the two pilots.

At 02:45 PM Pacific Time on the Indonesian continent of Oceania, two U.S. B-2 Spirit bombers, reserved for targets of the highest priority, honed in on the Birds Head Peninsula coordinates. What occurred next was apocalyptic as the bombs laid waste to what was the alien Kebun. Nothing was left behind but scorched earth. The Kebun's discoverer, the late Chief Metha of the Kweba Tribe, Gabriel, Dr. Sanjaya, his two assistants, Rafi Suharto, and Alan Cross would be the only humans to have ever laid eyes on its unearthly grandeur.

61

The nurse gently cradled his newborn daughter in Gabriel's arms.

"Congratulations, Mr. President. You have a beautiful daughter."

Gabriel looked at the child, and his eyes welled up. A wisp of brown hair topped her head. The shape of her almond-colored eyes reminded him of his mother's.

Smiling and quite pleased with herself, Catherine said, "If you agree, can we name her Rose Isabella Ferro? Rose was my mother's name."

"Yes, of course," Gabriel gushed.

"Now that we've settled that, Gabriel Ferro, you're in the doghouse for letting me do this alone."

"You weren't due for a couple of weeks as I recall."

"She's a bit impatient like her father."

Gabriel gently placed Rose by Catherine's side and planted a kiss on Catherine's lips. "Am I forgiven?"

"Kiss me again, and I'll think about it."

The following morning, they returned to the White House to what resembled a state reception. Every able body had lined up to greet them.

The explosion that had taken place in the Indonesian jungle made media head-lines around the world for the next week. The United States issued a statement that American geologists were confident it was the result of a meteor that exploded above ground like the one that destroyed the Stony River Tunguska area in Siberian Russia on the morning of June 30, 1908. Indonesians living many miles from the site thought they had witnessed a meteor streak across the sky just before the explosion. Although they had actually seen nothing, it supported the lie that it was in fact, a meteor. With no other feasible explanation, it was soon forgotten when the Indonesian government marked the area permanently off limits. It was left to the annals of history as another unresolved mystery.

Case closed.

When Rose turned one-month old, her proud father asked if Catherine would bring her to the Oval office so his staff could fuss over her. As expected, everyone, none more so than Betty, Dex, and Remy, did just that. Betty had arranged for a birthday cake with a big number one on top.

Betty asked Catherine, "The president changes diapers, doesn't he?"

"He did once—that was it."

"Hey you two, I *am* the president after all."

After everyone had left, Gabriel took Rose to the door of the adjoining office and asked Catherine to knock.

Catherine tapped lightly on the door. There was no answer.

"Open it."

Catherine swung the door open. Masma was sitting behind his desk.

"I wanted you to meet Rose Isabella Ferro." Gabriel said.

Masma said nothing

"She's one-month old today," Catherine said to Masma.

The closer Gabriel got, the tenser the little alien appeared to get. Gabriel dipped forward slightly so that Masma could see Rose clearly.

"Do you want to hold her?"

Masma eyes grew big. "I do not believe so."

"Oh, come on, she won't break."

Gabriel extended Rose to Masma, but Masma pushed back against his chair.

"Nothing to be afraid of... here, hold her."

Masma relented and allowed Gabriel to place Rose in his arms. With her eyes wide and bright, Rose smiled and made a gurgling sound. Masma looked to Gabriel, then to Catherine; his face splayed into a broad smile. The moment was magic.

"I... I had forgotten," Masma said just above a whisper.

"I know," Gabriel said, "I know."

Over the weeks and months that followed, economies around the world began to rebound and stock markets were showing signs of renewed prosperity. There were signs of hope after all.

The aliens had left behind one major contribution to the human race: all existing nuclear weapons and the materials to make more had been rendered useless. To ensure mankind would never again create such weapons, a United Nations resolution permanently banned their future manufacture. Nuclear, except for use in medical research and advancements, had become a dirty word.

Catherine returned to her work. From time to time, Masma assisted her by providing science and technology that would have taken her team years to discover on their own.

B.D. Sanjaya became the head of the National Archaeological Research Center in Jakarta, Indonesia, and Owen Jennings was promoted to the Director of CIA interrogations. He chose Rafi Suharto as his deputy director.

Life on planet Earth was showing promise.

Sadly, Gabriel received word that Skip Galinski had died of a massive heart attack while working on his beloved Huey. Since Skip had no family, Gabriel arranged for him to be buried in Arlington Cemetery with full military honors. Those in attendance were Gabriel, Catherine, Jennings, Cross, Betty, Tyler, Bonnie, and Skip's military buddies French Stewart, Jimmy Gillford and Harry Wilson. Fearing his presence graveside would be disruptive—the media was forever trying to obtain photos of him—Masma observed the service from a Secret Service SUV. Following the service, Gabriel hosted a reception in the White House State Dining Room where he gave a brief address:

"There are many who walk this Earth who are endowed with a sense of self and place that others can only hope to emulate. Skip Galinski was one of those rare individuals. His love and his loyalty to his country was beyond reproach. Those of you who knew him understand when I say, Major Skip Galinski was one of the finest men we were privileged to call our friend." He paused for a moment of reflection. "On a lighter note, there are some in this room who will recall the day when Skip, naked as the day he was born, raced across a sandy beach and into the Andaman Sea for a swim."

The following morning, Gabriel received his daily classified briefing. The reduction in worldwide population had totaled 2,148,113,048. Soon the effects of the alien's "birth control" program would wear off as Legna had promised and that would be that. A commission was assembled to study ways to ensure future population growth was in sync with the planet's ability to support.

On a worldwide television broadcast, Gabriel delivered the following speech.

There are many challenges that test mankind's will. The most important is: How do we live in harmony with each other and respect our fragile planet? It is my firm belief that to meet whatever goals we set for ourselves, they must be met by us, for us, as a unified society.

It has been a long, arduous journey from when mankind first walked this Earth to where we are today. We have achieved many technological advances never believed possible and there will be many more to come. Let us begin by putting the alien intrusion behind us, never forgetting that we are no longer alone in the universe and that one-day contact will be made again. Until that time comes, let us prosper and go forward as one, for the benefit of all.

The election to select a permanent President and Vice President was fast approaching. It was a time of soul-searching for Gabriel—to run or not to run. Many considerations, including the birth of Rose, entered the mix. He discussed it with Catherine, and with her full support, he withdrew his name from consideration.

"So, what do you do going forward?" Catherine had asked him. "You're not one to sit around and ponder your navel. Why don't you take those notes you've so meticulously kept and turn them into a book?"

"I'm way ahead of you on that one."

"Good, then it's settled. When we move back to the condo, you'll work from home, and we won't need a babysitter because I intend to continue with my research."

"Seems the Ferro's have a plan."

Gabriel met with Alan Cross to inform him of his decision not to seek the office.

"You plan to run?"

"No, I'm finished with politics. You?"

"I wasn't going to if you were," Cross said. "I'm going to give it a go"

"I appreciate that, Alan. If elected, who do you see as Vice-President?"

"National Security Advisor Charles Bregg. He's clean as a whistle—no skeletons in his closet."

"Is there such an animal in politics?"

"If there is, it's Charles Bregg."

Early one morning while signing papers, Gabriel received a visit from Masma. He carried with him the silver box of codes, which he set on the desk, then took a seat on one of the sofas. "Please join me."

Gabriel eyed the silver box suspiciously. "Shouldn't this be given to the new president?"

There was no response from Masma.

"Okay, then." Gabriel rounded the desk and sat across from Masma.

"You have shown me great kindness," Masma said. "We are comrades."

"Yes, we are comrades."

Masma fell silent, folded his hands, set them on his lap, and looked away.

That the alien was lonely and sad was not lost on Gabriel. It was becoming more evident each passing day. The one bright spot in Masma's life was his occasional assistance to Catherine. But even then, fearing for his safety, the Secret Service was forced to spirit him to and from her Bethesda lab for fear the media might exploit him. Gabriel and Catherine would often invite the little guy to the family quarters. He had become quite comfortable around Rose, and they delighted in each other's company; to Rose he was her playmate. But there was no denying reality; Masma was living on a strange planet residing in the White House.

"Hey, whatever's on your mind, you can be straight with me."

"I wish to live among the Mogen."

Coming out of the blue as it did, Gabriel was at a complete loss for a comeback.

"I am grateful for your friendship, your generosity, but I live as a captive, unable to move about freely."

"The memories are still fresh. When people come to know you as I have, they will accept you."

"I fear not, Gabriel, I fear not."

Gabriel thought for a moment. "If that's what you want, the Mogen welcomed you once, I'm sure they will again."

"You believe this to be true?"

"I do."

"Might you make arrangements?"

"It would be my pleasure."

"I will miss your friendship. I will miss Catherine and Rose."

"And we will miss you. But hey, we can visit you."

"I would treasure that."

Masma's eyes went to the silver box. "I am curious, Gabriel, will you open the box?"

"Shouldn't it go to the next president?"

"That would be your decision to make."

Gabriel smiled. "I guess you'd have to change the thumb print, huh?" He stared at the box for a long moment. "Maybe I'll just hang on to it for a while in case we're not ready to deal with its contents just yet."

Masma stood. "I will take my leave now."

"I would like to shake your hand, Citizen Masma."

"Yes, Citizen Gabriel, let us shake hands."

Gabriel wrapped his hand around Masma's. "Please give my warmest regards to Rahmat."

"I will do as you ask."

As Masma reached the door, Gabriel called to him. "May I ask you a question?"

Masma turned back. "Yes?"

"You once recalled memories of events that took place before the Transformation: The Great War, your mate and your offspring. Yet another time you expressed an emotion by placing your hand over your heart."

No response from Masma.

"And yet, Ecaepians were supposedly unburdened from both memory and emotions, that neither served a useful purpose.

Masma took several steps toward Gabriel. "You wish to know if I am conflicted?"

Gabriel nodded.

"I have observed humans sharing memories of joy, happiness, love, and sadness. I witnessed the emotional significance between you, Catherine and Rose. I have no explanation, but these once treasured virtues have returned to me. I realize now that memories are required to make sense of the present and that emotions can bring joy as well as sadness. Have I clarified?"

Gabriel smiled warmly. "Quite well."

Masma turned to leave again. When he reached the door, Gabriel called to him.

"Masma."

"Yes, Gabriel."

"Is there is anything else, anything at all I should know?"

Slowly, Masma lifted his head and looked to Gabriel. "You wish the answer to two questions, do you not?"

Gabriel smiled. "So, you can read my thoughts after all."

"I meant no malice."

"None taken."

Masma moved to the edge of the oval rug and stared at the white dove for a long moment. In what can only be described as an act of defiance, he stepped forward and planted both feet firmly on the dove. His eyes went to Gabriel. "We, like you, possessed catastrophic weapons of unimaginable force and destruction..." His words trailed off, his expression darkened. "Foolishly, such weapons were engaged in the Great War." He looked away as if it pained him to speak of such things. "Ecaep's surface was rendered infertile and our atmosphere poisoned. And enclosed Jubia City rose with necessity and urgency."

"But while on the ship, we saw the images of a healthy, lush planet."

"An untruth… all outside Jubia City remains uninhabitable."

"Then why were we lied to?"

"Our desire was to save from extinction a civilization that was by accident an extension of ourselves. If our past missteps had been revealed, we feared you would have rejected our hand. We were misguided in believing we could intercede, for mankind's future must be secured through natural evolution." He was thoughtful for a moment. "Perhaps in the end, we have awakened humankind to seek a unified society that one-day will live in peace, harmony, and balance."

Masma strolled to the door, stopped, and turned back. "Have I answered your queries?"

"Yes, you have."

"It would serve no purpose to reveal my destination to others."

"No, it would serve no purpose."

"Goodbye, Gabriel. I will cherish our friendship as a gift I had not anticipated." He placed a fist to his heart and smiled.

Gabriel stood and placed his hand over his heart and smiled back.

Gabriel placed a call to Rafi informing him of Masma's decision to live among the Mogen: would Rafi agree to personally escort Masma to Surin Island.

"Of course. It would be my honor."

"Take four or five cases of Sprite with you."

"Sprite?"

"Just do it as a favor to me."

Two days later, all arrangements had been made. Those who had spent time with Masma on Surin Island: Betty, Tyler, Bonnie, Cross, Dex, Remy, and Rafi, all gathered in the White House family quarters to bid him goodbye. There wasn't a dry eye among them as each wished Masma well—except Rose, who insisted Masma join her on the floor to play with her Baby Einstein Take Along Tunes toy.

"One day we will come to visit—I promise," Gabriel told Masma.

"I shall look forward to such a joyful day."

Masma went to each of the guests and hugged them. Rose was last—he held onto her just a bit longer than the others. She cried as Masma left with Rafi.

Alan Cross and Charles Bregg won the election with 312 electoral votes. Cross' first order of business was to ask Betty to stay on as his personal secretary and Tyler as his Chief of Staff.

"I'm flattered, but I'm ready for the retirement heap," Betty told Cross.

He laughed. "So am I, but here I am. If I can do it, so can you."

"Did Gabriel ask you to do this?"

"*I'm* asking you. If you pardon the expression, I need someone at that desk with balls who can keep me organized."

"Is that your way of flattering me? Okay, Mr. President, let's give it a try, but if you ever yell at me, I'm out of here."

"My reputation precedes me."

"Big of you to admit it. So, let's get to work and do some good."

"Deal."

"Oh, one other thing," Betty said.

"What's that?"

"I don't put up with any cursing."

The day of the Cross' swearing in, Gabriel and Catherine's belongings were transferred to their condo. Rose, however, could not understand why they had to move.

"It'll be a relief to be away from all the madness of this place," Gabriel told Catherine. "I'm looking forward to settling into the peace and quiet of our condo."

"But the Secret Service will continue to shadow us."

"I told them no more than a year—that's it."

"Not that I don't trust you, but I've hired a nanny."

"Which means you don't trust me."

"Have you spent a full day with an energized child? Trust me, you'll appreciate the nanny. You just concentrate on writing that book."

62

A month had gone by since they moved back to the condo. Gabriel spent his time organizing his notes; he had yet to write a single word.

Betty called one morning to invite him to a private lunch with President Cross the following day.

"What's this about?"

"I have no idea, Sparky, that's above my pay grade."

The next day, Gabriel showed up at the Oval dressed in his best dark blue suit paired with a red and white striped tie. Betty broke out in a wide smile and wrapped her arms around him.

"Sorry, I've been missing in action since we left; we've been busy getting resettled."

"You're forgiven. How's retirement?"

"Busy trying to turn my journals into a readable book."

"And Catherine and Rose?"

"Catherine's working hard at her lab. Much of the science provided by Masma helped advanced her research. As for Rose, what can I say? I get to be with the pretty little lady much of the day when she's not being cared for by her nanny. Nice lady, but strict about Rose's schedule. How's it going with Alan?"

"His temperament has improved; haven't heard him cuss once."

"By the way, Catherine and I want to have you over for dinner. Is Saturday night good?"

"Thanks, I'm there."

"There's something else. Rose, as you know, has no grandmother. We'd be honored if you'd take on that role."

Betty's hand went to her mouth, and her eyes misted. "Oh, my goodness, really?" Her arms flew around him and she kissed him on the cheek. "Thank you, Sparky, I accept."

"Still with that Sparky crap!"

She kissed him on the cheek again. "You'll always be Sparky to me, young man. Now, get in there, the President of these United States is waiting."

Alan Cross rose as Gabriel entered. "A month has gone by and not a word from you." He crossed the room and shook Gabriel's hand. "How the hell are you?"

"Good, I have my sanity back. How's it with you?"

"I'm losing mine." Cross frowned. "You stuck me with the most difficult job in the world."

Gabriel chuckled. "Tell me about it."

"Come on, sit."

They sat on opposite sofas.

"Are you up for an assignment?" Cross asked.

"Alan, I'm writing a book."

"Hear me out. Last week I met with the United Nations Secretary-General. He wants to explore the one-world government concept."

"I thought we were past that?"

"The Secretary-General believes it's at least worth investigating, and I agree. If we don't explore new ideas, society is back to square one. The way population reduction came about would not have been anyone's choice, but damn it, there's no denying it had to be done. The whole idea of one-world, one- people could be the next major step in bringing this cockeyed civilization together."

"What is it that I can do?" Gabriel asked.

"The Secretary-General has asked if you would study the possibilities and submit a report."

"Jesus, Alan, that could take months."

"Oh, I forgot, you're all of, what, thirty-nine now."

"Don't be a wise-ass—up next is 40. So why me?"

"Because I told the good Secretary-General the idea appealed to you. Am I right—did you not tell me that?"

Gabriel stood and ambled to the bookshelf and stared at the photo of President Conrad.

"He would want you to do this, Gabriel."

"I suspect the old boy would."

"You'd report directly to the Secretary-General—no committees. He'll see to it you get whatever administrative support you need, plus $75,000 for your efforts."

Gabriel lingered on Conrad's photo for a long moment before turning back to Cross. "If I do this, I do it from home. If I require administrative assistance, it's by phone or email with New York—I'm not traveling back and forth."

"I'm sure that'll be fine."

"I get to write it up the way I see it; no one edits, no one interferes until the Secretary-General reads it. From that point on, it's his to do whatever he decides. Agreed?"

"I can't speak for the Secretary, but I don't envision any problems. When could you begin?"

"Maybe in a week or so I can put some initial thoughts on paper."

Cross laughed. "I had faith you'd accept."

"You were that sure of me?"

"I know you better than you know yourself. You never could turn down a challenge." Cross smiled whimsically and stood. "Lunch awaits us. You'll tell me all about lovely Rose."

That evening Gabriel presented the idea to Catherine.

"You have to do this, Gabriel."

"I doubt if it will go anywhere."

"In the end, that's not for you to decide, it is? Pour your heart into it and then let it go."

And so, he began. He spent the first week conducting research to determine how best to frame the report. It was paramount that to validate a one-world concept he refrains from injecting his personal conclusions, expressing them only in a cover letter to the Secretary General. With a sense of purpose and urgency, he began with a quote from "One World," published in 1943 by Wendell L. Willkie, an American lawyer and corporate executive who had been the 1940 Republican nominee for President of the United States. Willkie's words would set the tone for whatever followed.

"Freedom is an indivisible word. If we want to enjoy it and fight for it, we must be prepared to extend it to everyone, whether they are rich or poor, whether they agree with us or not, no matter what their race or the color of their skin... Whatever we take away from the liberties of those whom we hate, we are opening the way to loss of liberty for those we love."

In another chapter, Gabriel wrote: *"We are one race despite our differences, skin color, or ethnicity. But from the very beginning of our time on this planet, we have banded into tribes with an us against them mentality. To achieve a lasting world peace, we must move beyond our prejudices, our false sense of nationalism, which causes us to pursue individual supremacy as a worthy goal. Although the universal contempt felt for the aliens, we would do well to heed their words; if we are ever to achieve lasting peace, harmony, and balance, our deep-seated tribal mentality must end. If we, the human race, do not find a way to reconcile our missteps, we are destined to become a footnote in the annuals of intergalactic history."*

Five weeks after he had begun, he had completed a 254-page report. He chose to end it with a quote from American author, conservationist, and activist, Terry Tempest Williams.

"The human heart is the first home of democracy. It is where we embrace our questions. Can we be equitable? Can we be generous? Can we listen with our whole beings, not just our minds, and offer our attention rather than our opinions? And do we have enough resolve in our hearts to act courageously, relentlessly, without giving up—ever—trusting our fellow citizens to join with us our determined pursuit of a living democracy?"

He printed the report, made a thumb drive copy, and delivered it to President Cross.

"Are you pleased with it?" Cross asked.

"That's not for me to decide. I presented the possibilities as I saw them. My hope now is that maybe, just maybe, it becomes a reality in my lifetime. It's in the hands of the Secretary-General now."

"No, it's in the hands of all mankind. You sure you don't want to deliver this to the Secretary-General personally?"

"I have a book to write, you do it."

Cross laughed. "And it's a book I look forward to reading. Hopefully, you'll hold nothing back."

"When it's published—if it's published—I may be tarred and feathered and run out of town."

"Stay in touch, will you?"

"Count on it. The minute I see you veering off course, I'll be on you like a hungry bug."

"I'm going to hold you to that. My best to Catherine and Rose."

When Gabriel had left, Cross opened the report and flipped to the first page. It was Gabriel's cover letter to the Secretary General.

Dear Secretary-General:

First, let me express my sincerest gratitude for the opportunity to have compiled this report. I trust it will serve in some small way to advance human society.

As we are all aware, sir, we humans possess unshakeable prejudices that affect our ability to think and act with absolute clarity. Society is over-run with conflicting religious, basic philosophical beliefs, economics, and values. However, it should not deter from the task at hand; to unite the world in peace, harmony, and balance. You will forgive me for quoting the aliens, but I believe you will agree their point was well made.

Holding us back from creating a truly altruistic society is our winner-takes-all approach in business and our personal lives; He who has the gold rules, as the saying goes. How then do we go about ensuring representation and opportunities for all people, regardless of race, creed, or religion? How do we encourage understanding, compromise, and equality, rather than a winner take all mentality? Instead of focusing on winning or losing, we must seek an alternative approach, a moral approach, one that maintains balance across all nations for all people if we hope to defeat the tribalism that possesses us.

In the end, the aliens provided us a gift, a first step-up, by cleansing our environment and providing food, clean water, and electricity to those most in need. Hopefully, we can now build on those gifts.

I thank you again for this opportunity, Mr. Secretary-General. It is my hope this report leads to a plan. As President Conrad once said to me, "A goal without a plan is just a wish."

Sincerely yours, Gabriel Javier Ferro (private citizen).

63

Gabriel glanced at the bedside clock, it was 5:00 AM. Catherine was sleeping as soundly as she always did. Slipping out of bed, he made his way to Rose's bedroom and stood quietly by the door, watching her chest rise and fall in peaceful slumber. Thankfully, when it came to sleeping, she took after her mother. He couldn't help but wonder what the future might hold for this precious child and all the other children to follow.

In the kitchen, while waiting for his coffee to brew, he wrote Catherine a note. *Although I question my life, I am certain of the role yours plays in mine. For that I am grateful.*

Quietly entering the bedroom, he propped the note against the bedside clock.

Barefoot with coffee cup in hand, he crossed the living room to his study. There he sat and pondered. "So now I have to write this bloody book; where to begin, where to begin?" After several sips of coffee, he smiled. "Ah ha, I've got it! I'll start at the end. Brilliant, Gabriel, brilliant."

With a clear vision, his fingers went to the keyboard:

We now know the "Big Blue Dot" is the "Small Blue Dot" floating in a vast string of universes with who knows how many civilizations out there. So, where does humanity go from here? Are we an invasive species that has reached its apex? Can we rise above our self-imposed limitations, or will we falter yet again, only to perish as the aliens predicted? To answer these questions, we must first define human consciousness, that elusive process responsible for our ability to think, to learn, to feel, and to love.

Although the world reveals itself in its physical form—I see it, I touch it, I smell it—why then do I feel so removed from it? Might it be that I see through flawed eyes? I am human after all, with all the associated flaws that goes along with being human. Therefore, I am less than what I hoped I would be by the very nature of what it means to be human.

Perhaps the Roman Emperor Hadrian summed it up best when he wrote: "It is not true that I despise men. If I did, I should have no right, no reason, to try and govern them. I know them to be vain, ignorant, greedy, cruel, cowardly, capable of almost anything for the sake of their own profit. I know because I am like them, at least from time to time, or might have been."

It's that last line we need to heed.

I do not accept the Ecaepians' belief in the Originator other than it is an extraordinary source of energy, one that I hope we too will discover. But like us, the Ecaepians sought answers to creation, and that is the one they chose for themselves. I believe that whatever is the true force behind all that there is, we are destined to discover it for ourselves—if ever.

I can never forget the contradictions so eloquently stated in the opening lines of A Tale of Two Cities, serenaded to me on that puffy white cloud by five angry aliens:

"It was the best of times, it was the worst of times, it was the age of wisdom, it was the age of foolishness, it was the epoch of belief, it was the epoch of incredulity, it was the season of Light, it was the season of Darkness, it was the spring of hope, it was the winter of despair. We had everything before us, we had nothing before us, we were all going direct to Heaven, we were all going direct the other way."

It will be up to us to decide. Will we choose wisely? Or will we mimic Sisyphus of Greek mythology, who revolted against the gods and was forced to roll an immense boulder up a hill, only to have it roll back, repeating the same action up and down the hill for ever and ever.

Let us hope not.

He sat back and browsed the photos covering the walls. The latest, which he had placed next to the one of his parents, was a portrait of him,

Catherine, and Rose, taken a two of weeks before they moved out of the White House. It brought a smile to his lips.

With renewed clarity, he continued writing.

What is most important to me now is my love for my wife and child. Beyond that, nothing much really matters, for life and its meaning remains the ultimate enigma, and maybe that's the way it is meant to be.

Now we come to the silver box of codes that, according to Masma, holds the answers all men seek. What if what is hidden inside is not what we are searching for? What then? It is for this reason I have decided against opening it, nor have I revealed its existence to anyone. Before leaving, I hid it away in the White House where only I know its location. Maybe someday, far off in our future, it will be found.

Note to self: Do not include this in the book!

Pleased with himself, Gabriel Javier Ferro, son of Isabella and Javier, sat back, smiled wide and sipped his coffee. "Okay then, on to chapter one."

THE END... or the beginning.

Turn page...........

"What we call the beginning is often the end. And to make an end
Is to make a beginning. The end is where we start from."

T. S. Eliot

1888 – 1965

British essayist, publisher, playwright, literary and social critic,
and one of the twentieth century's major poets.

"All things share the same breath - the beast, the tree, the man ...
the air shares its spirit with all the life it supports. Man does not weave
this web of life. He is merely a strand of it. Whatever he does to the web,
he does to himself. Take only memories, leave nothing but footprints."

Chief Seattle

1786 - 1866

Suquamish Tribe and Dkhw'Duw'Absh Chief.